Beyond our bowsprit I saw clearly the sky that opened before us, the avenue in the clouds at that joining of sea and sky, the archipelago of islands and the blazing channels of brightness between. It was not the same archipelago, not the same islands, as I'd sailed out through once before; they were paler, brighter, less grey, a hundred tropical pastel hues upon a sapphire brightness that seared the very eyes. The golden light fringed their edges with golden beaches, and upon those beaches white surf was beating; above them seabirds flew and cried their exaltation. The breezes that blew around us were warmer, caressing breaths with richer, heavier scents of cedar and cinnamon, cardamom and cloves, pepper, ginger, turmeric and tamarind, the languid muskiness of orchids, the sharp tang of dusty roads and crumbling soil.

For however long he lived, surely no man could altogether lose the magic of that moment when the deck began to skip higher still beneath his feet, and never quite dipped down again — borne aloft on the tides of light, the roads of the sunrise, into the sea of azure, the infinity of the Spiral.

'*Over the Dawn! Over the airs of the Earth! We're underway!*'

*By the same author*

RUN TO THE STARS

THE WINTER OF THE WORLD:
Volume One: The Anvil of Ice
Volume Two: The Forge in the Forest
Volume Three: The Hammer of the Sun

CHASE THE MORNING
*with Alan Scott*

THE ICE KING

A SPELL OF EMPIRE

# The Gates of Noon

MICHAEL SCOTT ROHAN

LONDON
VICTOR GOLLANCZ LTD
1992

First published in Great Britain 1992
by Victor Gollancz Ltd
14 Henrietta Street, London, WC2E 8QJ

A catalogue record for this book is available from
the British Library

ISBN 0 575 05202 3 (Hardback)
ISBN 0 575 05317 8 (Paperback)

Typeset at The Spartan Press Ltd,
Lymington, Hants
and printed in Great Britain by
Mackays of Chatham plc, Chatham, Kent

*For Marise, Philip and Lucy*

*Between the pedestals of Night and Morning,*
*Between red death and radiant desire*
*With not one sound of triumph or of warning*
*Stands the great sentry on the Bridge of Fire . . .*

Flecker, *The Bridge of Fire*

Too angry to wait for the creaky elevator, I went clattering down the dusty stairs, so fast that I outpaced Dave. I stalked across the little lobby, ignoring the receptionist's soft-voiced courtesies, and barged straight out into the sunshine before I stopped to take a deep breath. This wasn't the best idea. Rumour awarded the atmosphere here one of the world's lowest oxygen counts, and beyond the air-conditioned shade of the shipping offices the sunlight beat down on it with the brassy intensity of a gong. The roar of the city enveloped me, the growl of cars mingled with the deeper cough of the buses, the high-pitched fizz of the little *tuk-tuk* taxi-rickshaws and the flatulent mopeds. A thousand stinks smote my nostrils: smoke, exhausts, spices, street filth, sweat and all the other stalenesses of humanity. Round here they were pretty considerable, these offices being in a low-rent district not far from the riverside wharves. Just the kind of one-horse outfit who'd normally be falling over themselves for the business of a world-wide agency like ours.

Normally.

I was actually trembling with rage and resentment. I was fed up with this place. I just wanted to walk, to get away to somewhere less hot and stinking and uncooperative. I turned on my heel and plunged away through the counterflowing crowd. A sea of heads hardly reached my shoulder; I had to fight the feeling that I ought to be swimming. But for all the crush and hubbub, the eternal plastic pop blaring from Japanese blasters, there was none of Hong Kong's earsplitting jabber, nor the barging you'd find in Western crowds. By and large this was a quiet-spoken, courteous people; only their children and their rock bands screeched above the traffic. On the other hand, I became aware of nimble fingers probing my jacket now and again, and was glad I'd zipped away everything in inside pockets. But that was just this part of town. The crush cleared a little, and Dave caught up. 'All right,' I said heavily. 'You told me so. Anywhere else? Or is that the lot?'

'Nowhere else,' he said, just as heavily. 'Look, I only wanted you to see for yourself, that's all, okay? I'm new in the job, I didn't want you of all people to think I couldn't handle it. You're sort of a hard act to follow – 'specially when it's you I'm reporting to.'

I stormed on, still too angry to appreciate the compliment. Pounding the pavements suited my temper. 'Damn it, Dave! It's an everyday deal, this. Just a simple set of consignments to Indonesia, that's all!'

'Yeah, so simple nobody wants it.'

'But in god's name, why not?' We skipped back as a string of mopeds ran a light, spattering debris from the gutter, then we plunged across with the human barrier before any more broke through. 'I mean, we couldn't make it any bloody easier, could we? One or two shipments at most for any big carrier, but we can feed it through one container at a time if we have to. So how come none of 'em want it? Not the big boys, not the little boys – not the absolute bloody dregs back there! Air, sea, land – no matter how we finagle it, this is the nearest we get. That's hard enough; but from here it's just like running into a bloody wall!' I glared at him. 'I know damn well just how much pull we used to have around here! So how come you've somehow managed to lose it in a week?'

'That's unfair,' said Dave quietly. He flicked his gold-topped Zippo under a cigarette, shielding it between dark fingers, then slid the lighter carefully back into an inner pocket he could fasten. It underlined a point; he was no stranger here, either. 'Look, I'm slipping shipments through points East all the time, no sweat – as you'd know if you'd read my this month's sheets. Contracts all nitt and tiddy. Never a bother. It's just this one. And a pretty penny-ante job at that – or so you say. So why all the fuss? Not doing a little dealing on the side, are we, already? Arms? Nose candy?'

'For Christ's sake, Dave! You know damn well I'd never —'I caught the jibe, and reined in my temper. 'Look, I'm sorry, right? I know you can handle things okay, you're doing at least as good a job at Contracts as I ever did. That's why I found it hard to believe you could run into such a foul-up over this one – penny-ante, as you say. Even when you'd flown out personally. So that's why I came myself.'

'Yeah. When I couldn't fix it. And now neither can you. So you might as well spill it. What's so important about this pipsqueak account, anyhow, that it brings our new assistant managing director out and running?'

'Well . . .'

'Oh, c'mon. I work for you, remember? Why're you so interested – personally, I mean?'

I shrugged, and jammed my hands hard into the pockets of my light silk suit. 'Look, it's nothing like – nothing big, all right? It's just a favour. A Good Cause one of my political cronies talked me into. Kind of millstone you have to take on now and again, good for street cred. *You* know! Could be awkward if it flops. Bad PR. That's all.'

There was a short silence. Only between us; the roar of business as usual in Bangkok, that concrete lump dropped into the belly of Asia, filled in the gap.

'We're old mates, remember?' Dave informed me, reverting to his would-be streetwise manner. He blew a casual jet of smoke back at the street. 'C'mon, you're not fooling me, Fisher. I know you – workwise, anyhow. I know just how much trouble you'd take over any given punter – normally, that is. And just how much temper you'd lose, which is not much. This is something you want to go right, and not just because of your precious political buddies, either. Something you care about. And it's just like you to be embarrassed as hell about that, too.' He shrugged. 'Oh, don't worry. I like that. I like seeing you forget you're made of wheels and clockwork and cryonic chips, and getting involved with the human race now and again. It suits you.'

As so often with Dave, I was slightly taken aback. 'Well . . . I wouldn't say it like that. Making me out as some kind of altruist or something.'

'Sure. Could ruin your rep.'

'Thank *you*. I mean, this just fell into my lap – at a Rotary do, in fact. Someone suggesting we might be able to help out a foundation they were involved in – friend of a friend, that kind of thing. So I looked into it a bit further, and it sort of . . . caught my imagination. Barry and I agreed. Right in our field, dead simple, the sort of thing we could pass through in ten minutes before tea, so why not? At cost. No skin off our noses.'

9

'So you send a contracts manager jetting halfway round the world, then come chasing after him yourself? Boy, you sure are ruthless. But don't worry, I won't spill your secret – *if* you ever get around to spilling it to me!'

I hesitated. Not because I didn't want to tell him, but because he'd touched that same old sore point, asking a question I'd been asking myself for some time now. Why *was* I so interested? Not just because it was a good cause. Every business gets swamped with those and soon learns to be hard-hearted; if we responded to them all we'd be bankrupt in a month, and doing nobody any favours. So why this one, especially? I'd never come up with an answer – unless, as I suspected, it was one particular thing I didn't want to admit. Not even to myself.

My furious progress was cut short. Even with my eyes closed I'd have baulked at the sudden wall of stench that rose before me, riper even than all the other city stinks put together. Dave wrinkled his nostrils. 'Wow. Try charging across *that* crossing and you'd really be in deep – '

The street ended in one of the narrower *klongs*, the famous city canals that still serve as home, highway, water supply and sanitation – not necessarily in that order – for a chunk of the poorer population. A tour boat raised a churning wake, its cargo of tourists filming the uninhibited behaviour of the dwellers in stilt-borne shacks along the bank; and it said a lot for the dwellers that they didn't summarily drown the tourists, and even grinned curiously at the all-devouring lenses as they buzzed past. For us, too, they had grins, though they were inclined to stare askance at Dave; Africans were pretty rare in these parts, let alone Oxbridge-accented Africans in raw silk suits. Dave chucked his gilt cigarette-end into the turbid brown water, which swallowed it with a faint greasy belch.

'Yuk,' he observed.

'Yuk it is,' I agreed. 'But all the same, that's what it's all about, here or anywhere. Water.'

'You call that water?'

'To a lot of places it'd be lifeblood. Might even be glad to have it in California, these days. And Bali. You know, the island—'

'Which just happens to be our consignment destination, right. One more lush tropical paradise I never get sent to.'

'I haven't been there either. Not yet. Anyhow, you were born in one.'

'The Kano suburbs are a tropical paradise? Oi.'

'Paradise is relative. So is lush. Thing is, Bali's got little or no water of its own; and that's what this business is all about. It depends mostly on rainwater flowing down from the central highlands, and there's none too much of that. Fair shares make the difference between idyll and starvation. It's been that way for centuries now, so they've evolved a pretty sophisticated irrigation system to distribute water – so long it's become all mixed up with their society, their religion, everything. They have these societies called *subaks* to govern the community rice paddies, sort of local water-temples with complicated law codes and judge-priests to administer them. It's democratic, in its way, and it works. So far.'

Dave nodded. 'We had things like that back home, in some places. Pretty arbitrary, though – the chief or shaman or elders settling disputes under the banyan tree, that kind of thing. Or the District Officer, when you guys took over. This sounds more sophisticated.'

'It is. Complicated as hell. And Bali's changing, just like everywhere else.'

'Tourism booming in the eighties and nineties, sure. Rock stars getting married there, that kind of thing.'

'That – but not just that. The population's expanding – better medicine, hygiene, the usual reasons. And whatever the cause, global warming or deforestation or the natural cycle or whatever, the rainfall patterns are definitely altering. For the worse. The *subak* system's had its day; the *klian subaks*, the priests, they can't cope any more, or soon won't. A few years back this American college project thought they could get it to hold up by teaching 'em to put the whole damn system on little home computers! But there's got to be something serious done now, and soon. I can tell you, the central government's pretty worried. The island's going to need a whole new system, a couple of desalination plants like they have in the Gulf – and guess what those cost! Plus more efficient collection, storage, distribution, all controlled by a centralised computer network. Maximise the use of every last drop they can get.'

'The difference between idyll and starvation . . . ' repeated Dave thoughtfully. 'Seems like a shame. And how the hell are they going to pay for all that?'

'Usual channels – World Bank lending, aid from the Gulf

States, European Community, a lot of places. But it's all pretty tight, after the debt crisis; that's all earmarked for the desalination plants, and they won't be operational for maybe ten years. They were going to have to muck along with the present irrigation system meanwhile, and that could mean eight or nine crisis years – maybe even hard famine. A hell of a lot of suffering, plus infant mortality, environmental damage, maybe even epidemics. At the very least it'd kill the tourist industry stone-dead, and that means less hard currency, the central government less willing to spend money there – you see the progression?'

'I do,' said Dave grimly. He'd grown up in the aftermath of the Nigerian famine; he knew. 'Anybody doing anything?'

'They got one of the US college foundations to step in. It set up a project, finagled a bit more public and private funding – good PR. So the Project's buying the most expensive stuff, the sluice engineering and control systems, in the USA and Europe, and recruiting the manpower; but even there money's very short. This is an ecologically clean project; big money's not interested, because there are no massive returns to be made. The islanders will benefit, and the government's all for it – no political problem involved as far as we can see. Yet it seems that all along the line there's been trouble.'

Dave cocked his head. 'Now you tell me?'

I felt slightly abashed. I hadn't believed it could affect us, that was all. 'Well, I didn't fully understand it myself, not at first. All I was told was, the foundation was having a hell of a time shipping their stuff. When I saw what they could afford to pay, that didn't seem too hard to understand. So we polished up our haloes and said cost or below. And here we are.'

'Yeah. And we might as well be up to our necks in that damn *klong*. So it appears you've heard a bit more about this mysterious trouble since.'

'No, it bloody well doesn't! Just what all our friends and associates here – our *usual* associates – let drop when they turned us down. Only to me; they don't know you that well yet. Vague rumbles, worried mutterings; nothing too specific. But each and every one of them effectively stuck the black spot on the whole Project. And you've heard nothing else yourself?'

We fetched up at some huts, and absent-mindedly turned down behind them, away from the *klong*. Dave thought back. 'Well, now that you mention it . . . I didn't even connect it at the time.

12

But old Lee Wang Ji over at Taiwan Star just happened to drop into the conversation that guerrilla trouble on Jawa might be spreading to Bali. He didn't add anything.'

'Yes, well, Boonserb at Pacific C did. Hinted the terrorists might have their knives into the Project. But he was shipping right into Jakarta during the last big blow-up a couple of years back – and Sulawesi, too. Never stopped him for a minute. I looked up the Bali incidents, and they were just a couple of bushwhackings, nothing like the same scale. Probably by Javanese fugitives. You're not telling me *that*'s the reason!'

We strolled along in silence, thinking deeply. At last Dave stopped and fished for his cigarettes. 'So the shippers are just looking for excuses. Me with my wicked Third World up-bringing, I'd say any block as complete as this has got to be political. Bound to be. Maybe some other governments in the region . . . '

I felt a great tide of hopelessness surge over me. This was ground I'd been over and over these last few days. 'Which ones, for god's sake? What could any of them gain by scuppering this Project? Bali's about the most peaceful place in Indonesia. Peace, natural beauty, rich farming, good surfing – that's about the sum total of its resources. No threat to anyone, damn near impossible to invade . . . ' I sighed, and kicked at the ground. A great fan of dirt showered out. 'Dave, I don't know . . . I'm not just being paranoid, am I?'

'Well, we both . . . ' He finished lighting his cigarette, and blew out an irritable blast of expensive smoke. It dawned on us both then; no pavement underfoot. 'Damn! Just where the hell have we got to?'

We gazed around. Somehow or other the crowded little streets had melted away, and we were standing in some sort of back alley, barren and dirty and unusually empty. The walls around us were a wild assortment. Rows of rotting brown planks, patched with bamboo and rusty corrugated iron, ran right up to elegant old stonework, pitted and cracked. Pastel plasterwork crumbled away from the wall of cheap yellow brick that crowded up against it, shedding its mortar in loose flakes, or absorbed the sordid staining from a cracked downflow pipe, pooling in fetid puddles at its base. A wrought-iron fire-escape sagged drunkenly from windows that seemed to be mostly boards, grinning sharklike with shards of dirty glass. As a child, fascinated, I'd watched windows like that in old half-empty tenements, a strong wind setting the glass teeth chattering with a faint chilly icicle music. Now and again one would work loose and drop with a crash into the sordid lot behind, unregarded by those within. Here they rippled to a softer breeze, like a hot breath on our necks, to a more alien music.

We turned round. Behind us we could dimly see a complex warren of alleys kinking away in all directions, floored with mud and refuse, swimming with pools of accumulated unpleasantness. Dave stared appalled at his elegant brogues. 'Did we really come stomping through *that* stuff? Without noticing?'

'We must have got turned around somehow,' I remarked, and strode confidently around the next corner. 'So it must have been . . .'

I walked straight into a wall of mist. No other word for it; not a cloud, not wisps, just a single sudden wall, the way it looks when you come up against it on a nightbound motorway with too much on the clock and brakes squealing into lock. One minute I was walking in the late afternoon light, the next I was stumbling through obscurity where even sounds rang differently, where refuse piles I'd been carefully avoiding were somehow no longer there. It was warm, clammy, hard to breathe. Even my footfalls sounded different.

'Dave? You there?'

'If I knew where *there* is, I might answer that! I'm sure somewhere.'

'Can you see anything? What's underfoot?'

'Well, dirt . . . no, wait a minute. *Stone?*'

'Remains of one of the older buildings, maybe. And dammit, there's even a pillar of some sort, I just saw it over there . . . damn, it's gone now.'

'Over *where?*'

He answered himself by crashing into me. We staggered back against the pillar. What felt like very uneven stonework jabbed into my back. The mist was thinner here, and looking down I saw I was resting on uneven nubs of grey stone, its surface faintly cracked and lichen-encrusted; it was deeply carved, with what looked like hanging foliage. I looked up. Dimly through the whiteness I could see what must be other pillars, tall tapering shadows that seemed to stand alone, supporting nothing more substantial than the coils of mist. I was about to say something when Dave grabbed my arm. He didn't need to point. Between two of the columns there was now a third shadow, inchoate, changing. It took me a moment to realise it was a human outline, half turning, this way, that way, hunched up as if it was peering about. For an instant it loomed our way, and I found myself silent, short-breathed, desperately hoping it wouldn't spot us. Then, still in that concentrated half-crouch, it disappeared back into the mist.

If anything it left its feeling behind it. A horrible hunted sensation was growing on me, spreading like chilly lichen. I'd felt something like it once before, a burgeoning unease in my bones – but where? I looked at Dave. There was a grey tinge to his skin as if the mist had got under it. I mouthed *Let's get out of here*! and he nodded fervently. Slowly, quietly, keeping a firm grip on each other's arms, we sidled around the curve of the pillar. Ahead were other pillars, and we hadn't passed any on our way in; so this ought to be the best bet. If the normal rules applied, that was . . .

Why had I thought that? When didn't they apply?

Something was stirring in my memory, something formless as the shadow in the mist. Something that still woke me in the cold chill hours before dawn, confused, in conflict, still spinning on a sparking pinwheel of feelings. Less often, these last few years; but on a night not long ago one girl had put a hand up to my cheek as I sat there, panting. She'd exclaimed, wondering, 'You're all sweaty! Like a fever! And . . . '

Did the silly bitch have to sound so utterly dumbfounded? 'Steve, you've been *crying*!'

A few years earlier I might have thrown her out on the spot; even then I was tempted. But the strongest feeling in me was loss; only for what? Something definite, but something I struggled against, something I refused to give shape to. My great barn of a flat was in darkness; but in the living room below the gallery that was my bedroom I could see a gleam of light, that just seemed to hang there in the emptiness. I'd got up, padded down the steps past the clothes she'd scattered there – always a bad sign. The light was only the moon, shining through the open window on to the grey Portland stone mantel and the old broadsword I'd hung over it. My designer had shed bitter tears over that; it was right out of place in his glassy post-modernist vision. Most of my guests agreed with him, but I wouldn't be parted from it. I touched the

15

cool perfection of the blade, like still waters. Impulsively I laid my hot forehead against it, and that seemed to still the confusion. Then I'd mixed up drinks and taken them back to bed. She'd enough sense not to press me, so we'd had a pleasant time making the sun come up – but the darkness of that half-formed dream had lingered. And now, here, I sensed somehow, as with a hint of a long-forgotten scent or flavour, that it was out of that darkness all this had come boiling up.

With the pillar in front of us we hastily backed away, darting looks this way and that as each swirl in the mist threatened us with hidden fears. We'd rounded a corner; so if we went back—

With switching suddenness there was light around us again, the same warm light we'd left, the same soft dirt underfoot, the same compounded stinks. After that formless emptiness they were almost welcome, the stained walls gloriously solid and confining. 'It's the alley okay!' Dave's grin was a rictus of relief. 'Now let's get the hell—'

But as we turned around again, we saw that the alley wasn't empty any more. A minute ago I'd almost have welcomed company, any company; but these . . .

They were short compared to me, to Dave even; but there were a lot of them. They were Orientals, but oddly indeterminate, their faces so many scowling masks of light bronze; and even their own mothers might have called them ugly, seamed and scarred and broken-nosed, with gaping gravestone teeth. And their old-fashioned baggy blue pyjamas, bound with heavy black sashes, had an unpleasant hint of uniform about them, ragged and filthy as they looked. So did the long wavy daggers in their hands. Their heads lolled mockingly as they advanced, silently, flicking the blades with expressive, menacing force. Equally silently, Dave and I gave back; I saw the sweat gleam on his face, felt it around my own collar. They came on, steady and relentless, herding us back towards that crucial corner.

'Can't you do something?' hissed Dave, out of the corner of his mouth.

'Why me?'

'You, the hotshot leader in the strategy team! Wiped the floor with that Securities team, everyone saying what a fighter you were—'

'With a bloody paint-ball pistol, yes! I haven't even got that here!'

'There's my lighter! They might think . . . '

'Going to offer them a Sobranie? I somehow don't think a little flame's going to worry these guys. We'd need a bloody machine gun—'

But even as I said it, the image that sprang to mind wasn't a gun at all. It was that sword. I could have used that – couldn't I? In fact, I had. Somehow, somewhere – where the hell had I picked that thing up, anyhow? Down by the docks, wasn't it? Nearly eight years back . . .

*The docks*!

In a summer storm I'd seen a wave arch high over a seawall. It hadn't looked like much more than spray; but it crashed down on a street of shops and parked cars, and when the water-curtain pulled back it left a shattered chaos in its wake. So memory rose and roared down into my thoughts, spilling tangled images of sea fights and stark terror, of stars and drifting clouds and sails, of sea and fire and the jar of blade on blade, the touch of a woman who burned from within, with hair that rose like smoke. Of once upon a darkling field a swordhilt leaping doglike to my hand. These things had been. Beyond reason, beyond question, they had been. The certainty shone in me, gem-hard and with the same fire at its heart. And out of it, sprouting like a time-lapsed seedling, burgeoned the beginnings of an idea . . .

With a screeching yell the leading knifeman sprang, flinging his blade up to fall on my throat. Fear takes time – I had none. Instinct flung up my arms in futile self-preservation, but all I felt was anger, furious anger at being interrupted now, of all times, just when I'd suddenly seen what I had to do. The dark fire flared. Now, of all times *now*, to be distracted, killed even – that couldn't be. To fight back became an instant, all-consuming need, that sucked me into it like a flooding channel.

The red darkness of oxygen starvation roared in my head, faded to black. A tiny point of light glittered in the blackness behind my eyes, glittered and grew against a swirling dimness, turning in a great slow wheeling motion. A streak of circling light, it sparkled agonisingly against my closed lids, closer, brighter, larger . . . My eyelids flew open. No time had passed. The knifeman still loomed up in front of me, mouth agape; the knife hung at the top of its sweep, and came slashing down. And into my outstretched palm something slapped with stinging force.

The blow curled my fingers about it; they closed and held, tight. The descending knifeblade clanged against the massive blade I held across my breast, skipped along it and stuck at the hilt. I twisted the heavy blade viciously, tearing the weapon from the wielder's grasp with a force that whipped him around and dropped him face down into the mud. The knife clattered aside. With a yell I sprang forward, treading on his back, and brought the blade hissing down a hair's breadth in front of the next knifeman's flattened snout. It thudded into the mud, kicking up a spray. I tore it free and sprang again, sweeping my way clear with great circling slashes – horribly clumsy, but it made the ancient sword rush and sing like a child. The remaining bandits leaped back, back again, back at every swing till they reached the far end of the alley. Then I yelled aloud and charged at them, and with one massive slashing sweep scattered them into its shadows.

'*Dave?*'

'Yeah?'

'*Run like hell!*'

Which he proceeded to do, though he did look back once to be sure I was hard on his heels.

Not for long. He was younger and lighter, and if it hadn't been for sheer and utter terror I couldn't have kept up. No doubt fright was winging his feet, too. Certainly it made us both forget we'd no idea where the hell we were running to; any alley without mist and muggers seemed pretty pleasant just then. And I was almost as frightened of the sword in my hand, and of the equally sharp and lethal things that swarmed around in my head. Things I'd made a pretty good job of banishing, all told, these last few years; and yet never had the skill, or maybe the courage, to forget completely. When had I last made it back to the Tavern? Three years, was it? Or four?

Wheezing and panting in the sulphurous humidity, I rounded one more corner – and narrowly missed impaling Dave, who'd stopped stone-dead in my path. This was a gloomy hole, two small side alleys and a dead-end sink of scum and sewage the rickety buildings curved out over, their roof tiles almost touching, as if to hide its shame from the sky. Beneath the arch they made, as the tropical twilight dimmed the sky, the shadows hung in the sweltering air blacker than the coming night. Within those shadows, higher than our heads, something moved.

A mask, one of those processional things you find all over the East – a monstrous animalian face, long-jawed and triangular, that might have been remotely based on some bug-eyed nocturnal tiger. Its colour scheme was more natural than in most Eastern art, lacking the shrieking reds and yellows, a rich shading instead from autumn russet to glossy leaf-green, offset by glistening ivory fangs and its scarlet, lolling tongue; but gold-encrusted ornaments fringed its gaping jaw and sleek silvery mane. It was a rich, amazing sight, and I found myself wondering who in this lousy quarter could have hung out such an expensive-looking, vibrant work of art.

Then the staring eyes narrowed, the jaws spilled slaver and the scarlet tongue lapped it off yellowed leonine teeth. The gilt rustled and jingled as the monstrous head tossed, threateningly. A soft purring snarl throbbed in the air, as disembodied as a lion's cough and even more alarming. For Dave and myself, still jangling from the mist and the knife attack, this was too much. We yelled with one voice, turned and bolted for our lives. I plunged down the little side alley to the left, feet skidding on decaying garbage and worse, and around a corner stacked with boxes of empty bottles and gaudy food containers. I found myself looking at a wall faced with decaying concrete, blank except for one door, narrow, low and forbiddingly faced with a single sheet of zinc, dented, weatherstained but very, very solid.

I grabbed at the handle; it turned freely, but nothing happened. I hammered my fist on the door; the zinc thudded, but nothing stirred. 'No use, Dave . . . ' I panted, and knew even as I looked around that he wasn't there to hear. The alley was empty behind me, empty and silent save for my own sobbing breath. But beyond, as I listened, I heard distinctly a soft padding step, plashing delicately through the muddy staleness. I was about to call out, when I noticed something about the sound. My jaw clamped shut; the sweat started out in rivulets. Whatever was padding along that way had four legs. Frantically now I battered the door again, kicking it hard enough to mark the zinc and jar flakes of concrete off the surround, clanging on it with my swordhilt. At least I had that. Dave must have run the other way; he'd be all right. Probably. Better it had followed me, I told myself, and turned again, slowly, putting my back to the unyielding door, to face it.

The door opened, outwards, so suddenly it sent me staggering. A hand clamped on my flailing arm, and yanked. Helplessly I lurched into the dark opening, and the door swung to behind me with a solid slamming boom. I was left leaning against it, gasping in darkness; there was the soft dull snick of a key turning, the sharper snap of bolts being shot at foot and head. Then there was silence. I half expected an impact on the metal, or a soft curious scratching; but there was nothing. Then long nails brushed my hand, and I jumped violently. But the fingers that closed over mine were definitely a woman's, and they drew me away from the door. I was in a pitch-dark corridor, it seemed, with soft matting underfoot, and warm air heavy with stale, sickly perfume. A little way ahead thin threads of light outlined a door ajar, and the hand on my arm guided me towards this. A slim arm gleamed, sliding it gently open. A slender silhouette crossed the dim pinkish light, and wordlessly drew me in after her.

The door closed softly, and a bead curtain rattled back across it. The room beyond . . .

I blinked. It was low-ceilinged and shabby, over-decorated in the fashion of a cheap Chinese restaurant, encrusted with fake lacquer, plastic 'carvings' and peeling bamboo wallpaper. Except that these carvings wouldn't have graced any ordinary restaurant, that was instantly obvious; nor would the pictures on the wall. The heavy scent masked a faint animal smell, tinged with the musky sweetness of decay.

A soft voice spoke. 'You are safe here. You need fear no pursuit. Will you not sit and rest?' It was perfect English, with only the faintest tinge of Eastern staccato. I turned; and whatever I'd meant to say choked in my throat. She was breathtaking enough in herself; but there was still more to it than that. Maybe she saw my lips frame a name, for she stretched out a hand in a strangely elaborate, courteous gesture, bowing from the waist. That left me even more speechless. For a moment it seemed as if I'd summoned up still more of my past, as if a gentle ghost of my student days had stepped in to rescue me.

A delicate oriental face, delicate but strong; but the skin was the light honey-brown of a tanned European, and the mane of hair that framed it was ash-blonde, constant from root to tip, a subtle luminous shade that almost certainly owed nothing to any dye. Even the strong slender shoulders and the sleek curves of the figure beneath the loose batik wrap were the same strange mingling of Eastern and Western forms, strange, lovely and alluring. This could have been the girl I once knew; whom I'd come nearest to loving, whom I'd long ago thrown over for reasons that even now I didn't care to dwell on. Whose name, or one that could be hers, had leapt out at me from the staff lists of the Bali Project prospectus, and dragged me down into this whole lunatic business.

But though I'd never dreamed anyone else could look like her, it wasn't Jacquie. Like enough to shake me severely, to throw me back – what was it? – fifteen or sixteen years. To stir my blood, make my breathing shallow, my collar far too tight. Alarming, alluring – but not her.

This girl's face was slightly browner, her features smaller, neater, less of the Chinese in them, nothing at all of the European. Yet she was no Thai, either; and the same sharp intelligence shone out of those mild eyes, though her bow revealed that beneath that wrap she was dressed, or undressed, in the black bikini that was practically a Bangkok bar girl's everyday uniform. She repeated her offer, and I managed to find my voice.

'It's . . . kind of you. Very kind.' The English phrases sounded stilted, ridiculous. 'You got me out of real trouble there. There were these . . . characters with knives, and then there was . . . '

How could I tell her what there was, when I didn't know myself?

She cut me off with another gentle gesture. 'Yes. My pleasure. Sometimes people are found murdered in those alleys. It comforts me to have helped you. Will you not sit down? Would you like a drink? Whisky?'

I became aware how shaky my legs were. I let the sword lean against the wall; she hadn't even glanced at it. 'Y–yes. Thank you. I would, very much.'

She smiled, and her hand on my arm guided me to a shabby rattan couch, under a picture framed in fake gilt. It was one of those night scenes painted with fluorescent colours on black velvet. An obvious imitation of classic Chinese art, a Ming dynasty erotic illustration, but the naked figures were crudely modern, Westernised and very graphic. One man, three women, picked out in peeling paint in a stilted tangle of limbs and heads and groins that looked barely possible, let alone enjoyable. The girl followed my gaze as she handed me a double measure of yellowish fluid, and smiled demurely. I sipped, and was startled to find it was a single malt – not even Chivas, which was the usual status drink around here.

I exhaled gratefully. 'That's bloody marvellous!' She smiled again, and sat down next to me, stretching out her legs, letting the robe slip back off them. She looked at me as if she was expecting something. 'Er – my name's Steve, by the way. Steve Fisher.'

'And mine is Rangda.' She bit off the last syllable with an exquisite flash of pure white teeth, eclipsing her earlier smiles.

I looked at her more keenly. 'Beautiful. It suits you. Not a Thai name, though, is it?'

She looked down. 'No.' My turn to expect something more, but she didn't explain. I was about to ask where it did come from when she gave a sudden explosive giggle, snatched my Scotch and sipped at it. I got the message: don't ask. 'May I?' she added.

I wasn't quite sure why, until she began to stroke my hair. In this part of the world they consider the head sacred, not to be touched without permission; but why should a tart bother, and with a Westerner? Definitely she was something a bit out of the ordinary. There was no mark of age about her, yet she seemed much older than the giggling teenage bar girls of the Three Streets, farm girls most of them who age early in the city.

I looked around, shifted awkwardly on the lurid floral cushions. They had a faint greasy feel which gave me the urge to burn my suit; but it was a clash of feelings that made me really uncomfortable. I was strongly aware of her, this close, the warmth of her skin, the scent she wore as languorous as jungle orchids, far fresher and heavier than the dismal background odour. The surroundings were sexy in their way, but it was the blatant pin-up sexuality of the Phatphong bars. With the girl it was . . . different. She radiated sexuality, availability even; but another kind altogether, hard to fix on. I didn't know what to make of her; the closest I could get was that the room was what you might find in any brothel, the girl what you might dream you'd find. She didn't seem to belong. 'You . . . work here, then?'

She raised a sardonic eyebrow. 'When it suits me.' She stretched again, and her robe fell wider. 'Not . . . tied to this place; I come, I go, as I like.' She leaned over and tilted the Scotch to my lips. 'And with whom I like. Not . . . *necessarily* . . . ' She made a nice play of pronouncing the difficult word, and we chuckled. 'Not necessarily for business.'

She leaned her forehead against my head; blonde hair brushed my shoulder, lips brushed my ear. 'Though, I am at home here. You stay as long as you like. We are not disturbed.'

She guided my hand to the sash of her robe; her warm belly fluttered against my fingers an instant, and the sash fell away, the robe parted. Almost without meaning to, I slid my arm around her waist, drew her to me. Almost, because though my heart was racing furiously, so was my mind. Wheels and clockwork and cryonic chips, Dave had said. Others had said worse, women especially, and maybe they were not so far wrong. But there were times it served me well, gave me a cynical eye, a wary tread and a distrust of illusions – most of all my own. I'd never had much trouble with women, but I knew full well I wasn't *that* attractive. Yet she seemed to want to make me feel I was. Not for money maybe, but then there would be something else, some other thing she wanted, and after the shocks I'd had I wasn't sure I could cope. I hated anybody manipulating my feelings, no matter how they did it, power or money or sex or anything else; I hated any kind of possession. And somehow, surely, that must be just what she was trying to do.

There was Dave to think about, too; where had he got to? Had anyone helped him?

'No,' I whispered, because I was still having breathing problems, and slid the girl gently back on to the cushion. 'Not . . . now. I mustn't stay.'

'Oh, but please!' she breathed, where an ordinary bar girl might have whined and called me *honey*. 'Please stay! I need you, I want . . . '

I made as if to detach myself gently, but somehow I couldn't shift her. 'There was this friend of mine – in trouble too—'

She made a grimacing *moue* of impatience and slumped back, flicking her robe wide, splaying her legs and hooking one thigh over mine to hold me down. She seized my hand and slid it down over the smooth bikini, between her legs. I felt every detail through the thin glossy fabric, a radiant, thrilling warmth, a hint of moisture. She ground my hand against her, and writhed. Her other hand . . .

I swallowed; a blatant whore's gesture, but none the less there was a power in it, a devouring appeal to things a whole lot deeper than sense or inhibition. Wheels, clockwork, chips – and the pulse that beat beneath my ear, roaring in mockery. I pulled her to me, crushed her to me in an ecstasy of lust and anger, anger at having my strength so tested; anger that it had almost not been enough; anger that it had. 'No!' I croaked again, and wished I didn't mean it. 'You . . . I want you too. You can't guess how much . . .'

*Because you don't know how much you look like Jacquie.*

'But not now. I would . . . you. Everything. You're beautiful . . . but I can't. Mustn't.'

Abruptly she released me, swung to her feet so fast I winced, thinking she'd start a screaming tantrum or call in the boys from the bar. Instead she just looked around at me, slowly, expressionless, and gathered her robe around her. 'If you meant that,' she said slowly, 'you would come back.'

'I will!' I wheezed, infinitely relieved, hastily shoving my shirt back into my waistband.

'You owe me much. Do you not?'

'Well, yes! Of course!' Her hand stopped mine as it reached for my wallet.

'Not business. Not ever business. I took you through the door. I made you mine, and you will promise, and that promise will hold you. Promise you will come back. Soon.' She smiled again, and gently straightened my tie. 'You see? I do not bind you to a day and hour. There is no – necessity. I feel your need of me. You have much to seek in me, I in you. You will open yourself to me. Promise!'

I stared down at her, wildly uncertain. How much of me could she see? And by what sight? But she was right; something of me was hers, she'd made it so. 'I owe you more than a promise,' I said. 'Okay, I'll come back. Soon. I promise. Is that all you want of me?'

She smiled, and shook her head demurely. 'But enough for now. I will show you another way out. A busy street.'

She took my arm, and we were almost at the door when I remembered the sword. 'There's this,' I said awkwardly, and was startled; the glance she flashed me was impatient, almost malevolent. 'It'd take too long to explain, but – I can't just walk into a busy street with it. If you had something I could wrap it in . . . ' She cast about, then flicked up a long thin scarf or shawl from a chairback and coiled it around the blade. 'Thanks. I'll bring it back.'

She nodded, as if it was a statement, not a promise. And perhaps it was.

She led me out into the darkened corridor again, up stairs and down, across a creaking bridge over a malodorous little court where a black pig grunted in a pen, through a narrow door and along more corridors, lightened by dim oil-paper windows, beneath one of which a dark-skinned man lay snoring. She pouted in disapproval, and as we passed she kicked him with surprising force. Occasional noises filtered out from doors as we passed, but apart from him I saw nobody else in our passage till we came to a broad, dirty hallway, little more than a corridor, that pulsed and thudded with anonymous disco music. It ended in a heavy door, but to one side an archway with only a curtain of plastic strips opened on to a wide, dim-lit expanse of booths and tables, and beyond them a tiny stage where brown-limbed figures jerked and gyrated. A strong odour of sweat and stale beer and cheap cigarettes drifted out, mingled with disinfectant.

'Bar,' said Rangda, leading me past, her plastic sandals clacking on the cracked vinyl. 'Pricey drinks, cheap girls. Too much of one makes you buy the other. Either way, you get sick. You come back, you ask for me, drink with me.'

I looked at her once more. 'When will you be here?'

She gave a short laugh. 'You come, you ask, you will find me. Now go. *Go!*'

With that surprising strength she yanked the door open and boosted me through. I staggered out, blinking and gasping in the low light and sudden heat, straight into a bunch of giggling tourists, almost overbalancing a fat European in pink shorts who was wielding a video camera.

'*Sauvertrünkener!*' he snarled, spraying sweat and spittle. I glanced back at what he'd been filming. Framing the door and all along the sleazy mock-pagoda facade were tall pink placards with crude line sketches of girls with legs akimbo, a motif animated in pink neon along the roof ledge and racks of raw-meat photographs. The girls looked about fourteen.

*Bar Cabaret – Sex Show – Pussy Jim's.*

Most of the city's girlie bars and brothels are actually crowded into a small area of three streets and their interconnecting *soi*, all owned by one tycoon and even known by his nickname, Phatphong. This was one of the rare outsiders. The street was tiny, almost empty by Bangkok standards, except for those bloody tourists. The building looked less ramshackle than I'd expected, but old, positively ancient, with the traditional rising gable; there was no sign it had ever been anything but a brothel, every sign that it had been one for a long time. Maybe that was why it was tolerated, that and its out-of-the-way location near the wharves. Unable to fake aplomb, I slunk past the tourists, feeling the faint stickiness of the cushions still on my fingers, wishing the whole city in hell.

And of course everybody looked round at me again when Dave yelled and came running, pushing his way through the gawkers. '*Steve! Steve, damn it*!' He grabbed me by the shoulders. 'You bastard, you're all right! And what the hell happened? I mean, there we were, then there was – wow, you sod, you've just gone and fallen on your feet again, haven't you?' He twitched up the dangling end of Rangda's scarf, and whistled at the pattern. I hadn't even noticed it. It was one of those temple friezes from Angkor or somewhere, full of figures cheerfully writhing in erotic, athletic and apparently endless combinations. Dave lifted it to his broad nostrils and made appreciative sniffing noises. 'Hoo, some scent that is! Full of yer actual Eastern promise – knock over a carthorse, that would – so hey, I want to know just where you got that! I mean, here have I been, scouring the bloody streets, half out of my mind with worry, and all the time you've been getting yours with a vengeance – c'mon, what's she like?'

I snatched the scarf out of Dave's hand and wound it tighter round the sword. That was his idea of ribbing me, and right now I'd had a bellyful of it. 'Well, you'd bloody know where I've been,' I growled, 'if you hadn't just pissed off and left me to it – wouldn't you?'

'Ah, come on!' protested Dave. 'Last thing I knew, you were right wiv me! We both did a runner there, didn't we?' He shivered, and touched a hand to his temple, as if at some unpleasant but murky memory. His real accent surfaced again. 'Only thing we could do. Only sensible. Didn't know they just let lions run loose round the backstreets here. Shouldn't we tell somebody?'

He sounded very unconvinced by the idea.

'A lion,' I said. 'Is that what you think we saw?'

'Well . . . yes. A lion. In some sort of harness, maybe, like a circus animal, but . . . ' He was struggling. 'Christ, it gave me a fright! I . . . it's gone all blurred. And you know something? That suits me, right down.' He grinned suddenly. 'What about you? Don't tell me you weren't frightened, either!'

It wasn't possible to stay irritated for long, I was so relieved to see him alive and in one piece. 'Are you implying your superior is a rank coward?'

'No, just a sensible one. Listen, you're not going to believe this. I mean, I know how it sounds, but . . . well, I came thundering out on the street, this street, before I realised you weren't with me. And then I did go back after you. Or rather I tried to. But, I know it sounds crazy, but . . . ' He shook his head. 'Oh, shit. Forget it, you'd never believe it.'

'Try me,' I said, and there must have been something in my tone to make him look at me so sharply.

'I couldn't get back. I just . . . *couldn't*. Every corner I turned – it was the wrong corner, it was just another street. Till I was tearing my hair out . . . Those alleys. It was like, like they'd never even *existed*.'

I looked around at the little street, and set off towards the main road, the one furthest from those tourists. The sun was sinking, leaving a veil of dust and grime on the oven-hot air. My throat hurt, and I felt very tired; and yet somewhere inside me, throughout all this, I'd guarded that precious germinating idea. I wanted a rest, I wanted some peace and quiet to sit and think about it, and let it develop out of those turbulent, insane memories. But most of all I wanted a drink.

'Oh, they existed all right. Fifty – a hundred years ago, maybe. Before the Vietnam War brought in all the GIs for R & R and changed all the teahouse brothels into bars. Before bloody Anna Leonowens and all the rest of us brought this goddamned place all the benefits of Western civilisation. But they never really went away. They're still around. You were looking in the light, Dave. You should just have looked in the shadows.'

At some point in all that he'd opened his mouth to say something. Now it was hanging open, and he shut it with a snap, and said nothing at all. I could sympathise; a few years back it had affected me the same way. But I didn't feel like explaining now. At the corner I hailed a passing *samlor* and began the inevitable weary haggling over the fare. We climbed in and slumped back

27

under the little canopy, sagging in the airless heat of sunset. The covered sword clanked against the curlicued steel armrail, and the wiry little driver looked at me oddly. 'A souvenir,' I explained; and so it was, of stranger places than this.

He dropped us outside the hotel's well-shaded terrace bar. We didn't get any further. We sat there, and we drank, and it was a couple of hours and a good few leisurely gin slings later that we levered our weary bones off the cane chairs and shambled into the lobby.

'Suite 405? Oh yes, Mistah Fishah,' said the American-accented clerk, and produced a telegram. 'Come in for you momentarily,' he added.

'Don't tell me home office has found us a carrier,' I remarked to Dave, and ripped it open. But it was from my flat management company. Apparently the burglar alarm had been triggered by somebody breaking a window.

'But you live up in the bloody stratosphere!' protested Dave. 'Breaking a window in a fourteenth-floor penthouse?'

'Well, they say the caretaker and the security man found nothing else was damaged. Or missing.'

I blinked in sudden realisation. I was still trailing that startling scarf of Rangda's – much to the amusement of the lobby staff, I realised, having learned to spot a Thai poker-face. But it hung feather-light in my hand, no more than a wisp of printed silk. I looked around in sudden panic. The rickshaw – had I let it fall? Or the bar – had I left it there? But I remembered all too clearly the awkwardness of clambering out with it, of leaning the thing against my chair and manoeuvring it out as I stood up. Dave too was staring at the scarf, a weird range of emotions chasing each other across his mobile face. They settled swiftly into wide-eyed anger. By tacit consent we'd carefully skirted around recent experiences while we enjoyed our drinks, but that couldn't last. I rolled up the scarf, thrust it into my pocket, and headed for the lifts.

'Bandits,' grated Dave softly, hurrying behind me. 'Old-fashioned dacoits or whatever you'd call them—'

'That's a Burmese word.'

I could almost hear the twang as Dave grabbed at his overstretched self-control. 'It's good enough! Dacoits. Lions. Sex bars. Alleys that suddenly show up from nowhere and then *pftt!* away again. Into the shadows, say you. A hundred years in the past. Or more. You know all about them. And all you fucking well condescend to do is laugh at me! Okay, that's enough, you hear? I'm entitled to some answers, and by god I'll have them!'

I knew this mood. If he didn't get them I might be needing that sword again. I wasn't worried about it. The caretaker knew what it looked like; and it would have left a clear mark in the mushroom-grey paint. If it had been missing, he would have missed it. When I got back I knew it would be hanging there above the fireplace, as obstinately out of place as ever. 'I'm not laughing,' I said. 'In my room, though. In private. And before we go get any dinner. If need be I'll have something sent up.'

'You *know*!' repeated Dave, unmollified. It seemed to offend him; he glared at me with aggressive scepticism. 'What're you trying to sell me here, a ghost story or something?'

I shook my head. 'Something.' The lift sighed open, and we trod over thick pile, building up the inevitable static charge that would leap into the first metal we touched. 'Something,' I repeated as I slid the keycard into the lock, 'that happened to me, years ago now. Something not so easy to explain, or believe; so I know how you feel.'

The wide glass doors to the balcony showed me it was night. I crossed the room in three long strides and thrust them rumbling wide. The river breezes had dispersed the furnace airs of day, and this high the heavy traffic fumes could not reach. In the black-glass sky the stars were twinkling, and the great arm of the Milky Way arched across the city like trailing translucent silk. The arm of a spiral galaxy, I thought; and with dramatic suddenness I seemed to see, superimposed over that awesome image in my mind, that far mightier, immaterial Spiral of space and time. That swirling pool of being in which our own reality, fixed and regulated, was the solid Core; but along whose arms lay every infinite variation of it that the human mind could conceive, and more, far more. And among whose shadowy reaches dwelt powers that could play with humanity like toys. Through those same reaches, in immortal, timeless journeying, a man might become more than a man, more truly himself till in the end – if he survived – he might rise to rival those powers, rise as they must once have done themselves.

Rise – or sink; I had seen both. I had seen both, and trembled in awe and horror at the extremes they reached, and my own vulnerable helplessness in the face of either. For long years the scale of that vision had oppressed me, yet lured me with memories that tugged at my own innermost core, at the soul that once I'd let shrivel for the success I coveted. Those were memories I'd striven to suppress – never hard, when they were spawned outside the Core, where they found no roots. Yet I knew now why those dreams had tracked my face with tears.

Shown my own weakness, I'd been warned off. That warning I'd tried to heed. Yet now, it seemed, the Spiral had reached out to me, and in no friendly way. Countering it had shown me something new, though – a way I could make use of the Spiral's possibilities. Summoning a sword was a small way, admittedly; but if I still had the trick of that, there might be other things I could manage. And in a good cause, too; important, in a realm where motives really mattered. I would need help; but that I knew how to find, or thought I did.

What some called Spiral and Core, others, usually from an earlier time, called Wheel and Hub. Well, perhaps I could start that Wheel turning in my direction a little, at last. I raised my arms to the vision, as if to embrace it, turning there above me. I became aware of Dave, silently watching me as if I were a man he had never seen in his life before.

'Explanations begin here, Dave. They won't be easy. But if you think I'm insane, just fasten on what you've seen today – explain that some other way! But keep a firm grip on it; don't rationalise, don't lie to yourself. Don't just . . . take a step back. Memories like those, you'll find they slip away more easily than most. And you'll need them, Dave; because there may be one way open for our containers, after all!'

'Listen, tosh!' Dave waggled a finger in my face. 'You do not, repeat *not* , get rid of me that easily.'

I snapped home my seatbelt. 'I should've left you back out in the Far East! Dave, I know you're the athletic type, but you're going to have to run real fast to keep up with me now.'

He smirked. 'Uh-huh.' He dangled something that jingled in front of me, and whipped it away when I snatched. 'An athletic pickpocket is what I am. When we were coming down in the lift.'

I thumped the wheel. 'Listen, you stupid bugger! Give me back those keys! It's not that I don't *want* to take you along!'

Well, I told myself, not entirely. But the truth was, I was a little jealous of the Tavern and the people and all it represented. It was important to me, it represented a whole other side to my life, totally different from the cool crisp world of international commerce, with all its flash trappings. And flasher than Dave they rarely, if ever, came. Much as I liked him, I didn't want him to become mixed up with the world I'd found. I was afraid, in a way, that he might make it look smaller, shabbier, less glorious. Even if he didn't actually sneer at it – and he could be pretty good at sneering, when his better nature wasn't in gear – his very presence, his Isse Miyaki coats and cigarettes from the Burlington Arcade, might leach the warmth and colour out of the Tavern and leave it looking shabby, sordid even. Of course my jeans were Calvin Klein, and it wasn't exactly a pony-trap I was driving; but that was different, somehow. And there was a more immediate problem.

'It's – well, you remember you couldn't find your way back into those alleys? That's how hard this place can be to find!'

'But you said you'd been back there since that first . . . time out on this Spiral thing.'

'Yes. But not for years. I didn't exactly give up trying, but . . . well, it kept getting harder. For every time I got through there were ten more times I couldn't pick up the way, just went charging around street after street in the car, on foot, for hours, just *trying*. It's a horrible feeling, that. Sometimes you even see it, or what looks like it, in the distance, down a sidestreet or something. And then you back up and go after it, and it's just some clapped-out old paint store or something . . . You begin to think you're mad. Really mad, I mean. Begin to doubt everything.'

'Ever thought you might be? Okay, okay,' he spluttered, backing off in alarm. 'I saw the alleys, I saw the lion or whatever, I saw the dacoits, okay, if you're crazy I am too, see, here's the keys, nice keys, see? Only,' he added as I made a flying grab over the car door and snatched them, 'only listen to just two little points first, okay?'

'I'm listening.'

He made great play of mopping his brow with a silk handkerchief. 'Hey, you're lovely when you're angry, anyone ever tell you that? One, you yourself said how this Spiral thing's come out to you this time. Might do that again, mightn't it? Could be real useful, like, having someone else along. Two, if we have real trouble getting there, I guarantee you personally I'll let you drop me on any given street corner and make my own lonely way home, and you can try again. Now, tell me, how can you truly object to that?'

I swung back behind the wheel. 'Maybe I'll only get one chance. But . . . ' I glared at him, standing there radiating cocky poise and confidence in the damp evening. I knew him well enough to see the intelligence behind the poses, but I'd never thought of him as the courageous type. He'd made fun of my taste for rock-climbing and, more recently, fencing and sailing, claiming they were designed to appeal to caveman instincts. His sports were team games like football and basketball, not to mention horizontal jogging. He'd had as good a fright in those back alleys as he'd ever had in all his life; yet here he was, pleading to throw himself in the way of something that almost certainly threatened only me. 'What the hell. Get in, man. And put your seatbelt on, for once.'

'I hear and obey, oh deputy managing director of mine. We're taking enough daredevil risks tonight.'

32

I accelerated the Morgan smoothly out of the office carpark, turned right to head out towards the ring road, swung the long bonnet mercilessly around the roundabout and into the right lane. Between late afternoon and sunset was the best time, and all this gabbing might have held me up just a bit too long. I leaned on the throttle a little, though I'd have to play it carefully; this car looked and sounded a lot more conspicuous than the dinky sports saloons I used to drive, impossible to tell apart if you missed the plates. It was good to have an open car, though. Even in the traffic the air was cool and fresh, and I welcomed the hint of rain; I could feel my parched skin expanding as it drank up the moisture Bangkok had baked out of it. The traffic cleared, I changed up and put my foot down, turning to grin at Dave. He didn't look so happy, hunkered down in his seat, hugging his blazer close around his chest with his tie streaming out in front of him in the eddy the windscreen created. I found the cold air stimulating, thrilling even as it took on a first faint sea-tang. For once the lights were with me, and I had no time to look up at the clouds; but out of the corner of my eye I seemed to see a first faint suggestion in the low light, like the memory of a distant landscape among the peaks and gulfs of the air. With a sudden thrill I changed up, sent the car leaping ahead and into the left-hand lane, ready for the turn-off into the devious one-way system that had become the quickest way to the docks. It spat me out into the big roundabout at the bottom of Harbour Walk, and from there into the shadowy mouth of Danube Street. Between its massive walls night had already fallen, but the cracked panes of the upper warehouse windows mirrored the orange and crimson flames of sunset clouds, as if to mimic the gas lamps that had once burned there. A well-remembered thunder of tyres told me the cobbles were still there, as they had been – when?

Three, no, four years since I'd last been here, right enough. *Don't forget the docks, and Danube Street. And 'fore all, the Tavern!* So Jyp the Pilot had advised me. And I'd tried. I'd sought the Tavern many times, but rarely reached it. Most often I'd tried at times of stress or pain, at crises in my life. Sometimes I'd made it, then. Sometimes I'd found peace of a sort in the Tavern, food and drink and good company, tales the like of which you never heard; and I had one of my own to tell. I'd begun to believe, then, that it had something to do with my state of mind, that I'd get through when I most needed to.

But there were other times. Then I'd found nothing, not even a locked door. Only the lowering walls of Victorian warehouse and factory or the garbage-strewn vacant lots they left behind; bleak streets of flyblown cafes and moribund shops, or the empty elegance of urban renewal – empty facades restored and prettified, a saccharine mix of disco and gift shop, tapas bar and bistro with straw-wrapped bottles and pleated shades, as colourful, elegant and lifeless as a blown-glass butterfly. Yet those times, most of them, had been every bit as fraught and critical as the times I'd got through – or so they seemed to me, anyhow. Was it just arbitrary, the way out to the Spiral? My instincts told me it wasn't; and out there I had learned to trust instinct, when all else was chaos. But the rhyme or reason of it was still beyond me.

Now, turning slowly into Tampere Street, I felt a great electricity build up within me. It had hardly changed, the same shredded newspaper whirling down the gutters in the eddying breeze, the same torn polythene sheeting sliding along with a sinister dragging hiss. Dave broke his long silence, demanding, 'This is your wild romantic haven?'

I was too busy scanning the little alleys and courts. 'Watch the rooftops,' I told him, and turned left into a likely-looking sidestreet.

'So what am I supposed to be looking for?'

'When you see it, you'll know.' Right again, in the general direction of the sea; that felt reasonable. I seemed to know this street, and the deserted factory that brooded over the T-junction ahead; another good sign. Gull cries echoed through the still cool air, giving an edge of harshness and urgency. The long evening shadows lay stretched out like a lazing cat along the sidestreets, as sleek and as enigmatic. Which way to turn? I couldn't decide. There was nobody behind me, so I slowed to a crawl again and looked around.

'Nothing much so far,' said Dave in a bored voice. 'Dull as ditchwater. They might as well roll up the pavements round here, come evening. No wonder people watch so much TV.'

'How so?'

'All these aerials. Look at them. Must be bloody square-eyed, living here.'

I braked hard, and looked up open-mouthed.

'Hey! Now I know why you made me wear that bloody

seatbelt!' Dave complained. 'Nearly had me through the windscreen then! And flattened my ciggies!'

'You always did like Turkish.' I shot back through the gears again, and sent the car racing across the cobbles for the junction at the end, and around the right-hand corner. Not far ahead another road crossed it, and down the road lay a spiky shadow like some vast web. 'Dave, you idiot! Do they look like TV aerials, those?'

'Well – they must be down by the docks . . . Some kind of radar?'

'Aerials!' I laughed aloud, half drunk with the excitement of it, and the ease. I swung the car around that last corner, and sent it roaring away down towards the sea. Now he could see for himself; and as it dawned on him he said nothing, only slumped back in his seat with his jaw sagging, his eyes wide and foolish. And even I, who knew what to expect, found myself slowing the car gradually, till the boards of the great wharves drummed under its tyres, and I braked and pulled up. Together, silently, we stood up in our seats, leaning on the windscreen, staring in sheer wonder at the ancient harbour pool, and a sight that should have slipped away two centuries gone. A fierce joy leapt up in me, knowing it was no delusion, no fantasy I'd carried with me for so long, that mighty forest without leaf or root that lined them, with only tarry rope and ratline for its foliage, the clustering masts of a mighty host of square-rigged ships against a fiery archipelago in the sunset clouds.

A hundred types of hull, so many they were moored in rows, rose and fell and rubbed against rope fenders in the gentle swell, like great sea beasts scratching their flanks in idleness. The swollen curve of a cog lay alongside the sleek shark shape of a clipper, the tall castles of a galleon loomed up over the flat deck of a cutter. For the most part, though, the ships before us were square-riggers of the Georgian era or its likeness, builds of the late 1700s into the middle 1800s, shaped by the last great flowering of the age of sail. Along the hulls of lean privateers rows of gun-ports stared hungrily at rotund merchantmen, and here and there the dark even lines of a heavy warship loured over lesser craft with masterful menace. From out of the Spiral to the ports on the fringes of the Core these ships had come, bearing strange goods whose use one might often only guess at; even the warships were traders, though it might not be honest barter or convoy work that gained them their goods. And to the Spiral they would return, for lingering too long in any one place had its subtle perils. Meanwhile, though, their crews would go in search of recreation; and we would be able to follow.

I grinned at Dave, knowing full well that till then, as I would have, he'd been hedging his bets, postponing judgement, never really believing a word of what I'd told him, no matter what he remembered from Bangkok. 'Any comments, Mr Oshukwe?'

He shivered, though the breeze was light. All the flip affectation had fallen out of his voice, left it sounding thin and hollow. 'I didn't know what to think. Still don't. I know what I see, but I still don't say you're not nuts. It's just myself I'm not so sure about.'

'I felt the same way. But isn't it fantastic? Isn't it beautiful?'

'Beautiful? Jesus – was what hit us in Bangkok beautiful?' He scrubbed the back of a hand across his mouth. 'I used to think I could just about cope with the world, ride with the punches and all that crap. But if there's all this just waiting round the wrong corner, what else is there? What could I run into, back home in Kano? Or coming home from the office? How's anyone to expect it? How's a man to be ready? I knew you were a pretty strange guy, Steve; but if *this* just makes you sit back and admire, then you're a damn sight stranger than I thought.'

I grinned. 'Thanks for the reference! You get used to it. But not alone. We need some help, and that's what we're here to find.' I was scanning the aged brickwork of the wharfside buildings, where elderly painted signs bleached and peeled at the bite of the salty air. Above the door of the tallest building an ornate red sandstone plaque bore a legend in swirling copperplate, crumbling into unreadability – *Paramaribo Wharf*.

'This isn't one I know. We want the streets behind the Melrose and Danziger Wharves, as I remember; somewhere round there, anyhow. Come along, we'd better find a sign, or somebody to ask.' Dave left the car with the greatest reluctance, wincing when his feet touched the worn wharf timbers, as if he expected them to melt away and drop him in the greasy-looking water beneath. Well, he was probably the over-imaginative type. I'd been told, and not as a compliment either, that it was because I'd never used my own imagination much that I found it easier to accept the unimaginable.

Maybe so; but as I peered down murky sidestreets where daylight could never have meant much, it wasn't too hard to feel slightly spooked. There wasn't anybody around. The ships looked empty, but they'd probably have watchmen on board; I wasn't going to risk disturbing them, though. Suppose I chose a Wolf ship, or worse? I'd been told there was worse, much worse, though how was a little hard to guess. And now the first euphoria was melting away, I began to wonder if we hadn't managed to get through just a little too easily. It was rarely wise to trust to appearances, in this weird and shadowy suburb of normality.

Steps divided the wharf from its neighbour, apparently the Callão Wharf, steps that led down to a lower quay where ships' boats and the like might land; but it was crumbling and slathered in green weed and slime. Beyond them yet another murky alley opened, but not too far down it I was surprised to see a dim glow mirrored in the puddles. Unquestionably lit windows, but not very bright, showing reddish and sullen on the signboard that creaked back and forth like a gibbet above.

'Bloody hell!' muttered Dave as we trooped down towards it. 'Looks worse than a motorway service station.'

'On a Bank Holiday, right. Can't hurt to ask, though, can it?'

'I don't know,' he muttered, skirting an oily pool by the doorstep. 'This place gives me the heaves.' As I pushed open the door I was inclined to agree with him. The smell that poured out seemed to be mostly bad tobacco and greasy frying at first, till you caught the whiffs of stale drink, unwashed bodies, vomit and worse that made you grateful for the smoke. Inside it was small and dim, lit by smoky candle lanterns on the low rafters, the soot-stained ceiling soaking up their light. Men sat there in the shadows, hunched over tables. Some were black, others pale-skinned, but that was all I could say of them, save for the gleam of eyes that turned towards us. Talk faded to a low growl. A big pot-bellied lout clad in a ragged shirt and kneebreeches bound with a black sash surged to his feet from the nearest table and looked us up and down, sizing us up.

'¿Qué quereis?' Spanish wasn't his native language any more than it was mine, and the tone was just short of spitting in our faces.

I spread my hands with all the mild dignity I could muster. '¿Perdóneme, señor, queremos descubrir la Taverna Illyrica, por favor?'

Even in that bilious light I could have sworn he went pale. '¡No sé!' he barked, with the aggressive force of a man reacting against his own weakness. To my astonishment he stabbed out two fingers in the horned sign against the Evil Eye, and spat on my shoe. Almost any other time I might just have turned on my heel and left, but my blood was singing with the sight of those ships against the sunset, and the memories they awoke. I kicked out and wiped my shoe on his breeches with considerable force. He howled, hopped and grabbed at his sash. For a knife, I guessed; I grabbed his shirt and threw him back across the table. *Then* I turned on my heel. Dave caught at my jacket and practically hauled me out the door.

'Christ, what's got into you? Let's get out of here before they cut our throats. Or worse! How could you *do* that?'

'Don't run,' I said. 'That'd just bait them. Act confident.' Mirrored in a dirty window opposite, I saw the door of the den swing open behind us, silhouetting a figure against the red light – no, two or three. But they weren't coming out. Calmly I looked back. One of them waved, mockingly. '¡*Buenos noches, señor! Nos respetamos à los bultòs!*'

The door slammed. 'Lousy Spanish,' said Dave, with only a slight tremor in his voice. 'Worse than mine. Why're we supposed to give their respects to the . . . that word just means bundles, doesn't it?'

'They're not Spaniards, that's for sure. I wonder why they thought we were?' I looked back at the sign. '*Den . . . Vijnkeller* something. *Marowijnse*, maybe. Sounds Dutch. And the Netherlands used to be Spanish, once; some of their colonies, too. So maybe for those heavies using Spanish was an insult in itself. And *bultòs* . . . I suppose it does mean bundles. God knows why. Another insult, probably. Come on, let's find somewhere friendlier.'

But as we walked back to the wharf through the gathering darkness, it came to me that I did know something. *Bundles* . . . I'd heard that word, or something like it. From Jyp? Maybe; and in no light tone, either. Something bad – and it was just then that I heard the titter from the darkness ahead.

A titter, a very human sound, but high-pitched, piping; a soft scuffing of feet, as of stealthy movement; a faint dry rustle, and *that* sounded thoroughly insectile. Dave had heard it, too. His whisper was almost lost in the sea-hiss. 'If it's those bloody dacoits again—'

'I don't think it is,' I breathed. 'Whatever, it's between us and the wharves – but only on the shadowy side of the street. If we can sort of sidle round – then we bolt for the car.'

We moved swiftly, quietly, ducking back across the street and under the shadow of the wall opposite; but as we crossed, just for an instant we put the last glow of the sky behind what lurked there. At first I thought it was just a man, a bulky shape on thin legs – very thin – wearing something that covered arms and head. But then, as it swung about, searching, I saw it was solid, that there was no head or arm, only shreds of thin fabric that flapped as it moved, like an old-fashioned burlap sack. Then another one moved up beside it, and it was the same. I heard Dave's teeth grind with the strain. But just a few steps more and we'd be past them.

That hellish titter sounded again, right in my ear. '*Run!*' I yelled, but I could have saved my breath. Dave was already on the move. I panted after him – and behind me I heard a sudden savage rush of feet, one I'd heard before. We rounded the corner and ran for the wharf, for the car. The first night I'd ever come here, something had followed me back to my car – something that had trailed me, then come rushing after me. I'd never seen what; but it sounded just like that. We reached the car, piled in over the doors with fine disregard for the paintwork. There was an awful moment while I fumbled for my keys, and then the power of the engine roared out into the stillness. I spun the wheel, swinging the car round in a narrow arc towards the wharfside.

'Hey, hold it!' howled Dave. 'You're not going *back*—'

My offside tyres rose up on the timbers at the brink, barely making the turn, then bounced back down. I flicked my lights full on and let their beams sweep the wharf. There was nothing. Smiling grimly, I changed gear and we went bouncing off down the wharf. 'Didn't think they'd risk the car,' I grinned, and then we passed the mouth of the alleyway, and they came boiling out after us. Nightmare things, shapeless things swathed in rope and rustling mummy-wrappings, bounding with horrid energy on legs so bare and wiry they looked less human than they actually were. Out around the car they leaped and hopped, collided into it with heavy thumps that sent us skeeting and swerving wildly. One hopped on to the narrow running-board with a force that almost turned us out and over the edge, into the deep harbour; but Dave rose in his seat and aimed a powerful kick that sent the awful thing flying into the path of its fellows. This close you could see that within those wrappings things were stirring, bulging, threshing as if they were about to burst through the rotten-looking coverings; heads or limbs, maybe, but it looked less normal than that, and more malevolent. Out of the alleys they spilled, banging into the car like moths to a light, and I couldn't get up more speed. The windscreen shattered, and I punched it through, barely in time to see another set of steps loom up ahead. I flung the wheel around, the back end fishtailed and sent the monstrosities scattering. One wheel screamed over emptiness a moment, then we were bouncing and jarring down a narrow alley.

'It's getting *narrower*, Steve!' The rising note of hysteria in Dave's voice echoed my own fears. If we had to stop – if they caught us – would those ragged bundles burst? Would what squirmed within there be revealed to us? And what would happen then?

Dave yelled and pointed. Another narrow street opened to the left, and down it gleamed a spot of molten gold. I spun the wheel again, the tyres screeched on the cobbles – and just at the wrong moment a wall of the things hit us amidships. The wing crumpled, the car rocked, tipped up violently, then came crashing back down on its suspension and sped on. I peered through the shattered screen, weaving and dodging along the narrow lane. One of the things was caught against the wall, pinned, dragged – in my cracked rearview mirror I saw the ropes burst, the sacking explode outwards. Maybe it was merciful Dave caught my arm just then, and I missed a closer look at what came spilling out. 'There!' he screamed. 'That somewhere?'

Red woodwork, white walls, florid signboard and warmly glowing windows . . . 'Can't you see?' I shouted, unfairly startled that he even needed to ask. 'That's it!'

Across the road opposite the side wall of the Illyrian Tavern loomed up. Praying that there wasn't anyone else on the road, I launched the car out and hauled her round in a terrible screeching curve, right at the bottom of the steps. But even as I jerked the handbrake, the heavy door was flung back with a crash. Into the opening, clasping a scarlet mantle close about her, stepped the girl I knew as Katjka. In one hand she held a heavy ship's lantern, and as we jolted to a halt at the foot of the steps she swung it high, shouting aloud, and flicked open its stormshield with a clatter.

The light from within blazed down on her. Maybe it wasn't as bright as a magnesium flash or an acetylene arc, not quite; yet it made everything else grow dim. Her eyes glistened as the lantern swung, and the smile on her lips seemed strange. 'Look out,

Katjka!' I shouted, but the shout faded. She knew we were being followed; she understood. Her shining gaze was fixed on the lane opposite, and the things that clustered there; and they came no further.

She came one step down, outlined in that cone of bitter radiance; it threw deep shadows on her face, hardening her features into a pale glassy mask. The things seemed to bunch together.

Another step. The mantle swirled and glowed like woven flame, and they set up a high fearful tittering.

Another step; and her eyes, normally grey, suddenly blazed green and feral as a fox's, the hard lines round her mouth deepened in a sharp-toothed snarl.

She lifted one foot off the last step. There was a chorus of hysterical shrilling, and the crash of leaping feet.

She stopped, and looked down with a wry smile. She stood one step from the ground, and the things had fled.

A deft twist of her wrist flicked the lantern closed. We looked at each other. '*Devre naçz, Stefan!*' she said quietly. 'I'm glad you are come back. You look well. But a little older.'

'It's been a while, Katjka. A long while.'

She smiled slightly, shrugged. 'Sso? It does you no harm.' The mantle swirled back from her shoulders. I expected Dave's eyes to be out on stalks. Her braided red waistcoat and sprigged blue dirndl skirt were just that bit too gaudy, her cleavage too precipitous by far. When we first met I'd taken her for a tavern tart, and not been too far wrong. But Katjka was many things, and least of all of them simple. 'Good, perhaps, that you did not wait sso much longer. The *bultòs*, filthy things! Why were they at your heels?'

'I don't know.' I looked at her, uneasily. I'd never seen her the way she'd appeared then, nothing like so formidable. 'I don't even know what they are. But they're not the first.'

She raised a sardonic eyebrow. 'Best you come insside, then, before there's more! And make known to me your friend, *ej*?'

I'd been a bit worried about introducing Dave to Katjka, for all kinds of reasons. But his usual relentless line of groin-based innuendo seemed to have dried up completely, the last effect I'd have expected Katjka to have. He shook hands with her and smiled, but there was a sudden reserve about him, his normally open, cheerful eyes narrowing. If there was anything in his look as she led us up the steps and over the threshold, it might have been awe, and very deep distrust.

He stared into the warm spicy gloom of the Tavern's main chamber as if it was a deep well, but allowed us to lead him down to a booth by the fire. We'd hardly subsided on to the bench cushions when Myrko the landlord himself came bustling up to wring our hands in his leathery paws and welcome me back like a long-lost son. As he rolled off roaring for food and drink for his special guests I began to feel the terror of the outside slip away. Dave was peering around at the other booths, but though there were plenty of customers in that night it was hard to see them clearly. That was just how they liked it, and Myrko took care to see it remained that way. Shadows hung like draperies beneath that roof with nothing to cast them, drinking up the warm golden light from the oil lamps; but there was nothing sinister about them, snug and enveloping as velvet after the chill darkness of the streets. I leaned back and revelled in the old room with its smoke-blackened rafters, its hams and sausages and straw-bound bottles and bales of strange spices and dried improbabilities from distant seas. 'Really got your feet under the table here, haven't you?' said Dave quietly.

'It's that sort of place,' I said. 'That kind of people. They'll do as much for you, if only you'll let them. What's the matter? Don't you like this place? Don't you like Katjka?'

He scratched a finger on the worn tabletop, dented with swords and pistols hastily cast down, with bags of hard coin and stranger currencies, stained with drinks slopped in good cheer, rarely, but sometimes, spilled in anger. 'The place – and her – Christ, Steve! I mean, she's something to you, obviously . . . but don't *you* feel it about her?'

'Feel what?'

He winced. '*Weird* . . .' was all he had time to whisper. Katjka reappeared with a tray of two-litre beer steins and little flasks of *tujica*, better known as slivovitz, and flopped down between us with a gusty breath.

'*Whoo*! Now drink this! Drink, and ssay what brings you here with such hellhounds on your tails.'

'Hellhounds? What were they, anyhow? Where'd they come from?'

'Those? Have you not heard of them? They are from across the ocean, those *bultòs*. Haunters of graves from the mountainlands where the condor flies. The heathen priest-kings feared them,

42

thought them spirits of the displaced dead. Perhapss they are.' I
thought of the swathed mummies in Inca tombs, and shivered.

'From South America?' demanded Dave hoarsely, putting down
his beer. 'What're they doing here?'

She looked at him sombrely. 'What does evil anywhere? Some
greedy fool sought to smuggle them in, to use their terror for his
own gain. Much like a certain *dupiah* of the Caribbees, of which
Stefan can tell you more – though that was far more powerful.'

'Not here,' I said, feeling the hair bristle on the back of my neck.
'Not now. I thought you had . . . well, safeguards against that kind
of thing.'

She nodded, wryly. 'The Wardens laid a cold hand on the fool,
yess. And most of his flock, but like rats some esscaped, and still
haunt the shadows around the lesser wharves. Rarely in such
numbers, rarely sso bold unless another will seeks to stir them.
There are simple precautions one may take against them. Sso I felt
their presence even within here, and came out to seek you. Myrko
ssends out the word that the Bundlers are massing again, and there
will be a hunting and a cleansing.'

'*Bundlers*? Yes, dammit, Jyp did warn me against them, I
remember now. But he didn't say what they were – didn't want to
scare me any more, I guess, when I was new to all this.' I stole a
glance at Dave, washing down his second or third slivovitz with
beer. 'Katjka love, I've got to talk to Jyp. Or Mall. I need them for
something, or their advice at least.'

She shook her head. 'Two ssuch rovers, will you find them often
in one Port? They are not now, nor will be within foresseeable
future.' My spirits sank. When Katjka said *foreseeable*, she meant
it literally. They might not be back this way for years.

She smiled, leaned against me and rubbed my leg affectionately.
'Not sso worried, Stefan! I'll put out the word for them also, by all
the pathways. That may take ssome time, of course. But I am
always here, Steve. Always your friend.'

She looked at me with wide concerned eyes. Her hand no longer
moved on my thigh, but sat lightly, a promise without distraction.
Maybe she could help, strange creature that she was; advise me at
least, put me in touch with someone else. I looked to Dave, but by
now he was evidently out of it. Shock and slivovitz had taken their
toll, and he was sitting sipping his beer and staring into nothing,
paying no attention to us or anything else. 'Well,' I began. 'It's like
this . . .'

I left out nothing, except the little matter of Rangda. Not that Katjka had any claim to be jealous of me, but it seemed wisest. Certainly Katjka's eyes flashed with malign amusement as I described how a girl had helped me away. But she heard me out gravely, smiling only when I mentioned the telegram; modern communications always seemed to strike her as funny, though I could never figure out why. 'And thiss strangely born idea of yours?'

I gnawed a nail, hesitantly. 'Yes . . . that. Well . . . Look, it may just be me going paranoid, but – if we really are up against some kind of unofficial barrier, then maybe . . . just maybe . . . we might be able to bypass it. An unusual barrier, by an – unusual route.'

She nodded, alert as a vixen. 'Sso. By—'

'Yes. By the Spiral. Shipping our cargo east of the sunset. Out of common time. A lot of trouble, maybe even dangerous – but if it gets all those sluice mechanisms and computer gear and the rest through . . . '

Before I finished she'd already slipped out the pack of cards she always seemed to have about herself, warm and silky as her skin, and was dealing it out across the table. The three cards I turned over seemed to surprise her, the three of every suit except spades. She shuffled again, and handed me the pack. I cut it as she asked me, again and again, and started in surprise as she pressed the cards to my lips. They smelt faintly of her, not exactly unclean but strong; her origins I'd never dared ask, but I guessed they were somewhere baths were rare and soap a luxury. I'd managed to slip her some elegant Worth stuff once, as part of a larger present. She'd been delighted, but I had a suspicion such a rare treasure was sitting gathering dust in her attic bedroom high above, too precious for actual use.

This time I had to deal, three cards at random; and again she frowned, as King of Clubs appeared, then Queen of Diamonds. And as the second card fell I stared; for the faces on the cards seemed somehow to change, to take on the faint tremors of life, the hint of an expression. And it was not a look I liked – as if they were warring with their painted glances, fixed, hostile, implacable. I peered, blinked; and somehow, as I did so, those glances appeared to shift outwards, horribly aware, and fasten upon *me* . . .

Katjka's hand slapped down over them. 'One more,' she said softly. I dealt, and it was another court card, the Knave of Spades. I felt a sick chill inside me; once before I'd drawn a Knave from

44

Katjka's pack, a Knave of Diamonds, and seen within it a fearsome vision of an enemy I'd had to face, almost to my ruin. But this one was just the usually jolly, bovine figure on a card – or was it? It looked, in some indefinable way, like a door ajar, like curtains with a foot sticking out, the essence of a mocking, menacing concealment. A room is just a room, until you know a body lies beneath the floorboards; then everything about it changes, though not one dust-grain stirs. So it was with that card, until Katjka slid it on to the rest, and back within the confines of the pack.

'You are not paranoid, Stefan,' she said quietly. 'There are indeed great forces arrayed against you, in this venture of yours.'

I sat back with a sigh. 'I knew it! And who the hell is it, then? Competitors? Governments?'

She cocked her head, surprised. 'You ask? No, Stefan! I cannot be sure, but I think not. No mundane enemy of yours; for those you could have met long since with those arts and mysteries of which you are a master.'

'Then . . . who? Where from?'

Her answer was disturbing. She lifted her eyes to the shadowed ceiling, and her open hand traced a slow eerie arc across the air, around and above us. Dave, jolted out of his haze, sat up with a muffled oath, and I sympathised. The gesture seemed to conjure up a whole unseen world, pressing in. 'I cannot be certain; it is what my heart tells me. The attacks upon you might be from many causes, or none esspecial. But I believe it is from beyond here, from the outer sshadows that your enemies have come. That it is from the Sspiral that this barrier is raised against you.'

'Oh . . . *jesus.*'

I sagged against the high back of the bench, feeling the shadows gather around me, and not so cosily now. I realised now it was something I'd been half afraid of all along, and yet always dismissed with the comforting reflection that it simply didn't make sense. What interest, good or bad, could my little everyday affairs hold for forces from the wilder shores of space and time? Yet it seemed they did. I caught Katjka's arm. 'But who? Or what? And for god's sake, *why?*'

'Sso much is beyond me. Except that to the East it is strong, for that way my ssight is most clouded. It, or they; for there may be more than one. You drew in threes.'

'You mean . . . ' I snapped my fingers. 'That might be why I could route the cargoes to Bangkok and no further? Because further westward it – they – haven't the power to block me?'

She nodded. 'That may be sso. But Stefan – there might be other things they could do.'

Food arrived then, Myrko's friendly toad-face beaming over a vast tray of dishes. Dave showed some animation when the smell tickled his nostrils, and began shovelling great chunks of seafood and rice on to his plate. 'Hey, don't you want some of this?' he remembered belatedly, with bulging cheeks. 'It'sh fantastic!'

'No, Dave,' I told him gently, contemplating what he was tucking into. I helped myself to a skewer of *Husarjenspijtz* and a fiery mess of vegetables. 'You go right ahead.' After all, he'd twitted me now and again for not eating snails, so he ought to be perfectly happy with jellied sea-cucumber. But somehow I hadn't the heart to tell him.

Anyway, I had other things to think about, when the peppery food's first onslaught died down. 'So,' I said ruefully to Katjka. 'From what you've told me, it looks like this idea of mine's just about as bloody wrong as it can be.'

She arched her brows. 'Is it?'

'Well – if I'm having all this trouble with forces out on the Spiral, wouldn't shipping stuff that way just be, well, playing right into their hands? I mean, it seemed like a bright idea at the time, but it's not absolutely the only alternative. We could charter an ordinary merchant ship on our own behalf, sail the cargo direct. That'd be ruinously expensive, but if we went by some Third World carrier we might get government kickbacks . . . We could even send it piecemeal by air, though that'd be even pricier.'

'You mean – through the Hub? The Core?' Katjka shook her head sombrely. 'Not if you want to see your ship again, or your . . . aeroplane.' She pronounced every syllable very carefully, as if the word was unusual. 'And keep the lives of a crew off your conscience. There are too many things may happen to one ship in the open seas. Or to a machine that flies.'

'Not if they couldn't find the stuff. We could disguise it, snow out the end-user pretty well; there are ways, the arms boys do it all the time. Until we were under way, even. There'd be no slip-ups if I went along—'

'*Nyej! Njevecz!*' She shook her head so hard her blonde hair flew out from her shoulders, absolutely horrified. 'No–no–no! That you must not do, that above all things! Not within the Hub! Not alone!' Her anxious grey eyes flickered over me. 'Yes, you are older, you have grown; yet still within you are gulfs, emptinesses that leave you sso very vulnerable to . . . outside forces. And you have no other shields to raise against them, of art or knowledge, not yet. They have shown they can strike within the Hub, or at its margins. If they can reach so far, they will find your cargo however you can disguise it. You . . . ' She hesitated. 'What would you call it? If you go with it, you would only be a target, a focuss for their strike.'

My heart sank. 'The way I was for the Wolves, you mean? God. I thought their kind of attack was almost unheard of . . . '

'Sso open, so blatant, aye, it was. More likely they would come upon you ssecretly, subtly, in some out-of-the-way place where the outer margins of the Hub are thinnest, and by night. But come they would, and it would be . . . terrible.' She brooded, staring into the flames of the fire as if they held a memory of some ancient ill. 'No, not in the seas and airs of the Hub is there any safety, not now. Out here, yes, their power will be greater; but it must cover a wider range, to seek their prey, and so be spread far thinner. Your cargo will have to be protected every sspan of its way; but that is nothing uncommon. And here upon the Sspiral, most important of all, there are countervailing powers, if only you may find them. You will need advice and help – a mind of craft and might . . . '

I looked at her. 'Haven't I already found one?'

Katjka smiled a lot, but seldom laughed. It sounded nervous now, as if I'd somehow challenged her. 'No. Sstrengths are given me, maybe, but they flow in other courses. Of the East I know little. A greater adept than I . . . '

I thought of the old creature Jyp had found. 'How about Le Stryge?'

'*Nyej!*' She hugged herself and shivered, angrily.

'I know he's an old villain, a murderous one – and he smells a bit – okay, a lot. But god, he can do things—'

'*No!* Stefan, a hundred times I tell you and you do not seem to realise just how dangerouss that creature is! He is not to hand, anyway; and if he were he would not help.'

'I could pay him. Well.'

47

'I know only too well that you could. But in no coin you can afford to lose! Before, he aided you to clear a debt to Jyp, and because he ssensed a challenge to his own domain. You he owes nothing – the reverse, more like. He would see it so. And Stefan, he might try to collect. Are you ready to face that?'

I thought for an instant, then downed a great gulp of the plum brandy.

'Sso,' she said quietly, the sibilance of her accent suddenly very strong. 'Then put the old fiend from your mind, lest you draw him upon you. Anyway, he also knowss little enough of the East. You need someone who does know; but such great adepts rarely if ever come westward.' She sat for a moment, considering. 'There is one we might consult. He landed off a clipper from the Spice Isles some months past. He has been here, once. He keeps his own company and counsel, but he sseems amiable enough of his kind, well spoken of by Those who should know.' She smiled sourly. 'Which probably means he is less powerful than the greater ones like Stryge. But also less dangerous.'

'Then will you take me to him?'

She hugged herself again, and shuddered. 'Bothering even one of lesser craft in his lair, that is still a risky business. But . . . ' She shut her eyes, as if wrestling with herself. 'Stefan, for you I will adventure it. When we have eaten, then we will go to seek him. In your car.'

When we made our way out of the Tavern, Dave stood warily at the top of the steps, looking about the empty street, before sidling smoothly down to the car. I contemplated the battered wing and scratched paintwork rather ruefully, and thought of what else might have suffered from the jarring; still, I'd probably be away again for a week or two, time enough to get it looked over. The door clicked behind us, and Katjka came slowly down to join us. The shabby belted trenchcoat and beret she'd put on, together with her lean foxy features, made her look like something standing under a lamppost in a 1940s film. She too glanced around nervously. 'The air is cold,' she said, though to me it seemed a warm enough evening. 'Could we have the top up?'

When that was done, I turned the car about, following her directions. Dave, in the back, exclaimed in surprise and relief when they brought us out into Danube Street once again, heading away from Harbour Walk towards the Wharfside development area. 'Is it far, this?' I asked her.

'To me, yes,' was all she said, her voice small and tense. I glanced down at her, and saw she was huddled down in her seat, her features parchment-pale and tight in the yellow glow of the passing streetlamps.

'Are you all right?' I asked her, remembering Jyp's ambiguous reaction to modern cars. 'Shall I slow down?'

'The faster the better. I . . . do not go out so often. Do not leave the Tavern.' Her voice sank to an arid whisper, and she looked listlessly out at the gaudy little reconstructed shops and bistros we passed, as if trying to discern what they might once have been in their original incarnations. She said nothing about that or anything else, beyond the occasional crisp direction, but I felt it with her, the oppressive weight of a time-bound world. Nothing of her visibly changed, but the years seemed to settle about her like veils of dusty web. I thought at first it must just be culture shock, seeing all the changes time had wrought since last she dipped a toe into it – and god alone knew when that last was. It would have shocked and depressed me, at first sight, anyway. But I began to suspect there might be more to it than that, when she mumbled one direction so indistinctly I missed the turn and had to circle round the block. That brought us into a street overcast by the shadow of a high grim wall, the streetlamps no more than struggling red specks like dim eyes in the arid gloom. Katjka took one long look, then positively crumpled into herself, refused to look up or answer even the gentlest question.

'That? Just a museum now,' volunteered Dave. 'Course there was a prison on the site, once, three centuries back.' He chuckled. 'Used to string up witches off the gallows in the yard there!'

Katjka sat up with unexpected energy. '*Daj*! And upon the block outside they sold slaves!' she spat back at him. I winced. Dave had asked for it, but he was understandably touchy on certain subjects; and I was suddenly reminded that he came from a culture with a long history of witch-finding. This time, though, he just sat back and said nothing.

Perhaps, like me, he was surprised to find that Katjka's directions seemed to be taking us down towards a familiar area, the main railway terminus. All the old buildings round there had been torn down in the 1960s and replaced by bright new concrete, so the whole area was obscenely stained, crumbling and shabby now; but I couldn't imagine any of it providing a lair for some oriental wise man. I was even more surprised when her curt instructions brought us out into the streets alongside the actual freight yards.

More than half of this vast Edwardian enclave lay in permanent disuse now. We passed beneath the shadow of the old disused engine-sheds, round fortresses of stained yellow brick; one of them was still plastered with gaudy posters and would-be psychedelic graffiti, like a New York subway car. I remembered that; it had briefly been turned into a theatre, then an ethnic cultural centre till its directors pinched all the grant cash. That had been the end of any attempt to redevelop the yards. Now this whole end of the yards lay abandoned till they could find a desperate enough property developer, and the shed was boarded-up and mouldering like all the others. I could imagine Le Stryge lurking somewhere like that; perhaps that was where we'd have to look.

But Katjka let us come out into the wide-open street at the far end of the yards; a broad road, dim-lit in the dusk by widely spaced streetlamps, with nothing but dingy concrete-and-glass office boxes on one side, and on the other a grass-footed wire-mesh fence, topped with barbed wire, separating us from some rail sidings, rusty with disuse. Katjka seemed to be scanning the fence, for suddenly she waved us down.

'It's here,' she said, and closed her eyes for a moment. I switched off the engine and looked around. Sidings; offices; nothing. But as we clambered out of the car I saw she was looking at the fence, at a place where a torn and twisted gap had been roughly mended with a flat sheet of smaller mesh, now very rusty. She pressed it, rather nervously, and it swung back. I looked at Dave, and raised my eyebrows. He looked back.

'Railway property,' he said. 'I was warned off playing on the tracks when I was a little kiddie. And I'm not sure just how much more I want to know about this, anyway. I think, *if* you don't very much mind, that I'm just going to stay right here in the car and think improving thoughts.'

Katjka nodded. 'Probably that is best,' she agreed, neutrally.

But being Dave, he had to have the parting shot. 'After all,' he added, clambering back into the car, '*someone's* got to come bail you out. Or identify the remains. Have fun, now!'

Gingerly, avoiding the snagging wiretips, we clambered through the gap. Beyond it the lines were even less well-lit than the road, mere shimmering streaks in this grey corridor into night. The only thing that stood out among them was the remains of the old brick viaduct, where the long-dead city lines had crossed an access road. Now the road was disused and blocked off, the bridge girders had been removed. Only the two supporting inclines remained, isolated in a neglected little island of trees and undergrowth at the edge of the yards. Rust-rotted chunks of rail and girder, twisted, jagged, swathed with briar and bindweed, smothered by dock and nettle, stood out of it like the pillars of some ancient and terrible ruin half submerged in jungle. And behind them the brick facings of the inclines faced one another like a fallen gateway, an awesome threshold to the mysterious curtain of green beyond.

We picked our way carefully across the dead lines towards it. I too had been warned off playing around railway lines as a kid; but once or twice I'd chanced it, usually dared by other kids. I remembered how the gravel scrunched beneath my feet, how old and cracked the weathered sleepers looked, how rust-reddened the rails and fishplates, bright only at the passage of the points. And I remembered, too, how I'd hopped and skipped across them, imagining the sudden shift that trapped my foot, the faint rumble in the air, the vibration in the metal growing to a ground-shaking, all-devouring roar. I felt a faint prickling of sweat around my collar, even though I knew these points would never move again, not till they were torn up and sold for scrap. It wasn't a train I was half-expecting to leap out at me now; but something that bulked as vast and shapeless in my imagination, and as hedged around with morbid terrors. I'd seen enough to know that Katjka hadn't exaggerated the perils of disturbing – what?

Only one word for it, a word I'd been avoiding. A word I might have laughed at a few days past, letting all I'd seen slip lightly by beneath the flow of my more mundane thoughts, forgotten. Now, here, that word didn't seem one little bit unreal. It felt as hard and dark and dangerous as those rails.

A sorceror.

As we stepped over the last line Katjka called out, softly, and waited. No answer came. She hesitated, clapped her hands, and went on. We called again, together, as we reached the edge of the undergrowth; but still there was nothing, only the distant whir and rattle of a train shunting slowly through the still-used section of the yards. Something didn't smell too good, but we picked our way through the shreds of rubbish and pushed hesitantly into the undergrowth. It was as thick as it looked; briars and gorse snagged at my jeans, bracken leaves tipped water over Katjka's bare legs. The two sides of the roofless arch loomed up before us, and with one last call we stepped between—

Into a wall of mist. Slap. Again.

Only now, near us, somebody shouted, a single clear word. '*Ayang*!' We jumped, and almost lost one another. I reached out frantically.

'*Katjka*!'

Her bony hand clamped shut around mine. '*Quiet*!'

The mist rolled, and I was looking into her grey eyes – vital now, alive and young again, as if her weariness had sloughed away. 'This iss what came upon you in the East?'

'Looks like it! Now what—'

The thing sailed above the mist, an arcing streak of colour that sang close by our ears before I could move, let alone realise what it was. Its path swirled the mist, it struck stone with a loud steely ring and shattered. An arrow, a long arrow, its barbs strung with bright feathers—

'*Back*!' I shouted, and yanked Katjka's hand. But which way was back? More arrows sang through the mist, not so near. It billowed all around us, exposing tantalising glimpses of grey stone and dim grey sky beyond and whisking them away before we could get any kind of a bearing. The light was even and directionless, no guide, and the breeze – where had it gone? What had happened to the mild evening? This was hot, stifling even, and stickily humid. In Bangkok I hadn't noticed the contrast so much, but here it was utterly alien. And then the stone beneath me seemed to leap, as if a heavy weight had been dropped, some sacks of potatoes, say, or a *very* heavy footfall. Fear and anger danced a dizzy round in my head; but as I turned to run, Katjka reined me in.

'*Do not*!' she commanded softly. 'We have not moved three steps, we cannot be far from the way back. But move and we may never find it!'

'And if we don't bloody move? I've about had it up to *here*—' I tried to persuade myself I needed my sword – really badly – *now*!

Nothing happened, except another burst of arrows. They must be firing volleys at random; but this one flew uncomfortably near. My feet were jarring on stones. I stooped and picked up one that felt nicely fist-sized, and to my surprise found, shaped in my fingers, a fallen fragment of some carving with a leering face on it. No matter, it'd make a better weapon against any merely human jokers. Then that impact came again, and another – jesus, it *was* some kind of footstep.

Above the mist a huge humped shape arose, covered in glittering metallic scales and strips of bright fabric like fantastic banners, swinging this way and that with a slow, heavyweight nodding motion. Katjka saw it and hesitated, knuckles to her lips; then she flung her arms wide and yelled. There were words in it; they didn't sound like her own strange Slavic tongue, rolling and rounded rather than sibilant, more like a sonorous Italian or Latin. The mist heaved violently, as if a huge hand stirred it up; for a moment I saw stone flags, cracked, stained and mossy, a grey wall covered with intricate carvings, and beyond it a flash of sullen green. Then the whiteness folded over us like a surfer's wave, and we were enveloped.

Something shot out of it, vertically down. Not another arrow, but a pair of arms. That was putting it mildly; normal people have arms, but each of these would have made two of those. Massive, their naked skin showing pink under a coating of hair, they reached down huge hands with billiard-ball knuckles and clutched at us, hard. Before we could offer the slightest resistance they'd seized us by a shoulder each and hoisted us, for all our frantic struggles and kicking feet, right up into the heart of the mist.

Then they dropped us again. I landed, partly on Katjka, which was not too bad – for me, anyhow – and partly . . .

Over our heads the mist flared pink, and something exploded with a muffled concussive thud. The mist vanished, and darkness covered my eyes. I felt around. Grass. Wet earth. What felt like brick fragments. Not a trace of stone. I looked up, and saw, beyond the waving bushes, the dimmer darkness of the sidings – and, to either side of me, a pair of the broadest boots I'd ever set eyes on. Rearing above us, blotting out the sky and the yellow sodium lights of yard and road, loomed an extraordinary figure, blocky, square and hunched. He straddled us, holding his arms outstretched above us, massive arms like the ones that had seized us, but swathed in some kind of heavy greatcoat. Held out level from each heavy hand was a long straight rod; and at the tips of those rods there danced a pale, pinkish flame, that guttered and died even as I watched.

For a moment all was still; and then, with a heavy grunt, the huge figure unwound his arms from what I realised had been a single long staff, held yokewise across his rounded shoulders.

'*Dood ok ondergang!*' growled a deep voice. 'That makes the bastards hop! They dare try any such thing on my own dom doorstep?' With another earthy grunt he flexed his shoulders, then let the staff slide through his hands and hit the ground. It landed with a shaking thud, as if it was made of lead. The hands that reached down to help us up were definitely the same hands that had snatched us from the mist; but equally definitely the arms above them were swathed in clothes there'd been no time to put on. 'Why,' rumbled the voice. 'It's little Kat! What is bringing you so fars from the Tavern, hah?' A heavy finger no bigger than the average banana prodded her playfully in the ribs. 'And . . . what is *this?*'

Meaning me.

'A good man,' said Katjka, a little shakily. 'A friend. He needs your advice. I will vouch for him.'

'A man? Looks more like a clothes horse to me.' The finger flipped out my tie, held it out for admiration, then wound it up like spaghetti. 'Last time I see colours like that is somebody overturns a cartload of canteloupes!'

'It's hand-painted,' I said, rather stiffly, as I retrieved it. I was very proud of that tie. 'By Howard Hodgkin.'

'You sure it's his hand he uses? By dom, I think another part of his Hodgkin. Ach, well, put that thing away and come. Come!'

As I straightened up, dusting myself off, I was startled to see that this massive figure wasn't a giant at all. If he'd stood up straight, in fact, he still wouldn't have been as tall as me, but his shoulders were so rounded that his head hardly reached my shoulder, and he moved like an old man. Leaning on his staff, he ushered us in through the gateway of the old bridge, into the little copse of trees. The staff lifted heavy branches out of our way, and we ducked and scrambled through into a more open area, a patch of little clearings at its heart, hidden from the outside world. It looked as if he'd been tending these; some parts were cleared and cultivated, rows of plantings marked with little tags, while under the trees a small area was trellised over with a tangle of briars and other vegetation to make a solid, self-sustaining roof. Some derelict seats and sleeper benches from railway carriages had been hauled beneath it, evidently as beds and chairs, and a small

54

fire burned at the heart of a circle of blackened stones, with a heap of firelogs and bundled twigs beside it. But it all looked orderly enough, with none of the usual squalor of a tramps' camp.

The firelight showed me more of the man who came puffing through after us. What had I been expecting? Some old *sensei*, withered and harsh; a smooth-faced *guru* or sharp-eyed mandarin; the Abbot of Shangri-la, maybe. He couldn't have looked less like any of those. How old he was, was hard to say; but even in the flower of his youth he couldn't have been any beauty, and he looked like one tough customer now. The rolling walk was partly an old-fashioned sailor's gait, partly the effect of his low-slung bandy frame. And he wasn't wearing the saffron robe, or the peacock coat for that matter. He was dressed in worn seaman's gear, oiled-wool jersey with the stripes faded out of it, salt-bleached canvas breeches and some kind of navy greatcoat or pea-jacket, with a peaked blue canvas cap – like a seaman turned tramp, but cleaner. And both like and unlike Le Stryge.

'My little home from home!' he chuckled, gesturing around, then abruptly turned on me. 'Well – "good man"? Katjka I know; but not yet do you tell your name. What do you call yourself?'

'Stephen – Stephen Fisher.'

He studied me a minute, as if uncertain or taken aback, but then he nodded, and turning away threw another bundle of twigs on the fire. 'My name,' he said, 'or as much suits you to know, is Pendek. But you may call me Ape; everyone do.'

I found it only too easy, looking at him there in the firelight. His head was big, his face sallow-skinned, snub-nosed, heavy-jowled –what I could see of it, for a coarse red beard covered an out-thrust, aggressive jaw right up to the cheekbones, and bushy red hair billowed about his pendulous ears. All he needed to look really simian was heavy brow-ridges, but he didn't have them; beneath his cap a tangled red forelock fell low over a forehead that sloped, but evenly, back from bushy eyebrows. Where he came from was hard to say, but one look at the eyes beneath those brows told me something; they were large, with the narrow epicanthic fold Westerners mistake for a slant, and deep as a jungle pool, with a cold sparkle of intelligence. Another Eurasian, then; quite a contrast to Jacquie, or the Rangda girl, though. The effect was formidable.

He ushered us towards the benches. 'Kindly take your seats – and put them on the chairs! Yes? Hah!' I caught a whiff of him as he passed; at least he smelt slightly cleaner than Le Stryge, a strongly animal odour tinged with even stronger pipe tobacco, not entirely unwholesome – which wasn't something you could ever say about old Stryge. But there were other smells about on the evening breeze, wholly unlike the metallic stinks of the railyards; even the air seemed milder in here, as if the sun hadn't long finished warming it. I caught hints of spice in the air, and of woodsmoke very different from that sputtering little fire. And as they touched my nose, I became aware of other, fainter things. Sounds seemed to hover at the edge of hearing, sounds of voices – as if at any moment I might part those trees and see, not the grim linearity of the rails, but smoke rising from distant huts, and hear the shrill chatter of children at play.

Ape seemed to notice my response. He grinned, his beard parting over a set of teeth that looked capable of cracking walnuts. He took out a short, tarry-looking pipe, jammed it between them, and shook his head. 'We're alone.' He lit the pipe with a blazing twig, and its sour reek drove all others from the air. 'So – what brings you to seek the advice of Ape, Good Man Fisher?'

I told him the story as I'd told it to Katjka, carefully. At first his bushy brows lifted in surprise, as he heard who I was, and about the Project. He said nothing, only puffed away between clenched teeth as I talked; but I felt, as if it was a physical sensation, the atmosphere between us grow colder. The fire dimmed, the light died; only the coals of the pipe blazed beneath a sheltering thumb, and the condensing juices gurgled in the stem. When I mentioned the menacing mask, though, he sat up, spat a dark stream into the embers, but said nothing. My tale trailed to its end, with the girl helping me escape, and what Katjka had seen in the cards; but he said nothing, only smoked two more puffs. Then, abruptly, he knocked out his pipe against his heel, and ground in the fallen sparks.

'Don't see why the hell you come to me,' he said, his brows knitting. 'These aid projects, I say the hell with them. *Uitlander*, interfering, meddling in things they don't understand, making worse messes. Always something in them for somebody, always somebody loses. People they're meant to help, most often. But not the fat cats, not office boys, oh no. More bland they look, more

56

lilywhite bless-you-goodwill bull they spout, the more they are the ones. So, *Mynheer* Goodman, answer me this; what is in the job for you? And then give me one good reason I should lift a finger to help.'

If I lost my temper easily I wouldn't have been a professional negotiator. 'All right; there's some truth in what you say. Some aid projects have just made worse messes, big hydroelectric dams and so forth. But this isn't like that. The alternatives seem pretty clear to me, and what they add up to is misery for the islanders. And my answer is that there's no profit in it for anyone that I can see except them – least of all me. That's the plain truth.'

The burly man grunted sardonically, tamped down the half-empty pipe and began relighting it. '*Ah, jawel*! Man like you works for money and fast car and pretty clothes, and girls – *nie*? A man who is hollow, for those with sight enough – a man whom thought and feeling shine through like glass, leaving little warmth as they pass. Then suddenly he overflows with pity for the poor and needy – enough to run headlong into dangers he hardly even understand – *erg moeilijk te geloofen, knul*! Get him out of here, Kat, before I begin to loose my rug.'

I laughed, rather nastily perhaps, because Katjka laid a warning hand on my arm. But I didn't need it. I had my answer for him.

'Okay!' I said sharply. 'Okay! As it happens, you're too damn right. I *have* got a personal interest in all this. Maybe more than one. For one thing, there's almost certainly someone I used to know involved in it – somebody I wish well. Somebody I . . . owe a favour, you could say. But there's more to it than that. I was interested in this before I saw her . . . the name.' Katjka gave me an all too penetrating glance. Ape grunted, puffed smoke, and said nothing. I glared at him. 'Hollow – really flung that in my face, didn't you? Think you're the first? That I haven't had to endure it from better adepts than you? Well, there were a few things I could say about them, too. But maybe you're right. I've made a success of my job, a big success; there aren't many people my age at boardroom level, let alone deputy MDs. So maybe I've paid a price in other directions; I've seen it happen to guys I know. Maybe I'm just another self-centred workaholic yuppie like them. But I don't want to go on that way! And yet just throwing away all I've done, all the skills I've acquired – that doesn't make sense either. It's a waste. So maybe finding a use for my skills, that'll

57

help pull me out of it. A commitment – using what I've learned in a good cause – a bloody good cause!'

'*Bravje!*' applauded Katjka softly.

I looked at the bulky figure, squatting like a shabby Buddha under the bo tree. 'Who knows? You might try a bit of that, too! Instead of just sitting on your fat arse and carping!' Katjka caught at my sleeve, but Ape said nothing; and yet I sensed, somehow, that he was uncertain now, undecided. He took one more puff at his pipe, then rummaged by his seat, and leaned forward to the fire as if to throw in another log.

Only it was no log that left his hand, but a spraying handful of what looked like white sand. The little flames leaped to meet it, blazing up and outward in a great roaring sweep, a reaching hand that drove up between us. The grass-tips browned, the lower leaves crackled and scorched; I felt the withering breath of it sear my cheeks and smelt the first faint whiff of singeing hair. I leaped up, but Katjka sat tight, and pulled me back down again, holding me close to her. And as I hit the bench the firelight sank, then flared again in an explosive crackle, a burst of glaring light, white as a flashgun's at first but full of changing tints that slipped away before you could define them. It turned the little glade into a stark nightmare world of contrasts, of hard-edged light and wavering, shifting shadows. Beside me Katjka's face lost its lines, looked like a wide-eyed child's under pale, delicate hair; then they returned, deepened till every faint seam stood out like chiselled canyons of age and experience, till the hair seemed thin and colourless against that icy radiance, and she became an ancient, ashen crone; and then they shimmered, faded, and she looked her usual hard-worn late twenties. But next moment the light swelled again, till her very flesh no longer seemed to stop it, and it streamed right through her, skin and bone, like a figurine of milky glass. And all this time she was watching me, and from the look in her eyes she was seeing the same changes happening to me.

The flare faltered a moment, though, and there was Ape, sitting back as before, staring hard at us with those piercing dark eyes. Only he seemed unaffected by the light of change. Then, suddenly, he glanced up at the trees above my head. So did Katjka, and I felt rather than heard the tightening of her breath. The flare had hurled my shadow against those tall trunks; but as the warm wind waved them it split, into two vast looming shapes, solid and steady despite the wildness of the light. And between them, smaller and less distinct, another shape capered, wavering this way and that. Hunched and square, it could have been Ape's – except that he sat beyond the light, and could throw no shadow at all.

He flung out an arm again, scattered some dusty particles like a sower. As they drifted down into the fire the crackling subsided, and the flare died. Suddenly the air was warm again, and that hint of spices came floating back on the breeze.

Ape's pipe had gone out. He knocked out the dottle against his boot-heel, then suddenly turned a deep, sombre look on me. 'What Kat saw, so also I see,' he rumbled. 'And more. Indeed a power off the Spiral works against you, and against Project. In fact, two. Very great, very independent, but joining together in the blockading of the East. One, is largely confined there; but the Other . . . ' He shook his head grimly. 'Is muscleful enough to throw these curtains of mist before you, to try and lure you to walk through into the heart of Its own place where It can squash you proper at leisure. But It cannot long sustain them, or too often; or you find them behind the door every time you go take a leak, *hah*! It take a gamble, to stop you meeting me; It fail. But with such power It might just launch a real attack, right into the Core. With the means maybe to hand. Attempts lately to smuggle in forces from the East, past the Wardens – *nee*?'

'But surely all those failed!' exclaimed Katjka. 'Ssome idiot's always trying such things. What there was, was caught and . . . dissposed of. There has been no new peril loose along the Ways. Only the Bundlers, the Resurrection Men, *priculij*, Anioto, Gutterers – what was there already!'

'Maybe some get through all the same – and are held unseen, in readiness for one special attack.'

I whistled softly, to banish a shiver of remembered terror. 'The way the *dupiah* was.'

He cocked his head at me. 'What do you know of such?'

'It's a long story. But I helped discover one – and deal with the . . . man who brought it in.'

He looked to Katjka for confirmation, and nodded in surprised acknowledgement. 'So! Very like, then. But I think less perilous and powerful, less able to act on its own. Or the Wardens winkle them out, once alerted. What is small hides more easy. But at night and in loneliness, when you tire and falter – then even the small may be menace, when you are not ready to meet them.'

He lumbered to his feet, delving in his pockets, drew out a pouch

59

of some scaly leather. Each scale was bigger than my thumbnail. His palms rasped as he rubbed tobacco between them, tamped his pipe and stooped, wheezing, to light it yet again.

'There wass a third shadow,' said Katjka. He straightened up quickly, puffing.

'That you saw? Then what would you say of it?'

Katjka considered. 'A third powerful enemy, Stefan,' she said at last, softly. 'Nearer than the rest, maybe. More in your world, in the Hub – or closer to it, anyhow. And yet somehow less immediate – for now. But not to be forgotten.'

'There were supposed to be terrorist threats,' I said. 'Yet the terrorists hardly have any presence there – just now. Could that be . . . ?'

'It might,' said Ape darkly. 'It might well.'

I clenched my fists and swore, bitterly. 'That'd be all I bloody need! How the hell am I ever going to get the stuff through without help?'

'Probably never,' said Ape simply. 'So what is the matter with mine, hah?'

I gaped at him. '*Your* help?'

'*Juist*,' he said. 'Whatever is this Project, you I think are sincere. I can maybe advise you, maybe more; we see. So – we talk ways and means, *toch*?'

We sprawled on the benches, and talked. Ape polluted the warm evening with his pipe, and his horny fingers traced odd figures in the long grass. 'With *Katje* I agree,' he rumbled. 'This blockade, it costs these your enemies much strength, much *mana*. Once broken, they will not be able to hold it up longer. It fall down, like a prick.'

'Pardon?'

'In a balloon, *knul*! Your best bet, you do not try to barge a way through with all your load at once. You play it careful, take a liddle bit and break trail, open up a route.'

'A container – that's the smallest practical amount. The one with the computer gear, maybe; that's loaded and waiting at the supplier's. It's still a hell of a weight – tonnes.'

'So much the harder to run off with, *nee*?' He dragged a paw through his beard thoughtfully. 'In two places is the worst of danger. Here, this land, because they know of you here, and because the container is here; chance is, they know of that also, or at least whither it will come. Already they may be preparing that strike, at one or both. But if not, or if they fail, I think they wait till the East, where they have more power. Till Bangkok.'

'Will they not try and destroy thiss . . . container en route?' Katjka demanded.

Ape bared his nutcrackers. 'Not if I hide it from their sight! And set bars upon it that will drive them from its presence! But I cannot do that forever, not in their own realm where they are most powerful. The deeper into that realm, the more clearly they will be able to espy it, the more their arts will work upon it. But I cannot so well ward the container in the Core either, where all powers are weaker; they may well have tracked it down before I can get to it. So again, here is first great danger. We must get it past them, *whhhht*! – like grease eel, *nie*? So they lose sight of it here. Then, we send it off to Thailand, but not by special route. Just so it is hidden amid much other stuff the same – you can do that, *joengen*? And is stored so on arrival? So they would need much power and time to find it?'

'Yes, easily. The freight volume that way's pretty high. One container in a hundred or more, right in the middle of a hold. Or a plane's belly – routine.'

'*Jazeker*. No chance they spot it there – so long you are not with it, near it even. Best you do not make the arrangement even, yourself.'

'*Daj multito*!' exclaimed Katjka. 'Did I not ssay? You must travel separately, and by some safe means.'

'And after? When we get to Thailand, what then?'

'*Then*, friend, your idea is good! Then we seek a ship of Shadows, and slip it by beneath their noses when least they expect it!' His huge arm moved like lightning, his hand clamped on my arm with shocking force, a young baby's immovable grasp magnified into adult strength. 'But till then – hah! Your problems begin with getting your cargo out whole, and in one piece yourself also. That this One will attack, I feel in my bones. What may be brewing for you, I would not wish on my worst enemy's dog. This commitment of yours, will it stand up to so much danger as that?'

Time for the heroic answer, the jutting jaw. The idea of being stalked by these nameless horrors all the way eastward – I wasn't exactly entranced, to put it mildly. To put it not so mildly, I just felt sick. This wasn't my world, and I knew now why I'd dropped out of it, taken several steps back. But now I was caught. I knew just how important all this was to me – far more important than I'd admitted to Dave, to Ape, even to myself. For only I knew how much of a failure I really was.

Over the last few years I'd risen fast and far, and even the jealous and the backbiters couldn't ever deny I'd earned it; but there were mornings I'd had trouble looking in the mirror to shave, and they were becoming more and more frequent. Hollow, cold, self-centred – I'd been forced to face myself as that, when first I strove to find a way through the Spiral; the way I'd treated Jacquie, all those years since, most of all. If I'd stayed out there, left my own cozy certainties behind, I might have begun to change my spots; but returning to my old life forced me back into its mould. And since it was one I'd created for myself, it fitted all too well. It shaped me for success in one thing, my career; for anything else, for human relations, it was a horrible handicap. Even that might not have mattered; but I'd had bad luck, as well. The brief affair with Clare – that broke up soon enough, though it left us still colleagues and friends of a sort; of the horrors that brought it about, that set real bonds between us, she remembered nothing that I could tell. There had been others, over the last few years, once or twice even a hint of marrying, settling down; but each time something seemed to have got in the way. Luck – or guilt?

So I was left lonelier, more isolated than before; and the only role which gave me any comfort was the cold, hard-driving executive, the only fulfilment my career and my work. Something like this, this way of helping, was the only avenue of emotional involvement I had left that wasn't bound up with my own profit – the only therapy for a disability so basic that the world might never notice it. Partly, admittedly – irritatingly – it was because Jacquie might well be involved. But the one who really needed the help was me.

Once, long ago, I crossed the Earth and the stars on the wings of night, all to rescue Clare. I braved dangers and fought battles, and brought her back by my side. But now I had an even harder task, to rescue one who might be in a danger different, but perhaps – in its own way – even greater.

Once I'd gone in search of her, who might have lost her life. Now, adrift upon the infinite sea, it was myself.

'I'll risk it,' I said.

Ape released me so sharply I almost fell over. '*Goed dan!*' His frown didn't slacken, but I had the idea I'd pleased him. 'So you will not do it alone. I help.'

'You?' I hadn't expected that. 'If you're sure – you'd make all the bloody difference!'

'Maybe some. You make enemies with lots of muscle, *jongetje*.

Maybe more than you and I got between us, in these places. The business I had here, that's done. High time I head for home. I come with you at least part of the way – maybe all. You,' he jabbed a finger, 'you pay my passage; that's all the price I ask. And make sure we get to the Bali island before third of your May. That is the time I have to be there.' He looked ruefully at his little garden. 'I have to force on these beans. Shame.'

I glanced at Katjka. She looked as startled as I felt. I knew I ought to be delighted – I knew I'd damn well better *look* it. But remembering Le Stryge, I wasn't so sure. Ape wasn't remotely as foul, but he'd already shown he could be pretty uncomfortable company.

'What happens when we get to Bangkok?' I asked.

'We get a good ship, solid skipper – you can pay for those? Good. Must be in gold, mark . . . '

'I know. I've done it before.'

'Also good. So then, we ship out, east of the sunrise – hah?'

And that also I had done before; and I felt a great swelling joy at the prospect, so great I could almost feel the wind beneath my feet already. 'Great!' I said. 'But – how do we find them? Where do we start? I wouldn't have a clue who to trust!'

Ape bobbed his head, a peculiar gesture I'd seen often in the East – though not in Indonesia. It was the equivalent of a headshake. 'Maybe not so. But I help you – maybe before we get there, maybe once there. But first we have to get this container of yours away, past this first strike. And about that we must make plan, *nee*?'

We made our way back through the greenery and into the barren wastes of the yard, shivering in the sudden chill of the night air. I looked over my shoulder at the trees, waving in the wind, with no trace or clues as to who and what dwelt beneath them. And I wondered about other little islands in the industrial wilderness, whether trolls might still dwell among the Swedish ironmines, or ancestral spirits of the Delaware between the spoilheaps of the Pittsburg steel towns. And I knew even in the thinking of it that they did, and many other things in other places. For even the world most of our making is never entirely ours.

Back at the car Dave sat bolt upright as we ducked through the fence. 'You're a light sleeper,' I told him. 'Not nervous, were we?'

'Sleeper? Like hell, Steve – I haven't had any time to sleep. You've only been gone – what? – ten minutes.'

Some three weeks later I was looking back at those trees again, but from the far side of the yards. From the goods platform where I was waiting their tops were the only green and growing things visible, swaying in the fresh wind as if to greet the breath of the next shower. It had been an unusually wet month; milky puffs of pale cloud glided against a ground of thundery grey, heralding more rain to come. Then the freight car ground forward, slowly, and the big grey container it carried barred them from my sight as it was shunted slowly into the siding to await the make-up of its train. The haulage driver came running up with his clipboard to get the final clearance signatures. 'Nice neat job of unloading, that,' I told him. 'I wish all our stuff got handled so carefully.'

He grinned conspiratorially. 'Well, squire, if it all had you standing over it with that face on you, it might. It might.'

I grinned back. I knew they were a good firm, that was why we used them; but I'd been breathing down his neck all the same. 'Point taken. Counts as working with volatile or irritant substances, does it? It's worth a bit extra, anyhow.' As I was putting my wallet away I asked, casually, 'No trouble on the way over? Nothing unusual?'

His bright boot-button eyes narrowed. 'Should there'a been?'

'Just wondering.'

He shrugged. 'Clouds all the way, quite a few showers – right heavy an' all, bit o' thunder even. 'Course the forecast had sunny, didn't it? Bloke at the motorway services said it were all right till I came along. I must be towing it with me!'

I chuckled. 'When we start delivering weather you'll get the road contract, but we're not quite ready yet.'

'Still getting t'bugs out? Keep us posted. Well, must get on. Ta!'

I breathed a silent sigh of relief. This was the first container ready. Ape had thought it almost inevitable it would be spotted on its way here from the electronics plant, but he'd been sure it would be safe enough, provided it went by day. I didn't like the sound of that rain, though, and made a mental note to ask him.

We'd have about thirty to shift, all told, coming from various European sources; the others mostly held the special sluice gates, the control servos and other linkages, level metering devices and everything else that couldn't be manufactured within Indonesia. Some still weren't ready, and the rest, fourteen so far, were being held at source; but they couldn't wait indefinitely. If we couldn't shift them within a month or two the Project was not only going to be stuck with the manufacturing costs of gear it couldn't use, and salaries for staff sitting twiddling their thumbs, it would also be shedding serious money on storage bills, rental and demurrage on the containers, insurance – it didn't bear thinking about. And while my firm didn't stand to lose anything directly, it might just look as if we were responsible. Never mind that nobody else could do any better; that's not the way a company image goes. We had to start somewhere fast.

Ape and I had decided that taking the whole consignment on this first run would be an idiotic risk, and would narrow our choice of ships to the very biggest. We'd settled on one single load. A blockade like this was unprecedented. It must be a fearsome drain on the energies even of the godlike powers of the Spiral, even in tandem; break it just once, and the chances were it'd collapse altogether. What they'd do then was anyone's guess; but they'd be out of our hair awhile.

So the obvious choice, as I'd expected, was the computer equipment. At a pinch light engineering and the everyday electronics which made up the rest of the consignment might be despatched labelled as something else, or under fake end-user certificates – though how long that would fool our enemies was an uncertain point; but computer technology was still subject to stringent international security controls. The whole lot fitted nicely into one small standard container, with enough special packing to withstand anything short of a nuclear blast; this could travel by almost any means of transport known to man. On Ape's advice, again, it would be sent out by air, provided I didn't travel with it or even handle the despatching; the difficult part would be getting it to the airport. That we would do by rail – but not unprotected. An uneasy mixture of security and suspicion writhed inside me. There'd been no more incidents these last few weeks – no more unexpected gates into the mists of the Spiral; but I couldn't help feeling a growing nervous electricity, an inner tingle. Maybe it was an approaching storm.

As the container was brought to a halt and uncoupled, the rail freight manager, a tall enthusiastic Pakistani, came bustling across to greet me, brandishing a hand-held computer. 'You are the shippers' rep, aren't you? How do you do! Jamal Adhan.'

We shook hands. 'Stephen Fisher, hi.'

'Oh my goodness – managing director, isn't it? Yes, of course, I saw you on *Business Week*, didn't I? Speaking up for the rail lobby, too – excellent! Now this is a surprise, sir, to find you down here in person on this little consignment. And a pleasure – I hope there's nothing wrong?'

'Nothing at all – it's deputy managing director, by the way. Just a little job I'm especially interested in.'

'Well, well, you can be sure we'll look after it with kid gloves for you.' He scribbled furiously on the computer screen. We might be right in the forefront of the paperless society, but forms were still the life and soul of this business, even if they'd become electronic ghosts outlined in liquid crystals. 'You'll be completing the handover bumf? Yes, well, won't you come and have a cup of coffee in the office, then? Not the usual terrible stuff; I bring it in myself, you know.'

I cast a look back at the container. There were still plenty of people about this end of the yards. There wasn't much I could do just standing here. 'Sounds great. Thanks.'

It was exceptionally good coffee, and we sat by the hissing old gas-fire and whipped through leaves of multi-layered printout. I told him about the Project, which seemed to interest him, and he commiserated with me over the Third World bureaucratic obstacles we'd probably find ahead. 'Still,' the manager remarked, 'at least we can get you off to a good start with a through train, straight from A to B. No chance of being shunted off and left in a siding somewhere. Not that that often happens, of course!' he added hastily. 'But when it's something important – sod's law, eh?'

'Right. And it doesn't have to hang around long at the far end, so they can't lose it, either. We worked out the timing quite carefully.'

'As I'd expect from your company, Mr Fisher. Now, sign here, please . . . and here . . . excellent. That's the lot. Well, if you've finished your coffee?'

We strolled back out to the freight platforms, and I decided to take a last quick look at the container. It wouldn't be a last, actually, but he wasn't to know that. He grinned at my concern. 'Kid gloves, I assure you. Kid gloves.'

Then we turned the corner.

The container was still there, all right. Still very much there. In the grey light of the gathering clouds it was just about the thing most visibly 'there' in the whole yard. The manager could still speak, but he was so furious he kept sticking on the first word with the explosive effect of a small outboard. '*What . . .* what . . . what . . . what–what–*what*?'

All I could manage was a breathless giggle of disbelief. In the brief time it had been standing in the siding it looked very much as if the container had been swooped on by massed teams of vandals. From top to bottom, and including the clamps which held it on to its freight car, it had been covered with the most amazing mass of eye-aching swirls and squiggles of aerosol paint in lurid colours, mostly day-glo. The result looked like a cross between a sixties-revival disco and a New York subway carriage, with maybe just a trace of curlicued Malay script thrown in. I found myself fumbling for my sunshades.

The manager let off a howl of Urdu – not one of my languages, but I got the general idea of some pretty potent profanity. It seemed to clear the breech. '*What*— those little bastards, I'll have their balls for this! Bloody kids off the estates! It's their parents they should fine for letting them run loose! If it isn't pinching things, it's concrete blocks on the lines and footballs on the power wires! *Aaagh*! And skinhead racist slogans on the gates! I'll flay them—' Then he remembered me. 'Oh my dear sir, what a disgrace, what a disgrace! But don't worry, sir, don't worry, no! I'll be straight on the blower to the transport police, get them up here with a work crew and gallons, absolute *gallons* of paint remover. It will not delay your train more than a few minutes—'

I managed to get a word in edgeways. 'No, no – no need for that at all! Look, I think I know what's happened here, it isn't kids. Look . . . '

Steve Fisher, bare-faced lies at two seconds' notice a speciality.

'You remember the Project I told you this is all about? Well, there were these people who're, er, working with it, and we were having a drink, and they promised to give the container a special Balinese blessing as a send-off, and, er, I didn't know quite what they meant but this must be it . . . ' I ran down. 'They must have sneaked in and done it like this. As a surprise.'

Mr Adhan looked deeply disapproving. 'A surprise,' he said at last. 'Well, we can still get it removed.'

'Oh, I don't think that's necessary,' I said cheerfully. 'I mean, it's not doing any harm, is it? With the tarpaulin over the top it'll only be the sides that show. And it'd be such a shame to disappoint them, scrub all their hard work right off.'

'Mr Fisher,' he protested, wringing his hands in anguish, 'you are asking me to let *that* travel on my nice clean train?'

'Well, at least the graffiti aren't obscene or anything.'

'How do you know? Can you read them?'

'Well . . . no, but if we can't, probably nobody else could either. Anyway, it's my responsibility – all right?'

I got him calmed down eventually. 'At least it is a night train,' he said thankfully. 'And non-stop.' He contemplated the gaudy apparition for some moments more. 'A blessing? *That* is a blessing?'

'Balinese,' I reminded him.

'Hmmn.' He sounded extremely unimpressed. 'But they're Muslims out in Indonesia, aren't they? Like me?'

I ransacked my memory. 'That's right, yes. But from what I can make out, Bali's the last refuge of the ancient faiths – Buddhist, Hindu, homegrown religions, all bundled together. Quite a grab-bag.'

'Yes,' he said, with a wealth of meaning. 'Well, Mr Fisher, if that is a blessing then all I can say is I never want to see one of their curses. Good evening to you, sir!'

He didn't quite shake the dust off his feet, but nearly.

'We'll have to mend a fence there, Dave.'

'Sure. Gotta keep the local boys sweet. The usual?'

'Apologetic letter, yes, your secretary'll have that tomorrow. But *not* the customary bottle of scotch, right?'

'Oh. Right. What do we send instead?'

'I don't know. Who's a good Muslim in the office – Yilderim? See if he's got any ideas.'

'No, I'll ask Rafi. You know Yilderim, it'd just be bloody Turkish delight – yuk!'

'Yuk it is— Hey!' Like some immense grey-brown caterpillar with one gaudy stripe, the train was lumbering into life. I slipped Dave's car into gear, and we purred away slowly, a little ahead but keeping pace with it.

'Is it going the way your mate said?'

'Seems to be. But I wasn't worried about that.'

'That's something, then. You weren't worried; I was. He sounds barmy to me; they're all barmy, and that barmaid bint's the worst of them. How a bloke as sane as you ever fell in with such a crew of low-lifers I'll never know. Cards and tea leaves and table-rapping, bloody New Age stuff. Probably end up dancing naked round a bonfire and getting nicked for it. Can just see the headlines now. Or getting your block knocked off by those weirdo yobbos who went after us!'

I looked at Dave with a mixture of admiration and wonder. I was watching a process at work that Jyp had first warned me about, that I'd felt the roots of in myself; yet somehow they'd never quite taken hold. In the weeks since his first hysterical strayings on the margins of the Spiral, Dave had somehow managed to edit everything supernatural out of them, everything that didn't have solid roots within the Core. What didn't fit he'd forgotten altogether. Already it had become a pub crawl down by the docks, the Bundlers no more than a gang of odd thugs; soon even that would be just a blur. I remembered my own first experiences, waking up the morning after in sickness and bewilderment – what you might call a reality hangover. Unable to accept my memories, I'd found them fading, blurring, explaining themselves away; and yet somehow I'd hung on to them. As if I sensed subconsciously that here was something I needed, desperately maybe, and wouldn't let it go; whereas Dave and people like him, who might not need anything from their wider experiences, or couldn't benefit by them, would just take one step back, mentally, and let them go. And I . . .

Understanding flew in my face like a rush of chill rain, the realisation of how close I'd come to forgetting, how much I'd almost let slip away out of my life – maybe the last chance of changing it.

I accelerated, raced on ahead of the train, and turned off down an already countrified side road, empty at this hour of night. Ahead of us a bridge loomed, and I braked and pulled over. 'All yours, Dave!' I pulled a cloth-wrapped package off the back seat. 'Thanks for the lift!'

'Don't mention it. And listen, you take care of yourself among all those crazies, you hear?'

I laughed. 'What the hell are you worried about? You'd step into my shoes. You're the obvious candidate!'

He shook his head. 'Not like that! I'd sooner wait till you get Barry's job. We need you, man! Hurry back.' He clapped me on the arm, slid into the driver's seat and went purring off with a last beep of his weedy-sounding horn. I looked after him. It wasn't every subordinate you could trust in this sort of thing, whether he understood it or not. Not even every friend. But there couldn't be much time now. I chucked my bundle over the rusty fence at the end of the bridge, clambered after it and made my way gingerly down through the long grass beside the uprights. It was pretty unsavoury, full of plastic bottles, rubbish, and worse, but I couldn't help a thrill of excitement.

Under my climbing parka I was wearing the tough buccaneer gear that had been lying forgotten at the back of my wardrobe. Originally it had been Jyp's best, but he'd given me it as a souvenir. I'd forgotten how it felt, smooth black fabric, thick, slightly furry, immensely strong and warm or cool when it had to be, yet able to breathe better than all the patent porous fabrics in my parka. Merhorse hide, he'd said it was; one of these days I was going to have to ask somebody what the hell a merhorse was. With every step experiences that had grown dim and colourless came flooding back, the thunder of a seafight, the rush of a nightbound forest in storm, the voices and faces of friends. The office was a million miles away. I heard Jyp's dry chuckle, felt Mall's lips on mine – and the stinging slice of her sword. I felt alive again.

But they weren't here. I missed them, terribly. Alive I might be, but I was on my own. Even Katjka wouldn't leave the Tavern for long, or perhaps she couldn't. So there would just be me, and Ape. And if ever there was an unknown quantity, it was him. Affable enough, but alarming in the way such sorcerors seemed to be. He was helping me because it suited him, but I had the feeling that if ever I put a foot wrong, if something shady did turn up about this Project, or just something he didn't like, then he could just as easily turn on me. Katjka thought him less powerful than Stryge – but I wasn't nearly so sure. Less malignant, maybe. Maybe.

Around the curve in the rails ahead the train appeared. A little way beyond the bridge the lines divided, and the signals shone at *slow*, just as Ape had predicted; the engine was slowing, and in the dim-lit cab I could see the driver talking vigorously into his stalk microphone. Hunched in the grass, I let him go by, and the dull segments of the snake that clattered after him; but when I saw the container car I tensed, raced down the slope, threw my bundle aboard and leaped across the gravel. I landed just above the coupling, bruising myself on bits of oily metal, scrabbling for a handhold. A crane grab made of fingers reached out and hauled me effortlessly into the narrow space on the flatbed at the end of the container. The squat figure sat back with a satisfied sigh and a hollow clank. I gazed grimly at the mass of aerosol cans spilling from his knapsack and bulging out of his pea-jacket pockets.

'Now just how necessary was all that?' I demanded.

Ape looked at me, and growled, deep in his throat. 'After midnight you maybe find out,' he told me.

'You said you were going to make it inconspicuous, for god's sake! It stands out like a bloody carnival float!'

The squat man snorted his contempt. 'Inconspicuous to other eyes than yours, *knul*! And even that is not perhaps enough.'

'I never want to have to explain away anything like that, ever again! We were only gone for a few minutes, anyway – how'd you manage it all?'

A chuckle sounded above the slow click of the rails. 'Easy, *jongetje*! I just take *my* time.'

I said nothing, and busied myself unwrapping my bundle. The sword clanked against the container side as I freed it, and I set aside my little pack of flask and sandwiches. The train was accelerating on to the main line now, and up to full speed. I stood up, a little gingerly, and tried my footing as I swished the sword experimentally, a gleam that sliced the shadows. Ape looked on with interest. 'Fine weapon!' he observed. 'Where do you buy it, hah?'

'I didn't buy it, hah. I won it. In exchange for a boarding axe; I left that with the last owner. He was a bloody great Wolf buccaneer.'

'Me, I grudge one such even the axe.'

'Not me! I left it in his head.'

Ape made the nearest thing to an approving grunt. '*O ja*? Well, you maybe drive the good bargain then! For it is not Wolf work, that; and it is old, to my eye, old and age-strong.' But then his

71

scepticism returned. 'Even a fine weapon is not stronger than the arm that holds it, nor more artful. You, is such a boy fit to wield such a thing?'

I swallowed my resentment. 'I've been taught. I took up sabre a few years back, though I've let it slip a bit. But I had my first lessons from someone out on the Spiral, and she almost had the hide off me; that I won't forget in a hurry.' I reached up and slashed a twig from a rain-sagging branch in a spray of droplets. 'And you can look after yourself, I've no doubt. What really worries me . . .'

'Well?'

I stared out into the night. It was cloudy, but here and there the moonlight was shining through thinner patches. 'A purely material attack – in terms of the Core, I mean. You suggested we go along in case these mysterious forces launched an attack, and I agreed. But we were both thinking in terms of sorcerous muscle, sendings and stuff. But if they've so much power, why don't they simply rustle up a Core-style attack? Hired goons. Terrorists even, ex-Stasi or other secret police – there's a glut of them about for hire. That'd leave us looking pretty silly – I mean, even this sword against an Uzi. If you know what that is.'

'Sure I know,' answered Ape calmly. 'That kind of attack they will not trust. But if they did, still I would have power against it; you might, also. It could do better than you think, maybe, that blade. In the right hands.'

I swallowed that one, too. He had a point, the bastard. 'I know what you mean. The woman who taught me, I saw her split a pistol ball in midair once; but that was a flintlock, single shot. An Uzi or an Ingram on rapid-fire, that's like a hosejet of lead. I don't know if even Mall or Jyp could face up to a firestream like that.' I squatted down again, and hugged my knees. 'I could use them here right now – either or both.'

'*Mall*?' demanded Ape. 'She was your teacher?'

'Sure. Mad Mall Frith. Quite well known, I gather. And I picked up a lot of things from Jyp the Pilot. It was helping him that got me into this. And god, do I miss them!'

Ape snorted. 'You know little! Consider yourself shot with diamonds you find one of such folk to friend you for even a short time – let alone two! Even beyond the Core they take much seeking out, such, and are not to be met with round the corners of the streets!'

I laughed. 'Funny you put it that way. Because that's just about exactly how I did run into them, one after another!'

In the shadow I felt Ape lean over till I could feel his breath on my face. It wasn't a pleasant moment, though it didn't feel threatening.

'Is that so?' he murmured. 'Is that so? And to such a one as you . . .'

'I know, I know! Hollow. Half fulfilled. Bits missing. You don't have to tell me. I've felt what it was like to be a whole person – briefly.'

'Then you feel more than many all their lives long!' said Ape seriously. 'But I meant not that. Fascinating more and more . . . And as a coincidence, little likely. Did not these your friends ever say as much? Or hint of something special about you?'

I thought. 'Well . . . maybe. Once or twice. I didn't pay much attention at the time, I'd other worries. Le Stryge hinted something, but he was forever telling me what was wrong with me, in spades.'

'Those are what he would see,' said Ape, and for once he didn't sound quite so overbearing. 'About other things he would care little, unless they got in his way. And other things there may be – more than you yourself yet know. If you live so long, you may learn.'

The train raced and rattled on, following its fixed course into night. Twilight lingered in the skies, but the luminous blue was overlaid by a vast spread hand of clouded blackness that stretched from the horizon ahead. Only in the gaps at the tips of its blunt fingers did the lighter background glow through, so it seemed to float in the middle airs lit red there by the city lights beneath, trailing grey showery veils across the gloomy hills between. Below it dark wisps ran before the wind, as if afraid they'd be snatched and squeezed dry. The rising moon turned them to spectral traceries as they passed. They shone a faint eerie pink, as if they were trying to look alive. Time lagged, the rails clattered as we swept through bleak little stations with only a few lonely figures dotted along their dim-lit platforms. We ducked back into shadow, shivering, and VDU screens and Victorian bracket clocks told us how slowly the hours went by. Midnight came and went, heavier black clouds arrowed in overhead, and the glowing background was hidden. I emptied the last drop of coffee from my flask, relishing the brandy that had sunk to the bottom; the salmon and cream cheese sandwiches were long since finished. Cold and monotony took their toll on my alertness, but there was no way even to doze on this narrow car. And then, very lightly, it began to rain.

I felt the train slowing, but my watch told me it was hours away from journey's end; just another local station. I watched it slide by, empty and faceless, its few lights ringed with blurred haloes in the murky drizzle, mirrored in the slickly gleaming platform. Nothing moved, except at the extreme end of the platform, where below a flickering light the great mail sack hung. I heard the soft thump as it was automatically swung aboard the last car.

'And that's the first damn thing that's come aboard this train since we did,' I told Ape, who was sitting scoffing nuts he cracked between his fingers.

'What is?' he mumbled.

'One bloody great mail sack, into the guard's van. Just now.'

Ape grunted, uninterested. Then suddenly he spat out a great spray of nuts, and hauled himself to his feet. 'The hell you say! This is no dom mail train! And what guard's van? There is not one! Only a second motor unit! And they do not load mail automatic so, no more!'

Our eyes locked. Then, together, we turned and stared down the length of the now speeding train.

Dimly I saw it, the huge humped bulk plastered against the top and flanks of the last car, like some fallen fruit, half-rotten. Very like, for the lump was seething, dissolving at the edges, shedding small things that crept from it, a crawling infestation that moved out quickly along the cars.

Ape, perhaps, saw more; for he sucked in his breath sharply through his mobile lips. '*Kuro-i! Het smaakt slecht, jongen!*'

'What the hell are *those*?'

He managed to snort softly. 'Trouble! Would you know more?'

'I mean, are they human or . . . ?'

'If you are not too picky, *ja*, human of a sort. Vicious little *stinkeners*. Fit servants of a greater adversary.'

'So what d'you think they'll do?'

He looked at the oncoming creatures. The leaders were only two cars away now, scuttling effortlessly along the metal rim of a hopper. 'They head for the top, seems to me. So! They will seek to cut loose the container, so that it may be carried away . . . '

74

'What, off a moving train?'

Ape growled. 'You are going to stand there and arguefy while under our arses it is done? And we are rolled over in the process? Up on to the top with you, *jongetje*! So then we see if you truly are worth that Wolf-sticker of yours – *nee*? Hah!'

On to the top – easier said than done. There weren't any of those convenient side ladders you see in the movies, there were just the ribbed walls of the container. And this wasn't any especially smooth stretch of track; the train was really bucketing along now, and at every bend and points we were being swung and shaken from side to side. But the things were creeping closer, like blight on a branch, and the thought of them dropping on my head like spiders was almost unbearable. Thrusting my sword back in my belt at a safe angle, I caught at the slippery metal of the end rib protecting the container's door, my grip aided by Ape's tacky paint, and swung my foot up high to rest on the lock flange. Too high – the train lurched, my weight fell on my bent leg, my muscles strained in agony till I almost screamed. Then the car tilted back again, and seizing my moment I pulled up and straightened my leg together in best climber's style. That brought my head level with the top, and I threw an arm out like a grappling hook across the slippery plastic tarpaulin and frantically clutched at one of the further ribs. If I hadn't been a rock-climber and one-time mastheader I might not have made it; the train swung violently again, and for an instant I was back aboard a lurching masthead, legs dangling over an infinite gulf. Then, sweating and shivering, I hauled myself up on to the cover, retrieved my sword before it severed anything important, and crawled over the rain-slicked plastic to give Ape a hand.

I should have known better. He simply shinned up one of the clamping straps with a fluent hand-over-hand that would have made him a great speed climber, and his tombstone grin arrived over the rim of the container without apparent effort. He swung himself up one-handed, tossing what looked like a small stick in the other. I hauled myself upright, struggling for balance on the swaying surface, hoping there were no tunnels or anything else too close. I fought not to flinch too openly from the skein of high-voltage wires above my head, seeing the pantographs at front and rear of the train skid along them in a faint crackle of sparks and ozone. Beyond them, in the skies above, I could see two or three birds wheeling, like crows who scent battle and pickings. There was something odd about them, but I couldn't have said what exactly, not at this distance; something funny about the perspective? Perhaps . . .

But Ape's sharp exclamation called me back to earth.

'Jesus!' My mouth felt very dry, and the coffee was making a direct strike for my kidneys.

On the roof of the car behind the *kuro-i* were piling up. Piling up; there was no other word for it. They clambered chittering on top of one another like so many lemurs, which they rather resembled – both the primate, in one of its spookier nocturnal species, and the ancient Greek demons. Their gnarled little bug-eyed features, like giant walnuts with an accidental human resemblance, fixed us with glares of manic intensity. They wore shapeless sacks of some very coarse cloth, and I saw they hefted little weapons, sheaves of spears or darts and what looked like stone axes, about as formidable as bee-stings. I would have laughed if I hadn't been so flustered by that goggling gaze. That set off a sudden flush of anger.

'Well?' I shouted. 'Weren't expecting to find us, were you? Go on, get out of it – scram! There's nothing for you here! Piss off!'

Ape, still twirling his stick – no, a short baton – grunted approvingly. The *kuro-i* paid no attention. They continued to stare, wide-eyed. They blinked, all of them in unison, once – a horribly disturbing effect. Their black lips drew back over yellowed rodent teeth, the fine whiskery hairs at the corners of their mouths twitched – and they shrilled at me, a loud rat-like wailing cry that froze me to the spot. Then the air was suddenly alive with little spears, and they sprang.

One spear I swatted aside, a second narrowly missed, a third nicked my ear so finely I hardly felt the sting. I hesitated to use my sword on these grotesque little creatures, so I lashed out with my boot as the first one landed, to kick him off. But the little swine slid like quicksilver over the edge and hung there by one short arm, while the other clutched at my foot with a strength I'd never have believed. He tried to sink his teeth in my ankle, but even as they closed Ape's stick crashed down on his head and sent him bouncing and squalling into emptiness. It sang back again, catching two more in mid-leap and swatting them aside like casual pitches; but three more, ducking under the blow, seized his legs and toppled him, right at the edge of the container top. They went swarming over him, raising flint-tipped spears that suddenly didn't seem like such a joke. My sword slashed, the spears splintered and their wielders fell screaming into the dark – but I nearly went after them, sliding along the top in a threshing mass of yelling, clawing, stinking little fiends.

That took care of my inhibitions. Desperately I hacked and chopped and tore and throttled, afraid that one of the bits flying might be part of me I hadn't missed yet. But I emerged intact, pulled my dangling legs in, and looked desperately for Ape. He had troubles of his own, the little brutes seething over him like ants out of a hill, beating at him with axes and chain flails, so he couldn't do more than tear one off before another took its place. I charged into the middle of the flow, sword swinging, and that gave him the second he needed. While the little brutes were overwhelming me, he ducked back, tossed his stick in the air – and caught the great staff I'd seen him wield before.

He cast about, then touched one rounded gold tip to an oily patch on the tarpaulin. There was a dull explosion, a rushing sound, and he swung it up with a fireball burning at the tip. To left and right he cut, swinging the staff one-handedly with enormous strength, slashing fiery trails through the wind that howled around us. Flames roared down on the *kuro-i*, and they scattered, screaming; flame jetted to left and right of me, and I was free.

'I hold them off at the leap!' bellowed Ape. 'Ones that get past, you stomp!'

Easier bellowed than done; some of them were coming along the side and up the clamps. One of the little brutes leaped back to rake at me with a flail; I cut him down, and saw another fit one of those slender spears into a long grooved stick. He swung it back over his shoulder – then sharply down.

A blur, a hiss, and something plucked violently at my parka and jabbed me in the side. A *woomera*, an *atlatl* – almost as fast as a bow and arrow, in the right hands. If I hadn't seen a spear-thrower in a movie once, I might not have moved fast enough, and taken its missile in the heart; it was a matter of inches, even so, and my stroke missed him altogether as he scampered off down the roof. He stopped, aimed again, then vanished in a roaring jet of flame that blew him off the top and down like a meteor into the cutting. A stone-tipped axe, flung from below the container's edge, caught me a glancing blow on the temple; another, reaching over, missed my leg, but its haft barked me agonisingly on the shin. To left and right I cut and chopped, forgetting whatever skill I had, flailing into this seething mass the way you try to beat away a bad dream, skidding on blood and offal as the train lurched, fighting desperately to keep my feet because if I fell once a hundred little spikes and slashes would come raining down and there would be no getting up. My blood would run with the rest, and my insides spill among the trampling feet. And what of Ape?

My brief glance away was a mistake. A hard head rammed me in the groin, and I almost went over – would have, if his aim had been better. Speechless, I doubled up and grabbed the little creature by the throat; teeth sank into my thigh, I tore him free and held him, kicking and screaming, like a shield against his fellows while I leaned on my sword to recover. I had barely enough time; spears quilled his side by my arm, axeheads thudded into his body around my fingers, all on the chance of a lucky hit. He kicked and squalled; I struck out with him like a club into his murderous relatives, then sent him after them. His body was sucked between cars by the slipstream and dashed against the metal hopper with a reverberating gong sound. As if that was a signal, the malignant dwarf-things sprang back, looked over their shoulders and scuttled away.

Fire washed in their footsteps, thin spider-thread sprays of it that clung and writhed wherever they fell. Thrashing and clawing at themselves, the *kuro-i* hopped and scurried back, and I fell to my knees on the stained tarpaulin, wheezing.

A heavy hand landed on my shoulder, and the light of a thin flame dancing on the end of a much shorter staff. 'They back off – for a moment, I guess. You have no hurt, *nee*?'

I chewed down an angry answer, and just shook my head. I took a deep breath before I did say anything. 'About two inches further up and I'd never have played the cello again. Otherwise okay.'

'You play cello?'

'Forget it. The rest are just cuts and bruises—' Something tweaked around my left ribs. I reached into my sadly mauled parka and jerked out the spear that had struck me; the flapping parka had slowed it enough so the crude barbs hadn't quite gone in.

Ape looked at it, then tossed it away. 'Not poisoned! Most times they do, though the rain would wash it off – enough not to kill, anyhow. Their filthy bite is worse to be feared!'

78

'Great. I've got plenty of those. I thought you said they were human!'

'So you are picky! You, genus *Homo sap*, that they are not. But did you think that was the only kind of human around?'

'Well, no. The Wolves are a mutation—'

'And so of many! These, their ancestors are a fierce tribe, harvesters of heads whose long-suffering neighbours combine to drive them forth into the deep of deep jungle. There they suffer much, dwindle maybe in size; for that is not a good place for men to live. But something else is there, maybe; and out of the Core it lead them, on to the Spiral. And they return . . . ' he made a fluid, moulding gesture with his fingers, ' . . . other.'

'God. Like the Wolves?'

'Not so corrupt; but terrible malign, hard to keep on lead. True men fear them, where they still live on, for them they hate, and delight to plague. And they are apt to be turned against an enemy of Those they respect . . . ' His voice sounded hollow and dark, suddenly far less sure of himself. I braced myself as the car swayed beneath us at a bend, and discovered the sides of the cars behind to the moonlight.

'Here they come,' I said, and the words fell out of me in hopeless exhaustion.

Ape growled, glancing here and there over the offal-stained tarpaulin. 'You see any more benzine? *Nee? Verdom!*'

'But just a smear like that – it couldn't have fuelled so much flame—'

'This is the Core! I need like to breed like, power to breed power! Now little is left, I must have more. I look to use the paint cans, it burns good, but they all fall out, the rest is dry.'

I looked around at the tarpaulin. 'They almost overran us, last time. Would have, if there'd been more room up here. They couldn't get hold of us quickly enough, not with you at the gap. But it was the fire that saved us. There must be something else!'

'There is wet offal,' he said dourly, looking around, 'but that I cannot burn. Make ready, *jongen*! We do what we must!'

And then the rain came on, with a vengeance. A night-grey curtain seemed to billow over the wall of the cutting we were entering. With a rattle like steel chain it fell across the train, sizzling and steaming off the pantographs, thudding in the coke carts, drumming in the hoppers. It lashed our backs like leather, and bowed them under its weight. Spray rose like smoke, and through it, chittering and wild, rushed the *kuro-i*.

Ape's staff spun in his powerful fingers with an ease any majorette would envy. It swatted the goblin-things from midair and dashed them down between the rails, while my sword stabbed and slashed at any that ducked between his strokes. The ones coming by beneath shrank back from the tumbling bodies; that gained us a moment. The rain was scouring the tarpaulin clean, and that too was a gain. Dark blood washed down over Ape's designs.

'Waterproof paint!' he growled. '*That one! There! Catch*!'

It kicked and snarled on my swordpoint, as I lifted it high, stomach heaving, to hurl it away. I ducked furiously, only just in time. As the train swept out of the cutting a shadow stooped out of the rain, lashing it aside, a vast wing that almost swept me away with negligent ease. The birds – but I barely believed the thing I saw, dark plumage suddenly iridescent in boiling light, angry gems glaring out over a savage hook of a beak. Ape's fire flickered, and the monster wheeled up again, with a croaking scream like chalk scraping a board, times ten.

'The last of it!' he growled.

The others were waiting, vast idle wing beats keeping them in pace with the train, so they seemed to hover like roadside kestrels. The moment these little bastards cut the container loose – 'I don't believe it!' I yelled. 'They're the size of small bloody jets!'

Ape laughed, harshly. 'A *garuda*! There is worse and harder to believe than that out on the Spiral!'

'I know, damn it, I've seen plenty! Out there, sure, I'd expect anything! But if this is the Core, *how are things that size flying*?'

Ape stared at me a second. That triggered another surge of dwarfish horrors on to the car, but they fell back when he struck at them. It was little more than a feint to keep us busy. The main body were holding back beyond spearshot range, hanging on car sides, shivering and glaring, while still more came flowing up to join them. They had attacked too soon; but the numbers they were assembling now could just wash over us like a tidal wave, without Ape's flame. He hunkered down, and stared at the birds.

'You have right, by dom! For those to fly, we must be here at the very margins between Core and Spiral! To hold them so close, that is a hard and terrible thing, but it gives the monsters oomph to go flap!'

'Then there's nothing we can do?'

He grinned. 'You forget, *jongen*! The closer they are to me, so I am to them! I also am of the Spiral, and where it touches is more oomph mine also!' His grin faded, and he pounded out his words on the glossy shaft of his staff. 'But still–must–I–have–*power*!'

My mouth was drier than ever, my kidneys working overtime. 'There's power all around you,' I told him. 'If you've only the strength to wield it.' And I pointed, and his face grew slack with wonder and furious thought.

But he was given little time for it. The *kuro-i* were still beyond spearshot; it was heavy curved bows that sang, and bamboo arrows that came rattling down on us. Ape roared and sprang up, and swung his staff high as the horrible tide raced forward. At the last moment I saw what he meant to do, and shouted, 'Not down! Not to earth! Or you'll fry the lot of us! To the p—'

The word was lost in the sound, a deafening, crackling sizzle and squeal as a fat spark leaped from the wires overhead to one golden tip of Ape's staff. And the staff swung in his fat fingers, so that the domed end of the other tip traced an arc in the air, at just the height of the scuttling *kuro-i*.

The bolt that leaped down the train was a river-delta of force, forking into a million hair-thin strands, channelling radiant energy; and into its path the *kuro-i* leaped. Right through the midst of them it lanced, a fearsome, unstoppable web of blue-white fire that leaped to earth itself along the rear pantograph. How it managed not to blow every fail-safe in the train, I don't know; I saw the cab lights flicker violently, and smoke erupt from the misused pantograph. But for our small attackers it was infinitely more devastating. They writhed, shrilled, leaped or sprawled in that single hellish flash, dancing like sickening puppets on strings of spiking sparks. More hellish still was the momentary blindness after, the roaring furnace of after-images, the stink of smoke and roasting and the fear of what might still burst through it and throw itself upon your sightlessness.

Nothing did. That single bolt had broken the back of the attack, and as my eyes cleared, blinking, watering, squinting in pain, I saw the top of the opposite car scorched and smoking, clear of crawling things, save where a few crouched over the far end and watched us with impotent hatred. Some half their number must have died there, or against us; and the rest drew back, scared and sullen, to the vantage of the cars further back.

But by the same token . . .

Ape wasn't a crisp. Not even slightly singed. He stood there, legs braced, breathing like a blast furnace, staff braced to hurl another such bolt if he had to. I looked at him, awestruck. 'More oomph!' I panted. 'You weren't just kidding, either, were you?'

But he still looked grim. 'I expect no enemy so strong-mean as this, not by half, by dom! Out on the Spiral I have force of my own, I like not to use these sparky weirdnesses you drive your clankety machines with – too dangerous! I am lucky, that is all, you with me. And we are not down from the trees yet. For sure they try something more.' He glanced up at the birds. Could he fry one of them so easily? He might. But two would be harder, and there were at least four wheeling up there, like nightmarish carrion crows.

A new fear hit me. The drivers were far enough ahead not to have heard any of this, but they must have noticed the rear unit falter, seen their dials go haywire under that appalling power surge, suspected a fault on the wires if nothing worse – why hadn't they stopped? And what would happen if they did? Then I guessed why, and a glance at my watch confirmed it. 'Hey, the little bastards haven't got much time left! We're due at the airport depot in, god, practically minutes now—'

But even as I spoke there was a twang, and I staggered sideways. The tarpaulin shifted violently under our feet, slackening and sagging against the ribbed top of the container.

'They're cutting the lines!' I said, or possibly screamed. I could see the same look on Ape's face as mine – a vision of a billowing mass of heavy plastic fabric, suddenly cut loose, flapping and wrapping itself around us, whirling us off to hell . . .

'Down!' he roared. 'Down and make chutney of them! Or we lose!'

Scowling back at the *kuro-i*, hunched up with his staff, he looked very unhuman indeed. But even as I swung my legs over the edge, I saw the birds peel away and plunge down the wind. Ape and I both froze. He could handle the birds up here – maybe. But he would have nobody to guard his back. Nor would I, down there on that narrow rim of car. The *kuro-i* would have me alone.

It was insoluble – they had us. We were losing. And the time it took to realise that was time we hadn't got. With their abrasive screeches the birds were on us. Ape, raising his staff to the power lines, was bowled over by a hooking claw and sent skidding along

82

the container top. I sprang up, stumbling as the train began to brake, and slashed at the root of the cruel beak that stabbed down over him; hot blood spurted among the feathers, and the vast thing flapped away, squalling. I panted with relief. Only a scratch, it'd be back, but—

I'd forgotten, in the heat of it, that there were others. Ape's eyes went wide, he pointed desperately, opened his mouth to yell; but slow and tired as I was, I reacted and spun around only in time to see the sweeping blackness of another wingtip blot out the lightening sky. It caught me with the stinging impact of a vast door slamming in my face. Stunned, I was swatted backwards, sent flying straight off the container top and out into empty air.

Whirling confusion—

A sudden roaring flash of impact, and I was sprawled in a tangle of something with an aching, roasting agony in back and sides, fighting frenziedly for breath. It came, and I rolled over, trying not to yelp aloud. I'd done my best to land as I'd been taught to in climbing, rolled up but relaxed, shielding head and belly. The undergrowth had been an added bonus; men had fallen parachuteless from planes, thousands of feet, into that and survived.

But the train! I expected to see it vanishing into the distance; but instead the car was only a hundred yards down the track, and slowing all the time, almost to walking pace. That must have helped save my neck, too. The moment I could move my limbs I scrabbled about for my sword. I was on a steep slope, and, looking down through the undergrowth, I saw it gleam faintly in greying light, lying clear of the tangles in the lineside gravel some way below. I swallowed; I'd had the best of it, knocked more or less straight from top of container to top of slope. If I'd fallen straight down that far, I might have been a lot worse off. I slithered down to it, scooped it up, swung it about – not even scratched!

The grey light was growing. The great winged shadows still wheeled above the train, but I saw them rise suddenly and scatter. I thought of Ape, still holding them off on his own; I couldn't just leave him. Holding my ribs, seeing stars at every breath, I went after the train at a sort of limping lope.

Beyond the wide bend in the tracks, as my vision cleared, I saw the cutting was opening out, the gravel opening out into a wider network of lines, with others joining it to either side. No wonder the train was slowing so. We must already be in the approaches to the airfreight terminus – and that would be lit, that would be secure. If we could only have held out a minute longer.

'*Joengen!*'

I almost cannoned into him as I rounded the corner, running back along the tracks. He gripped me by the shoulders. 'You are not hurt, *nee?*'

'*Nee* – I mean, not badly! You?'

'A scratch, a peck – *gezond!* I do not see you fall, I am too busy – but then they leave off sudden, I see you are not there, I hoop down and leg it back to see we do not at least lose you!'

'What do you mean, they left off? You didn't do that?'

'If I could, by dom, I do it sooner!'

'Then—' Gasping, I stared back at the train. A swarm of squat little figures was streaming off it, down on to the line, back towards us. Ape hurled me into the bushes almost as hard as the first time, and dived after me himself. A cry tore the air ragged, great yellow claws raked and tore at the bushes. 'On your feet!' growled Ape, and not waiting for me to move he dragged me upright. 'And run like bloody hell, *joengen!* It is not your crate they have been after, this little while – it is *you!*'

I didn't stop to argue. Wheezing, limping, we staggered and scrambled up the steep cutting, through briar and bramble and bags of broken bottles, mostly on all fours; Ape was good at that. 'For the top!' he shouted. 'If I can get near enough the wires . . .'

But the undergrowth gave out before the top. We hesitated a second, then made a mad dash out across the open space – too late. Out along the crest of the ridge scuttled a line of small figures, drawing bows, notching spears into throwers; and others were crunching along the trackside and thrashing up through the bushes further along, moving to encircle us. There was no gap between them and us now. And overhead, against the grey clouds, predatory shapes were gliding down.

Ape spun his staff in his hand. 'Maybe was something in those bottles – alcohol, gas, kerosene. I should have looked.'

'Yeah. Sorry I got you into this, Ape.'

'I am the one to be sorry. Little enough they can do to me. My task is to help protect your cargo and you, and I can no more. Could we have held them off minutes longer . . .'

'What then?' They were closing in now, menacing shadows against a pale bright sky.

84

'Dawn. But the sun is not yet in the sky.'

'Ape, we're in a *cutting*!'

He thought an instant, laughed aloud – and suddenly hurled his staff high into the air, wheeling in what looked like slow motion. And as it rose the golden tips glittered and blazed like mirrors, afire with the first scarlet light of the sun's edge, rising over the edge of the outside world. With that light they blazed in their turn, and the *kuro-i* shrilled and staggered blindly as it rained down among them, as it woke iridèscence from every drop of the misty drizzle.

Winged shadows glided over. I flinched – and looking up, saw there was nothing there. Nothing except four drifting wisps of dark stormcloud, lit red around their lower edges. Away they drifted on the fresh cool breeze, across the great archipelago of black and gold that dawn awoke among the clouds. Nor was there any line of goblins along the crest, or along the line below, or along the tops of the cars – only a spray of what looked like dead leaves, dry and feathery, whisked up and away by the same quickening wind.

Exhausted, Ape and I staggered down the track, and into the scant shelter of an empty signalbox, watching the freight cars glide slowly towards the airfreight terminal. Dave would be waiting there, to see the container taken off and speed it through the formalities.

'You think it'll be safe, now?' I demanded.

Ape gave his odd oriental nod. 'More than always. They draw back now, those forces of the Spiral. More power they spend than I believe they could, and to no gain. They will be weakened for long now. And all that . . .' He cocked a sharp glance at me. 'All that for you. No poison on spears or arrows; attack, but not kill. The container, yes, if they can; but when it comes to choose, they want you most. You know what that says?'

I was almost too tired to speak, let alone think. 'I can't bloody imagine!'

'They think that through you they could get the container anyway, and maybe more – is what. They must think they have some hold over you – that somehow they will be able to make you do what they say. That if only they can get you, they have you – *so*!'

His staff stabbed down on one of the drifting leaves, pinning it to the gravel. I looked at it – long and thin, withered almost to disintegration, the narrow leaf of a giant bamboo.

The hotel clerk knew me from back when. He somehow managed to make the elegant Indian-style *sawaddee* gesture and still have my keys and my messages on the counter before I reached it. An emaciated-looking bellboy trotted up with a trolley and began loading my cases, but I kept back a long elegant package covered with FRAGILE – ANTIQUE labels and carried it myself. I might have had a hard time passing the sword through airline security and customs, but it's amazing what you can get away with in a Harrods wrapper.

Like a lot of Thais, the bellboy belied his small and fragile appearance. He heaved my bags around as if they were feathers, poured me a drink, slipped me a card for an incredibly obscene cabaret and added proudly that he was moonlighting at a Thai boxing club tonight, and not as a waiter either, and would I like to come along and bet on him?

A reasonable tip got rid of him, and as soon as the door closed I began leafing through the sheaf of envelopes. Greetings from our Bangkok agents – a fax from the office saying there was nothing worth faxing me about – Dave's report, confirming the call I'd had from him on the plane, confirming the container's safe arrival – nothing more. I sat back, contemplated my beer, swallowed it in one gulp and grabbed another from the bar. All very well, but the one I was most nervous about wasn't there; nothing from Ape.

He'd insisted I would be safe on the plane. 'They lose the container, for the now. Which mean, you are their only way back to it – *klopt*? Right now killing you is the last they want.' He chuckled. 'Safe? *Jongetje*, your ass is wrapped in cotton wool. At least till you get to Bangkok, anyhow.'

'Oh, so?' Ever since he'd taken that leap off the train after me I was a lot more inclined to trust him; but there was still too much I didn't understand about him – his motives, and the true extent and reliability of his powers. 'Then why aren't you coming out with me?'

He shrugged, did his best to look embarrassed, retreated into Dutch. '*Reis niet so graag met de vliegtuig, hoor – het is niks voor mij*! I find a ship will get me part way, to Ophir.'

I blinked. 'Ophir?'

'Sure. By Tartessos and Ashkelon.'

'Of course, silly of me, where else? With a cargo of ivory, Apes and peacocks, I suppose.'

Ape grunted and gave me a very old-fashioned look. 'The ivory, *ja*, as it happens – walruss, mammot', *eenhorn*. The peacocks, no, since I leave you behind.'

'*Touché*!' I said gracefully – like the Thurber cartoon. 'And you'll have no trouble getting another out of there?'

'*Nee*, it is a trade route long established, there to the East. If not, I can always cross to Baghdad, find one there for sure. I want to start my looking for a ship before Bangkok.'

Despite generations of storytellers and film-makers, Baghdad is hundreds of miles inland and has no trace of a seaport – at least, not the Baghdad I know. I kept quiet about that, though. The Baghdad Ape was headed for was a long shadow cast by history and legend both. It might owe at least as much to tradition as to reality – or be the source of that tradition. Truth was a two-way traffic along the Spiral. 'It's a slow way round, though,' I objected. 'How long'll I have to sit cooling my heels in Bangkok?'

Ape grinned. 'You never hear one about the *jonge* lady called Bright? Chances are I am there before you, *knul*! And looking around. You stick to your hotel and wait. You hear nothing, you come to this address, these times. And by this route, only.' He thrust a grubby scrap of paper at me – the printed label of a sardine can, still with its margins untrimmed, never attached to the can. It was covered with beautiful copperplate handwriting. 'A place like the Tavern, on the margins of the Spiral. If I am not there – *then* you start to worry. But all above, you stay away from the container, *hoor*? Well away!'

So that was all I had to do here – sit around and stare at the landscape. And wait for Ape to turn up, and wonder, still, if he ever would. I mooched over to the picture-window of my executive suite – fortieth floor, next best to a penthouse – and gazed out moodily at the afternoon skyscape of glass and concrete towers, broken only by the nearby pinnacles of the Grand Palace. Beyond the glass, even this high up, a haze of dust and fumes hung in the tropical air, and something of the heat and clamour penetrated through even to my air-conditioned haven. A couple of days till my rendezvous with Ape, if he didn't come through sooner; what to do till then? I'd been here often enough before. I'd even had time to play tourist, which I didn't always. There was nothing new I wanted to do. I even considered turning on the television, but I wasn't that desperate yet.

My gloomy reverie was broken by a discreet knock. That bloody bellboy again, with a card for something called the Thigh Bar – as in Thighland, no doubt. But almost as an afterthought he had another envelope. I ripped it open eagerly, but it wasn't from Ape. The paper bore the Project's Aquarius logo; the Foundation had heard from Dave that I was out here, and a representative from their local office would be contacting me shortly, to act as my personal liaison over the shipping arrangements to Bali. If that was all right, of course.

I sighed. Very obliging of them, but I needed a personal liaison the way I needed another set of orifices right now. I could just see myself trying to explain to some earnest aid worker how exactly I was proposing to despatch their precious computer gear; it might be via anything from a Spanish galleon to one of those giant Melanesian outrigger canoes, for all I could guess. Probably it'd be something much, much worse. Even the thought brought on my jetlag. I shambled into the bedroom and sprawled flat on the enormous bed. At this rate I'd be watching Thai TV yet.

Hunger got the better of me, though. I could have phoned down for something, but I remembered that the ground-floor restaurant would be better. Brimful of a cheerful *satay* and *kaeng keow wan kai*, plus a couple more Thai lagers, I was just heading back to the lifts when the desk clerk caught my eye. With a discreet cough he informed me that some gentlemen from Bali were asking the favour of an interview (that was how he put it). They were waiting in the east lounge just now. So here were the local reps already; I groaned inwardly, but admitted I was expecting them. I wondered why he looked so surprised at that. I almost asked for drinks to be sent in, but remembered they might be Muslims. I pinched a mint from the basket on the counter to kill the beer on my breath, straightened my tie and walked in as nonchalantly as if nosy-parkering client representatives were just what I'd been dying to see right now.

What I did see brought me up short. The little group of men in vaguely Indian-looking costumes who rose as I entered didn't look a whole lot like representatives of an international project. In this air-conditioned kennel of Western values they seemed totally out of place in dress, face, everything. It was as if a bit of the real East had thrust up like a gnarled treeroot through the endangered-forest mahogany parquet. Gnarled indeed; they were none of them young, grave, responsible-looking men in jackets of white or dark blue cotton, with – no, not trousers, but elegant, neatly folded *sarongs* of cotton or silk. Beneath their neat white caps there was hardly a black hair among them. White or steel-grey, it was always swept tightly back, highlighting the hard planes of the face and skull, and tied in short knots, on top of the head or at the nape of the neck. Some wore neat whiskers or short chinbeards, and one ancient had long white moustaches that stood out from his wrinkled face like straggly feathers. Their skins were browner than Thais, their faces rounder. Oh yes, these were Balinese, all right.

They all bowed in unison, a low sweeping bow with right arms extended, angling the short staves they all carried, so gracefully that I had to echo it. That gave the elderly gentleman with the moustaches a chance to set the ball rolling.

'*Selamat malam*! Good evening! You are *Tuan* . . . ' He hesitated. '*Fee-sha*? Indeed. I am *I Pemangku* Wayan Sadja. Gives me greatest pleasure, *Tuan*, that you so kindly consenting to see us.'

He pronounced everything as oddly as my name, so it took me a moment to realise that his English, however ungrammatical, was pretty good. No getting out of it now; I murmured the usual nothings, and offered refreshments. Most of them chose Coke, a couple Singha beer and mekhong whiskey, a fearful paint-stripper based on sugar cane, but one tall grey-maned character, who sat easily by himself in the centre of a settee while the others perched decorously in armchairs, ordered a Guinness. As he bowed his thanks he met my eyes with an ironical smile, which is the Indonesian equivalent of spitting in them, and lolled back with the ease of a relaxing lion. His steel-grey hair framed a hard, high-cheekboned face with a neat moustache and goatee, and heavy eyebrows shadowing deepset yellowed eyes. I put him down at once as a Brahmin, probably a temporal aristocrat as well, some *raja*'s relative or sultan's son showing off his knowledge of Western ways – and almost certainly the dominant spirit of this party.

We sipped our drinks and studied each other in courteous silence. At last I took the initiative. 'Well, er, gentlemen – you've no great cause to thank me, because as yet I don't know who you are, or the purpose of your visit.'

'But is not obvious, *tuan*?' demanded the white-haired spokesman. 'We are priests of our island. We are coming to Bangkok as delegation of conference of priests. All priests, not only *pedandas* who are Brahmins, but also the *pemangku* such as I who serve temples, and *sungguhu* who are priests of lower world. Even many *balians usada* and *dalangs*, who are for simple folk. But most of all, many *klian subaks*, who are priests of water.'

I nodded politely, though I didn't like the sound of this. 'I've heard of them. How can I help you?'

The old man drew himself up. 'We are chosen for our age and rank, but also because we may speak to the workers of this Water Resource Management Project in *Ingerrish* that you understand. We ask you hear what we come this way to say to you.'

I spread my hands politely. 'Thank you. Certainly I'll listen to what you have to say. But perhaps you should have contacted me in advance, and saved yourselves the journey; I'll be visiting Bali very soon, anyway.'

The old man bowed again. 'I thank you! So we are aware. Now is when you must hear us. It is important, very, very. This meeting of priests is unhear of before. So many come together, to protect what so precious to us. This water project – at all costs – and we come to ask, no, beg of you, *tuan* – at all costs *we want that it stop!*'

He didn't emphasise the words, almost sang them in his soft liquid accent. But all the same they thudded down between us like knives, and stuck there quivering.

I sat up. I resisted the temptation to ask why. This was going to take some very diplomatic handling. 'Then, gentlemen, I don't understand at all why you've come to me. I'm not a member of the Project, my firm is only one of its contractors. Your government, the Foundation, the Project staff themselves—'

The old fellow gestured with his staff. 'We appeal many, many times to the government in Jawa. They pretend to listen, but not. Then to the Project, to the Foundation; they listen, but not heed.

But we hear they cannot get their machines bringing to them, and we rejoice. Then you come, and will bring the machines to them. Without you, they are helpless. So the choice must be yours.'

'I believe otherwise,' I said briskly – about as sharp a contradiction as was still polite. 'My firm could withdraw, yes. At some financial loss, in penalty payments – though that hardly matters. But at an even greater cost to myself, to my standing, to the firm's. And I know how important standing, honour, face, call it what you like, is in your culture; you will understand. I'd need a very good reason to incur such a penalty. So far you haven't given me one. Or any reason why you object to the Project at all. We undertook to help only because it seemed such a good cause.'

They looked bleakly at one another, buzzing remarks back and forth, too low for me to catch. They understood, all right. The old fellow's face twisted unhappily, and he seemed about to say something when the tall man leaned forward sharply and rapped his staff on the floor. Like one or two of the other staffs it was tipped with a small ball of clear glass, but this one was set in a richly ornate clasp of gold, four dart shapes arranged as a stylised claw. His own hand looked clawlike, its nails grown to astonishing length, the mark of a man of leisure with no need to work. I realised that he must be a *pedanda*, one of the high priests of Bali's own strange Hinduism, and by the look of it a wealthy one. Wayan and the others shut up at once.

The old man rose and bowed to me – stiffly, as if he felt I didn't deserve it. And maybe to intimidate me a little; he was my own height, very tall for a Balinese, and longer and leaner of face than most, as if the blood of the ancient Indian lords of Bali ran purer in him. It was a hard face, long and strong-jawed, with a narrow curved blade of a nose; small gold ornaments dangled from the large ears half hidden among the gathered hair, but they seemed more votive than decorative. Hard and serene, unlined, untroubled as an animal's by doubt or strong feeling – a fanatic's face. 'I am *Ida Pagus Mpu* Bharadah,' he said, and though his accent was strong his English was even better than Wayan's, cold and clipped and precise. 'Are we to understand you are ignorant of the true purpose behind this good cause you claim to support? That it is no more or less than the ruin of our island?'

His voice was calm; open anger loses you face all through this part of the world. But the outright insult was almost as unusual, even from a *raja* to a streetsweeper. I had trouble staying suave myself. 'As I understand things, sir, what'll ruin your island is the Project's failure. Its only purpose that I can see is to make sure precious water is conserved and fairly distributed.'

'Conserved! Fairly distributed!' He snorted. 'And yet you say you have heard of our ancient *subak* system! Its temples have kept our island in the Divine Balance for untold centuries; yet now it is to be cast aside in a matter of a year or two by the machines you are bringing from over the sea! And not only the *subak* temples will go, but all else with it! All the sacred checks and balances of our island life, all our kinship with the gods and our sacred ancestors – all thrown away! All to be replaced by control from without, by the corrupt appointees of an alien government, that seeks ever to shape Bali in the apostate mould of Jawa!'

There was a low murmur of agreement. This was sticky ground. As the railfreight manager had said, most of Indonesia – the bit I knew – and hence its central government, was staunchly Islamic. They'd been sensibly tolerant of Balinese faiths, up till now, but rumour had it fundamentalist pressure groups wanted to change all that. And evidently the intolerance wasn't all on one side. I chose my words very carefully. 'I'm sorry if that's so, but I'd have no business interfering; that's got to be between the government and yourselves. But like it or not, this is a changing world. To keep Bali alive at all, there must be some adjustments, some room for new things, for progress—'

'Must there?' Nobody else spoke. The lounge was large and empty, but this Bharadah's personality seemed to fill it out and press against the walls. 'All that is new, is evil. The hand of the government reaches over us from *kelod*, from the sea, the breeding ground of all evil. Their accursed schools teach the Bahasa Indonesia tongue, so that young folk no longer learn the High and Low speeches, no longer know the castes and what address is proper to each, speaking at best a bastard middle tongue that pleases none and offends all. They are taught to cover their bodies in shame, where once they could walk lightly clad or naked as our climate demands. They are taught to forget their ancestors and live only for the present, to despise the wisdom of the past for the uncertain science of today. They no longer know their place; the sanctity of the *desa*, the life of the community, is torn apart.' He tossed his head scornfully, a familiar gesture somehow. Did it remind me of somebody – Ape, maybe?

'To you, child of a faceless, inhuman city, that may mean little. But had you visited our land ere you saw fit to pronounce on right and wrong, you might have learned better wisdom. Our temples are our land in miniature, from the *candi bentar*, the split gate which is the sea, to the shrine of Gunung Agung at the northernmost end, our sacred Great Mountain. And just so is each community and each household within it a macrocosm of the human bodies it contains. That is rightness, that is fitness; that has endured unchanged from ancient times.' He smiled coldly, and stalked across to the window, where Bangkok fumed and festered beneath the giant orange umbrella of the sinking sun. He lifted his staff in a gesture of rejection. The glass ball caught the light, and hurled it blazing into my eyes. 'That, out there, that is a new thing, that is *progress*. Do you bid us abandon our ancient unities to make way for *that*?'

'Of course not!' I protested, blinking away the fiery after-images. 'But – a growing population, tourists, mass communications, the climate . . . It's not just this Project or any other. Things are changing whether you or I like it or not. You need the other side, the better side of progress, to help you cope – modern medicine, modern education, modern irrigation . . . '

'We *need* none of these things!'

'But you'll get failed harvests – famine – sickness, otherwise! People will die!'

'There are worse things for people than merely dying!' He rounded on me, then seemed to remember his dignity. He lowered his staff and traced out a wavering outline on the parquet. 'Once the sea was a thing we shunned, the darkness into which all evil was washed, from the high heart of our land. We turned our eyes away from it, and raised them to the high purity, the abode of our gods. And now, *now* tourists have made our own children so ashamed of their own ways that they seek to ape them, and waste their time and substance to ride the unclean waves.'

'Oh, surfers?' I smiled. 'Yes, I'd heard. They caught the fashion from the Aussies, didn't they? All right, a bit loud and mindless, but surely there's no real harm—'

'Is there not? When they beg and scrape and steal and sell their bodies to be able to buy cast-off shirts and worn boards from the tourists of Australia and America, and radios that are cheap junk to the Japanese? When they dance the ancient dances and the timeless rites in piecemeal, perfunctory forms to please those tourists, like performing apes? Is that a life to be proud of, a prancing whore to the world outside?' He leaned on his staff, and his face was bleak and hard.

'Does *Tuan* Fisher also know what the word *puputan* means? I will tell you. Barely a hundred years ago, in the early 1900s, when the army of the *orang blanda*, the Dutchmen, came to overrun Badung, our greatest kingdom, its *raja*, together with his heirs, wives, courtiers, servants and all their families and households, marched out to face them. And in the face of the invader, with their holiest *kris* knives they ritually slew one another, the servant the master, the father the son, the husband the wives. The *rajas* of Tabanan and Klungklung did likewise, shortly thereafter. At Badung alone more than three thousand five hundred people slew themselves in the space of an hour or two. That, that is *puputan* – the honourable ending.'

He paused to let that sink in. '*Tuan* Fisher, there are men, there are whole communities who would prefer such a fate to having the balance of their ancient culture, their time-hallowed livelihoods, wrested out of the hands of the ancient gods of Bali, and placed into the grasping and unsympathetic hands of mere government officials. It could still happen today.' The staff flashed in my eyes once more. 'Will you bear responsibility for any such horror?'

Nobody'd ever accused me of being over-imaginative; but anyone who travels a lot sees things – shattered limbs in the rubble of an IRA bombing, machine-gunned bodies on a beach after an African coup. And I remembered only too clearly now the Wolf with the severed arm falling shrieking at my feet, the dark blood running across a broad blackened deck, steaming and stinging on my own bare arms as we cut our way free; and the hacking and squealing on the container top during that manic midnight ride. The horror burgeoned in my mind, a monstrous mound of corpses, sprawled and twitching, reeking, all the horrors I'd seen compounded a hundred times and more. Over it, crushing it down like a triumphant procession, rode the trucks blazoned with the Aquarius emblem. And always I was at the wheel . . .

I thumped the chair-arm. The other priests jumped, as if they'd been as much in thrall to that vision as I. This Bharadah was a powerful speaker; but he was wielding the rawest kind of emotional blackmail. I hated that wherever I found it, hated it like

94

hell itself, from advertising to preaching to corporate nego-
tiations; it was a kind of invasion, of manipulating and
dominating what ought to be your own feelings, a kind of
possession almost. I could taste the resentment on my tongue, and
I met the *pedanda* eye to eye. He held my gaze easily; only in those
relentless old eyes was there any hint of the fires within.

It took an effort, but I parried calm with calm; though you
could almost hear the air clink between us. 'Responsibility?
What's that supposed to mean? I know where my responsibilities
lie, and they're to my firm's clients – unless and until you can
prove they're doing something wrong. You've hardly even tried.
Instead you've come peddling the old days and the old ways
wholesale, never mind whether they're still able to keep your
people alive. You haven't shown a hint of understanding or
compromise. You've insulted the motives of people who only
want to help, without offering one shred of proof. And you've
resorted to threats—'

It was an actual spasm of anger that shook me. 'Well, my
friend, if you're thinking about inciting your people into some
kind of lunatic grand gesture, then that's nobody's responsibility
but yours – and theirs, if they're crazy enough to listen to you. But
I suggest you just sit down first and think damn hard – is it really
your people you care about most, or your power base? If you
know the term.'

I rose to my feet, fighting against that yellowed gaze as if it was
a physical pressure. I looked around at the other priests, but it
was as I'd expected; they'd deferred to the old man at first, but
even he was looking uncertainly to Bharadah.

'It's not that I don't understand your views,' I said, more to
them than him. 'Even sympathise with them, in some ways. I
don't always like what this world's become. But I'm not that sold
on famine and death, either; and I'd be damn slow to inflict them
on other people in the name of any belief, however worthwhile.
That's speaking personally. On behalf of the firm, there's only
one answer I can give. The Project's been officially approved.
That makes it a matter between the people of the island and the
national government, in which we've no right to take sides.
However, the terms of our contract allow us to withdraw if we
have good evidence of corruption or other ill-intent; so get us that
evidence – legal evidence, mind! – and we'll consider it, seriously.
We'll put that in writing if you give us the address of any

campaign organisation. Thank you for letting us have your views.'

Mpu Bharadah gave that angry toss of his head again. The skin over his cheekbones seemed to draw tight with fury, his mouth pulled back in a wide snarl. He clutched his staff till it quivered, as if he was about to brain me with it, and the long nails stood out like claws. There was no mistaking the growl in his voice now. 'You merely split hairs to serve your own ends. You *are* taking sides! Against the convocation of priests, and against all the uncorrupted folk of Bali! Prepare yourself to face the consequences!'

'Mpu Bharadah, my firm has faced threats before; and as then, it will do its utmost to fulfil its commitments. But speaking personally again, I don't take to being threatened one – little – bloody – bit!' I felt my smile twist as I looked at him again, more like a snarl. 'Any more than you would, I'm sure. *Bukan adat kami!* That's all. *Maaf, saya harus pergi sekarang!*'

They hadn't realised I spoke any Bahasa Indonesia. Assuming I didn't had lost them some face; now I'd said I had to go, they couldn't make any attempt to detain me without losing more. Automatically the old men rose and bowed politely, and I had to return it; but Bharadah just stood there, still fuming. For his benefit, if he was so clued-up on Western manners, I couldn't resist adding '*Selamat siang!*' Which means, roughly, 'Have a nice day!'

I fled for the nearest elevator. It turned out to be one I'd never used before, a glass-walled exterior model, slow and scenic. Not that I'm afraid of heights, I just didn't find the idea of a Bangkok panorama exactly thrilling. Seeing it now surprised me. The neon-crusted concrete I loathed did dominate the skyline, at first, interlaced with street-wide advertising signs, Tokyo style; but then you noticed the older buildings, the temples with their white-walled towers and tiled and gilded roofs, the halls and pavilions of the Grand Palace complex with its carefully planted gardens, the airy Victorian elegance of the 19th century Western buildings, the 'spirit house' at the base of every glassy office block. They poked up through the concrete like more of those roots, only here and there at first, until you realised how many of them there were, and how superficial the glitzy modernity really was. Roots, or shoots? Would these survivals live on and grow, till they cracked the modern crust and flourished again?

It did look impossibly hot and gruesome out there, the dust of long-dead forest earth settling in a thin noxious cloud about the city. In here, of course, the air-conditioning cocooned me in cool clear air; a shame it couldn't do as much for my mind. I stood and brooded.

Another fine mess – the local ayatollahs take a hand. Had there been some truth in what they claimed, those fearsome old men? I'd been in Indonesia just once – before the present government came to power. I didn't know much about internal politics, except as they affected trade, but I had heard there were serious strains between local and central government. Bound to be, with one of the world's largest populations, getting larger all the time. Economic factors, religious factors . . . And terrorists, of course. For all my bold words I'd had more than a few dark thoughts about those. Could there be a connection? Maybe not with all the priests, not the old fellow, I'd guess; but with a fearsome old firebrand like Mpu Bharadah, there might well be. But the fact remained –without the new irrigation schemes, Bali would be in for a pretty terrible decade, maybe longer. It might never recover. All the same, I ought to talk it over with the Project rep, when the real one did turn up.

Back at my suite, I shut the door on the outer world with some relief. I was too edgy to sleep, so I raided the mini-bar and searched for something remotely watchable on the satellite channels. After an hour or so of desultory switch-flipping I settled on a superannuated Hollywood blockbuster, circa 1933. The lantern-jawed hero was just stumbling his tongue-tied way through a love scene on the deck of the old freighter when the phone rang. I made a flying dive for it. It wasn't Ape, though. It was the desk clerk again, to tell me that the Project representative was here. I groaned inwardly; but I'd have to see him – and up here, in case the Sunshine Boys were still hanging around downstairs. I told the clerk to send them up, and wondered why he sounded amused this time. Perhaps it was better manners here to go down and fetch them; well, the hell with that. I needed the time to sling my jacket and tie back on, not to mention scurry about collecting abandoned socks and beer bottles and hurl them into the bedroom. I'd barely finished when the knock on the door came, but I was almost my usual self again. Until I opened it.

Another time – almost any other time – I might have been impossibly cool. Insufferably cool, maybe. But tonight I'd had just too many shocks to cope with one more. I don't think I gaped like an idiot; probably I just looked blank. Certainly there was nothing at all reflected on Jacquie's face. The level eyelids which were the only drastically un-European thing about her didn't even flicker.

'Good evening, Stephen,' she said calmly. 'May I come in?'

'Of course,' I said, feeling – what was it? – sixteen years peel away around me, onion-skin layers of accumulated experience, well-constructed lines of defences, barbed-wire uncoiled, minefields laid down and trenches dug by a dozen or more abortive affairs. Not to mention tin tacks scattered by god alone knew how many one-night stands. And when they were gone, what was left at the centre?

Stunned, uttering reflexive politenesses, I watched her as she swept past me, the walk as poised as ever, the figure as slender – no, a little fuller maybe, or fitter. She looked active, brisk, encased in a smart little charcoal suit, Versace maybe or a bootleg copy from the Chatuchak market, with a wide bow at the neck of her cream silk blouse. Nothing at all like the loose flowing things she used to wear. She slid elegantly down into one of the armchairs and sat back, crossing legs encased in some ghostly pattern of gossamer sheen, swishing her bobbed hair about her shoulders, the same ash-blonde mane of old now under severe restraint. She smiled up at me expectantly, and I was already sliding reflexively into the routine of offering her a drink when the strain told, my tongue broke its traces and bolted off out of control.

'Jesus H Christ, girl! This is just too much!'

She raised a polite plucked eyebrow. 'What is?'

'This! You're not asking me to believe . . . I mean, Christ, I refuse, that's all! You turning up like this! It's just too much of a coincidence!'

She frowned. 'Of course it isn't!' she said sharply, sounding suddenly very Chinese. 'I saw your name in the Public Relations documentation, found out it was you, and asked to be your contact. I'd some fundraising contacts to see in Bangkok anyway. That's all.'

That just left me more stunned. 'You asked? Jacquie, frankly . . . ' I couldn't think of a better way to say it. 'Frankly, I'm surprised you'd want to.'

She shrugged, and steepled her long fingers, presenting a long phalanx of delicately peach-shaded nails. 'Why not?' As brusque and businesslike as could be. She might have been dismissing some minor contract concession. Smooth, elegant, every bit as beautiful as she'd been as a student – and turning me right off. 'We broke up like mature adults, didn't we? Agreed to remain friends? Well, then. Aren't you going to offer me a drink? I'd like a vermouth and tonic, long – French, please, if these hotel bars have any.'

Friends? That was how we'd dressed it up, that was the lie we'd told each other. I'd done a pretty good job of believing it, till Mall kicked it out from under me and made me realise that Jacquie wouldn't have been fooled. Yet had she? I forced my battered mind to function, enough to oil the social wheels a bit, anyhow. 'Chambery? They give me that when I come here, they know I prefer it.'

'Marvellous, thank you. Yes, you would.' She smiled coolly. 'Remaining friends, yes. A shame you never did get around to coming out to Singapore, as you promised.'

I poured myself a stiff gin and tonic. 'Yes, isn't it? Just never worked out that way, with the business and all. Shame.'

*I've been to Singapore lots of times, lady; but I ain't telling.*

The shock of meeting her at all was bad enough, after all the others I'd had this evening. But encountering her like this, this glassy impenetrable persona so unlike the bright, bubbly, open girl I'd known – it was horrible. Time brings changes, okay; but what on earth could have changed her so much? Was she always case-hardened like this now? And if she was, what on earth could have done it to her?

Me?

'A shame,' she echoed me. Was there irony in it, or anger aimed at me? Jacquie was a quarter Chinese to three parts Scandinavian, and could be one hundred per cent as inscrutable as either when she chose. 'Still, there's no reason we can't work together now.' She smiled a slow, poised, casual smile, as neat as a painted mask and every bit as meaningless. 'Is there?'

I slumped into my chair, staring at my gin and tonic. Too late, oh lord, too late. 'None,' I said, and even to me I sounded utterly concussed.

Jacquie tilted her head slightly. There might have been a subtle change in her voice. 'Steve – you *are* all right, aren't you?'

I grimaced. 'I haven't been drinking, if that's what you mean – well, only a couple of beers to get over the journey. It was – well, it was just those damned priests . . . ' I mumbled.

She smothered an astonished giggle. '*Priests?*'

99

Awkwardly, gulping at my drink, I spilled out the whole account. 'So you – the Project – ought to know. That gabby character's a fanatic if ever I saw one. I mean, talk about Muslim fundamentalists – he could give an ayatollah a run for his money any day!'

'Mmnnh.' She nodded abstractedly, as if deep in thought; but she was watching me.

'Look!' I bridled, sitting up. 'I didn't make this up, I mean not in some alcoholic stupor or something! So you needn't sit there weighing me up like so much social work, okay?'

She smiled and looked down, a little apologetically. 'I'm sorry. Yes, of course you didn't make it up. I'm on the PR side, I've spoken to them, often – mostly the little old man, Wayan Sadja. He's rather sweet, isn't he? Not this Mpu Bharadah character, though; I may have seen him, I seem to remember the name . . .' She gave a slight shrug, elegantly dismissive. 'No, I suppose I . . . well, I was looking at you. I did think a lot about this before coming along. I'd heard a bit about you from some people who'd met you, in the shipping business. I was curious – naturally! – about how you might have turned out. Whether you'd have changed. How much.' Momentarily her smile was human – dry, guarded, tinged with cynicism and something more – but human. 'Well – go on, admit it! Didn't you feel the same?'

I contemplated her in some wonder. 'I didn't imagine you changing. I couldn't. Now . . . honestly, I'm not sure. I wondered if you'd be just as beautiful. You are. More, if anything.'

The smile glossed over again. 'You always were a salesman. Are you like this with all your clients?'

'I wasn't trying to butter you up,' I said irritably. 'Just saying what I see. That's all. No harm in that.'

She made no comment to that, only leaned her chin on her hand – an old familiar gesture. '*You* have changed,' she said judiciously. 'How, I'm not quite sure. But definitely you have.'

I managed a smile of my own. 'Any particular way?'

'Well, for one thing, when I knew you . . . *I think you'd never have let a bunch of bloody priests get you that het up!*'

My turn to think. She'd deepened her voice, put a sort of impatient, incisive edge on it. Imitating somebody. Guess who? 'Oh . . . Er. Well. Maybe not. And er . . . you? How's your husband?'

Much I really cared, the little creep.

'I don't know,' said Jacquie detachedly, smooth as glass again. 'And I don't much care. You don't know that we're divorced, then? No. Obviously. Two years after we got married. My idea. That's why I came back to the East, to my family. And got involved in this kind of work.' She looked down into her glass, and smiled, faintly. 'Speaking of which . . . '

'Right, right. It's not getting any earlier. Er – shall I freshen that up? As before? Fine, fine.' I scrabbled my thoughts together in a rush of hasty embarrassment. I'd been about to open my great big mouth and let something fall out, something that would have rung mawkish or insincere or just plain empty – how sorry I was, something like that. The Hollow Man strikes again. She'd neatly forestalled me, calling us back to business. Maybe she did it deliberately, maybe she was just sliding off the subject to suit herself. All the same . . .

All the same, I had a more urgent puzzle – how to tell her what the hell we *were* doing. Actually this hairy sorceror I'm working with has booked your consignment in on the *Marie Celeste*, but don't worry, we got a *great* late-delivery clause . . .

The truth could hardly sound any dafter. Or did it depend just how you told it?

'Well, here's the situation,' I said. 'Don't mind telling you, we've had the same difficulties as the other agencies with this first load, and then some. But I, er, more or less stood over the thing, beat off all comers, and we got it through. It's here now, safely in store in the warehouses out at Don Muang.'

'Ah,' she nodded. 'The new complex? Supposed to be all very high-security, aren't they? Everything electronic. And from there? Are you flying it out?'

'Er . . . it doesn't really look like it. We'll be taking it by sea, by a roundabout route; should cut out the problems the others had. One of our local experts is setting that up right now, I'm just waiting to hear from him.'

'That's fine. You'll let us know who to contact?'

'Won't need to. I'll be going with it, all the way there.'

Her eyes went wide. 'You? The Big Boss in person? Well, you're certainly giving us our money's worth, aren't you? I was surprised you'd trailed all the way out here. You must have responsibilities.'

I shrugged. 'Not so many. The office will run itself for a week or two right now. And if it doesn't, there's the Even Bigger Boss

Barry to take care of things; he likes it. Just the same way I like getting back out into the field. Nothing like a nice little sea jaunt.'

She sighed ecstatically. 'Oh yes. When you've been stuck here in Bangkok for absolute bloody weeks . . . mmmh.' She stretched, closed her eyes, then blinked and sat up sharply, as if an idea had struck her. 'Steve! I suppose it would be possible to book another berth on this ship? With this first container, I mean. I'd like to come along. Keep an eye on things.' She must have read the look on my face, because she rattled on smoothly. 'You see, I've got to get back to Bali anyway, soon. I could pay my way and everything, obviously.'

I massaged the back of my neck, where one nice headache was taking root. Keep an eye on things? I didn't like the sound of that. 'Look, I mean, it's nothing against . . . *I'd* like you to come along, old friend and all that, but . . . well, we could be taking this some hard ways. Tramp steamer, crew of roughnecks, that kind of thing. No nice cabins and sundeck and so on.'

Her glare was instant and glacial. 'You haven't changed that much! You think I haven't messed around in some rough enough places? One project, they sent me out on a three-day trip in a godawful old scow with a crew of Trobrianders! Nice boys, those Trobrianders. Never took me for granted. I even fixed the engine when the oil feed went; I'm good with engines.'

How'd she be with sharp-toothed homunculi and stone-tipped arrows? 'Look, sorry, that just came out patronising – really. I've known women who could rough it ten times better than I ever could!' And nearly cut my throat when I kissed them. One, anyway. 'But . . . well, a lot depends on the people Ape, er, my agent, is dealing with. What they think. You know we've not had any chance with the ordinary carriers, big or little. So we might be using some pretty, er, unorthodox types.'

'Oh.' Her expression darkened again, mistrustfully. 'You mean . . . like smugglers . . . gun-runners?'

'I didn't say a word. I don't know anything. My agent . . . '

She radiated cool disapproval. 'Make sure you can trust him. Drugs – you know they hang you for that, here!'

I spread my hands. 'Do me a favour! Look, it'll be clean, don't worry. Just . . . well, backdoor.'

She shook her head with detached, kindly concern. 'Be careful, Stephen. There're some really horrible types around. It wouldn't do the Project any good to be mixed up with them – or your firm,

I'm sure. Still, it's your business, you know best. You will let us have the ETA, though? We have to know because, well, there have been some . . . threats.'

'The terrorists?'

She sighed, and looked up at the ceiling. 'You've heard.'

'Just rumours. But the way you were reacting there, it wasn't hard to guess.'

'Well, at least you know about them. Yes. Oh, it's nothing much.' She rubbed a hand along her thigh, another gesture that sent the years tumbling away. But she didn't seem to notice anything like that about me. 'Just a few Jawanese extremists, trying to curry favour with the islanders – the Robin Hood bit, defenders of the oppressed – *you* know.'

'Defenders of the—' I sprang up. 'Look, what is it with this bloody Project? I spent ages looking into it, I couldn't find one good reason anyone could object to it! Then these holy rollers – now you're telling me there is one?'

'*No!*' Her tone was suddenly urgent, upset; the mask slipping a little, maybe. 'None! At least – not a *good* reason. I don't think it's one you'd recognise, anyhow.'

'Ahhh. But one you would?'

She shrugged. It was still a studied, guarded gesture; but I thought I detected real disquiet there behind the mask. 'I don't know. When I got into it, it seemed so marvellous, so necessary – oh, it still does, or I wouldn't be here! But they say there's always a price for progress, don't they? Those priests – I don't agree with them, but still I wonder . . . The terrorists say the Project's just an imperialist front to extend central power over Bali. Well, that's just balls, of course it isn't *meant* to. But in the end – I don't know. I've got some doubts. It might open opportunities; not so much for the politicians, even, it's the administrators, the bureaucrats, the little men. They're almost all Jawanese.' She let out a soft whistle of impatience between her teeth. 'But then there's no way around it, you see! Drought, overfarming, famine – they'd be worse, with more suffering, children dying . . . ' She shook her head, as if to scatter a vision taking shape.

'But that's not something the islanders can appreciate?'

Jacquie blinked. 'I didn't expect you to understand that . . . yes.'

I shrugged. 'I've seen things like it before. Something's got to give, somewhere. Give it time.' I stretched, sighed. I'd hoped I was lifting a burden; now I seemed to be squashed under an even bigger one, getting heavier all the time. I'd had enough of it. '*Anyhow,*' I said decisively. 'It's not my problem. We just do what the contract says, don't we? I'll get our ETA to you as soon as I know it – and yes, I'll be extra careful.'

Jacquie nodded, looked at her watch. 'Oh yipe! It's that time. Steve, I've got to hit the road.' Peach claws sent a card spinning across the coffee table. 'You can get in touch with me at my hotel, when you've some news.'

'Okay, but listen, it'll be dinnertime before you know it, and I'm starving all over again – jetlag, probably. There're some great places further down Sukhumvit, or on Silom Road.' I saw her hesitate. 'Or I could have some sent up here . . . '

She smiled – the impenetrable smile again – and shook her head. 'I've really got to be going.'

'And leave an old friend to eat alone?'

'Poor Stephen!' She gave a delicate chuckle, and added pleasantly 'But this is Bangkok, after all. I'm sure you won't stay lonely for long.'

She reached up and patted me on the cheek. Amiably. Warmly? Not especially. 'Must run. *Sawaddee kha*!'

She seemed to glide past me, as if borne away on some invisible current. The heavy outer door clicked shut behind her. I put my palms flat on its cool wood and rested my forehead between them. I'd desperately wanted to say something – but what? I hadn't a clue. Maybe the time for saying anything at all had been sixteen years ago; and what kind of idiot was inhabiting my body then? If anything – if possible – she was more beautiful now, with that ageless oriental touch in her features, and the uncertainties of youth ironed out. Too much iron, maybe; that horrendous gloss . . . And yet it wasn't constant, it dropped like a mask at times. She must cultivate it; why? To fend off men?

That set off a sudden sinking feeling. She'd heard about me from some of my business comperes, she said. Right, I could guess what *they'd* say; good friends and sore losers, every one. Maybe they wouldn't be too far wrong, either. Maybe their identikit image might match up just a bit too closely with the Steve Fisher she remembered. She'd been curious about me, nervous, uncertain. So she'd put on all that protective coloration, the image, the manner – all for *my* benefit, so to speak. A front to impress me, to keep me at bay, maybe. So everything I'd found so repellent about her was *me*.

And what made me even sicker was that if I hadn't known her already, if I hadn't been expecting somebody different – I might even have gone for that cut-glass exterior. And never once guessed the reflection in every facet was mine.

I needed a drink. But I also needed food. And my first rendezvous with Ape was between ten and eleven this evening. I scowled at my watch, then went and threw on my jacket. I could pick up something in the hotel's snackbar grill; it wouldn't be great, but neither would the company. I'd be eating with the person I least wanted to be alone with right now, and that was my own sweet self.

Over the meal I re-read Ape's directions, and the more I studied them the more it seemed that directions were the one thing they weren't. There were no street names, only turnings and buildings, and the turnings didn't make any kind of logical sense that I could see. Still, what could I do but follow? I scribbled my suite number on the bill, tossed down a few extra *baht* on top of the service charge, and the glass doors sighed their synthetic regret as I stepped out into the hot breath of the night.

It didn't seem long before my misgivings began to look justified. Ape's route took me smack dab into a crowded late-night street market; then, just as I groaned with relief at getting through the sweaty sweltering crush, that damned piece of paper directed me right back down through it again, jostlers, pick-pockets, pimps and all. It wasn't written on a sardine-can label for nothing, I thought. But this time the turn-off was different, a little alley I hadn't noticed behind an exceptionally smelly dried-fish stall. Just the place for a really fine mugging, or worse; I wished I'd brought the sword along, though I was wary of carrying it too openly. Maybe I'd be able to call it again, and maybe I wouldn't. I heard the chatter of the market die away behind me; this was a pretty long alley, with lots of handy twists and turns. I had things like clouds of mist on my mind when suddenly I saw, on the wall ahead, a flicker of pink light. And I remembered, suddenly, the red-eyed mask, and the heavy lids that opened and blinked . . .

I went on. I was walking Ape's road, and I hadn't any other. But I flattened myself to the wall – or as near as I dared, given the filth of it – and peered carefully around. But when I saw what it was, that light, I laughed aloud. And then, looking again at Ape's instructions, I stopped laughing altogether. *Here?*

But it was natural enough that there should be more than one kind of place along the borders of the Spiral, as there were all kinds of people. And okay, the Tavern had its louche side – some of which was Katjka. But this one . . .

Even for Bangkok it was sleazy, sleazy as hell. There was nothing timeless about it that I could detect, nothing but the ageless stink of vice. I propped up the bar, because it was cleaner than the barstools, and drank the beer – not because it was much cheaper than the liquor, but because it came out of sealed bottles, and I opened them myself. In between times I fended off the desultory attentions of under-aged bar girls, ignored their jibes, and did my damnedest not to think about Jacquie. What was laughingly billed as a cabaret didn't help – though calling it a sex show wouldn't have been that much more accurate. Even the fat-bellied Germans in their cut-off jeans, waggling the little hostesses into their laps, were watching only in the jaded quest for novelty, a new angle, a new cigarette or banana trick. At the moment it was razor blades, no less. An ancient blaster squealed out cheap rock from worn, wow-ridden tapes, the sweaty crush around me swayed with gloating sadistic brinkmanship, and I felt a million miles removed from the human race. Not the healthiest thing to be contemplating, not with Jacquie on my mind.

And that was pretty crazy in itself. Not as if she was somebody I'd just met. She was my past, a closed chapter – one I'd closed myself, and pretty harshly at that. So what could she mean to me now? Why was I mooning after her like this?

Could it be that after her nothing seemed to go right, every relationship somehow managed to misfire? As if I'd skipped a vital page, missed a clue as to how things should go, how feelings should work. The freeze had set in around me. The less involved, the emptier an attraction was, the better it suited me, till over two years, perhaps, there'd been nothing but one-night stands, practically anonymous. And the logical end of that process? Maybe it was here.

I contemplated the cabaret. Topless dancers were padding out between acts, wiggling around plastic pillars in an awkward parody of excitement. Emptier than this you didn't get; I ought to like it. And I might have ended up that way; except that, somehow, Mall and Clare between them struck a sudden spark of warmth back into my life. But right from the beginning Clare and

I had known it wouldn't last. We liked each other, we worked well together, we were too much friends to be lasting lovers; and she wasn't a deep person. In some ways she could be as empty and career-centred as me. However close we came, we were parallel lines; we never collided. With Jacquie, somehow, it was different. Only it was also too late.

And I kept seeing her – and behind her, like a shadow, teasing, available, the girl called Rangda. Because it was here, in this place that Ape had chosen, that I had first met her; and it was to its back door that I'd been hunted, all those weeks ago.

I drained my beer, and got another. Maybe it would quell the headache, stop my psyche tying itself in knots. If Ape didn't show tonight I'd have to come back, tomorrow, the day after. I didn't know if I could stand it. Another act started. I closed my smarting eyes . . . And opened them again, at a sudden outburst of noise, an almost wordless animal snarling. A pack of men were lurching through the door, up to the bar, baying at the cabaret, knocking over tables and barging other drinkers aside, grabbing at hostesses already with clients. Six or seven of them, big men mostly, Aussies by their accents. They towered over the little waiter who rushed up to remonstrate with them, and when he kept on shouting one smacked out a ham fist and sent him flying. Drinks scattered, dancers and hostesses screamed, the crowd around me seemed to surge back like a living animal gathering itself to spring—

I ducked back, right to the wall, and stayed there. It wasn't the first bar brawl I'd run into. They make people laugh on TV, but they're not at all funny to get caught in, especially in a confined space. Fists were flying, aimless whirling punches that did little damage at first, but spread the fight further. Tables toppled, glasses and beer bottles sailed through the air on trails of sticky drinks and exploded like meteors against the wall, or burst the strobe lights with a deafening pop, spraying smoke and hot splinters. Other bottles were being smashed against the counter to make daggers of jagged glass. A bit too direct and lethal for me – I like to have a choice about killing, when I can. I tried one of the tables – too flimsy, too cumbersome; I snatched up a barstool. Built to take the weight of bloated European backsides, so it should suit their skulls nicely. A shouting shape reeled towards me, and I swung the stool; a crack, he staggered back and was sucked back into the brawl. But then the whole crowd reeled my way, cutting me off from the door. The fighting animal spread its shapeless tentacles and trawled me into its chaotic belly.

I fetched up against one of the Aussies, and got a shock; he was hugely bearded, wearing frock coat and neckerchief and battered high-crowned bowler, straight out of the old photos from the Yukon or Kalgoorlie. His punch nearly felled me, but clanged off the chromium stalk of the stool; I swung it around, clipped his ear and socked him in the stomach. The bowler stayed where it was, but he howled and fell over. I lunged past him, looking for the door; but it was out of reach. A row of small shadowy figures blocked my way. I whirled around, swinging the stool, but they were beside me, behind me, a circle closing fast. A knife gleamed; others leaped out in answer, dark jagged blades covered in strange circular facets. No metal, but obsidian, razor-edged volcanic glass. As quickly as that, the *kuro-i* had me surrounded.

Panic, faster than thought, lashed out with the barstool – connected – felled one. I sprang for the gap, a slash whistled past my stomach, the stool slammed down into a wrinkled grinning face – and they were on me, kicking, twisting the legs from under me, knives forgotten, slashing with hands, teeth, anything that might bring me down. I staggered, tilted, crashed down on to the greasy lino of the bar with a dozen dead weights on me, landed hard, winded. Cold bony hands clamped on my struggling limbs. Wide bloodshot eyes gazed down at me with gleeful malevolence from behind strands of lank black hair. Strands of saliva escaped the thin dark lips and drooled down among the sparse brown bristles which covered the dirty pockmarked faces to the cheekbones. One, perched on my chest, reached down, and a sharp cold flake of glass traced a delicate line across my Adam's apple. I've known longer instants, but not many.

And then something whistled in the air, a sharp singing whistle, and the evil little creature gloating over me vanished as if a hurricane had whisked him away. There was a noise like an overripe melon splitting. A white shape swept over me like a rushing cloud, swirling this way and that. The other *kuro-i* scattered back, chattering, before the awesome shape, and the leering, terrifying painted mask above it. It looked like polished mahogany, streaked with lines. It rolled its eyes, it lolled and waggled a painted tongue – then the rush of air sang by again, ending in solid sickening thuds. Something glinted, like a dark blade gleaming, full of fantastic vents and curlicues. It hovered over me, not menacingly but defensively; and I saw, in the dim light as the brawl died down, that it wasn't a blade exactly – a kind of edged club of some dark wood, carved and polished into what was practically sculpture. But along those edges still darker stains suggested plenty of use – and not just decorative. The *kuro-i* gave back, staring, snarling incomprehensibly. The sword-club whistled a vicious little note, back and forth, and they bolted, screaming.

A hand reached down to me. An immense paw, that could have been mahogany too, enmeshed with the same snaky interlace of tattooes that gave the face its masklike look. My hands aren't small, but that enormous grip swallowed them up like an old-fashioned boxing glove, and hauled me effortlessly to my feet. The white shape rustled. A vast stiff cloak, spread wide over what looked like T-shirt and jeans, heavy seaman's gear; just an ordinary man, if being that size is ordinary. A pair of huge liquid eyes, gentle as a cow's, looked me over.

'Strewth! That was a hot 'un, no mistake! You okay, sport? No bones broke?' The voice resounded like something in a hollow mountain, but the actual words were strangely high and nasal.

'I'm okay, thanks. Bit bruised . . . Okay, thanks to you! They really had me there!'

'Ah, don't mention it, sport! Hate t' see a fella down that way. Anyway, 's kinda my fault.'

I stiffened. '*Your* fault?'

He shrugged. 'Well, yeah, sort of. You're Steve Fisher, aintcha?'

'Never heard of him. Who're you? Bit far from home for a Maori, aren't you? Even one with a Queensland accent?'

Imagine a frog in a rain-barrel and you have his chuckle. 'You gotta good ear, sport. My monicker's *Toa te Kiore*. Call me Ted if you'd rather,' he added unenthusiastically.

'I'll stick to – *te Kiore*?'

'Toa te Kiore. Means Champion Bush Rat – and before we have any wisecracks, that's a very honourable title, that is. Means the advance-guard of a war party, see? The ones who can fight like hell *and* keep their eyes open, scout around. And that's what I was supposed to be doin' – keeping an eye peeled for you, I mean. Only I got a bit distracted – the show, see? And then the bluey.

You gotta be careful in this joint – not that these little gumsuckers were much of a bother. One whack – *pow*! – and the rest, they run like buns. *He kai na te ahi*!' The frog again. 'Know what that means? *In the old days they'd've got et*!'

'They might be a bit ripe for that,' I said, contemplating the little heap of extremely late goblins at my feet. The Maori sword-club had made a horrible mess of their heads, and I wasn't a bit sorry about that. But it couldn't account for the way their whole bodies were changing, swelling and bloating and turning a horrible shade of yellowish grey, rapidly and nastily decomposing.

'Do look a bit past their sell-by date,' admitted te Kiore. Even as he spoke the skin on one arm split with a puff of gas, and we both jumped back, gagging. 'Aw jeez!' He clapped his hands with earthquake effect. '*Hey! Boys*!' The small wiry bouncers who'd just finished casting the Australians into outer darkness came trotting up, to stop short with yelps of revulsion. 'Shift these, will yer – out the back door, eh?' They dragged the bodies off in an ancient plastic tablecloth I suspected was kept for the purpose. 'That's done! Better be coming along then, eh?'

A giant arm settled around my shoulders, but I stayed where I was. 'Along where? And who sent you out to look for m— for whoever this Fisher guy is?'

He whacked himself on the forehead with a force that would have put me in hospital. 'Aw shit! I mean, strewth, should'a told yer, shouldn' I? The skipper, that's who; and your mate Ape. Sitting back there getting smashed on arrack.'

'The skipper? You're a sailor?'

'Yeah! You want a ship, don't you? Well, we're it. C'mon, let's go see 'em!'

I looked at him. He gave what was evidently meant to be an encouraging grin. It looked like the 'In' door of a carnival Ghost Train, quite capable of eating me or anyone else; but that was mostly the tattooes. He'd probably saved my life. And if it came to the crunch he wouldn't need to decoy me; he could probably just tuck me under his arm and run.

'Lead on, te Kiore,' I said.

'That's my job,' he grinned, ushering me towards the shadowy rear of the bar. 'First mate, quartermaster and sailing master, all three. Also ship's Peacemaker-in-Chief.'

'Long as you're not the cook,' I said, and he gave a great explosion of a laugh.

'Only when the stores get low – and you'll be paying for those! So better not get too stingy, see?'

'Or someone I disagree with might eat me? Okay, I'll bear that in mind.' We walked out into a shadowy corridor I remembered, but past the stairs she'd led me down, and along an even darker corridor that seemed to have innumerable shadowy side-branches. 'This is some warren,' I commented.

'Too right,' grunted the Maori, his stiff cloak brushing the walls on either side with every stride. 'Used to think I'd meet myself coming back, one of these days. But you're okay with me; never gone too far astray yet, here or anywhere.'

'That so? Isn't a Maori in darkest Thailand a bit out of his way?'

'That's all you know,' he said scornfully. 'Used to get around a bit, we did, even with your old outrigger canoes. Just we never found anywhere better'n good ol' Newzee, that's all.'

'Then why'd you leave?'

'Too full of bleedin' *pakahes*, that's why – nothing personal, you understand. Spent two miserable years herding sheep round the rainy Raukumaras, see, then when I was sixteen said the hell with it, ran off to Tauranga and away to sea.'

'That where you picked up the accent?'

He coughed slightly. 'Well, no. Got stranded. Lost my ship, see?'

'On a reef?'

'Me? No! On a bender. On account of forgettin' where I'd left her, or what her name was, even. By the time I came to in a Brisbane nick she'd probably sailed, anyhow. Couldn't get another, so I carried my swag upcountry and did a two years' spell back staring at bleeding sheep's arses in the Darling country, another five along the Diamantina. Then a couple as a lifeguard on Bondi. After that the accent kind of stuck. Can't stand prawns, though – well, here he is, boss!'

Without breaking stride the huge man flung open a door and swept me through. The air took me by the throat and set my eyes streaming, but I managed to make out a sort of snug or parlour furnished much like Rangda's room, with cheap rattan furniture and the oriental equivalent of saloon art. In the red glare of a plastic Chinese lantern a group of figures was gathered round a table littered with empty bottles and tin ashtrays filled with cigar stubs. One of them had his boots up on it, enormous boots. He swung back in his chair and waved a glowing stogey at me.

'*Dag, jongetje*! You see, we meet again with no trouble, *nee*?'

'Like hell!' I said. 'I've just been jumped by a pack of those *kuro-i* things – right here in this godawful dive! I thought you said they wouldn't try to kill me, if they didn't know where the container was! If te Kiore here hadn't been there to get me out . . .'

Ape looked surprised, but he nodded his shaggy head grimly. 'Here you stray out of Core and into their domain. Is easier for them to strike. I did not think they would; but nothing is certain. Which is why I send te Kiore out to look out for you. Is always some risks, hah? I say that, don't I? So. They try to kidnap you, is all; not kill you. They have nothing to gain—'

'Like hell! They damn near cut my throat!'

Ape's eyebrows twitched, and he looked sharply at the Maori, who nodded. 'They weren't playing around, boss. Their lead stinker was just linin' a *kris* up on his joogooler. Lucky he stopped to make a neat job of it, or I mightn't have reached him in time. It was a slick trick.'

Ape blew out a stream of obnoxious yellow smoke. 'Does not make sense! Unless . . .' He frowned. 'If they killed you here, very careful, maybe they make some use of your death. You might still be made to go find the container for them – uncertain, but it might be done.'

'You mean like a zombie . . . Christ!' I'd met zombies, too close for comfort, husks of living men and women, some I'd known even. Even the bare thought of going that way myself brought me out in a sweat of sheer terror.

'Not good,' agreed Ape. 'But also not for them. Too risky, too uncertain; too much to lose. As if . . . almost as if you have done something to offend them, to make them less cool, less certain. To make them so mad, they sooner take the gamble of killing you. Otherwise makes no sense,' he repeated, rasping a gnarled thumb through his beard with a sound like crackling brushwood. Then he sat up straight.

'Anyhows!' he barked. 'He does get you out, and I got us our ship like I promise.' He kicked a chair towards me. 'Sit down, have some *arak* on the strength of it. *Tuan Kiap* Batang Sen, I have the pleasure of introducing *Mynheer* Stephen Fisher, who is maybe not quite so wet behind the ears as he looks and is very bad news for Wolves, among others.'

Behind the table a little old man with a face like a pickled walnut stood up and eyed me suspiciously. '*Selamat datang!*' he piped.

When I replied '*Selamat malam!*' and gave the deep Indonesian bow, he flashed me a tremendous grin full of betel-stained teeth, seized my outstretched hand in Western fashion and gave it a whipcracking shake. Not so old, I reflected, unobtrusively massaging my joints back into place. I was even more startled when he added, 'Absolutely delight to meet you, old chap!' in a pretty good go at an old-fashioned Oxford accent. 'If you are a fighter of Wolves, always welcome in these parts. You like *arak*?' He poured out a huge glass and pushed it forward. Actually I hated the stuff, a hellishly fiery rice mash fermented with toddy-palm sap, but I guessed it was better not to refuse. This was important, bread-and-salt time.

'*Tuan* Batang, he is well known,' rumbled Ape, sipping his own glass. 'It was him I was hoping to find. He sails all over these waters in the local schooners, the *prahu*—'

'Hold on a moment,' I objected, coughing as the *arak* got me by the windpipe. 'This is a full-size container we're talking about here, remember? No *prahu* I've ever seen would have the capacity, hold or even deck.'

'True,' grinned Ape. 'But he since comes into possession of a bigger vessel.' He leaned over and delivered a deafening stage whisper that must have been audible right across the room, 'Best you do not inquire how, exact. The captain, he is a bogeyman.'

'Beg pardon?'

Te Kiore roared. 'Don't mean he lurks under beds! Bogeyman – Boegie man, see? Ever hear of the Boegies?'

I snapped my fingers. 'Yes, begod! Islanders, great sailors, sea traders all round the Malay Archipelago. Traders and—' I broke off. I'd been about to add *pirates*.

'And pirate, yes!' added Batang Sen, and tittered. 'English sailors fear us, they threaten their children with us. Say Boegie man get you if you are not good!' He tittered again, and topped up my glass. He seemed to like the role. 'But no Boegie man has ship as good as mine, old fruit. The *Ikan Yu*—Massachusetts-built, schooner rig, steam auxiliary. Plus four cannon. Strong hold, steel derrick, take one, maybe two container. Top-hole, my word yes!'

It sounded like some kind of Grand Banks schooner, though no doubt much messed around with. I raised an eyebrow at Ape, who nodded vigorously. 'Sounds promising. And the rates?'

Ape tossed a greasy piece of paper at me. 'Nothing to worry you. You post a bond against loss, though.'

Quite a hefty one, too; but even allowing for the gold

standard that seemed to apply out there the whole thing, shipping and all, only came to a few thousand, well within our budget. 'Great. Where do I sign?'

Batang Sen rose and made a courtly bow, European rather than Indonesian. 'Sir, that is not necessary. You are gentleman, you leave bond with stakeholder here, for the rest we have gentleman's agreement, yes?'

I was so surprised I could only rise and bow back, though it made my bruises protest. 'That's pretty kind of you, *Tuan Kiap*. And flattering. You're a gentleman yourself.'

Another bow, and he topped up my *arak* again. 'I was once in service of great *Ingeriss* gentleman, Rajah of Sarawak. I learn my ripping good English from him.'

'Rajah of— Right, of course!' That made me blink a little. 'That must have been, what was it, Augustus Brookes?' Even if he'd served there as a child, that made this old fellow well into his eighties. The last of the Brookes family, the 'white Rajahs' of Sarawak, must have been about the time of World War II.

He shook his head, eyes twinkling. 'Not Augustus. *Tuan* Harry. First, not last.'

I swallowed my *arak* in one gulp. Harry Brookes had founded the dynasty, some time in the mid-19th century; so . . . So it explained something of Batang Sen's Victorian idioms, anyhow. But you got used to this kind of thing on the Spiral. At least, everyone kept telling me I'd get used to it. I wasn't so sure.

'*Goed dan*,' rumbled Ape. 'You fix to get container delivered to the river wharves, this address, tomorrow evening, round sunset. I meet you there again. Till then, you stay away from it yourself, you hear?'

'As before,' I said. 'What will you be doing?'

'I go to shield the ship, as much as I can. There may be unfriendly eyes about.'

'Great. What about me?'

'Back within the Core again, quick as flasher! Once you're out of here they will have less power to harm you, and nothing to gain. Go to your hotel by the path I gave you, stay there till night is past, and you should not be assailed in any other way. Te Kiore, you go with him to the door, eh? Call if there's trouble. And take a good look around outside before you let him go!'

'No sweat!' The huge man rose to his feet, and the stiff cloak folded around him. 'Finished your *arak*, mate?'

Some blind demon of machismo made me gulp down the last glassful. On top of all those beers it didn't settle too well, and I had to fight not to let my legs go rubbery as I stood up.

"'S fine,' I said, feeling as if my guts were on fire. At least my bruises were suitably anaesthetised. I managed another shaky bow to the skipper. 'See you all tomorrow, then. *Sh – Selamat tidur!*'

Te Kiore peered into the corridor before ushering me out, lifting his cloak over one arm to clear the sword-club that hung at his belt. 'Not a cheep!' he said cheerfully. 'C'mon, let's scram!'

We traipsed back through the dark corridors of the ancient brothel. Te Kiore never hesitated, however tangled they became; he seemed to know exactly where he was going. Maybe he was a natural navigator, like my old friend Jyp the Pilot, my first guide and guardian on the perilous paths beyond the Core. In fact, he reminded me of Jyp, though he was as lumbering as Jyp was mercurial; he had the same easy warmth of manner. Now and again his massive arm halted me as voices sounded ahead, but there was never anyone around the next corner. Once, though, he yanked me urgently back into the shadow of the stair and stood rigid there, motioning me to curt silence, almost holding his breath, even. There was a moment of tingling silence. Footsteps approached, the light swift step of a girl, and behind it a slower, heavier tread, almost soggy-sounding. A light brittle laugh, as they passed; a low flatulent rumble. Then it was quiet, and he motioned me on. But across our path, moving from one dark sideway to another, ran a long trail of dampness, a faint smell of stale seawater, like a polluted beach. The girl's bare footprints were clear in it; but alongside them, spaced at almost double hers, were broad, vaguely triangular shapes, and dotted ahead of them the clear points of claws. I caught at te Kiore's arm and pointed; but he only shook his head sharply, shuddered, and pulled me on. When we were round the next corner I changed the subject.

'Nice cloak,' I remarked quietly. 'Thought it was fleece of some kind, till I touched it . . . Are those really feathers? All of them? The whole thing?'

'Too right,' he said, cheerfully again. 'Had to go a long way to get this cloak. A real Tanaraki, that's where the best ones're made.'

'What is it, then? Kiwi feathers or something?'

'Not far off. Moa feathers, albino, on a backing of flax *taniko*. Bonzer, 'solute.'

'*Moa*? But they've been extinct for . . .'

'Too right! Can't get them any *moa*.' I groaned, and he grinned. 'Told you I had to go a long way. Guess you didn't realise just how far.'

We were at the front door now. He opened it carefully and glanced around for a few minutes before he let me go, peering into the smallest shadows. 'Not a flamin' sausage,' he said cheerfully. 'But listen, shipmate, if I were you I'd skedaddle real fast, once you're out. This mate of yours, Ape, I reckon he's a bit too sure of himself. Could be whoever's after you is playing a deeper game than maybe he realises.'

I looked at him. I'm not usually quick to like people, but I found myself inclined to trust this great hulk of a creature. He really did remind me of Jyp, as if that kind of character was natural to people who had an unusually good instinct for where they were going. And when Jyp was uneasy about something, it was as well to listen to him; he had a lot more brains than you'd ever have expected to look at him. Maybe this one did, too. 'What makes you say that?'

'Well, deciding to bump you like that – doesn't make sense, like he said, unless they'd something to gain by it. Or unless . . . unless they wanted to stop someone else gaining. He's one smart fella, this Ape, but he didn't think of that.'

'What the hell are you getting at?'

'Well, he didn't tell us much – but he did say there was more than one enemy yappin' at yer shirt-tails.' He glanced around again, quickly. 'Ones that mightn't be too fond of one another, either. So, suppose there's one lot think they've got the drop on you somehow – found a way to get the container for themselves, through you – then mightn't the others be desperate enough to kill you? To stop 'em, y'see! Playin' dog in the manger!'

Suddenly my mouth was very dry, my bruises stiffening. I saw the sinister shadows cast by Ape's strange fire, longer now, reaching halfway round the Earth. That mysterious third power – what hand was it playing? Who were its agents in this dark game? 'Nice thought,' I said. 'You've got a mind for this sort of thing.'

He winked. 'It's in the genes, see? In old Maori times the absolutely dinkumest thing a warrior could do was to invite his enemies in for a peace feast – weapons at the gate, all that kind of thing – then smash in their heads during starters. Al Capone could've taken lessons, no kidding. So some little gene deep inside knows how this sort of thing can go.'

'Well, thanks,' I said. 'Skedaddle I will – for the moment. But I'm still coming with you, you know – come hell, high water, dacoits or demi-humans!'

Te Kiore wagged his head. 'Okay, shipmate! Till tomorrow evening, then – I hope!' The frog croaked in the rain-barrel again, and the door closed behind him.

I stood looking for a moment, ready to bolt back for the security of that door. There wasn't anybody actually on the doorstep, nothing but greasy hamburger wrappers and other trash stirring in the warm wind. Te Kiore hadn't thought anything of the three or four girls down by the kerb, a few more over by a rickshaw coke stall, or patrolling back and forth under the lights. That was all right; I knew *that* kind of danger. I fumbled woozily in my pockets for Ape's directions, but just as I was pulling them out and unfolding them a sudden hot gust plucked them from my hand, sent them skittering away across the unclean pavements. I ducked unsteadily after them, knowing I must be attracting attention. Inevitably a pair of heels came clicking over towards me. I seized the paper and straightened up – to find myself looking into Jacquie's face.

Only it wasn't.

'*Sawaddee!*' The voice was softer, more rasping. And yes, the face was browner, more oriental, the features smaller – though less so, perhaps than I'd remembered them; but it wasn't only the face, the heavy blonde hair that framed it. The slender shoulders, the full breasts and sleek hips, the slightly haughty tilt of the head – I hadn't realised just how startling the resemblance was.

'Good evening, Stephen!' said the girl called Rangda. 'I am very glad to see you back in town. You were coming to keep your promise to me?'

She took my hands in hers, clad in sheer sleeves of black lace. I couldn't say anything. This was Jacquie. Even the fragrance around her was so much alike – or was that simply a conventional perfume, plus her? She wore a Chinese *cheongsam* of black silk, everything to her that Jacquie's sharp little suit was not; it shimmered and sparkled like harbour waters under the garish signs, but it only highlighted the likeness. This was Jacquie, but Jacquie available; Jacquie eager; Jacquie as much a toy of my will as any little creature in that bloody cabaret. As far as my money would stretch, maybe -- but so what? Where was the difference, now the original Jacquie was lost to me? Was this Jacquie of my world, my values?

I wavered drunkenly. It was the original I wanted, the original whose image had tormented me all evening, all through that bestial little travesty of a sex show. But what chance did I ever have? What chance to undo a mistake of sixteen years ago? I thought I'd dumped Jacquie, then, dropped her flat, for reasons that had seemed so important then. Not unkindly, not harshly, so I'd told myself; deftly, maturely, as adult to adult, no fuss, no tears. A neat and gradual cooling-off, a slow severance, an easy distancing. Not without a few regrets, maybe; but for the best, all for the best. And then, years on, a woman, a terrible, wonderful woman had woken me up, the way a shaft of sudden moonlight in your eyes can wake you, and shown me in that awful clarity what I really was, what I'd really done.

But one thing she'd left for me to discover, the worst, the funniest thing; that I hadn't really wanted to do it at all. That however much I'd hurt her, I'd hurt myself ten times over; and all the success and all the pride and all the machismo in the world couldn't cover that up, all the drink couldn't blot it out. And the reasons? Adolescent, puffed-up, self-important bullshit – meaningless, irrelevant to the way my life had worked out, just as I should have realised they'd be. That was the funny bit, utterly bloody hysterical.

Bruised, half-drunk, wrenched this way and that by regret and shame and sheer stupid lust, I toppled a mass of inhibitions and restraints like loose bricks, felt them go tumbling down in confusion. I had no defences, no hopes; only the web of bitter alienation that cabaret had thrown around me. If I'd cheated myself, if I'd left myself only the meanest dregs of what might have been, if I couldn't even shake off this emotional maelstrom she'd thrown me into just by showing her bloody face – if I couldn't have Jacquie, then maybe somehow I could still exorcise it all.

'*Sawaddee Krup*, Rangda,' I said, and grinned. 'You were right, that was a lousy show. Much better to see you.'

She smiled back, languorously. 'We should have a drink on this, perhaps. To celebrate.' And still smiling, she clasped my hand in hers and drew it over her shoulder, taking my weight, moving with me towards the door of the bar. I wasn't that drunk.

'Rangda . . . not back in there!'

She smiled again, a little sadly, and looked up at me, eyes wide and wise, pools a troubled man could sink into. She drew my hand down between her breasts, and leaned softly against me. 'Rangda, no!' I protested hoarsely, 'I have to get back to my hotel . . . ' That scent coiled up around me in a dizzying cloud. 'But . . . we could have a drink there. If you'd like to come along . . . '

She pressed herself against me, and ran a delicate finger along my lips, as if tracing out the path for a kiss. No delicate peach-tint on these nails, but a brilliant fresh blood-red.

She conjured a taxi out of nowhere, a proper closed-in car, not a *samlor*, and we sped back to the hotel, necking and huddling in the back like a pair of teenagers, unable to keep our hands off each other. She was instantly aroused, less inhibited than any girl I'd ever met, animalistic and snaking under my devouring hands, sending her own ranging, one minute subtle and tickling, the next fiercely direct. I slid my fingers round behind her knee, ran my hands back and forth, each time a little further, climbing the greasy pole, till—

*Smoke. Heat. Pressed bodies, waving limbs. Razorblades—*

I scoured the vision out of my mind, closed my fingers over the moist lacy cotton, massaged it as her thighs butted hard against my hand, then slid it out of the way and wormed beneath. Her fingers, busy against my own thigh, clamped tight, rippled suddenly like a fluteplayer's, clamped again. I buried my face in her neck, saw her nipples peak against the black silk. We hardly knew it when we reached the hotel, staggered through the empty lobby before the elaborately unseeing desk clerk, and ground against each other to the point of bruising agony in the soaring lift. My hands trembled so much I could hardly get the punchcard into the lock. But the door sprang open and we tipped inside, my hands tearing at the taut silk of the *cheongsam*. With panther strength she threw me back, hunched down and straightened up in one writhing serpentine shiver that cast the black silk like a skin, left her standing in scraps of sweatstained lace that existed only to be ripped away.

I stood there panting, almost in awe. The world around me fell away, I seemed to exist only in the essence of that vision. I stepped forward, felt her claw at my clothes. Her eyes were clear green pools; I tasted their freshness on her lips and longed to dive in them, to be swallowed up, to drown and to hell with all things else. I kissed her breasts, ducked my head in fierce homage between her thighs, found oblivion there, as beneath rain on green leaves. We rolled on clean cool sheets, and I felt myself borne into her, drawn deep. I drew her to me in my turn as she wanted, held her close, held nothing back till our skin seemed to melt and merge together like wax in a furnace. My last clear memory is of her hunched above me in a brief breathless truce, whispering as our locked thighs churned again, slowly, '*My name – my love – my real name – my name is Kala'narang!*'

The rest is velvet. And claws.

But opening my eyes, a whole world afterwards, that was sackcloth and ashes, sackcloth shot through with little fiery threads of pain, ashes with embers still glowing. My eyes hurt. My head throbbed so hard my temples bulged with the pain, or felt like it, anyway. My mouth tasted vile, vomitous, as if I'd been sick several times and choked it back. I was stiff, I was leaden cold, my muscles shrieked with misuse at the slightest twitch. But it was too cold to lie here, and the *noise*—

It was cutting through me like a bandsaw. I forced one eye open against the terrible grey light. The wide central window panel stood open, in defiance of all the notices about the air-conditioning. Through it, even forty floors up, all the mechanised howls and growls and smells of a Bangkok day gathering momentum were coming. I groaned, clutched at my head and tried to look at the clock. Half past five. Wonderful . . .

Then it dawned on me. I was starfished right across the bed; and I wasn't touching another body. I lifted my head a little. I could see into the bathroom from here – nobody. I twisted about. The door to the living room was open, too. She might have been lying flat on the seating, or out of view; but I knew, somehow, that she wasn't. The suite had that kind of feeling about it, that stillness which is greater than silence. '*Jacquie* . . .' I croaked, and then corrected myself, horrified. 'Rangda?' But I knew I was wasting my time.

I tried to raise myself on my elbows – and yelled, and fell back. When the agony *that* caused subsided, I found they were scraped raw and bloody, clotted and caked with grit or something, the way they'd looked when I fell off my bike as a kid. It was horrible, nothing to see on a stomach like mine. God, what had I been doing last night? All I could remember was the intensity, the animalism of it. It left me with yet another sickening ache. I felt used, abused, swallowed up, dragged down somehow. Used and degraded – was this how whores felt? And she hadn't even hung around . . .

A flash of anger overrode my weakness, and I snatched at the bedside table, yelping at the pain it cost me. A little pile of foil wrappers scattered; I'd had some sort of sense left, anyhow. My watch was still there, too – and it was worth far more than my wallet held. Wallet? I rolled over – and yelped again. My knees were as bad as my elbows, or worse. There wasn't much blood on the sheets where I'd been lying, though – odd. Wincing, I leaned out of bed and plucked at the discarded jacket lying on the floor. There was my wallet, with cash and credit cards still visible; beneath it my cheque books, my passport. Nothing missing that I could see. I was as glad as I could be in that state, but a bit puzzled. She'd just upped and gone, like that, and taken nothing.

My skin felt shiny and taut with what had dried on it, sweat and other exudations. My innards were unstable, to put it mildly. The air was already getting warm and noxious. The bed stank; the room stank. *I* stank. No chance of going back to sleep, not like this. Blundering, wavering, I swung my rebellious body to my feet and shambled up. The window was too far, but I might just make the bathroom, step by faltering step, steadying myself on the wall. After the most immediate matters, I managed to start up the shower, and once I'd got over the pain of soaking my cuts clean I began to feel a bit better. I let the warm water steam and pummel away all the pain and filth, outside and in.

And of course, just as I was coming to terms with it, the phone rang. Cursing, I reached for the speaker button. If this was the clerk being funny . . . It was an outside call, an excited Thai voice gabbling his English. '*Khun* Fisher?' I deciphered. 'Captain Souvanaphong, Airport Security, Don Muang! A container here in bond for trans-shipment? Was register to your firm, yes?' And he reeled an interminable consignment number.

'Well, yes,' I began. And then, 'What d'you mean – *was*?'

'*Khun*, you will please come out here right away, a car is on its way to fetch you! *Khun*, it has been stolen!'

I reeled and cursed as if the phone had reached out and punched me, then staggered, still cursing, out of the shower and in search of a towel. The unfiltered air wrapped itself stickily around me, and I lunged for the window. There were scuff marks and stains on the sill. For god's sake, we hadn't been up to anything *there*, had we? On the fortieth floor? But I'd other things to worry about now. Rangda? Could she have stolen something of mine, some identification or document somebody could use to get at the container? But I didn't carry anything like that. All the details were on computer at our agency office in town; you couldn't just turn up and demand something, whatever IDs you could produce . . . My head was aching like a triphammer now.

It was still doing it two hours later, out at the airport. The ride out to Don Muang didn't make it any better, with the siren going all the way, and two lean, grim officers in plain uniform firing questions at me about the container, its contents, the Project, everything. They wore Tourist Police flashes, but after the first minute I was sure that was just a cover for their good English. It didn't help, either, that I'd listed the Project offices among the people to be informed in any emergency. As I shambled red-eyed into security headquarters a little buzz-box cab drew up. Out burst Jacquie in jeans and denim jacket and striped jersey, launching another volley of questions, which of course started the cops up again.

We ended up in the captain's office, facing him across the desk, with the 'Tourist Police' leaning disapprovingly against the wall behind. 'Our security is among the best in the world,' the captain protested, glancing around at them. 'The government insists on it, both for the protection of trade and as part of the war against drugs. At three-eighteen this morning our centralised monitoring equipment logged a disturbance – I cannot reveal details, but infra-red appeared to show something unclear, perhaps one man. A warehouse watchman, armed, was instantly warned by radio to investigate, and upon his sounding the alarm an officer ran to assist him. The officer was struck unconscious from behind, and saw nothing. By the time others arrived, the door was broken, one container gone, no other. So little was disturbed we had to check the manifests to be sure something actually had been taken. The watchman . . . ' He hesitated. 'He perhaps was also struck, although there is no serious injury. But he appears to be disturbed – shocked. He is babbling some fairy tale vision . . . strange creatures, I cannot tell what.'

I felt that deep sinking feeling again. One paper cup of ill-dissolved instant coffee and milk powder had done little enough to heal the damage of last night. God knows what sort of impression I was creating. 'This guard – does he speak English? I'd like to hear his story for myself. Can I see him?'

The captain drummed his fingers on the desk. 'We have finished interrogating him for now. He needs treatment. An ambulance is on the way.' He stood up. 'But why not? He might remember some other detail. Come along, please.' He picked up a small tape-recorder and ushered us along the corridor. The room was obviously a sickbay, but one officer stood guard outside, another sat in the dimness inside. On the stretcher-bed someone lay curled up in a foetal crouch. The captain shook him gently. 'Tran!'

The answer came in a moan.

'Speak English, Tran! The gentleman who owns the stolen goods would like you to tell him about what happened to you . . .'

I leaned over. 'If it's not too much of a strain . . .'

The head jerked round. The eyes glared. There was foam on the lips, rictus baring the teeth. I suddenly remembered what I'd heard about going *amok*.

He let out a blood-curdling screech, '*Poo 'chai farung*! *Farung bpleu'ay bah*!' and all but threw himself off the bed and at the window in one motion. But the officer grabbed him, and he crashed into the venetian blind, blubbing and gibbering and sobbing.

'Westerner!' said Jacquie quietly, looking at me. 'That means "crazy naked Westerner!".'

'It does,' said the captain heavily, as we settled back into his plastic chairs. 'The gist of his ravings is this – an idiotic tale about a train of spooks and spectres, and a European leading them. Pale-faced, rigid, like a dead man walking. Oh yes, and stark naked, apparently. These things attacked and laid hands upon him, he says, while the European operated the warehouse machinery himself, loading the container up on to some creaky old flatbed truck – wagon, even. When they left, he ran after them—'

That made him a pretty brave man, in my book.

'—but turned a corner, and was abruptly lost in mist. This is an international airport, *Khun* Fisher. There was no mist last night. That is all he told us. But he has indeed added one further detail.'

'And that is?'

'He identifies the European, *Khun* Fisher, as you.'

124

The next couple of hours were not happy ones. Of course I was the first European the man had seen since the incident, the captain admitted, but even so, and simply in the interests of inquiries, would I be good enough to explain what I was doing at the time . . .

And the narcs chipped in, and Jacquie sat there radiating bitter distrust and the lowest possible opinion of my character and motives. If she'd poked a finger in my face and shouted, 'You're in this just to make some kind of dirty profit!' she couldn't have encouraged them more. And here was I looking like just the kind of broken-down wreck who was quite capable of doing just that. There were an awful lot of very awkward questions, and I could see myself being hauled off for a session with the rubber truncheons and crocodile clips, until somebody had the sense to check with my hotel.

That turned the whole thing on its head. Yes, the night clerks had observed *Khun* Fisher returning around midnight last night, somewhat, er, excited – and alone. Yes, he had gone up to his room, and yes, he had stayed there. Could they be sure? Absolutely. They maintained a firm security watch after midnight, logging everyone in and out by the one main door. Cameras were recording the entire time. *Khun* Fisher neither left nor came back after midnight.

'Unless,' crackled the speakerphone, 'unless he somehow scaled down from the fortieth floor – ha ha!'

'Hahaha!' roared the cops, suddenly relieved they wouldn't have to try beating the bejasus out of this influential foreign businessman, with all the hassle that could cause.

'Ha ha,' I agreed, with a sickening vision of myself crawling stark naked down the outer face of the hotel in the small hours. My god, maybe even head-down! *And* back up. King Kong, in the skinned-rabbit version. The first-aid kit distributed around my knees and elbows stung guiltily with sweat.

The captain shook his head. 'My apologies, *Khun*. You must understand . . . ' He spread his hands. 'But evidently the man was totally delirious, insane from shock. And of course you Europeans look so very much alike. He has been a good worker. Let us hope he recovers enough to be more lucid. In the meantime our inquiries will continue.'

'Let us indeed,' I echoed him. 'He was trying to protect our consignment. I want him to have the best possible treatment, the best of everything. And see his family's looked after, if any. My company will foot the bill. Fix it up with our agents today, please.'

The captain nodded his thanks. 'That is most generous. Well, *Khun*, all this has kept you from your breakfast, if nothing else. I will have a car take you back to your hotel—'

'I'll get a taxi, thank you all the same. I want to go and see my, uh, chief associate about this – at once.' If I could find him, before the agreed time.

'Of course,' he said, and turned to Jacquie. 'And you, Ms Kven-Svensen?'

She stood up, her mouth set in a hard line. 'I,' she announced, 'am going with Mr Fisher. We are his principals, and we have a say in all this too. And so far I am not in the least bit satisfied. Wherever he goes, to consult whoever he consults, I am going along; and you gentlemen are witnesses, in case for some reason I should fail to come back. Do you hear me, Stephen? I am going to get some *answers*!'

There wasn't a hell of a lot I could say to that. There was no way now I could try to explain anything to her, least of all that having her along might make finding anyone impossible. It hadn't with Dave, but that might have been dumb luck, or just that I still had enough feeling for the way. I couldn't rely on that here, or on anything else. Morning and evening were the best times to pass from Core to Spiral, from Hub to Wheel. Because half-light made us less dogmatic about what we could or couldn't see, perhaps; but that was just rationalising. Now, anyway, it was full and glaring day, and getting back into the city was hard enough, let alone any more unusual transitions. Two hours' expensive cruising around couldn't find me the bar, and the taxi driver had never heard of it; so I decided to go back for a rest and something to eat, and try later on foot.

All this time Jacquie sat like silent thunder, accepting my offer of a meal with the curtest of nods. When I said I'd like to go and lie down for a while, she snapped out, 'I'll come with you!' and her look when I chuckled was like a slap. She trailed along up to the suite, which had been restored to its usual immaculate self, and after prowling around it, peering at everything, she announced she'd rest in the living room while I could have the bed. I lay there now, staring at the ceiling, drifting in and out of a doze. I was deadly tired, but the worry and the whirling in my head banished any real sleep.

Mercifully, that little pile of wrappers had been removed. It worried me, that heap. I couldn't have been as smashed out of my skull as all that — so why couldn't I remember a damn thing? I'd returned to the hotel alone, said the clerk; and he wasn't just being tactful. I'd lay a heavy bet that was what the security tape would show, too; me staggering back in with my arm around someone who wasn't there. As well they didn't keep cameras on the outside of the building, too. What had made me do something that was barely possible, let alone sane? And why did I feel so ill? It felt less like drink, more like some kind of poisoning, mental as well as physical — not a subtle nerve poison, either, but an Elizabethan kind, fierce, burning and corrosive. As if it had burned out half my insides and left me as hollow as an unfilled tooth. As washed out as when . . .

I sat up. The last time I'd felt like this was after Somebody had more or less invaded my body, shared it, possessed it, you could say. I'd been warned, once, that I might still be vulnerable to something of the sort if I strayed back into the Spiral. It had been bad enough, that, afterwards; not as bad as this. But then that possession had been almost willing on my part, and got me out of a terrible hole. Whereas here I'd been forced to act against my will, against good sense and self-preservation and everything I wanted. I shuddered, and my gorge rose. No wonder the clerk hadn't seen her. What came back here with me last night was some force of the Spiral, pursuing many purposes, maybe, but most of all her own. So she'd decoyed me, seduced me — and read me like a book to do it, playing upon my worst weaknesses. And in seducing me she'd wormed her way past my defences, into me, under my skin. I sagged back into the cool pillows. All through sex. Used. Abused. In effect, I'd been raped.

The door flew open. Jacquie stood there. 'What is it? What'd you say?'

I just blinked at her.

'I thought . . . ' she said slowly, 'I thought I heard you cry out, or something . . . ' She looked at me, and I could see her mind working. No, smooth crooks like Stephen don't go crying out. She shut the door again, then swung it back open as she heard me clamber out of bed. 'Where do you think you're going?'

'To have another shower!' I said curtly, because I was standing there stark naked. Nothing she hadn't seen long ago, but I like my privacy. '*If* you don't mind.'

She caught her breath. 'Your arms . . . and your legs . . . ' She stared at the patches of dressing, spotted here and there with blood. Then over to the window. Then back, her eyes widening, as well they might; forty floors. Smooth crooks don't do that, either, very often.

'If you want any answers,' I told her, 'you're going to have to start believing some pretty impossible things. And the first of them is that I'm not doing anything crooked.'

She snorted. 'Maybe you don't think so. Just good business, I suppose. What is it, drugs? No, too risky for you, too openly crooked. Insurance, then, maybe. A clever coup, something you can boast about to your drinking buddies. I suppose I shouldn't blame you, it's like blaming a deaf man for not hearing. You just wouldn't see that anyone could actually *care* about something like this, would you?'

'And that's what you think, is it?'

She followed me into the bathroom, glaring. 'I should have told them the moment I saw your name – if *he's* taken this on when nobody else will, there'll be some reason to it, some advantage. But I thought, well, why not, as long as it gets the job done? Why shouldn't he pick up whatever it is on the side, and good luck to him? That's his way, and there are worse ones – I thought!' I didn't say anything; what could I say? I twisted the big shower handle and stepped in, wincing in anticipation. 'I thought you might have changed a bit – I was curious! And I thought, if he hadn't, well, it'd be all right with me there to keep an eye on him – I thought! And then when I met you, you seemed so much more . . . ' She shook her head. 'I could almost have believed you'd changed. But if I'd realised you never meant to get the stuff through—'

She stopped as I burst out of the shower in a cloud of foam and grabbed her by the arms. The hot water had hit the dressings and with them my self-control. 'Listen to me will you? All these assumptions you're making – what evidence have you got?' I shook her, scythed one hand out in a flat plane. '*None*! What bloody *reason*, even, have you got? The way I dumped you, years ago? The stories you've heard about me from business friends? Christ, could I tell you a few about them! And I wouldn't need to exaggerate, either! And yet you . . . ' Words failed me. I shook her again. And then I saw her face, and read everything that was there, fury and doubt and worry, a horrible boiling brew. Maybe she was right, at that. Maybe I didn't know what it was like to care for something that way.

'Everything I'm doing,' I said more gently, 'is for just one thing
– to get the container and that computer gear in it back and to the
island, if possible on time. And all the other ones to come after it.
You may not believe me now; but I hope you will, soon. Stick
with me, sure; but try to believe in me, give me the benefit of the
doubt for now, at least. That'll make it easier.' I glanced out at the
sun. 'Afternoon. We can't do anything till early evening. We
should take the time to get a good meal on board.' A thin thread
of red trickled out into the dissolving soap on my arms. I winced.
'And after I finish my shower I want to change these bloody
bandages. That'll take time.'

'Not so long,' said Jacquie, 'if I help.'

The truce lasted, for a while. I found that scrap of paper still
tucked into my jacket; Rangda hadn't noticed it, or hadn't cared.
And together this time, we retraced my steps; only this time, the
road I came up wasn't the same as the one I went down. 'As if the
spatial relationships are constant, but what fills them isn't . . .'

'What on earth?' demanded Jacquie. Or was it just because I
was with someone who wouldn't see the sense of doubling back?
Who wouldn't believe in it?

'Just rambling,' I said, picking my way through the various
unpleasantnesses along that winding alley. 'It should be round
here . . .'

'Wow,' said Jacquie sardonically. 'I really like your friend's
taste. I mean, not the sort of place you'd find crooks hanging out,
is it?'

'Save it. Let's try inside.'

But after a while I began to wonder if Jacquie wasn't still my
millstone. The bar was its old sleazy self, though this time of day
the speciality acts were off, and only a couple of bored
bump-and-grinders filled their place. The shadows at the back
were just shadows, the doors solidly closed. Attempts to pump
the solitary barman about them got nowhere; he'd say nothing
about anything, even when I offered him increasingly outrageous
bribes. 'Best kinda health insurance in these parts, a tight mouth,'
he volunteered, cheerfully. 'Better'n Blue Cross.'

We got tired of waiting, and went out and drifted round the
docks, but I got the same response, except when I asked for
Batang Sen by name. By the reactions I might as well have been
asking for the Flying Dutchman. And Jacquie, of course, got less
and less patient, more and more into her acid Chinese manner. I

tried looking among the *prahus*; there were plenty of Boegies there, lovely little craft, long of bowsprit and top-heavy with sail, gliding gull-white and gull-fast across the choppy estuary waters. But there was no sign of any larger schooners at all, let alone a Grand Banks type with the space for even one container, let alone two. 'This is all very interesting,' commented Jacquie. 'But may I remind you, evening's coming on, and this isn't the healthiest side of town for Europeans after dark – or even a mongrel like me! So why don't we go back to your nice clean hotel, and you can rehearse a few answers on me, eh?'

I looked around the deserted boardwalks that bordered the docksides, leading out to old wooden quays. The sun was almost at the horizon now, sending long rays out across the water, deepening the shadows. Here and there harbour lights were winking on, and small boats hauled up. 'Back to that bloody bar! I said I'd have the container here now, and I don't! I've got to find them, tell them what's happened, get help – help that'll do some good!'

Jacquie closed her eyes, for patience. 'Steve . . .' she began, and then they flew open again, staring behind me. I turned, and saw the three youths who materialised out of a side alley. They were smiling, and their jaws rotated slowly, chewing gum; their shorts and shirts were American or Italian flash. One held out a hand, as if to offer me something; but as he opened his fingers there came the click and flash of a switchblade.

He'd chosen the wrong time, and relied too much on the knife to terrify me, as it might an ordinary tourist. This was the limit. I grabbed his wrist and sank a fist into his face with all my fury and frustration to propel it. The knife fell through the boardwalk. The other ones jumped me, but one hopped and staggered, yelping, as Jacquie delivered a ringing kick on the shin, then landed a neat one-two in his mouth. She hadn't my weight behind her, but as he rocked I hit the third one hard, then grabbed them, one after another, by the scruff of the neck and the seat of their pants and hurled them bodily out into the *klong*-mouth with a muddy splash.

The first one pounced from all fours, like a rugger tackle, and carried us both over the walk's edge on to the short slope beneath. I grabbed his throat, twisted us over and jammed his face into the shallows at the edge. '*Kiap* Batang Sen!' I barked, lifting him up by the hair. 'Where do I find him? Here? Or where? Speak up!'

He couldn't, only bubbled a bit. I was just putting him back when I looked out across the water, past his floundering friends. The sun sank and, instantly, though the skies were still rich and golden, the harbour lights stood out against a papery greyness. And in the clouds, extending out into infinity, I saw peak and promontory, peninsula and islet of bright cloud, gold-fringed as if with glittering beaches, grey-crowned with craggy rocks – an archipelago in a sea of fire. Fire that spilled out in a track across the mirroring waves, right down the seas towards us, scattered at last in the rippled wake of the thugs as they scrambled ashore, exhausted. But in the shadows on either side of it a dark sea mirror reflected the harbour lights, more and more clearly.

I let the struggling body fall, swung myself back up, seized Jacquie's arm and dragged her after me. We ran, our footsteps rattling down the boardwalks as the evening haze closed in. They seemed to grow rougher, half-rotten almost, as if this part of the dock had never been renewed. It wasn't far, a couple of quays only, and I stopped before a half-ruined gate, and pointed.

'What . . . ' she breathed, her voice dry, shaky, uncertain. 'Were they after us? Were there more coming?'

'No! Them? I wasn't running from them! Look!'

She looked, not where I pointed, but at me. 'What . . . what do you see, Steve?'

'Not me – what do *you* see, there, in the water? Reflected there in the dock?'

She stared, puzzled. 'I don't know – lights, maybe . . . Too many lights, as if something was reflecting them high above the water – but there isn't—'

'There *is*! No, don't look up, not yet – look into the water, harder – *harder*! D'you see it?'

'Something . . . two, three . . . can't make it out. And lights.'

'I can! Two masts . . . no, three – or is that a funnel? Rigging, with lanterns . . . god, look at the height of it! That's it! *Come on*!'

And pulling her after me, I strode through the gaping gateway, out on to the quay. But my foot fell, not on worm-eaten wood, but on ringing flagstone. And I heard Jacquie cry out, and pull hard at my arm; yet in the dense swirl of white mist that billowed around us she was lost to my sight.

A cage of silence dropped around us. The only sound was Jacquie's jagged gasp, her panting breath. I clutched her arm tightly, and hissed a warning.

'Whatever you do, don't—'

'Let me *go*!' she spat, and hammered a numbingly accurate blow on my biceps, the sort of thing they teach in self-defence courses. It mightn't have deterred a rapist, but I wasn't expecting it. She tore her arm free of my tingling fingers, and her footsteps pattered off back into the mist.

I trailed after the sound, cursing – not her, myself. I didn't blame her one bit for reacting that way. I'd given her reason enough to think me crazy already, or worse; and then this. Of course she'd think it was something to do with me. And she'd run back in the direction I would have, off to the left – which made both of us wrong, because the mists weren't getting any thinner, and there was still stone underfoot. A muffled thump and an exclamation up ahead made my heart leap, till it was followed by a scrabble of feet; she'd tripped over something. Then I almost did, too – a step, a wide stone step, dished with wear, slippery with moisture. A stair! Which might lead higher than this mist – or might end in emptiness. I climbed, cautiously, one hand outstretched, hoping Jacquie would take care, too. I didn't dare shout, mindful of arrows; and it might only drive her away, too.

The stair was steep, and before too many minutes passed I began to see the steps ahead of me, dull smudges in the mist, and around me, looming above me, immense shadow shapes suggesting columns and domes. Then, quite suddenly, I surfaced like a swimmer in a dazzling sea of milk. And looking up, I stopped in awe. The stairs climbed up to towers and galleries against a blazing blue sky, encrusted peaks of carving in weathered brownish stone, bell-shaped domes of stone lattice enclosing shadowy sculpture-shapes, shrouded in columns of steam as the sun at its zenith boiled off the mist-slick like a sacrifice. At its zenith; and its heat fell like a heavy hand on the back of my neck. One step, one gate, had taken us from evening to noon.

Further up the stair stood Jacquie, still as the statues around her, staring outwards, giving no sign she'd even seen me. Still thigh-deep in the mist, I turned and looked where she looked; and, like her, I was transfixed.

The mists were lifting. It was only round this vast shadowy edifice of cool stone, encrusted with age and lichen, that they lingered so thickly. Beyond it, they dwindled to ghostly wisps that trailed among the treetops of a vast swathe of jungle, an endless ocean of brilliant greens that stretched unbroken, becalmed, as far as the clear air carried our sight, to a horizon of rolling hills.

I turned back and went racing up the steps. Jacquie retreated, but only a step or two, slowly, her mouth open, her eyes flickering between me and the impossible landscape.

'Not me!' I panted, clutching her arm. 'Not my doing! Somebody that doesn't like the Project, I think – but how, don't ask me! Or why, or where—'

Jacquie shook me free, but absently, turning away to stare around her. Behind us rose another gallery, and she suddenly pointed to the vast carved friezes. 'Look!'

They were stylised and badly weathered, but even so I could see why she was impressed. Swirling across the age-darkened stone like a widescreen cinema ran an epic image of a smoothly human figure entangled with a battling mass of monstrous figures, all tusks and staring eyeballs. I thought of the mask-thing, and shuddered. It was a savage image for what looked like a shrine of some kind; but it held Jacquie hypnotised.

'I know this!' she said dazedly. 'See there, this is the story of Buddha – he's being attacked by the demon Mara's armies – and down there, below, that's a *Jakata*, a Buddhist folktale – that one's about the monkey king, a bit like Hanuman in the *Ramayana*—'

'The epic, you mean? Don't know where you get all this stuff.'

'Oh, I read it all, years ago.' She smiled dazedly. 'Looking for my oriental roots. And the Buddha stories and the *Ramayana*, you keep tripping over them out here, where you get Buddhism and Hinduism piling on top of one another. Common stock in dances and puppet shows, that kind of thing.'

'And temple walls. I see. And you don't happen to remember just which temples in the Bangkok area might have a Buddha biography carved all over them like this?'

She laughed. 'Oh, there's nothing this size anywhere *near* Bangkok—' Her hand flew to her mouth. 'Oh my god . . . '

'Yes.'

'I must have been loopy, I didn't think . . . '

'You had a hell of a shock, is what.' I stared at those carvings as if they'd tell me something. They didn't. 'Don't blame you. It hit me just as hard. It's been happening to me since I got into this bloody Project!'

'To you? Already? But . . . where *are* we?'

There was a sound, a shock, faint but clear, thudding through the stone. 'Somewhere I don't think we ought to hang around . . .'

I took one step down and stopped dead. In the sea of mist below us something swam like a gigantic fish, scales glittering beneath the surface. It rose slowly higher, towards the steps; and a high sharkfin shape broke the surface. As it swayed I realised it was the same shining hummock I'd glimpsed once before above the mist; the shape on its back was broad and solid, like a turret. Not a fish; more a submarine with its conning tower. Then, rearing up on to what must be the bottom step, its head showed clearly through the mist, a glittering mass of scaled, encrusted armour, slowly swaying, beyond which wide grey things flapped like fins indeed. Not fins, though, but ears; and below the armour something swung and two great curving prongs of whiteness protruded, tipped each with a jagged steel dart like a gigantic spear. Over the arched back more armour glittered, a sawtoothed backplate falling away to a cascade of spiked and barbed scales and heavily ornamented chain mail jingling and clanking in time with that massive stone-shaking tread. The thing on its back was a cage of metal plates, octagonal, laced with narrow perforations, topped by a trailing banner.

A war-elephant. The ultimate weapon of the Hindu conquerors of southern Asia – the largest elephant by far I'd ever seen, a gigantic creature that dwarfed any zoo-bound beast, decked out in full fearsome panoply. Its ears flapped as it surged nightmare-like out of the mist towards us; they too were shielded by plates of silver mesh, and from them, dangling and dancing, hung earrings of jewelled skulls. As an emblem of fantastic wealth and power it was unparalleled, more terrifying than a tank in its solemn, majestic advance. And from the armoured howdah it carried, long arrows trailing gaudy streamers sang out and skipped across the stones around us.

One whined right past my ear, not close but startling. If it hadn't I might have just stood there, stunned, till it was too late. What was going on? At this range they should have skewered us by now. They were firing to miss, to pin us down as prisoners. I risked a glance up the steps; there was at least one more terrace up there, but I thought I saw movement between the domes. And at once another arrow hummed right over our heads and smashed into the steps higher up. Point taken; they might stop firing to miss. Anyway, wherever our way out lay, chances were it was back in those mists somewhere. Behind the advancing elephant tall spears were rising and dipping, and here and there a bowstave. The searchers were gathering to cut off their prey. That left just one thing to try, and it had better be fast. Jacquie was standing there goggling, mouth open, breathing in great gulping gasps like a drowning woman. She was teetering right on the brink of screaming hysterics, and no wonder. I seized her arm, and she gaped at me.

'*Down!*' I yelled, or maybe screamed. Yanking her after me, I went cantering down those steps so fast I almost lost my balance, and we blundered on in that headlong rush which is just fractionally short of a fall. Nothing less would have saved us; the bowmen acted fast, and arrows spat and splintered on the steps where we passed. But our runaway descent brought us down to the one spot where they couldn't fire – right in front of the elephant. It was well trained, though, for just this; the massive head ducked to widen the field of fire, the barb-tipped tusks tossed menacingly, the trunk lifted in a challenging trumpet. Another step – two – one; and I jinked sharply aside, heaving Jacquie after me. She stumbled – then squealed and ducked. The trunk flailed past her head and slammed against the side of the stair, long spikes glittered on a huge encased leg as it lifted and stamped, swinging its whole bulk sideways to catch and crush us. But we were already past, dodging the spear a *mahout* hurled down from his perch. He began belabouring the elephant with a hooked stick, but on the stair those stiff pillar-like legs wouldn't let it turn fast enough. He started yelling, the elephant squealed angrily, and we ducked down into the mist. A vague figure materialised in our path, shouting a challenge, lowering a spear; but I was already ahead of its point, letting go of Jacquie and launching a flurry of fists at the dim face. He spun around and tipped back down the stairs with a scream and a clatter; someone else fell over him. Suddenly there were no more stairs underfoot, only level flags. Another man rushed up, lunged at me and shot by, to crash against the stairfoot with an agonised yell. Jacquie, beside me, was biting her lip and limping; she'd tripped him. 'Nice one!' I said, scooped her up and scuttled as best I could back out on to the terrace, in something like the direction we'd come from. Behind us the shouting and shrilling grew louder.

But almost at once another bulky shadow formed in front of us, high and hard-edged in the swirling cloud, so close we ran more or less right into it. For a horrified moment I thought the grey, slab-like side was another armoured elephant; but my out-thrust hands touched it and came away flaked with peeling paint. The realisation was almost worse. 'It's the bloody container!' I cried aloud.

It was mounted on a battered, decayed old flatbed truck, a rusting relic of the 1920s by the look of it, no make I'd ever seen. It looked barely able to carry the weight. I ran around to the cab and flung back the door. 'No keys! And god knows how you'd hotwire something like this – I don't think it's even got an electric starter!'

'Wha— what're we going to do?' cried Jacquie.

'What can we do? We can't lift the thing on our own – that damn beast could hardly do it!' And as if I'd summoned it, I felt the flagstones shiver with fast striding footfalls, as near a run as an elephant can manage. They'd placed us.

'Leave it!' I yelled, reaching out to drag Jacquie along again. She shook me loose and raced off on her own, around the container and out into the thinning mist. Any moment now I expected to run into foliage, feel the whip and snag of leaves and vines and rootlets tangling about my ankle, dragging me back into the path of that awesome tread. But instead I felt something else, a springy hollowness underfoot that wasn't the soggy spread of soil; our footfalls drummed and creaked on wooden slats. In the same instant the mist lit with one blinding pink flare, a blasting hiss and crackle like a log exploding in a gigantic bonfire.

I reached out to Jacquie, caught her hand – and tripped and fell, pulling her down with me, rolling over on the splintering wood. Overhead, where the sun of noon had blazed only moments since above the mist, the sky was clear; and there were stars. Against them reared the shaft of a pillar; but it was wooden, and covered with flakes of paint, and shattered, at its summit, to splinters that still smoked and smouldered with that pink fire. It was the remains of the old archway; and its falling splinters stung my hand. I looked across; the other side was the same, smashed and scorched. Of the crossbar there was no trace. The gateway had been blasted to a stump.

Jacquie raised herself on one elbow, blinking. Ape came rolling down the boardwalk, shouldering his staff. 'By dom!' he roared. 'The colour of stale *advocaat*!'

'Wh . . . what?'

'Your lousy faces!'

I took a deep luxurious breath. I hadn't heard any explosion; but the air still seemed to be ringing with an aftershock. 'Don't worry,' I told Jacquie. 'He's on our side.'

'God, that's reassuring,' said Jacquie drily. She was doing her best to sound in control of herself, but the corners of her mouth were trembling. 'And what is our side, exactly?'

I took another deep breath, but then Ape came stamping up, flushed and scowling with ill-contained fury. '*Nou, Mynheer Idioot*? So what do you go and bugger up now, that you waste all our hard labours and throw away all we achieve, hah? And for a bonus let them get their paws on you yourself?' He snorted deafeningly, like a scornful carthorse. 'By chance only I find you, you know that? You don't turn up, or the container! I worry, I go look ashore, and what do I find?' He hawked and spat copiously. The planking resounded with the impact. 'You hand it them on a platter and serve up yourself for afters! Maybe I should leave you stew in your own dom folly! Maybe next time I will!'

'Stop that!' shouted Jacquie, her voice fraying. 'It wasn't Steve's fault!'

I peered at her. That was a pretty different tune to the one she'd been harping on all day. Ape cocked his head on one side, considering her. '*Wat*,' he inquired insultingly, '*is deze*?'

She bridled.

'This is Jacquie,' I said hastily. 'She works for the Project—'

Ape's manner softened slightly. 'So,' he said, considering. He lifted a massively calloused finger to his tangled hairline. '*Dag, mevrouw*. Not his fault, you say, yet somehow he is mixed into it. I think some explanations called for, *nie*?' He swung up his staff, and a single flare of pink light crackled into the sky. 'Te Kiore and his men are looking also; I recall them. We go to the ship and have a drink or six, which you look like you need.'

'The ship?' inquired Jacquie suspiciously, picking herself up.

Ape gestured. She turned, and caught her breath. The harbour was a glowing curtain of coloured light now, mirrored in the calm dark water; but over it, like a tracery of shadows, lay the rig of a large sailing ship. She caught my arm as sharply as she'd refused it a moment since. 'That . . . ' she began. 'That's what you were seeing . . . when I couldn't . . . or thought I . . . '

'Like the man says, explanations are called for.'

She shook her head, in bewilderment, not denial, and as she leaned against me I felt the shiver that ran through her. She looked up at me, wide-eyed, and I nodded. I knew how she felt. Just as I had, just as Dave had, she had stepped over a threshold into a wider world; and she was feeling the chill wonder of it, right to the depths of her being. 'Yes,' she said, only a little tremulous. 'I'd say so. But first . . . '

'Yes?'

'That drink.'

Then she looked over my shoulder, and her face stiffened. Te Kiore was trotting down the boardwalk with his sword-club slapping at his side, waving and shouting various totally incomprehensible greetings. He was minus his feather-cloak, leaving his latticed neck and chest all the more visible. In the dim light of the dockside streetlamps, widely spaced and intermittently bright, the tattoos turned him into a sort of shadowy lacework gargoyle with an Ocker accent.

'Strewth, mate, we been turnin' the joint arsy-versy lookin' for you! Threw a proper bloody scare into us, you did! An' where's this overgrown jerry-can of yours got to, too?' He saw Jacquie, and pulled up short. 'Oh, ah. Hey! Who's the lovely lady, then? G'day, Miss, you comin' on board with us? Great! Got the longboat 'long the walk here – hop on down an' we'll whip yer out slicker'n spit off a hot stove!'

'Make that *drinks*,' Jacquie amended wearily.

A multinational band of chattering cut-throats bore us off

down to the boat and more or less heaved us bodily aboard. But for all their malevolent appearance I noted that they practically flowed to their places at the oars without confusion, and the moment te Kiore freed the painter and leaped aboard they pulled away in perfect unison.

'Old hands,' I remarked to him, as the longboat traced a spreading arrowhead across the dark harbour calm.

He studied me a moment. 'Too right! Not straight off the quay yourself, exactly, are you?' He turned round in the bows. 'Well, there she is! An' ain't she a living beaut?'

Ahead of us, as we curved around to come alongside, the looming shadow was slowly filling out into solid form. Beside me Jacquie gave a breathless half-giggle. 'I don't *believe* it!'

I was pretty startled myself. An old steel engraving was lifting off a page. About a hundred and thirty feet I made her, a long lean hull like an ancestral clipper ship, sleekly flush-decked except for a small poop and wheelhouse, and a larger hatchway which must cover the hold – easily big enough to take a container. Her three masts held something like an old-fashioned schooner rig; but between foremast and main there was space enough for a fourth mast, might once have been one, in fact. Only now in its place there lifted a high thin smokestack, gleaming black with snaky gilt traceries, and crowned with an improbable oriental dado, like an early locomotive's. And right beside it the hull's clean line was broken by a low rounded box, like the mudguard of a vintage car, covering what looked like a many-bladed millwheel. 'It's a paddle steamer!' breathed Jacquie. 'God, is it *safe*? It must be a hundred years old!'

'I wouldn't bet on that. And it's not even a steamer; the paddles are too small. They must just be auxiliaries, added on to a basic sailing vessel. Right, te Kiore?'

'Sure is!' he agreed. 'That's how we like it, old man Batang and me. Wind's free; fuel ain't. They won't exactly zip her away on their own, the ol' millwheels, but they'll get her out of harbour without a tug, jolly her along in a flat calm, and hold her in a heavy sea. Or help her outrun a pirate longboat. And that's worth bloody gold-dust in our trade.'

Jacquie shook her head again in utter disbelief. 'But . . . paddles? Steam? Why not use diesel, a screw propeller?'

Te Kiore's tattooes writhed good-humouredly. 'Because there's no diesel agency in Tir nan Og, or Arcadia, or Terra

Australis, or Tar-Shish. Because Prester John's divers can't hoick off a cracked screw, and there's nowhere can fix it nearer than Nibelheim, or the Cyclops' forges, and you might not like their prices. But you can shape and fit a new paddle blade in an hour or two, with your own two mitts, east or west of the sunset. That's why, beautiful!'

Jacquie looked wildly from him to me. 'Arcadia? Prester John? Cyclops, for god's sake – are you two trying to wind me up? Because if you are, you bastards, you can—'

'Explanations!' I said sharply. The boat pulled in under the lee of the hull, an elegant outward curve quite unlike the pot-bellied tumblehomes I'd clambered up, sometimes under fire. 'Like it or not, Jacquie, this world's a lot stranger and wider than most people ever imagine – let alone see.' At te Kiore's hail a long boat-ladder came creaking down. 'It opened out for me, once, years ago. Ever since then it's closed in again. But, for better or worse, nothing was ever quite the same again.'

I helped her out on to the platform of the stair. It looked positively luxurious, all polished mahogany and brass rail, like something off a Victorian yacht; which it might well have been. 'Nothing,' I repeated. She looked back at me, once, and away back to the shore. It wasn't so far, but it had faded into an indistinct haze of scattered light, insubstantial, out of reach. Then without another word she went up the ladder.

The *Ikan Yu*'s saloon was a shock. I'd expected the crude comforts of a Malay pirate; but instead Batang Sen sat half curled up and grinning in the embrace of an enormous armchair covered in rich red brocade, smoking a long German pipe on a silver rest. *Arak* in a cut-glass decanter and a copper bowl of leaf-wrapped betelnut and lime sat on the battered rosewood table between us. The carpet under us was worn Persian, and the batik hangings covered beautiful maple panelling that suggested an origin not a hundred miles from Newport, RI; at intervals hung a dispirited-looking stag's head, a dusty little stuffed crocodile and a few faded landscapes. Silver-chased lamps swung gently in the estuary swell, and the oil they burned smelt of sweet herbs. Their light mellowed Jacquie's hair to gold as she rocked slowly in a threadbare but elegant hammock chair, built perhaps for the wife of an East India merchant or one of his captains, turning her second gin sling in her long fingers. Very good gin slings they were, too; Batang Sen's steward could have taught Harry's Bar or the Raffles a thing or two. But she was saying nothing, only humming to herself, and her eyes were looking at nothing in particular.

That worried me. I'd tried to tell her about the Spiral, and after a few minutes of breathless or angry disbelief she seemed to have accepted it at last. But I remembered how the whole thing had affected Clare, left her in a sort of dreamy daze of irresponsibility. It had led her to do things shockingly out of her English-rose character – on the surface, anyway. Jacquie was older, of course, and probably a lot brighter; but the day's events must have given her a hell of a jar. They'd left me pretty shaky, and I'd had some idea what was going on.

And now she was hearing me explain them to Ape, which wasn't the most enjoyable thing I'd ever done. With her there I was trying to play down the business with Rangda as much as possible. 'Just one of the bar girls, that was all. I'd met her there the first time, after that bit with the dacoits.'

Ape snorted again. 'And it never for one moment enters that dried pea you have for a brain she is maybe decoy?'

'No! Anyway, I was . . . upset. I'd been beaten up, I'd had the priests badgering me with doubts about the whole business, I'd got a bit drunk, and . . . there were other pressures. I was upset.'

'So you go look up a slice of cheap *bumsen!*' said Ape witheringly. 'Make it so easy for them, you just as well hand them the keys!'

'I wasn't looking for anything or anybody! She was just there, she picked me up! Don't think I'd just go off with any little tart, do you? She—' I stopped.

'*Ja?*' Ape pounced. 'What is it, then? What's so special about this one, that you forget all your caution?'

I glared at him. 'For you to gloat?'

He thumped a gnarled hand on the table. 'I? I gloat over nothing, this least of all! I seek to understand what happens to you! So I may guard against it, perhaps even find back what you so foolishly let slip! So you tell! Or I scrub my paws of all this and you with it!'

I backed off before the fury in those strangely hooded eyes. 'All right! All right! I'd met her before, she'd been pretty nice to me. I knew she fancied me, or seemed to. But most of all, it was because, well, she . . . looked like somebody, that was all.' I stole a glance at Jacquie, but she still stared out into space, humming softly. No way I could come right out and say *I wanted the woman because she looked like Jacquie and I couldn't have her*; but it was the truth. 'Somebody I'd known. Somebody I'd begun to realise I was missing, missing rather a lot. There she was; and I thought the container was well out of harm's way.'

'And you didn't warn him,' added te Kiore.

'I also do not tell him not to stick his head in a meatgrinder!' snapped Ape. 'Or any other of him! Though I may!' He dragged his sausage fingers through his hair, and grew calmer. 'But so much is what I need to know. She had some way to you, this girl, to that of you which is yet empty. She opened that way – and Something flowed in, and filled you, and bent your knowledge, your very being to its will. Whatever this thing is that this girl serves, it has you going off to seize the container you most want to protect.' He reached out and prodded me in the chest with a heavily ridged nail. 'So, at the behest of that within you, yes, you did climb naked down a wall of forty floors – aye, and back up. Yes, you did lead a horde of who knows what creatures, minor powers or worse. The watchman, he saw and told true. You were possessed.'

I gave a great shudder of nausea. I felt as if slugs coursed along my veins, as if my innards were filled with trails of bitter slime. 'I should've known! That little *bitch* . . . '

'Perhaps not so human,' contributed Batang Sen, and puffed at his pipe.

'Possessed!' I grated, hand to mouth, fighting to suppress the retching. 'Christ, just the idea of it – hate it – makes me sick—'

'It would,' nodded Ape. 'Those who are not vulnerable it does not much concern. It happens to you before, has it not?'

'Not against my will! Not in the end.'

'Because to help others, yes?' The cutting edge left his voice, a little. 'But this also you wanted, though you know it not. She uses the very emptiness you feel of your life, and this loneliness.' Behind me the chair creaked abruptly. 'Her way to you is through your desires. In slaking those, so she breaks through your inhibitions, your defences.' He sighed. 'True, I guess not they have such hold over you, or I take more carefulnesses. A bitch she is not, this girl. More like a Trojan whore, for who knows what powers! But now we have no way to finding out.'

'What puzzles me,' remarked te Kiore into the crashing silence that followed, 'is why these bleeders went and used a flamin' ute to wheel off the container. I mean, when they'd all those *garuda* birds and things – eh?'

Ape looked as distant and blank as Jacquie. 'The birds? That is another attack, of another origin. Remember, more than one power is ranged against us here. One fails to take the container from us by force. Another, subtler, prefers subterfuge.' He shrugged massively. 'Seems they are right.'

Very carefully and coldly I placed my empty glass down on the table, afraid I was about to crush it. I choked down the nausea, and the anger rose instead, till my temples pounded and I felt a red haze hovering around my sight. 'Let me tell you one thing, Ape! Whatever powers they were – all the powers of Hell standing in my way, even! – I am *still* going to get that container back.'

'*Bonzer!*' whooped te Kiore, and clapped his huge hands. But Batang Sen stirred, leaned forward and squirted a stream of scarlet betel saliva into the ornate silver cuspidor at his side.

'*Tuan* Stephen,' he said with delicate seriousness, his weathered face crinkling uneasily, 'a bargain you make with us for gold, and we are not bounders to go back on it, no? What you ask us to face, we face with you. But of all the powers of Hell you speak – that, and no less, indeed may be the problem.'

Jacquie stirred. 'Oh, what's the point of just sounding off, Steve? You know they'll only go and smash open the container before we or anyone else could get to it. What's to stop them?'

Ape suddenly bared his kerbstone teeth to the gums. 'I, *Mevrouw* – I am! They cannot harm it, not while my charms are marked upon it. Even to carry it is hard! Why they use the truck, I think. And why they leave it where it is, for the mists and rains of this holy place to wash them little by little away. Till then, even they drop it into the sea, it floats and may be found! By means I know of, if no other!' He glared at me from under beetling brows. 'You are serious, you still want to take them on? Okay, maybe I give you one more chance! *Steward!*'

His roar brought the little fat Indian running. Ape kicked the captain's spittoon. 'Go bring me another like that, a bowl, a pisspot even, so it is clean! And water, much of it! *Maar en schiet op, we hebben hast*! Or you make quick rebirth as a mangy baboon!'

The steward winked at the rest of us and toddled off;

evidently he didn't take Ape's threats too seriously. He reappeared with a startlingly ornate silver punchbowl on an equally florid tray, and a heavy pitcher. The inscription on the bowl was almost impossible to make out, except for what looked like a ship's name, *Quedagh Merchant*, in something like 18th-century script. I glanced at the captain, who smiled seraphically. 'Present from very old friend, now decease.'

'I can imagine – hey!' Ape's massive fingers had clamped around both my wrists.

'Definitely you touch the container?' he rumbled.

'Yes – I've still got paint under my fingernails, look! So?'

He nodded his head. 'Then it is you will tell us where it lies!' Still holding my hands, he tipped some of the water into the bowl, gestured over it a minute and muttered.

'What does he mean, you?' whispered Jacquie behind his back.

'I don't know. I saw the old man, Le Stryge, try something like this, but not quite—'

'Sssh!' said Ape sharply, and gestured again. He drew my hands forward and over the punchbowl, and snatching up the pitcher with his other hand, he added, 'Now think! Of where you were, of what first you saw there – and of the container!' With a soft hissing word he slowly poured the remaining water over my fingers. I struggled to think, to recapture that shock of recognition, the impact in the mist. For an instant nothing happened, then with an impatient spitting growl Ape bent down and blew sharply on the water. That quickly, it boiled. Steam drifted across its surface, and suddenly I was thinking of that menacing, formless whiteness that had swallowed us. 'Hard!' panted Ape, his own brow trickling with sweat. 'Bend your brain till it creak! Harder!'

And it did feel as if I was straining against something, till my whole body shivered with the tension; as if I was somehow a conduit for an interplay of conflicting energies, torqueing this way and that.

A drop of sweat trickled down behind my ear and into the steaming water. Something raced across it like spreading oil, the mists cleared, and I saw, clearly, not the base of the bowl but the tossing tops of a forest, smoking now under a lashing rainstorm, and just at the rim the merest edge of dull grey stone, water spewing above it out of a gargoyle's mouth. The dribble of cold water across my fingers changed abruptly, became stinging hot and slanted, tilted as if some invisible wind drove it off course. Right over to the bowl's rim it drifted, still falling at that impossible angle, struck the silver edge and sizzled into stinging steam droplets.

The image vanished. Ape flung loose my hands, pushed me back and rocked back into his own chair. A blast of steam cannoned out of the bowl and splashed against the coachroof. As it dissipated, I cautiously peered over the edge of the punchbowl. It was dry and empty.

'Careful!' Jacquie exclaimed. 'It must be red hot!'

Ape grinned at her again, seized my wrist in that impossible grasp and pressed my hand flat against the rim. It was pleasantly cool. He slid it around; at one point droplets still clung to the surface. He glanced at te Kiore. 'There. That way. You, sailing master, you say what? South-southeast?'

Te Kiore shrugged. 'Southeast, more. Indonesia. Bali, even. You couldn't get any closer?'

Ape released my hand. 'Ask *Mynheer* Stephen here. He felt it. They fight hard to turn away prying eyes, them. But not hard enough, this time.'

'Yeah, I sort of noticed,' the Maori admitted, glancing up at the moist patch on the saloon ceiling. 'Just as well you weren't reading entrails, eh? Southeast's the best I can do. What the hell's down that way that fits your description? Place is lousy with temples.'

'Not like this one,' Jacquie insisted, frowning intently. 'So large, and so alone – I thought of Angkor Wat, but I've been there, it wasn't the same at all, not the style, even. Southeastward . . .'

She was accepting what she'd just seen – divination, magic. Entering into the spirit of it, in a way neither Dave nor Clare ever had. What was she going to make of the Spiral, or it of her?

Batang Sen had clambered silently out of his chair and over to a cabinet at the end of the saloon. He came back holding what looked like a pair of carven-headed staves, and sent one rolling across the table with a flourish. A huge chart of Southeast Asian seas, a Victorian-looking affair on linen with names in Dutch, unrolled between us. We all leaned over it. Southeastward from Bangkok . . .

The three voices were simultaneous, a kind of unholy chord – Jacquie's squeal, te Kiore's whoop and Ape's satisfied grunt. Three fingers stabbed down, Jacquie's dwarfed by two massive paws. They looked at each other, and said in unison, '*Jawa!*'

'Many temple,' nodded Batang Sen. 'Buddha temple, Shiva temple. Borobodur, Prambanan, Ratu Boku . . . '

'*Borobodur*!' breathed Jacquie. 'The Temple Hill! It could be! I've read about it – but I've never seen it. It could be. It was huge, all right. And it had *stupa* – you know, those bell things – they cover Buddha statues, usually. But it was all surrounded with jungle . . . No, it couldn't be. Damn and blast. Nothing's overgrown like that on Jawa nowadays.'

'Nowadays?' echoed Ape, his guttural voice softened to a sort of eerie croon. 'But now lives shorter than a mayfly, and all the past is one. For many long centuries forest surrounds the Hill *stupa*, before it is found again and made clear by foreign men. And so forest surrounds it still, its essence, its eternal self, the long shadow it casts, far out into the Spiral. The forest . . . and more. Borobodur is always a place of mists. Often, even at noon.'

Jacquie looked again. 'Wait a minute. Borobodur. Jawa . . . ' Her voice sounded a little unsteady. 'Jawa's an island. In Indonesia. It's hundreds of miles away – halfway to Bali, isn't it, or more? You're telling me that an hour or two ago we just . . . *stepped* there? And back?'

I nodded. 'That's the way it seems to be.'

She retreated from the table, sat down hard in her chair. The fingers she put to her lips trembled slightly. 'Can . . . anyone do that? Out . . . out here?'

'No. Ape was saying how much power it must take.' I leaned on the chairback, rocking her gently, and ran a hand over her hair. She hardly seemed to notice. 'He probably could, though.'

Ape lifted his shaggy head. 'Do not believe it! The Borobodur, that is a place of great—' he made a heavy punching gesture, and a deep visceral grunt, '*mmmph*! Last remnant of old faiths outside Bali. Hindu and Buddhist both, and within them what is older than either, what is of the Ancestors. Who dares make such use of the Temple Hill is not lightly to be meddled with; their *mmph*! must be great also. Yet even they have not the force to just carry you off from where you sit; they must open gateways for you to walk through, and Gates that are gates already, and they cannot do it often. Me, that is not in my powers at all.' He looked sombre. 'They have limit. Both in space, and in time. We must work fast.' He bent back over the chart again.

I found myself wondering what Ape's limits really were. Everyone had said how powerful Le Stryge was; yet, remembering his divination and Ape's, if anything, Ape's was more impressive. And I'd never seen old Stryge do anything so direct as blasting that gate. In fact, I was inclined to suspect Ape of being a very powerful sorceror indeed, next to Stryge; or had I never seen Stryge's fullest powers? I shivered again.

'Work fast? But . . . what are we going to *do*?' demanded Jacquie.

'We go there, of course,' I said. 'And we bloody well take the container back.'

She cocked her head suspiciously. 'We, meaning you? Plus of course me?'

Ape darted a fierce glance at us. '*Ja*, if you are tired of life! Now they have the container, what use have they for *Mynheer* Fisher alive? So they have no more fumblings through their blockade, him, if they can, they will now kill. *Platch*! Squash like flyspit.'

'Boy, you're encouraging,' I told him. 'What else is new?'

'Steve,' said Jacquie sharply. 'He means it!'

'Sure I do. And not just him. Better you take yourself off, *haastens*. Yourself, who is part of this Project, if they find you with him, also they'll kill.'

Her eyelids fluttered, and she looked down at the tabletop for a moment. 'I don't care.'

'Jacquie, listen—'

'*I don't care*! You came to this Project a month or two back, and I still don't know what it is you're expecting to get out of it—'

'*Get* out of it?'

'—but *I've* been working on it for the last year and a half! I've been on Bali and I love it, and I've got a bloody big score of my own to settle for that last little episode, and if there's something enough to make *you* risk your precious neck for it then there ought to be a damn sight more for me, oughtn't there? *Well*?'

'Wind's gettin' up a beaut, eh?' remarked te Kiore, into the ringing silence. It didn't work.

'So,' snapped Jacquie. 'If we've got to get there so fast somebody'd better start some practical organisation round here! I'd better see about scaring up some plane reservations, hadn't I? Or charter an executive plane – I could even get a Learjet in from Kai Tak. If your ante's high enough to make you spend that kind of money, Steve?'

'What bloody ante – oh, stuff it, Jacquie!' One minute support, the next back to the old cynical bit again. I couldn't figure her out, and right now I couldn't take much more. 'You don't understand. Not me, not any of it, not yet. *This*—' I stamped my foot. 'This is our fastest way to Jawa. Right here!'

I felt suddenly weary, and rather scared. I turned to the captain. '*Tuan* Batang, you said you'd go along with our deal. And we bargained for some trouble, yes. But getting that container back, it means a trek ashore, a search. And the chances are it could mean a fight, maybe a really bloody one.'

Batang gave the smile of the wise serpent, and spat scarlet saliva into his spittoon. 'Not first time, old chap. Bargain's bargain.'

'But the crew? How about them?'

'Bunch of bloody desperadoes,' contributed te Kiore cheerfully. 'Pay 'em high enough, they'd do anything. Or anyone. Cut their own heads off for a ten percenter off the top, no clawbacks.'

I grinned. 'Now for *that* I came prepared! I've had my friend Dave active in the gold market, he's rather good at that kind of thing. With what he's left me in the hotel safe I think we can manage a bit more than ten per cent.'

'Put it to 'em,' suggested the Maori. 'Show 'em the colour of your cash. Nothing like that for whippin' up a bit of the ole rag! But best you do it fast. If we're going to catch these bleeders, we gotta spread canvas for the dawn wind – right, skip?'

I stood up. 'Then you'd better put us ashore. Somewhere we can cross back into the Core again without too much trouble. And no goddamn Gates! I'll go back to my hotel, show up again on shore in about four hours, okay? Come on, Jacquie, we'll drop you off on the way.'

She rose, slowly, her eyes narrowed, her lips compressed. Her voice was cold and steady, and she looked Oriental as hell. 'I told you, didn't I, Stephen Fisher? I'm sticking with you till you get that container back. Whatever this weird world is you've wandered into, whatever you've got mixed up with – gods and devils and magicians, and whatever your own little game is. Because I knew you once and I know you still and you've *always* had some little game going!'

Surprisingly, her breath caught a moment, her lips trembled. 'Maybe it's bad and maybe it's good. Or part of it is – or harmless at least. Or that's what you think. But now you're playing it with the lives of a whole island, a people, a culture. And I'm just a PR person in the Project, a fixer, a small administrator – but I'm all of the Project there is, right here. And so I'm sticking with you till you get our bloody property back! *Right*, Mr Fisher?'

'Now there's a mouthful for you, sport!' said te Kiore amiably, rolling his bulk to the cabin door. 'Take my advice, you don't say one bloody word an' just does as the lady tells you. *Boat's crew! Leap to it, you pack of gimpy joeys! Two to go ashore!*' He grinned over his shoulder, a ghastly mask in the lamplight's deep shadows. 'And if my arse ain't entirely out the window, two back aboard, an' all!'

The night was hot and humid again, and the streetlamps flared in a stifling haze as the lone taxi cruised slowly down the dockland street, its loose exhaust tinkling over the uneven surface. The driver tossed his head back, face twitching in a rictus that was not a grin. 'You no like I go faster? Man could get a-hurt aroun' here!'

I shifted the lumpy airline bag that was cutting off the circulation in my leg. 'It's not far now. I don't want to miss the spot. Then you can go as fast as you like.'

He slapped one hand on top of the wheel and waved the other in wild protest. 'You no getting out here? You tourist, you no know! Muggers here, dope guys, crazy man, all! Me, I live tough, I no get out an' walk here! No girls here, no gamble, no music, no nothing – I take you nice place, very safe! Friends of mine they run it, they no rip you off – no so much . . . '

'Here,' I told him. 'Just at the alley, here.'

He braked hard, but caught my arm as I was offering him a suitable note. '*Khun*, I mean it! I got wife, kid – how I go home sleep tonight, I leave you an' lady here this crappy place? I drive you anywhere, no more charge – huh?'

He obviously meant it, and I was touched. So, by her face, was Jacquie. 'We know what we're doing,' she said. 'But thanks anyway. You go on home and don't worry about us.'

'That's right,' I said. 'No, no change. We'll be all right.'

He hesitated, doubtfully, eyes flicking around. 'Is not just men here,' he said unwillingly, wincing as he expected us to laugh. 'Other things, too, very bad!'

I smiled, and reached down to our baggage. I dug my fingers into the paper of the long parcel, and tore it away with one sweep. I held the sword up, and it glittered, far brighter than the distant streetlamps could account for, glittered and flashed with the cold light of stars that never shone in the skies overhead. Jacquie stared, sucking in her breath as if ice had touched her, and the driver lifted his eyes to it with a dazzled awe.

'You heard the lady,' I told him softly, and swung the great blade once, twice with a soft singing rush. 'We know what we're doing. We're of this place – though you probably couldn't guess how.'

To my surprise, he seemed to. His mouth hung open a moment, but his eyes took on a relaxed, remote expression, as if he stared into great distances, or into memories long forgotten. He nodded in quick understanding.

'Go back to your wife and child,' Jacquie told him. 'Sleep in peace. Don't worry. *Sawaddee kha*!'

He nodded again, slipped the taxi back in gear and roared off with the exhaust jangling in protest behind him. We looked after him. I wondered what long-buried memories we'd sparked off there, what sudden recollections of strange passengers picked up for even stranger destinations and soon forgotten, leaving only a faint and haunting unease. Then Jacquie looked around at the black alley behind us. 'Well, we told the man,' she said, only a little shakily. 'We know what we're doing. Okay, let's do it.'

We heaved up our small pile of baggage, and looking very carefully around us, ready to leap back at the first touch of any thicker mists, we stepped into the muggy darkness of the alley. The laden flight bag cut into my shoulder with every swing; I hoped the strap would last out. A sewer miasma rose around us; I heard Jacquie choke, but her mind was evidently on something else.

'You – when you held up that sword there – '

'Yes?'

'You looked . . . I don't know. Not different, exactly. Almost more yourself. As if you really were what you look like . . . a champion. A – a paladin.'

My turn to catch my breath. I'd given that name once, half jokingly, to someone I'd suddenly begun to admire, someone I was drawn to. And she'd been vastly flattered by it. To hear it of myself; and from . . . But the very intensity of the feeling made me want to shrug it off lightly. 'Thank'ee for them kind words, missie.'

'Oh.' I could almost see her lips curl impatiently. 'Don't worry. I know it's just appearances. But it'd be nice if you could only live up to them now and again . . . Isn't that the harbour?'

It hadn't been, but suddenly, it seemed, it was. Or maybe I just wasn't looking hard enough; but the margins of Core and Spiral were full of such tricks. What had been darkness at the alley's end didn't change, visibly; there was no one moment when it was black, another where there were lights. It was more as if those spots before your eyes, that faint filmy shimmer of blinked-away moisture, turned out to have been the distant lights and the ripple on mist-shrouded water all the time. Maybe they had been; it was past saying, now. A second later we had boardwalk beneath our feet, and a boat waiting at the quay's end. From out on the water came a faint chuffing, and between the masts a dull gleam of red-lit smoke. The *Ikan Yu* was firing up.

We hailed the boat, and within moments our luggage was expertly swung aboard, and ourselves after it. Batang's bosun, a huge New Guinea tribesman called Walan, glanced alertly at my drawn sword and up at the darkened quay. 'You go have trouble, *kiap*?'

'No. Just ready for it.'

'Figures. Pull away, there!' Silently, as if the oars were muffled, we glided out across a pool of greyness towards the darker shadow of the ship.

Te Kiore and Batang Sen were waiting on the poopdeck as we came clattering up the ladder. It was pulled up after us, and the boat hoisted swiftly to the davits. The captain, still smoking, was leaning on the heavy brass-capped binnacle that held wheel, compass, speaking tubes and the engine-room telegraph, while the Maori mate eased himself up from the helmsman's bench and lumbered across the deck to greet us. 'Nice timing, mate! We was just wondering whether t'set the ole Ape scrying for you all over again!' He moved closer and added quietly 'Glad we didn't have to. Your mate doesn't seem himself, quite.'

'Ape? What could be the matter with him?'

'Oh, nothing much. Just sort of, well, low. Depressed an' impatient at the same time, as if he's got something real important to do an' can't get on with it, and it's gnawing away at him. Like if he were an abo, it'd be walkabout fever, when they get the urge t'just wander. An' sometimes if they can't, like they're in jail or some'at, they gets sick.' He shook his head. 'Lot of 'em die in the white man's jail, aboes. Not that your mate's dying or anything. He just . . . ' He shrugged his massive shoulders.

151

'I'll have a word with him in a moment. How long before we sail?'

'Not long!' chipped in the captain, sniffing at the mist. 'Light soon! And Lady Ushas brings us our wind!'

'So have we time enough to get all hands together?'

Te Kiore glanced at the captain. 'Sure!' He picked up a brass speaking trumpet and bellowed, '*All hands! All hands aft*! Shift, you louse-licked scubberlutchers! I'll tar your scuts and light 'em for lamps! Aft with you!'

The crewmen I'd seen had looked hard enough. Now, as they joked and jostled together below the poop rail, they looked absolutely terrifying. Jacquie recoiled as she saw just what she'd shipped with, and I didn't blame her a bit. There were Malays in colourful shirts and baggy trousers, hair bound with anything from rags to gold fillets, there were Polynesians in *lavalavas* and various Indonesian tribesmen in *sarongs*, flashing filed teeth; there were New Guineans like Walan, a lot of them, black-skinned and frizzy-haired, wearing anything from ornate shirts and breeches of 18th-century cut to bits of grass apron. There were Indians in loincloths and gold ornaments, Japanese in coarse cotton prints, there were even some Westerners, though it was hard to tell them apart, their skins tanned the shade of old oak, their clothes a weird amalgam. But each and every one of them carried at least one sword, and a selection of knives about their belts, from which their hands never strayed too far. Some had small crossbows, Chinese-style, slung across their backs; one grizzled Westerner leaned on a longbow shaft, with a sheaf of flights lifting above his shoulder. Some of the New Guineans had stabbing spears, and there was the odd blunderbuss or flintlock pistol here and there, though firearms, like steam engines, were hard to maintain in the Spiral, among whose mazes no major industry could flourish.

But white, black, brown or yellow, whatever the shade there was a common cast to their faces. It wasn't one I liked. It was made of lines and scowls and scars, the marks of the wrong kind of experience; it went just too well with those weapons. So did a habitual catlike stance, too ready to pounce, too afraid of being pounced on, or both. They fitted te Kiore's definition exactly – a bunch of bloody desperadoes. I was glad they were on our side, and I wanted them kept there; there was no way I was looking forward to cajoling this lot. Suppose they started heckling – with arrows?

But I needed them ready and willing. They were risking their lives, but that was part and parcel of survival out here; you could live a long time, but you had to eat along the way, and nobody's cash lasted forever. So, since they had to risk themselves, better they knew why and what for. When you thought about it, it became just a management problem like any other, no different in principle from motivating an office or pep-talking a sales force. In fact, it occurred to me, these guys had a lot in common with some sales forces I'd seen. You don't know carnivores till you've faced a roomful of commission-only men.

At Batang's nod I stepped forward. The sword was still in my hand, and as I laid it on the rail the hubbub died away. 'Yes!' I said, loudly. 'I've got some fighting to do. Some son-of-a-bitch has stolen the cargo you're meant to be carrying this run – cargo that means life or death for a people, island people like many of you. And in stealing it he made a monkey out of me! Getting that thing back's my word, my honour. But I'll be needing help – your help! It won't be easy. We've got powerful enemies; we'll have spells and swords to face. That wasn't altogether in the deal your skipper and I made – so every man who's with us in this gets extra. A bonus!' I dug open the flight bag, tore at the packet within and dripped the coins it spilled through my fingers, sequins and thalers and crowns and florins, Spanish ounces and little Chinese bars, with a low clinking music. 'In gold!'

Something like a wave washed over the crew as they crowded closer to see, a rising rumble of excitement.

'Every man's share, twice over, for helping us in this venture now! Every man, skipper to seaman!' A low rumble rose on my words, and a breath of excitement which carried me away with the rest. 'And if we get it back,' I roared, 'and to its destination, safe – then I'll give as much again! See it here!'

I snatched a double handful of the stuff, impossibly weighty, maybe two thousand's worth or more, and thrust it high above my head like an offering. Maybe it was accepted; for I saw it spring into sudden flame in the eyes of the crewmen, sear through to their minds and set fire in their hearts and their guts, not only for the worth of it but the challenge and prize that alone can make a longer life worth the living. It flashed and flared in my upheld hands, a brilliant beacon flame, caught in the first forerunner ray of the swift tropical dawn.

'*Ushas!*' cried Batang Sen, and pressed his gnarled hands together as if in prayer, lifting them as I lifted mine. Then he flung them down and slapped the brass binnacle like a gong, shrilling out orders in his cracked old voice. '*Hands to stations, by Jove! Mis' Mate, weigh ankahu! Fu'steam!*'

'*Capstan crew!*' roared te Kiore, striding across the bridge. '*Stand by to weigh anchor! Topmen up, stokers down, jump to it! Or I'll stuff you in the boilers and fry my rice in your dripping! Fit those bars lively, capstans! Lively, damn you! Lean now, and heave away! Heave!*'

The noise was appalling, orders shouted, feet thundering on the scoured white planking, throbbing and stirring in the very deck beneath our feet. The anchor chain came rattling and clanking up to the cathead. The slender smokestack thrummed and belched a sudden puff of soot and cinders, high enough so the rising breeze took it and cast it clear of the decks. A bell rang, and the engine-room telegraph swung.

'*Full steam, skipper!*' shouted te Kiore. Batang Sen yelled something, grabbed a lanyard on the binnacle and heaved. At the crown of the stack a steam-whistle loosed its earstabbing blast. Jacquie, clamping her ears tight, stumbled and almost fell as the deck lurched. I caught her, steadied her in my arms, and that felt good, one with the other old exhilarations that came coursing through me. The thudding beneath our feet changed its note suddenly, became a deep slow chugging, and from overside the mist boiled and thrashed suddenly as first the port and then starboard paddles began to turn and bite. I heard them swish and thresh in water, but from their blades as they lifted only the mists ran in ragged streamers. Slowly, ponderously, the great schooner began to turn, circling around to place her bow into the light, heading into the sunrise as if it were the harbour roads.

I held Jacquie tight, her back against me, my arms clasped around her slender waist; the throb of the paddles pulsed through us as one. The bows dipped and lifted, dipped deeper, lifted higher as we rode out beyond the harbour on to the endless swell, entered the ancient rhythms of the seas of all the world and beyond. We turned our bows towards the open ocean, that one great infinite Place that holds all others in its clasp; and where sky and sea met, each took its colour from the other, mirrors of mirrors, till all boundary between them vanished in the blaze of dawn.

Then beyond our bowsprit, for the sails were still furled, I saw clearly the sky that opened before us, the avenue in the clouds at that joining of sea and sky, the archipelago of islands and the blazing channels of brightness between. It was not the same archipelago, not the same islands, as I'd sailed out through once before; they were paler, brighter, less grey, a hundred tropical pastel hues upon a sapphire brightness that seared the very eyes. The golden light fringed their edges with golden beaches, and upon those beaches white surf was beating; above them seabirds flew and cried their exaltation. The breezes that blew around us were warmer, caressing breaths with richer, heavier scents of cedar and cinnamon, cardamom and cloves, pepper, ginger, turmeric and tamarind, the languid muskiness of orchids, the sharp tang of dusty roads and crumbling soil. In my arms Jacquie stiffened, eyes wide with overwhelmed wonder. I remembered how that sight had first moved me, the daunting vastness of all things, the thrill of limitless possibility, the chill wind out of infinity that blew through your very bones yet woke a troubled sleeper to tingling life. I remembered the words that Jyp had cried. I echoed them, and with me te Kiore, and others among the crew. For however long he lived, surely no man could altogether lose the magic of that moment when the deck began to skip higher still beneath his feet, and never quite dipped down again – borne aloft on the tides of light, the roads of the sunrise, into the sea of azure, the infinity of the Spiral.

'*Over the dawn! Over the airs of the Earth! We're under way!*'

As if in answer canvas broke out on the foremast and main, sails fell, billowed and boomed tight with a jerk that shook the ship. On the mizzen a gaff rose up and a triangular steadying sail swung out, its whiteness shining against the stream of smoke that trailed out above, till the wind whipped it to nothingness. I felt almost as light, as immaterial, as if any breeze could whip me away; but Jacquie weighed against me, bone and muscle shifting with every gasping breath, the delicate solidity of coral wrapped in silk. She struggled suddenly like a protesting cat, pulled my hands apart and wriggled loose. She clutched the taffrail, panting; I was about to touch her shoulder when a heavy hand landed on mine.

'Skipper's compliments to you both,' rumbled te Kiore, 'and once the steward's shown you your cabins, will you come and drink a glass or two to a profitable voyage?'

I caught Jacquie's eye and nodded. Ceremony and ritual could be very important out here, and manners always were.

She smiled weakly. 'Tell him we'd be glad to, in just a moment. I could use it – only not arrack, *if* you don't mind!' She straightened her shirt, hitched up her jeans, smoothed her hair, avoiding my eye. I didn't press her. We had a lot to talk about; but not there, not then.

A folding tray-table was set up out on the overhanging stern gallery; there Batang and the Maori were sitting, and with them Ape. They rose when Jacquie appeared, rose and bowed, Batang in the formal Malay manner, te Kiore in such a Victorian way I began to wonder when he'd got his education; but Ape barely looked up, and mumphed something that might have been Dutch or double-Dutch. It was so unlike his normal robust energy I thought at first he must be seasick. When Jacquie acted concerned, though, he roused himself enough to deny any illness. '*Gezond bin ik*! A time approaches, that is all. My time, by when I must be back, as I agreed.'

'We'll get you there,' I said. 'Don't worry.'

He nodded. 'I know. But more and more I think of it, and of how this homecoming shall be. Already I am gone too long; and a task awaits me there also. Over that I have no choice but worry.'

He would say no more; but from then on he made an effort, and roused himself, and we soon forgot his black mood. Soon, because Jacquie suddenly looked up, hand to mouth, and exclaimed, 'It's getting dark!'

Te Kiore jerked a thumb astern. 'Kind of a habit, I understand, when the sun sets. Any complaints, you take it up with the proper authorities.'

'Oh . . . of course . . . when the . . . but it was dawn just a . . . less than an hour ago . . . *you're laughing at me again!*'

'Just the same as everybody did with me,' I chuckled. I couldn't help it. Batang was tittering like an apprentice ghoul, and even Ape was snorting and snuffling into his beard. 'And that's the answer they all gave me, too. East of the sun and west of the moon, remember? Across the dawn and into another night. But it was no use telling you till you actually saw it. You wouldn't have believed it any more than I would.'

Jacquie swallowed the remainder of her last sling in one gulp, and then stood up slowly and with great dignity. 'I think I am getting a headache. And I am therefore going to my cabin to lie down. And whatever side of the sunrise we happen to be on, you are a typical pack of bloody self-satisfied males. That is all I want to say at this juncture.' Her shoulders jarred with a stifled hiccup, and she wove an extremely careful path down the poopdeck. I went after her to see she didn't fall down the companionway, but she was already stalking through the saloon. The door to the guest cabins slid closed with a crash that must have hurt her more than me.

'Well,' remarked te Kiore, stretching, 'she's about got me to rights, anyhow. Fancy another? *Steward*!'

'At least she'll be comfortable. Those cabins of yours—'

'Ain't they something? Must've set the bloke who built 'er back a bob or two. Not so big, but real extravagant stuff, those marble heads and all. He was right to spend it, though.'

'How, especially?'

Batang grinned, and it wasn't a grin I especially liked. 'Te Kiore, he teach me one of your sayings – *You can't take it with you*! Okay?'

'Oh,' I said, thoughtfully. Very thoughtfully. 'Okay.'

As the night wore on the wind rose, and after a while the paddlewheels were disengaged and the engine fell silent. We were making good headway, and Batang was conserving fuel for later. I didn't feel like going to bed. I was too busy savouring the feel of it all again, the taut song of the rigging, the stars overhead, the strange formations of the clouds around us, sunk in shadow under the brilliant moon. And beneath our hull, stretching out to an infinite horizon, a sea as insubstantial as a vision, a calmly undulating expanse of mist. Perhaps, beneath it, there was glass-calm water; or perhaps we truly were above the airs of Earth. The sight didn't disturb me the way it did once. It was as if now, here, I had Jacquie to do all my doubting and my disbelief for me, where I had only to accept the reality of things that had faded, like faint recollections of a once-favourite book. This was the night that lay behind every dawn; this was the shadow of each new day, that trailed it around the world, of all days, through which one could pass, if one only had the skill, from any one to any other. This was the shadow of time itself, the infinite seaway of the Spiral.

Walan at the helm was singing softly; a song from the Trobriands, he told me, about their legendary race-mother Imdeduya.

*Imdeduya, Imdeduya, kwanuwedi bakenu*
*Avila yokwai e! yegu Yolina*
*Laula o la Neamu, laula o la nebwogegu*
*Newa wegu kesaie, nemtamata wowogu*
*Imdeduya, Imdeduya!*

*Imdeduya, let me lie on your breasts,*
*I am the Midnight Sun,*
*Lashed by the waves of the sea,*
*I waste away,*
*By night and day I yearn for you, Imdeduya!*

I leaned on the rail and thought of what might have been, of
how I might have lingered out on the Spiral and gone home late or
never, of what I might have become then. I was so deep in thought
I jumped, startled, when someone leaned on the rail right beside
me.

'Oh,' I said with breathless originality, 'it's you. I didn't expect
to see you up.'

Jacquie sighed. 'Those bloody paddles! I couldn't get to sleep
for them at first. Eventually the noise fell into place somehow,
lulled me asleep. Then they went and turned them off, didn't
they? And now I can't get back to sleep again.'

'You're better off out here in the fresh air, anyhow. It's
beautiful, isn't it?'

Her sigh this time was very different. 'Oh yes. Disturbing,
though. I can't believe someone like you . . . no, that's unkind. I
just . . . didn't think you'd appreciate anything like this. Didn't
think you were the type.'

'Neither did I. But I seem to be, underneath.'

'I wonder . . . ' she said, surprisingly timid. 'Listen, Steve, this is
probably stupid, but . . . you said that out here, beyond the Hub
or the Core or whatever, it's full of *shadows* of places?'

'Shadows is a word. You could call them projections, maybe;
the images the Core throws out into timelessness. Overlaid on
one another, often; so you find all sorts of times side by side, or
muddled up. I've sailed with a seventeenth-century captain who
could drive a car, or claimed to.'

She shook her head. 'That sounds confusing – jumbled.'

'What little I've seen, it isn't. Often the shadow seems more real
than the actual place, I'm told.'

158

'Truer, you mean?'

'You're getting the idea quicker than I did. Yes; a sort of distillation of its special qualities. What makes it what it is. The idea, the archetype of a place. Even one that never actually existed.'

'It fits,' she said thoughtfully. 'You see, I was wondering – could that be true of us, as well? Of people who come out here? You – I see something like that in you. You can be the biggest cold-hearted bastard—'

'I know. Don't rub it in. That was years ago. I'm not the same person, any more than you are.'

'Not just to me, I mean. But that was never all you were, or how on earth do you think I'd have fallen for you in the first place? What I see out here, it's still the same you, but it's more so in some ways, less in others . . . Oh, sh— sugar.' She leaned her elbows on the rail and jammed her chin into her hands. 'It's not like that at all, not so simple. But the more I try to pin it down—'

I raised an eyebrow. 'In Spiral *veritas*, you mean?'

She tossed her blonde hair almost in my face. 'There you go. Back home you could have come up with something like that, you just wouldn't have bothered.'

'I'm not so sure,' I remarked, feeling a strange churning turbulence somewhere, as if the paddles were starting again. 'I have changed, I know that, since we . . . Hell. Since I dumped you. But I mean, that's natural, it's been – what was it – sixteen years, who doesn't change? Though okay, maybe it was the Spiral that put me on the right road, started me caring about other people a bit more. But then it was one bit of caring that got me out here in the first place.'

Her hair rippled silver under the moon. Level eyes peered sidelong up at me. 'You know, Steve dear, I have not got the faintest clue what you're drivelling on about.'

I drew a deep breath. 'What I'm on about is . . . You may be right. People do change out here, intensify, become more their essential selves. I've seen it happen – in both directions. So – since that's so – maybe I can say something and have you believe me. Something I wouldn't say otherwise.'

A shrug. 'Never hurts to try.'

'All right then! I . . . ' I swallowed. Come on, boy, speak up! 'I must have been raving bloody mad to ditch you. I've known that for a long time; maybe always. But I never quite admitted it;

afraid to see myself as such a total jerk. So I rationalised it, I suppose. Till I almost rationalised any real feeling out of my life altogether. I screwed up. Then I froze up. I hurt you horribly, and got my own fingers scalded. Almost lost my sense of touch.'

She was still leaning on the rail, face away from me. She lowered it, and her hair hid her face. Instinctively I reached out to stroke it. 'I'm not saying forgive me or anything like that. What's done's done. But . . . ' Instinctively, again, my hand slid down that smooth hair to her neck, her shoulderblades, her spine. Suddenly she straightened up, and my hand fell to her waist. She let it draw her closer, into my arms for the second time that day, facing me now, looking up, breathing my breath. Pale hair, pale skin, white silk shirt; in that jewelled light she became a glistening sculpture of snow. Yet her breasts pressed gently against me, the warmth of her body came to me through the strange soft hide I wore, and seemed to spread. My hand lay loosely on the waistband of her jeans now; I tightened my grip, and drew her to me, the other hand brushing the strands from her face, from her parted lips. I pulled her close, unresisting, moulding her supple slenderness against me, and her own arms slowly closed around my back. I pressed my lips to hers, felt the flicker of her tongue— '*Deck! Deck there! Sail hoi! Sails!*'

We flew apart, shaken, staring around us. But there was no time to find words; people seemed to be pouring on deck. The urgency in that voice was jarring.

'*What you mean, sails?*' yelled Walan.

'*In our wake! Three sail, maybe four – one more!*'

'Blow me, the beggar's right!' said te Kiore tautly. He swung his telescope slightly. 'I'm seeing at least two from down here, maybe another. Dead clear in this light. Two masts, ketch rig with tops'ls, three goddamn jibs – strewth, I know what I make of that! What about you, skipper?'

'I say! Rotten luck!' barked old Batang, more staccato than ever. 'You see? *Pinisi!*'

'Er – *what?*' exclaimed Jacquie.

'*Pinisi!*' insisted Batang furiously, flourishing the telescope in Jacquie's face. '*Boegies! Pinisi!*'

Te Kiore coughed. 'What he means is, those sails back astern are local schooners, *prahus*. But not just ordinary ones; they're all of them Boegie *prahus*, fast designs they call *pinisi*, right?'

'Oh,' said Jacquie, relieved. 'He had me a bit worried there. But the Boegies, they're the captain's own people, aren't they?'

'Too right! And, well, that may be the bloody problem. For one thing, most of them are Muslim, but Batang's old-fashioned – about six hundred years that way. He's still a Hindu.'

'Big, big problem!' nodded Batang. 'Could be cousin, could be friend. Could be all-round pirate sonuvabitch. Could be both. Out east of sunrise, could be old Boegies from evil time. If they follow us, maybe by chance. Maybe not.'

'But those are tiny craft compared to this,' I protested. 'Couldn't you just outrun them or outfight them if you had to?'

'Maybe carry big crews, many guns.'

I nodded, shivering with a double dose of adrenalin. 'And you can't send them a stay-away shot or two, can you? Not without finding out—'

A dull thud resounded down the breeze. 'Maybe we just did.'

But something burst in the air, with a loud popping crackle, and it was off to starboard. 'Firecracker!' barked Batang.

'An SOS?' said te Kiore, surprised.

'*Deck hoi!*' yelled the lookout. '*Distress call, to starboard! Pinisi, no sail!*'

We could almost see it ourselves, without telescopes, when we knew where, a white dot tossing against an empty, greying sky.

'The others must be headed out to help it!' cried Jacquie.

'Looks like it!' admitted te Kiore.

'But we're nearer – couldn't we get there sooner?'

'Yeah, with steam up. Just what I was wondering – skipper?'

The captain sucked his teeth impatiently. 'Ape? You get wizard, you ask!'

The Ape lumbered up to my side, groaning and grumbling about his broken sleep. When I told him about the *prahus* he stared blearily into the dimming darkness and sniffed the breeze. 'There is something about them – but they too are voyagers east of the sunrise, that is to expect. No strong magics – more I cannot say.'

Batang pondered, but only for a moment. He snatched up a speaking tube, and set hand to the telegraph. '*Steam up!* We go look, okay. Careful!'

As the paddlewheels chugged into life again Walan slowly turned the wheel, and overhead the yards creaked in the chilly dawn breeze as they were swung around. Jacquie and I stood close together, silent mostly, tangled in a web of inner feelings and wider worries, watching the disabled *prahu* as it grew more distinct. It looked in trouble, all right, one mast askew, listing heavily even in that gentle swell, wallowing as if ballast was shifting or water coming in. The light was growing, and I remembered with sudden vividness that strange fleeting transition, that leap between ships when infinity seemed to open beneath my feet, and then was only sea.

My unease grew, until at last I brushed a hand against Jacquie's shoulder, asking her to wait, and disappeared below. There were two reasons for that. I wanted my sword; but that was only one. At least here the guest cabins had private indoor heads, in the same slightly tarnished luxury as the rest. On the way back, the sword bobbing comfortingly along my leg, I met te Kiore, buckling the polished sword-club at his side. We exchanged slightly shamefaced grins, like two party guests looking for the back way out. 'Just a touch of the collywobbles, most like,' he said apologetically. 'Still – that hap'worth of tar never hurt, did it?'

I agreed, and we clambered back up to the deck. The light was growing now, the sky grey, the mist spiralling up in strange ragged swathes. We could see the other sails clearly now, huge top-heavy sharkfin shapes tacking in towards us at speed. The only one aboard who didn't seem to be at all excited was Ape. He was still on deck, sitting against the rail with his legs crossed and his huge boots hauled up on either knee in a sort of lotus position, like a gross and hairy parody of Buddha; but his gingery beard vibrated with very unmeditative snores. Batang himself was at the wheel, chattering incomprehensible orders; he seemed to be bringing us the long way around, circling downwind of the distressed craft. It was wallowing horribly, and figures clinging to the gunwales and dangling from the rigging flailed and shrieked at us as we closed in.

Batang gave an order, the paddles slowed and men came running up with lines; but he gave another, and I felt a familiar rumble underfoot. 'What's that?' demanded Jacquie nervously.

I gestured up the deck. A long gun-carriage, gaudily painted green with red and yellow flames, was being trundled back from the rail; a barrel of greenish bronze covered in gilt scales, with two handles cast like wings and a great gaping reptilian mouth. Men busied themselves around it. 'Not taking any chances with his relatives, is he?'

'Probably judges them by himself. Well, he's closing in. Why from the windward side? Here goes anyway – hang on!'

We lifted, clumsily, on a sudden swell; the line-men began to swing their weighted grapnels.

All hell broke loose.

The noise was stunning. I thought for a moment the cannon had gone off prematurely; then I saw it on its side, with a screaming man beneath, and smoke billowing from the deck below. Men who'd been dangling helpless a moment earlier came swinging out on ropes with demonic screeches, lines from their deck whistling up to ours; a human tide surged over the side in a clatter of steel and popping pistols. A tide of Boegie-men, right enough; instant nightmare.

Jacquie screamed, te Kiore yelled some amazing oath; maybe I shouted too, and Batang Sen jerked the whistle lanyard. But he also did something else; he spun the wheel, hard, and we swung about. The wind caught our sails, heeled us over; the swell lifted us and we tore inexorably away from the decoy ship, breaking lines and spilling half the horde of boarders in mid-leap. It was a brilliant move, one he'd obviously planned for in bringing us round to windward. Battlecries broke into screams of terror as the Boegies fell – where? The dawn broke about us, on an expanse of glittering unarguable blue sea, with never a trace of mist in sight. The paddlewheels threw up a dazzling cloud of spray as they threshed back to full speed.

Without that crucial move they would have overwhelmed us in minutes, or at least kept us engaged till the others could catch up. There must have been a hundred Boegies or more aboard that *prahu*, enough to make that very convincing list just by gathering under the gunwales. But we still had half of them, at least, and the deck became a milling battlefield, too much so. 'If they cut the stays or spike the paddles, we're mutton!' yelled te Kiore. 'Come on!'

Together we raced to the poop rail, but already the Boegies were swarming over it, popping off pistols at random. I yelled to Jacquie to get below, swung my sword and cleared three of them off the rail, then leaned over and started slashing at heads beneath. Te Kiore had reached the ladder, and was clearing his way down it with great swinging hacks. His sword-club's edge of inlaid stone simply smashed any lighter metal weapons he crossed with in a shower of sparks. He reached the deck, the Boegies swayed back and I vaulted the rail into the space they cleared, stabbing and slashing as I landed. It wasn't scientific, but it sure as hell shifted them. Te Kiore ploughed into them with great thudding blows that shattered limbs and popped skulls, sweeping their cutlasses aside like chaff, clearing a great avenue along the deck. Roaring and bellowing, he gathered the scattered crewmen in a spreading wedge behind him, like a wake, gathering up others as we passed. Pistols might have stopped him, but they'd mostly been fired off in that first mad rush; there was no time for reloading now. Charging along beside him, hacking and stabbing to either side, I saw one Boegie in our rigging take aim, only to be plucked neatly from his perch by a singing arrow from behind us. The tall longbowman was clambering up the poop ladder, choosing another mark; but a yelling Boegie sank a boat axe in his stomach and he folded.

Then I saw Jacquie still on the deck, with a pistol in both hands, levelling it at the oncoming axeman. Both barrels went off, and it flew up out of her hand; but the axeman's tunic exploded, he spun around and fell. I heard Batang's hyena cackle. To my horror Jacquie, shaking bruised hands, went cantering down the ladder right into the melee. I turned to race back, but a Boegie hacked at me with a cutlass. I parried once, twice, kicked him on the kneecap and ran him through the throat. Jacquie was picking up the longbow.

'Leave that, you idiot!' I yelled. 'You can't just use those things like a gun—'

I stopped. One fluid movement nocked an arrow, rested it on her thumb, drew back the string to line her nose and chin, then loosed. A pirate toppled from the hold hatchcover with a gargling shriek and fletches sticking from his throat. Another ran at her and I cut the legs from under him. She shot another dead in his tracks as he turned to run.

Then te Kiore and his wedge circled the hatch and came driving back through, herding the pirates into the starboard side of the deck, with nothing beyond but the railing and the sea. In that, at least, there was a chance they'd be picked up; on the deck here we were slaughtering them piecemeal. Most of them took the chance, broke, turned and leaped for their lives.

It was a pity, maybe, they'd forgotten about the paddles. The note changed, the shrieks were cut off in the dull thudding, then it was back to the same strong beat again. Jacquie winced, let her

164

bow sag and was abruptly and uncontrollably sick where she stood.

I pulled her back, tried taking her in my arms. She shook her head, but I didn't let go. 'Jacquie! You all right? Not hurt? You – I didn't know you could handle a bow!'

'Haven't for years,' she said thickly, her breath sour with fear and disgust. 'Never shot anything more than a target before. Less than ten yards – couldn't miss. The way – in his throat like that . . . ' She shook her head, as if in panic, but I held on to her. She closed her eyes a moment, and a great shudder ran through her. She felt rigid and light, like a balsa carving, hardly breathing.

Heavy hands clamped on our shoulders and forced us apart. 'Hate to break up the happy party,' said te Kiore. 'Nice work with that there one-string harp, miss. Might as well hang on to it, poor old Gamble Gold's not gonna have much use for it. But you might. We're not just outa the bushes yet. See back there?'

Three tall rigs bearing in on us, oversized sails like white sharkfins. Circling back had brought us well within their reach. And that 'distressed' schooner was hastily re-stepping its mast to come join them. Suddenly we all flinched as something screamed between the masts, a wind riffling our hair; a thump and a sizzle rang across the sunny waters.

Te Kiore swore horribly. 'In bleedin' range already! Gun crew!'

But there wasn't any gun crew. A charge of grapeshot, fired upward at point-blank range from the pirate's deck, had splintered the carriage, made shreds of the gun captain and crew on one side of it and toppled the gun on the rest. Bloody and broken, they were being hauled out now, and even with the healing powers that could be drawn upon here their outlook didn't look good. A deep revulsion swelled in me. Here were men who'd lived maybe four or five times my life or even more, being spilt like so much offal, and for what? For me, for the good name of my company? Or for Bali's rice paddies and green woods and the ancient, delicate culture they supported?

'Okay!' yelled the Maori. 'Port watch, four men! Wheel the flaming port gun across, lash her down at the mizzen gunport!'

'Port *gun*? You've only got two? And I thought the *Defiance* was a bit lightly armed!'

Te Kiore glared. 'We're a cargo boat, not a flamin' privateer! Two twelve-pounders and swivelguns at bow and stern, that's a lot for these parts. Those *prahus* must be laden to the bloody gunwales! Anyhow, we'll make it hot for them!' He beckoned crewmen to him. 'Wutai – yes, you! You're acting gun captain! And Shortass Chen, Bag O'Nails, Rukuni . . . one more . . . '

'Hey!' I said tentatively, 'I've worked a gun once or twice—'

'With ole Pierce? Bonzer, you're in! Well, don't just stand there, poxbrains! Run in, load, fire as she bloody well bears and don't stop for the formalities! Topmen, get aloft, undo those reefs and give us more canvas! Bosun, go below, break out the muskets! *Run, you festering bloody plague pustules!*'

We didn't need telling; shots were singing left and right now, and a charge of grape came spattering like hail through the steadying sail above the poop. I grabbed the rammer pole as we clattered across the deck, and even before the gun was lashed into position I was jabbing a torn cartridge down the gaping dragon-throat, following it up with rough wads of what looked like pith, on to which somebody toppled a rattling ball. More wads, and the leathery old Chinese gun captain angled the gun on our leading pursuer, opened the powder horn and was just tipping grains into the touchhole when he spun around suddenly and slumped down across the gun. I caught the horn as it fell, saw him scrabbling at his chest, coughing blood; a faint crack came down the wind.

'Muskets!' muttered the rotund Westerner called Bag O'Nails, snatching the rammer.

'At this range?'

'If they've sharpshooters. With more'n just sights to guide their lead, if I know them! Heads down, lads!'

Wutai's linstock, a length of sputtering slowmatch, rolled off across the deck; I caught it, blew on it and swung it to keep it alight. How much more powder in that touchhole? I glanced at the others, but they didn't volunteer a damn thing. I tipped in a small cone, held my breath as I tried to match the rise and fall of both vessels, made the best guess I could and gingerly touched the match to the touchhole.

A sheet of flame spurted up and all but curled my eyelashes. I felt rather than heard the crash of the gun, a spasm in the air, and dazzled as I was, saw nothing of the ball's flight. Then from astern came a thump like a huge hand beating on a barn door, a great cheer went up, and dimly I saw a mainsail fly loose from the *prahu*'s foremast, its sheets cut. The yellowish craft swung sharply into the wind, sails flapping loose, and the decoy *prahu*, next nearest, swerved narrowly out from astern and overhauled it. But almost at once the stricken sail was caught and hauled in, and they were on our tail again. There was a sudden whistle, a crash and a cloud of splinters; Chen fell screaming with one in his leg, the rest of us dodged as the gun snapped free from its anchorage and trundled like the original Juggernaut back across the deck, gathering momentum, heading for the lip of the hold. Bag O'Nails threw himself on the trailing line, I followed and we were towed yelling across the deck with others clinging on. If that weight dropped down into an empty hold . . .

Walan grabbed the abandoned rammer and jammed the pole between the carriage and the wheel, like a cart brake, and the gun screeched slowly to a stop against the lip of the hold, too slowly to break through it. We heaved a sigh of relief, the ship heaved and we barely got out of the way as the gun came trundling back again. Other crewmen fell on it with wedges, but I'd had enough; I staggered up and bolted for the poopdeck.

'If we fire that thing again it'll go straight out the starboard side!' I shouted to the captain and te Kiore. 'Or through the bottom!'

The Maori looked to the captain. 'How long to lay in more bolts?'

'For cannon tackle? Two hours, begod!' Batang chewed his stringy moustache. 'And we have not one, even! See, they come!'

'That's it, then!' muttered te Kiore. 'Another beaut of a barney! Only from two flamin' sides this time! With a backup not far behind! Wish I was a contortionist.'

'Why so?' inquired Jacquie, still hefting her bow.

'So I could kiss my bum goodbye. I'm clean out of ideas.'

'Me too,' I said heavily.

Batang Sen said something I suspected was comprehensively obscene.

'You're not just giving up?' yelled Jacquie. 'There's got to be something we can try – somebody who can think of something . . .'

A long, satisfied-sounding snore rumbled up between us. We turned round as one. There behind us, still in his contorted lotus position, Ape rested as peacefully as a baby, spluttering mildly through his whiskers. With a yell Jacquie threw herself on him and shook him, and te Kiore and I, with military precision, seized him by each arm and dragged him upright. That didn't stop him snoring, and cannonfire and carnage on deck hadn't woken him. Batang Sen, with unexpected strength, heaved up the helmsman's water butt and slopped the whole lot straight into Ape's broad face. His eyes flew open in the kind of horrible glare you see in Hindu art, cross-eyed, buck-toothed and dripping malevolence; he flexed his arms, and te Kiore and I, both larger than him, went crashing to the deck.

'*Dood ok ondergang!*' he bellowed. 'Why you lousy asshole leeches—'

'No!' yelled Jacquie. 'Look! Back there!'

Ape's pale eyes widened, took in the oncoming sails and smashed sides and blood-slathered deck, all in one.

'So,' he muttered. 'And what do you expect I do over this?'

'Can't you take the wind out of their sails or something?' I demanded.

He glared. 'Just how I do that, you care to tell me?'

'Le Stryge did it! But maybe he was a real sorceror!'

'A real lot of things!' spat Ape. 'You want him, you go get him! I do things my own way!' And, turning away, he calmly vanished down the companionway, leaving the rest of us staring.

There was a sound of blundering and crashing from the saloon below, chairs overturning and hoarse oaths, and finally what sounded like a satisfied bellow. I sidled nervously over to the hatchway and looked down. There was a sudden rush of feet, a clatter on the steps, and Ape's bulk exploded out of the hatch like a demented hippo, simply bowling me aside. I sprawled on my back, and he went rushing at full tilt for the stern, roaring excitedly and waving something over his head. It looked as if he was planning to take on our pursuers single-handed, armed only with – what? I just had time to register a vague impression of something brown and shrivelled, before he gave it a final wind-up and pitched it flying out into our wake. I was afraid he'd jump after it, but he only stood clutching the taffrail and leaning far out with an air of intense expectation. Of course we rushed to join him, then ducked hastily as musketballs cracked and whined into the wood around us, amid a chorus of derisive shrieks and catcalls. Only Ape stood unmoving, the wind riffling his coarse hair; then he stretched out a long leisurely arm and pointed.

And there was something there, something in the churning green water at the margins of our wake, something floating just beneath the foam-flecked wavecrests. Something long, very long, with a ridged, jagged surface that gleamed momentarily at the surface; something that moved, a lazy sculling motion that somehow suggested immense strength. The leading *prahu* evidently saw it a lot better than we did; the cries turned to alarm, and the high masts heeled as the wheel went hard over in a desperate attempt to turn aside. A good try, but they didn't quite make it.

We saw the shock clearly as the knifing bows sideswiped the thing in the water, the masts flexing, a shuddering ripple across the sails, a grinding rumble of hull planking. There was a sudden convulsion beneath the surface, and the sculling end, lazy no longer, lifted like a whip and lashed at the exposed flank that had struck it. The splintering crashes were so loud they left no room for doubt. The water must have come rushing in through a dozen shattered planks, torrential, unstoppable, filling the bilges in minutes. The *prahu* wallowed an instant, heeling in genuine distress this time. But with full sail set it could not support that angle long; the top-heavy rig threshed, sagged to the water and pulled the whole ship over. Men were pitched screaming and howling into the creaming sea, almost on top of the monstrous thing that had holed them. It plunged among them, wide spearhead jaws yawned and shut, and it seemed to roll over, threshing and striking among the struggling pirates, beating the water to a pinkish froth. It was only then we saw clearly what it was.

'*Bujang Senang!*' screamed Batang Sen. '*Bujang Senang Raja!*' His weathered features turned an extraordinary cheese colour, he fell to his knees and began beating his forehead on the deck.

The next pursuer, only seconds behind, couldn't have seen what was happening. Perhaps they thought we'd hulled the leader, because they put their helm hard over, just managing to avoid the wreck, hoping probably to slip around it and bring their own guns to bear. Then they saw what was going on in the sea, and in evident shock they turned into the wind, a sailing ship's swiftest and simplest way of shedding forward speed. But they'd been going so fast they couldn't possibly lose enough; momentum carried them on, right on top of that horrible spectacle, right into collision with the foundering hull. The shock must have alerted the thing in the water, already in a feeding frenzy, for it hurled itself forward with appalling speed, jaws open like a gaping trap. The collision jarred the second *prahu*, its foremast whipped and snapped as if it had been shot off and slid across the deck, sweeping men screaming into the stained sea. Somewhere astern muskets were crackling, but that was a definite mistake; lead balls could do little more than sting those warty armoured scales. The monstrous jaws gaped and closed, there was a sickening, tearing crunch; it rocked its head, almost casually, and *bit* loose a whole great chunk of the deck and hull planking. This time I saw the water go boiling in. The second *prahu* began to founder.

'I don't bloody believe it!' was about the most intelligent thing I could find to say. Some kind of sea-serpent would have been easier to accept than the monstrous thing that rolled and snapped there.

'I think you'd better, mate!' said te Kiore shakily. 'You do get the odd salty in these waters, I've seen a few. But never anything the size of *that*!'

'Salty?' I inquired faintly.

'*Crocodylus porosus*,' said Jacquie hoarsely. 'The salt-water crocodile. You get them everywhere from North Australia to Sarawak. One bit the transom off a fishing boat on the Queensland coast last year, and that was an 18-footer; I read about that. But the largest one measured was almost 40 feet; and apparently they grew a lot bigger than that before they had to compete with men and guns.'

'I believe you,' I said. 'Indeed I do.' We were pulling away now, and the third *prahu* was nosing cautiously up to the scene, with the fourth one on its traces. Either they were genuinely concerned about their fellows, or they were glad enough of any excuse not to tangle with a prey that could unleash such forces.

'But how on earth did you summon one so quickly?' she demanded of Ape. 'Or – I know! All that time you were pretending to be asleep, and you were actually calling one up?'

Ape's grin was mocking. '*Zoals je segt, mevrouw.* Just as you say.'

The second ship was wallowing lower and lower in the water now, though someone had had enough sense to cut the yards free before they could pull it over. They were trying to launch a boat now, but like the decoy they'd been carrying too many men; they were fighting to get into it, with fists and knives and teeth by the look of it, and when it pulled away moments later it was so overladen it toppled at the first wave. I shuddered as the Boegie men were tipped wholesale, screaming, into that fouled sea; the greasy stain was spreading, and other teeth were at work there, or would be soon. Like most large ships we had attracted our small complement of sharks around us, and other high-bladed fins could be seen nosing in from all directions. I was glad we were drawing away so fast now.

A sudden thump followed us across the waters, and another; plumes of smoke arose, and instinctively we ducked. But the shot wasn't flying anywhere near us; the other *prahus* were standing off and cannonading the monster crocodile.

'That'll finish it,' Jacquie said heavily.

'You think?' Te Kiore shook his head. 'My money's on the croc. Those bastards are bloody hard to kill. Ten to one he sinks the lot long before he's handbag meat.'

'No takers,' I said. 'Anyhow, it'd depend how long it would take the water to get to the sawdust.'

'*What?*' demanded Jacquie.

'The sawdust,' I repeated. 'Assuming that was what's in it, of course. Straw's possible, or maybe kapok in these parts; but I seem to remember they mostly used sawdust.'

Jacquie shook her head. 'What're you on about? Used in what?'

'In stuffing the crocodile, of course. The one from the saloon downstairs. That was what Ape threw in – though I didn't recognise it till I saw it. That was why I said I didn't believe it.'

'Oh god,' said Jacquie weakly. 'But that was only about two feet long. A baby! You're not telling me he . . . he . . . and brought it to . . . '

'Maybe he was just calling one up, like she said,' suggested te Kiore.

'Using the little one as a symbol? I don't think so.'

Te Kiore glanced at Batang Sen, who was still knocking his brow on the planks and babbling. 'I've a feeling he's guessed. I've half a mind to join him.'

I looked at Ape, still leaning on the taffrail and humming to himself, a shapeless, rather dismal little tune. 'That was pretty damned amazing, Ape. Thanks again. But just what *did* you—'

He snorted. The lines on his face had deepened, and he looked and sounded depressed. 'You go ask Le Stryge, the next time you bump into him,' he said quietly. 'But if I am you, which thankfully I am not, *jongetje*, I leave that bump particular for about as long as you possible can. All okay now?'

And without waiting for an answer, he shuffled off, shoulders hunched, back down the companionway. Nobody followed. But later, exhausted from helping clean and patch up the ship, we clambered down and found him, boots on thighs again and hands on knees, pink palms turned outwards, sitting comfortably snoring in the centre of the saloon table.

Everything was sudden, in those drizzling mists. Everything seemed almost to leap out at us, a half-fallen tree poised threateningly above our heads, a dangling vine or creeper swinging snakelike into our path.

Such as it was. The undergrowth had tripped and snagged our steps all the way out here; now, as we crawled, it was taking a positive delight in tangling all over us. And we had to restrain our *parang* blows; with everyone on all fours and shoulder to shoulder, half-hidden by soggy greenery, the heavy jungle cutlasses were too likely to chop off more than the odd tendril. So it was hellish hard going, we sweated more than ever and the drizzle delved through every layer of clothing and clung there, sucking away the warmth. It was amazing how cold you could feel like that, even in this steaming mist. The salve the Dyak had given us to smear on melted and ran in sticky little rivulets down every crack and crevice in the skin, an incredibly unpleasant feeling. After the fresh sea air this heavy humid soup seemed almost impossible to breathe. But there was no help for it; we were getting near, or so te Kiore claimed, and we had to keep low.

'Look on the bright side!' whispered the Maori, scrabbling eagerly to help Jacquie flail at a thorny creeper. When he'd realised we weren't sharing a cabin he'd begun to show an elephantine interest in her. I tried not to let it irritate me – after all, why should it? He draped a massive arm around her, ostensibly to unwind the plant. 'At least it's too cold for the mozzies to come out.'

'Yes,' muttered Jacquie irritably, unwinding the arm in much the same way. 'They've got more brains. What about leeches?'

Te Kiore didn't seem put out. 'Aw, no sweat, not this low

173

down. Above about a thousand feet's where they bother you, in this part of the world. Anyway, you bet that Dyak junk'd take care of them. And all those manky little bastards in the soil, skin burrowers and stuff.'

I felt the slight shudder in her shoulder as it touched mine. '*Larva migrans*? It prevents that? What's in it?'

'Don't ask. You might settle for the leeches— *Hey*!'

Leeches and larva forgotten, galvanised by the soft exclamation, we raised ourselves and stared ahead. For a moment, as our eyes struggled to focus against the whiteness, it seemed as if he'd been seeing things. Then, slowly, we made sense of the faint tinges of grey at its heart. The trouble was, it was just too big. We were expecting a building, a large one even; after all, Jacquie and I had been climbing up it. But when you're looking for a building and you find a good-sized hill, you tend to look over, or around. The slow circulation of the mist showed us a tower one moment, conical and encrusted with carvings, then an angle of stone blocks, a shattered *stupa* half smothered in vines, a worn section of frieze, a handless statue. They seemed to glide out of the grey vapour, one here, another there, hundreds of yards apart, as if some spooky joker was sticking up random chunks to confuse us. But as you realised that they did all belong to one building, you began to see the symmetry of its outline, and the size. It *was* the hill.

With that misty immediacy the Borobodur loomed over us. Its lowest terrace hidden, it floated midway on the mist like some supernatural island, a vast mass of age-dark stone. Tower and pinnacle sprang from it as trees from a natural hill, a symmetrical forest of stone that led the eye upward to the needle summit of its central spire vanishing into the cloud. The bulk of it oppressed our minds, as if any moment its awesome shadow might glide out over us and its weight descend, obliterating us unnoticed in one crushing instant. And yet for all its massive burden of stone it was not threatening in itself, it was not made to threaten. It had nothing of the glittering thrust of the World Trade Center or the brutal blankness of the Kremlin walls; only detached, contemplative, godlike stillness, divinely calm as the stone Buddhas who gazed down upon the swirling sea of whiteness. I felt it was we who might break against that petrified serenity like an over-eager wave, dashing our cares and fears and petty concerns against the indifference of Nirvana, shattered by our own energy alone. It was made to awe, to overawe, and that it did to us all. Even if there'd been no peril, our voices would have been hushed, our eyes forever watchful. A power dwelt here.

I looked at Jacquie, and whispered in her ear. 'This is it, isn't it? This is where they shanghaied us to.'

'Yes. Yes! I knew it must be, but now I'm sure. The way it feels . . . '

'Yah, too right!' put in te Kiore's bullfrog whisper. 'See anywhere you recognise? Any mark as'd tell us where you were?'

I stared, along and back, alert for the slightest trace of motion. If there was anything alive there now, it seemed to be lying very low. 'Maybe. It's hard to be sure, in this mizzle. We might have been on the other side, mightn't we?'

'Nope. Said you were looking out over flat jungle, didn't you? Other way's hills. So it was here somewhere.'

'Right. We ran down a narrow stair to get past the elephant. Then a wide terrace, wider than the ones higher up, then a bigger stair, really wide.'

'Uh-huh. With an arch over it, with kind of a face on top?'

'Not that I noticed. But in that mist . . . '

'Yeah. It sounds like the main gate, that'd be over there. Best not go blundering in blind, if they've the force you say. A few minutes and we'll be able to see . . . '

'But it was noon then,' said Jacquie uncertainly. 'And dry.'

'Not far off noon now,' said te Kiore. 'And the rain's slackened off a fair old bit while we've been walking. Should give up in maybe a quarter hour or so. We'll lie low a minute, and keep an eye out.'

We huddled together, staring at the vast edifice and trying to imagine which part of it we'd landed in. But every shift of the mist seemed to unveil another stretch of labyrinthine terrace, another flight of stairs, all symmetrical, all alike, except where a patch of green marked the overgrown edge of a tumbled terrace, or a bush or shrub poked through a cracked carving. Grey patches of lichen spotted every surface, gleaming slickly under the drizzle. Yet here and there among the carvings I saw splashes of brighter colour, yellow and crimson and a faded-looking purple; they'd been painted once. That set me thinking of the colours on the container; how well were they lasting? Or had Ape's charms already been broken?

Jacquie shook her head confusedly. 'All this – I can't even relate it to any of the books or pictures. It was restored, years ago. But this?'

'This is the spirit of it, remember? This is its timeless self, its shadow. Just as the Surabaja we put in at isn't today's . . . '

Wooden quays, dusty unpaved streets, high walls of dried clay brick and only a few pink faces besides ours, a pompous-looking Dutchman and his wife in a European carriage weaving its way through the chattering market crowds, turning up their noses at the lively women, bare-breasted in their bright *sarongs*. And nothing of Europe in the buildings, from stone temple to wooden hut. Yet the huge ox-wagon we'd hired, primitive as it was, had steel axles and turned bearings of a sort, crude but serviceable, and the harness, though tooled with traceries like the Wayang puppets, was certainly European in inspiration. An earlier and a later Jawa blended and met, uniting the essence of both; and perhaps, if I only knew which corners to turn, there would be traces of a Jawa that was yet to be.

Jacquie nodded. 'Yes. Strange. I thought . . . this might be still clear, still in use. But then they abandoned it almost as soon as it was finished. So this is its true self, all overgrown like this. Or worse than overgrown; it feels . . . '

She didn't finish. 'Yes?'

She turned those level eyes on me. 'Don't laugh. It feels haunted.'

'I'm not laughing, believe me. When was it built anyhow? And who by?'

'When? Oh, the ninth century. The Saliendra princes. Buddhists, bringing in a new faith on top of Hinduism, which was already mingled with local beliefs. Just about the time my father's people were sailing down from Sweden to rape and pillage the British coast.' She grinned suddenly. 'Chopping up yours on Lindisfarne, probably.'

'My mother's, maybe. My old man's ancestors must have been somewhere along the civilised side of the Rhine, then. Probably selling job lots of odd boots and dented armour to Charlemagne's army. They came over from Germany with George the First, or maybe earlier.'

'Oh? I didn't know that. They weren't building anything like this in Charlemagne's time, were they? The big cathedrals came later. And they weren't as big as this.'

I smiled to myself. Jacquie hadn't changed that much; she'd always pushed the Orient whenever she could, as if to bolster her own Eastern blood. 'No. Nor as spooky! But we kept the cathedrals going, didn't we? Why'd these princes let all this rot? It must have cost them a fortune to build.'

'Nobody knows. They just did.'

That thought became a veil of silence drifting down on us. There was only the hiss and patter of the drizzle. Gargoyles even uglier than the usual Western model were dribbling water down stone that was already worn and streaked; they'd been doing it a long time.

The mist brushed spectral tendrils across my cheek. Was that the air shifting? At least the drizzle was slackening. There was a sudden flurry in the undergrowth. Skinny legs and arms flailing, Batang Sen came up beside us with the energy of a scuttling spider. Back at the road I'd wondered how someone so old and fragile would stand the trek; now, moustache bristling and little black eyes alight, he looked about ten times fresher than me. 'Wind changes!' he hissed. 'Ape, he say something near, something strange! You take care, old fellow!'

I nodded tautly. Ape was our rearguard, in case of nasty surprises. The rest of us were laden with weapons, but he had nothing – except, no doubt, that peculiar staff of his. And he was right about the wind. The mist swayed seductively as a supple dancer now, swirling, peeling back from the upper reaches of the temple, the circular terraces that made up the centre of its *mandala* plan, and the tall *stupa* at its heart. The needle tip of its spire was suddenly visible, some forty metres above the plain, and behind it, for an instant, a patch of blazing blue sky. Then the heavier mists below boiled sluggishly across, and hid it; but in doing so they lifted a moment from the lower terraces. I saw it then, the space we'd run across, the pools of water and the slick flagstones; and beyond them over the stairs, an arch, half crumbled, so that the gaping beast-face above seemed to hang like the Cheshire Cat's grin, upon nothing.

'The *kala*, the devouring demon!' cried Jacquie. 'The gate is its mouth, when you enter it swallows you! So you can be reborn spiritually—'

'It does, does it? And that's the way we ran out, when Ape blew up the arch – so just outside it – *there!*'

The fold of mist had revealed it, standing lonely and

incongruous on the dished flagstones little more than the length of a football field away – an ancient, battered lorry trailer. Upon it, its bright colours smudged and peeling but still gaudy under their dewy coating, stood the container.

We'd agreed what was best, a quick dash-and-grab job – run in, seize the truck, tow it out by main force on to the forest paths away from the temple itself. Whatever lurked there ought to be weaker beyond its bounds, as our escape had demonstrated, and we could defend the container better; if we couldn't start the truck we could couple the oxen to it. But with the aura of the place around us, confronting the sheer numinous mass of it, nobody seemed too eager to make the first move. Batang Sen half crouched, frowning and chewing his moustache furiously; te Kiore, face working, glanced from him to me, and to Jacquie. I was just nerving myself up to give an order when everybody whirled around at the sudden crashing in the trees behind us. Muscles tensed, hands flew to weapons; then we saw it was Ape, living up to his name, half running, half swinging through the tangled forest towards us, his great arms hurling him through the greenery as if it was so much cobweb.

'Well?' he half screamed. 'For what do you wait? The nuts to drop? *Vorwaerts! Ayang!*'

He hurtled in between us like a hairy comet, grabbed the scruff of my neck in one hand and te Kiore's in the other, and with one great heave propelled us forward. The two of us hurtled out, arms flailing; if there'd been a cliff in the way we couldn't have stopped. If we'd tried we'd have fallen, on our own swords probably; so we ran, to let our feet catch up. Behind us the merry men, galvanised by Ape's appalling energy, sprang up and hared after us with a volley of whoops and screams, Batang Sen hopping and cackling in their midst. There's nothing like facing down fear to set the adrenalin flowing; we covered that hundred yards at Olympic speeds, hurdling the loose stones in our path, and fetched up behind it in a gasping mass.

'Strewth, it's an ole Holden!' panted te Kiore, springing up into the cab. 'Grew up with these things! Starting handle, where's the bleeding handle?' It was in place, protruding from the radiator grille; I tried swinging it, nearly put my back out, only to hear it cough, splutter, die. Again, with the same result. Te Kiore pushed me aside, then gave a heave that could have overturned the truck. The engine wheezed asthmatically and died again. He kicked the grille.

'Right! Round the back and unhitch it!'

Hands scrabbled at the towing hitch, hammered at the ancient brake with cutlass hilt and cudgel. With a protesting squeal the trailer came free; ropes were thrown around it and made fast, men threw their weight on, and the heavy mass began to turn away from the cab, to swing out towards the jungle and freedom. But as it ground around on the stones there was a sudden swirl in the mist, a convulsion almost; the faintest of cool shivers coursed down my back. We all felt it; we all gave the kind of guilty start that makes you drop things, we all of us, even Ape, looked up as if we expected thunderbolts. But there was only a blazing sunbeam that the churning mists seemed almost to focus and direct, a spear of light that touched the stone of the central *stupa* and slid down it, down the still-shadowed face of the temple, across the terrace and down the steps towards the stones where we stood.

A sunbeam; but it might have been some frightening super-weapon, a hair-thin laser or particle beam that could slice rock seamlessly, without smoke or waste. For as it played down the centre of that whole vast building a line of light ran behind it, a thread, a seam that cut tower and stair and gate exactly down the middle, the median line of the whole immense temple. There was one noise, a sharp, stony, explosive *crack!* But then there was silence.

With the ponderous gravity of the gates of Hell, the whole front wall of the temple split down that seam, neatly, cleanly, and glided apart. The line of light expanded. If fire had leapt out to engulf us I wouldn't have been one bit surprised. But what blazed out of those dark depths was brilliant daylight, the light of another place, another sky, clear and cloudless, without the faintest strand of mist.

Except in one place, a hazy purple slope, far distant, from whose whitened peak a skeining stream of thin smoke arose. I knew it, that slope, not from life but from photographs. By her stifled cry, Jacquie knew it also. It was famous, unmistakable, a shrine for natives, a lure and a penance for ambitious tourists. Gunung Agung, Navel of the World, sacred mountain and sleeping volcano. But not here, not in this area; nowhere near it. Not even on this island of Jawa. Gunung Agung lay at the heart of the destination so fiercely denied to us, the holy summit of the island of Bali. And Bali was a good two hundred miles away; yet Gunung Agung, and all the lands about it, spread out beyond the sundered gate of the Borobodur.

Amid the shock of that unbelievable sight crazy hopes whirled up like dry leaves from a bonfire, flaring and falling apart in the instant. This was no gate we could hope to pass. It opened before us, a temptation, a taunt and a challenge. Beyond it another stone terrace stretched out, high above the distant lands; and along it a terrifying array of force was rising up, a tide of power spilling up over the step. That bright sun blazed down on streaming banners of silk, glanced in unbearable flashes off spearpoint and breastplate, encrusted helmet and painted shield. Warrior generals in demon masks with white moustaches bristling glared down across their ranks of troops, a bristling fence of spear and shield, their archers with streamered arrows half drawn and poised, and in the front rank, in coarse blue cloth and red sashes, gaggles of dacoits with wavy *kris* sword-knives. And above the ranks the shielded howdahs tilted on the armoured backs as great war-elephants coiled up their trunks in contemptuous challenge between their blade-tipped tusks.

'Those banners I know!' breathed Ape beside me. 'Mataram! And Warmadewa! Ancient and bloody lines, *rajas* of Jawa and Bali both. War and tyranny that once sweeps the island – its blood-drunk spirits, awoken, thirsting, come back to war!' There was a growing fury in his voice. 'Who does this thing? Who *dares* do this thing?'

But I hardly heard him. I had seen, crouching among the front rank of dacoits, insignificant, invisible almost amongst that menacing tableau, a figure, slight and uniquely fair of hair. She half rose, and across that distance, however great it was, our eyes met. It was Rangda.

I clutched Ape's shoulder. 'That's her! The little bar girl – their decoy! Those sons of bitches, they've stuck her right in the front line!'

Slowly – reluctantly, I thought – she stepped out between the men around her, her gaze fixed, her face blank. Even at that steel-taut moment the sight of her made me breathe a little faster. Her hair glittered and the sun gleamed golden on her skin, for she wore almost nothing, a skimpy *sarong* of plain white, a necklace of heavy pearls that fell in loops between her bare firm breasts and across her belly, a white band around her neck. And I remembered from somewhere that in the ritual killings, the *puputan*, even in the murders after the 1965 coup attempt, both victims and executioners had donned ceremonial white. Which was she?

There was a slight gasp at my side. 'That? That's *her*? The bar girl you . . . ' Jacquie looked from me to her, then back again. An angry tide of red rushed up her cheeks, and she dealt me one tremendous stinging slap right across the face. 'Why, you – complete and utter slimy *bastard*—'

At college Jacquie had moonlighted as a life-class model – one source of our quarrel. She'd seen herself in more than mirrors, scanned, scrutinised and recorded through the eyes of a hundred artists and photographers. She knew better than most of us *exactly* what she looked like.

And seeing the two together, looking from one to another in the same harshly brilliant light, the resemblance was eerie, alarming. The others saw it, too, and gaped. But Ape, though his eyes never left the girl, reached out and clutched me by the collar with strangling force, and he was glowering like a madman.

'*This* is your little bit of *kutje*? This? *This?*'

I was literally choking, clawing at his fingers till the blood roared in my ears. As well paw at a steel grab. 'Y–yes! S–so *what? So bloody what? C–capital crime?*'

His grip slackened. He laughed, once, hollowly. 'I would not think this could be! How can it? *Idioot*, do you not know who she is?'

'I know her name—'

'You know nothing! *Niks!* Of Bali she is, though not of its bearing. A bar girl, you call her? A princess this is, once – Mahendradatta, a conqueror the ocean washes up, like all evils, to Bali. A warrior princess at the head of hosts! A witch queen, a warlike, destructive force of ancient days! So, then!' His small eyes narrowed. 'But then, at least, she is human!'

'What're you on about – *princess*?, *human*? Of course she's bloody human!'

'Now what is she?' A taut hush seemed to dry out his voice, thin it to a thread. 'To the wild lands she is banished, and to the evil-tainted ocean! She is all that drains and is negative, all that threatens order and grows fat on discord, all that devours and diminishes. She is the spirit of the dry lands! She is the parched flakes of the dried-up river mud! She is the dead leaves hanging from the tree, the hot blast that tears them from their bough! She is the gasping voice of children!'

'*You're crazy!*'

Ape's eyes glittered. 'Am I? Maybe. But I do not share my bed with *that*! Long ago she passed beyond what was, became part of what may be. Mahendradatta she was, till her footsteps set her on the Spiral road, from ill to evil and beyond. She is Kala'narang, the enchantress! *She is Rangda!*'

'Yes!' I gasped angrily. 'She told me her name! So what?'

Ape gave a convulsive start. 'Then she learns to speak truth to you! Learns and is wise, for truth breeds greater power where lies breed small! For know this, infant in the world – of the powers arrayed against you, surely among the greatest is she!'

He was shouting now, so loud she could hear him; I saw her cock her head as if amused, or complimented. '*She is mistress of the Netherworld, princess of the undead, daughter herself of Shiva Lord, the Destroyer! She is the Guardian of the Graveyard! She is the Queen of the Night! She, the white-haired whitebone demon!*'

It began to dawn on me then just how that ash-blonde colouring might appear in oriental eyes. But all Rangda did was throw back her head and laugh, the thin, piercing oriental giggle. It might have made me laugh, too, caught up in it, if I hadn't once heard such laughter in another woman's throat, and sensed the strength behind it. No answering laugh arose among her ranks or ours, who stood stunned, eyes wide and horrified. That eerie laughter rang off the stone *stupas*, rippled along the encrusted terraces like splintering glass, growing stronger and stronger till it seemed that slight throat could no longer be its source. And the glass shards stabbed our ears, agonising needle-points of hot agony that made us clap hands to them, shake our heads and shudder, unable to think or act. Held by that swelling, mirthless laughter, pinned and kicking where we stood, we saw the slight blonde girl begin to change.

She grew. She didn't stretch or swell unnaturally; she grew as any living thing grows, in proportion. If an adult human body were a child's in its turn, so it might grow; but not so fast, nor so strangely. As if she was expanding, extending from cramped confines to a towering height. Her hair fell in pale winding curls about her as she shot up, writhing around the curves of her body, hiding her face. The *sarong* about her waist slipped, stretched, shrank to the skimpiest of loincloths beneath that smooth belly, barely hiding the few pale wisps of hair. The tanned skin stretched taut over strong sinews, the slim legs tensed and splayed like a dancer's. Veins stood out on her arms, and her fingers curled. The strings of pearls bounced sullenly against her taut breasts, and rattled hollowly. They were old and yellowed human skulls, still hung with patches of dried and flaking flesh; but the thong they were strung on glistened a fresh sticky red, a rope of entrails.

More than twice mansize she stood there, head hanging, face hidden, still sleekly beautiful in shape as the bar girl she'd been – and yet a vision of power and menace to make my heart falter. I found myself praying frantically she wouldn't show her face or open her eyes. But the curtain of pale hair stirred and lifted, and from within it the worst shock of all. There was no face, as we understand faces. Pushing out through the curtain was a long animalistic snout, pale-skinned, the eyes above it huge and staring, dark-rimmed, bloodshot, with great dull black pupils – utterly inhuman. And the mouth beneath was a beast's. Black lips curled back from yellow fangs, and between them lolled a long red taper of a tongue.

I wanted to scream, to bolt, to beat my head against the trees to blot out the sight I was seeing. *Rangda*! This thing, this monstrous bloody abortion of a thing! Yet what made that face so horrible was its very half-humanity, the reminder of kinship. On Madagascar, those ghoul-faced night lemurs, *ai-ais* – they were the closest I'd seen. Eerie, a hag-thing, but not quite monstrous – a sort of self-justifying grace to it, a species in its own right, even a shadowy kin to mankind. That was in her also, and it was terrible; as if she expressed some monstrous truth about us, some tendency taken to its fearsome extreme.

But above all there was power, riveting, radiant, dominating power. Because nothing else could have held me there when my shaky limbs ached to run, when my sphincter muscles were about as much as I could control and I'd the gravest doubts about *that*. None of us screamed. None of us ran. That gaze nailed us down where we stood.

The creature stood there, legs splayed, arms akimbo, in the attitude of a native dancer; and then the closed fists flew open. Great shining nails flicked out from the fingertips, uncoiling like silver springs until they stood, stiff and quivering, long metallic claws that gleamed and flashed in the sun of Bali. Then, out of that clear light, that eternal noon, the creature took a wide, posturing step forward, and another. Beneath her feet the terrace boomed and quivered, as if stone trod stone. The elephants tossed their heads and trumpeted in fright, but behind her the banners dipped to the advance.

Like a dancer, still, the creature came on, swaying on splayed legs to unheard rhythms. But beneath those feet the stone rang, each footfall louder than the elephants', and the steps cracked and split. Behind her, in a hesitant arrowhead, the ranks swayed forward as if they too feared to come too close. The metallic claws on her feet struck sparks from the stair. A Buddha statue toppled forward from a *stupa* and fell flat on its smiling face. I felt myself shuddering uncontrollably, with fear, with rage, with the sheer horror of her presence. This was what had lured me, seduced me, possessed me – and that thought all but made me vomit where I stood. I felt defiled, within, without, humiliated, unmanned in every sense. She was advancing on the container. Were enough of Ape's charms worn and washed from it now? They might be. Then she could probably pick the thing up and run off with it – or crush it in those arms. Smash in its walls, scatter its precious cargo of electronics out of the shockproof packing and sow the earth with them like tares. And then throw the remains down shattered in front of my very eyes. Or into them, I realised with a jarring chill; for with it destroyed, only we stood in her way. And this, too, she'd managed through me.

The thought of that raised a rush of real fury to overwhelm the chill. Right then I'd have wrung the lying little throat right out of the girl Rangda, if I could have laid hands on her. I recognised her all too clearly still, the body I'd thought so like Jacquie's mocked me. Somehow that thought seemed to loosen my limbs a little – to think of her as human, as limited, confined, fragile even. As I'd known her; as once she really had been, maybe. Neat, small, delicate as a butterfly and no more dangerous. No harder to *crush*—

The staring eyes swung towards me. But they were too late. I shook free of their spell; and where minutes earlier I would've just run like hell, I screamed out the rage and revulsion that was in me. And I tugged my sword from my belt, and dived between her and the container, daring her to come on, slashing in furious challenge at the air and the glittering, mocking sunbeams.

Then it was as if I really did cut something, that severed with a soundless recoil and the force of a stretched steel hawser, so the air thrummed and juddered with it. Just behind me Jacquie fell to her knees with a yelp. Ape stumbled, rubbing at his eyes as if he'd been dazzled. But cries of dismay went up from the crew, and even te Kiore. The hag-creature and the hordes bearing down on them, outnumbering them by hundreds, was just too much. They began to back away, straggling around the end of the truck, ready to cut and run; and I didn't blame them one bit.

Ape rounded on them, as if he'd eyes in the back of his head. '*Hé*! *Waar zouden ju'gaan, hoor*? You want something to run from, by damn and devils I give you it, I! In spades!'

'*Aduh*! *Orang bebal*!' croaked Batang Sen, tugging at my arm. 'Complete off your chump! You cannot fight! Not this!'

'You gotta get him away!' said te Kiore hoarsely. 'No point him just standin' there t' get mashed flat! And the girl – yourself too! C'mon!'

'No!' snapped Jacquie, equally hoarse. 'It's our last chance! We can't just—'

'*Stand*!' said Ape, his voice abruptly louder than it had any business being. Even the banners on the steps above flailed and fluttered wildly, as though in a sudden change of wind. Suddenly an arrow came hissing down out of the ranks above, streamers trailing in its deceptively lazy arc – not at me, at Ape. Mouths opened to warn him, but it was already on him. He threw up a hand – I couldn't see more than that, it was so fast – spoke a harsh word, and something spun in his palm. The arrow glanced off like light on a mirror, and sang back into the ranks lower down. There was a noise like clattering kettles, and a body came rolling down the steps at Rangda's back – one of the armoured captains. His limbs flailed loosely, and one after the other arm and leg flew loose and rolled on their own, bits of armour fell off scattering, and finally, as he crashed to the bottom beneath the hag-creature's feet, his helmet went bouncing off. From inside it, trailing a few bare hanks of hair, a withered skull bounced free and rolled to a halt, grinning hugely at its own ghastliness.

Ape chortled. '*Niet zo gezond*, your cohorts, Princess? Eh? Not in the pink, exactly? You should feed 'em better, by damn!'

Vastly heartened, I suddenly found myself chuckling, and heard the crewmen joining in, the sudden dull clink of swords and *parangs*. 'They all gone off like that?' demanded te Kiore.

'The more you think of them so!' Ape answered quietly. 'What they were, She shows you! What they have become, is for us to see!'

I strained my eyes, staring at the bright ranks, striving to see the spots of rust on the armour, the bare bone grasping the bannershaft. Eyeless faces behind those daunting masks, behind those snarling mouths that last, perpetual grin. To see even the elephants as mouldering cages of bone, hardly able to bear the weight of their rusty armour, pathetic, sorrowful relics that should never have been disturbed . . .

And I saw the first change come over them, the bright banners turn bleached and straggling and eaten away. But so evidently did Rangda, and knew she must move fast. With a hideous screech she waved one taloned hand, and like a sudden tide race that whole great force of ancient might came rolling down the steps upon us. Rusty arrow was fitted to mould-stained bow, its string drawn back in bony fingers, loosed in a flurry of fragmenting streamers; spears were couched against withered flanks. Te Kiore roared a command, and the crewmen swung in around us, a tight circle, instants before the first wave fell on us.

If they'd been whole, alive, there would have been no fight; we would have gone under in those first few seconds. But these bony scarecrows were no fighters, for all their rotting finery; many flew apart at the first touch, or hewed each other in their uncertain haste. But others were more solid, and we found ourselves fighting a fierce hack-and-thrust fight simply to keep from being overrun by sheer weight of numbers. The broken dead piled up around us; and every so often a rusty spear or chipped battleaxe found a good mark in our line, and somebody dropped down. We dragged or just heeled them back the moment we could, or they would have suffocated in that carrion mass for sure. But the more we saw of shattered skulls and half-fleshed limbs the easier it was to believe in them, and so the weaker the fighters got. I crossed swords with one captain I'd seen resplendent in the rear line minutes earlier; now he fought like a clockwork toy, without the weight to block and thrust, and the rusty rims of his breastplate bent and dented as even my lighter blows got home. Cross, right, parry – and I rammed my fist in the basket hilt into his demon-mask. It caved in, he swayed and folded like a heap of dead leaves. Another, fresher-looking, leapt over him with a mace whirling, but before I could react Jacquie startled me by stepping into the gap and sending his head spinning off with one blow of her *parang*. No doubt about it; we were winning. Or so, for that moment, we thought.

Through the mass of undead those dacoits came gliding, and trying to see them as anything else had no noticeable effect. They were recent, maybe even living. They had more will of their own, that was noticeable; they didn't just rush in, but used the ancient troops for cover. Ape caught my shoulder and Batang's. 'Watch yourselves! These are her own, her votaries as today terrorists are, more dangerous by far. The time comes to strike back at She herself! When I give the word, be ready to rush in!'

He reached up, spun a little rod in his fingers – and his hands were suddenly full of staff, twelve feet long or more with rounded golden endcaps glistening. He twirled it in one hand, and it hummed in the air – then lashed out at an onrushing warrior, who more or less exploded at the impact. He stumped forward, out of the ring; a dacoit rushed him, caught the tip of that spinning staff and was sent flying. Ape swung his arm over his head, a golden cap fouled one of the tangled old kenari trees at the forest's edge and tore loose a branchtip. But it was no accident; Ape caught the branch by its straight centre, touched it to his lips and with that astonishing strength hurled it hard at Rangda. It flew like a javelin, but curved down to rattle on the flagstones at her feet. Disappointed, I hesitated; but Ape swung his staff again in one slow wheel and struck the flagstones before him.

For a moment I thought he'd summoned a plague of snakes or worms or something of the kind. From every conceivable crack, every niche between the worn stones, things came wriggling upward in one tremendous surge. But in the same heartbeat I saw them for what they were, plant and seedling positively exploding up at an unbelievable rate in a direct line from him to Rangda, where the branch had flown. And the branch itself actually leaped from the stones into midair with the force of its growing, root and twig and tendril shooting out like springs. Right in front of Rangda it sprang; next instant its foliage was wrapped tight around her, still burgeoning as she screamed and threshed.

'*Now!*' yelled Ape, and his staff swept our way clear. With a mind full of red murder I raced ahead of him and out, and at my heels came Batang, te Kiore and the others, sweeping our faltering attackers aside, closing in on our entangled enemy. But even as I came up to her I saw those animal jaws open, that tongue loll out;

and next moment a blast of fearful cold swept over me, so cold I barely clapped my hand to my eyes in time. My own breath froze to ice on my upper lip in that rushing instant; and then it ceased, I looked up and saw those silvery nails ripping at the ensnaring foliage, as grey and brittle now as ground glass, ringing with icicles. She had frozen it with her breath.

One arm snaked free, and in it the long white scarf from around her neck. It seemed to drift out over me like smoke in a wind, and I saw the strange characters that were painted along it somehow, white on white. But when it reached its full extent, it cracked like a whip; and that crack seemed to shatter the world.

My sword went mad in my hand, bucking, wheeling, twisting like a live thing to be free of my grip. I hopped hastily as it almost sliced me on the shin. I staggered, fighting it, and dimly saw the others doing the same. My world was full of that shimmering menace at arm's length, fighting to disobey me; it was like having a cobra by the throat, an angry cobra. Only my eyes told me that it wasn't moving at all, straight and stark as ever; it was my fingers that were doing the writhing, as if they'd taken on a life of their own.

Very abruptly, as if it'd just been manoeuvring for position all this time, the sword actually reversed itself in my hands. Or they reversed it; but that wasn't how it felt. It just swung over and lunged straight at my chest. If it'd had an invisible Basil Rathbone behind it, it couldn't have been more vicious or direct. I held it, barely, with arms outstretched, my hands against the hilts; but the sword was longer than my arms, and it was already stabbing me slightly. One slip and it'd run me through easily. I staggered this way and that, struggling to throw off the force that drove it, shake loose the unseen hand – no good. And no wonder; no wonder my arms were shaking with the tension, the muscles twitching and trembling. They were pulling, as well as pushing. I screamed aloud with the agony of it. I was fighting myself.

Even as I realised it a great white curtain billowed up between me and the outside world, between me and myself even. I was lost, isolated, thrashing with a blind mad hatred at a formless wall. Somewhere in there, somewhere behind it was the bastard who'd got me into all this—

—who'd tangled me up in this horrible web of dangers . . .

—who'd wasted half my life, robbed the rest of meaning . . .

—who'd ruined me, made me half a man, an empty emotional cripple . . .

—who'd palmed me off with cheap casual sex and hollow success instead of a real relationship . . .

—who'd trailed me down the path of failure . . .

*Somewhere in there.*

And all I wanted, all I had left to want, was to strike out at him, to cut him down. Half myself was somewhere in there, the front I put up, the weaknesses it hid, all the things I might have sneered at in somebody else. I knew it was me, and I wanted to stab it, maim it, kill it, silence it, scrub out the thing I despised, shunned, spat on, ground underfoot and scoured my shoe sole . . .

I could hear myself shrieking, and other voices with me. I flailed frantically to shake free of that rippling whiteness that cut my brain in two. Something struck me painfully on the back, and my sight cleared. A crewman blundered into me, screaming hoarsely in Malay as he struggled to fight back the *parang* blade that was trying to slash at his throat. One hand drove it on, quivering with the effort; the other held it back with only a bare palm, spouting blood. Another crewman sagged to his knees with his cutlass deep in his stomach, and folded over it, retching. Batang had buried his cutlass in a tree, but seemed to be trying to jerk it loose. Te Kiore wheeled in a nightmare dance, slapping away the whirling sword-club as it swung at his body and chest and face, sometimes connecting. Jacquie rolled on the flagstones, crying out in fear and anger as her *parang*, clutched in both hands, made little jerking leaps at her throat. Ape sprang forward, unaffected, and a sweep of his staff knocked the blade from her hands; it clattered harmlessly away, but her hands stabbed violently with nothing. There was no magic in the blades; we were doing this to ourselves.

A shadow blotted out the sun. Rangda loomed over us, free now of the entangling branches; and she seemed to dwarf even that ancient man-made mountain behind. Ape, caught unawares, lashed out with his staff; but her claw caught the blow. It rocked her back, but it knocked him spinning. In desperation I struggled to twist my sword around again, but instead I almost lost control. My hands convulsed, and about a finger's breadth of the point sank into my chest. I screamed in pain and fright, tore it loose and sagged, feeling the spurt of hot blood. The sword clattered on the stone, but I had no strength left to lift it. Weakened with shock, I fell down at Rangda's feet. She stalked by me without a look, some fourteen feet high, as if I was no more than another insect on the jungle floor. Yet as she passed, terrifying thing that she was, I still saw the body of the slender bar girl, arched over me on that night of foggy and deceitful memories. I howled aloud with the anguish of the memory, desire and ecstasy and shame and terror weirdly blended.

Only Ape stood between her and the container now, splay-legged, tense, spinning the staff in his massive fingers as if it was a featherweight baton. She hesitated an instant, rolling her head strangely, as if she was studying him; and instantly he lunged. But fast as he was, that huge hand moved even faster. A blaze of pink flame scattered across the stones, a rain of hot sparks hissed and spattered down into the trees; the silver nails sprouted a foliage of fire. But the force of the blow slammed undiminished into Ape, picked him off his feet and sent him sprawling over the end of the truck. He went crashing down like a bulky meteor into the first line of bushes.

I grabbed my sword and struggled to my knees. Anger poured down over the shock, but I was still shaking. One rush, one strike – if I could only manage it. Eyelids sagging, I heaved myself up, but she was almost at the container. Then another figure stepped around its end. For a moment I thought it might be Ape, swiftly recovered; then I saw who it was, and could only gape. A tall elderly man, neat in plain white shirt and trousers, goatee and moustache groomed, steely hair in a careful knot – and in his hand the crystal-tipped staff he had brandished back at the hotel. Rangda came to a dead stop, eyeing the old man – Mpu Bharadah, that was the name. He lifted his staff in his claw-like fingers, and I winced, expecting him to be swatted flat.

All he did was gesture. A sharp, unmistakable gesture – *Get back! Leave it!*

But no more than that. After the fright and hysteria of the last few moments it was oddly impressive. Even more so, that curious toss of his head again. It was the oriental headshake, like Ape's, a refusal, a denial; but there was something more to it than that, something both aggressive and absolute. It was then I noticed the silence that had fallen, making the gasps of tortured breath unnaturally loud. The weapons no longer fought their owners; no more warriors or dacoits ran forward over the slathered stones.

Rangda still didn't move; but I did. I hobbled up, half falling, and aimed a massive hacking cut at her. She whirled, I missed, and staggered desperately to get my balance before she could swipe my head off my shoulders. She didn't even try. Instead she let out a scream of rage and frustration, whirled about and charged with great sweeping strides back across the stones, back into the ranks of her followers, scattering them like chaff. In the wake of her flight they ran after her, ants scuttling back to their lair. Up the steps they poured, kicking down corroded fragments and a cloud of dust; and even as they passed there was a sudden rumble and creak of stone. Slowly yet inexorably, shutting down the sunlight of Bali's noon like a snuffed candle, the sundered flanks of the Borobodur moved once more, grinding softly as if they moved on heavy marble rollers, closing like a gaping wound. The two halves met and shut with a force that sent the last shreds of mist billowing up into Jawa's hazier sky. The grey masonry was seamless, unbroken.

We were alone.

We stood there, in the spreading light of a bright midday, on the ancient stones of Borobodur. The piles of rotting corpses were suddenly no more; the stacks of armour and weapons had vanished. From their *stupas* above the stone Buddhas smiled down serenely – all except one that lay prostrate, as if atoning for the violence that had been committed there. Crewmen were lying around groaning, possibly with serious wounds. Two at least lay sprawled and still, one with a cutlass handle sticking grotesquely upright from his midriff. Almost everyone was bleeding from lesser ones, myself and Jacquie included. But she picked herself up cheerfully enough, and limped over to the container, with the remains of Ape's hex signs trickling down its battered and dented flanks.

'Well,' she said brightly, 'we've got it back.'

My head was still churning. That *creature* . . . The night I'd spent with . . . *it*. No, *her* – or whoever. Gods, who or what *had* I made love to that night? Christ, the things I'd *done* with it. I hardly remembered, but the few fragments were enough, sweaty, twining, enveloping things, a salty sensual taste upon my tongue. What had I really been doing? I prickled with a breathless sweat of panic. I couldn't have done myself some kind of permanent damage, could I? Maybe I should see a doctor, fast. I was almost grateful for the distraction of twinges from my chest wound. It hurt, but I'd had worse; a couple of ribs had stopped it – much longer and they might not have – and an ugly clot was sealing it now. 'How are the others?' I asked te Kiore, the symmetry of his tattooes spoiled by a puffy black eye.

'Two goners. Two more mightn't make it back for help. About fifteen could use a spot of serious darning and patching – you included, I'd say.'

'It's not as bad as it looks. Damn! *Damn!*'

He shrugged. 'Got your box back, didn't we? And most of the fellas got off light enough. Whatever that scarf-thing was she used on us, they held out pretty bloody well.'

'The *anteng*,' rumbled a voice from behind us. Ape was limping around the container, gingerly feeling his neck and jaw, and rubbing his massive backside.

'Some whack you took!' exclaimed te Kiore feelingly. 'Lucky all the bits're still attached, eh? *What'd* you say that thing was?'

'The *anteng*.' Ape laughed, that rare chattering laugh of his, an eerie, humourless sound. 'The only weapon Rangda herself wields; and she needs no other. The mind-breaker, the cradle of spells. Yet the name means only a baby's sling.'

'Some baby,' grunted the Maori. 'Mind-breaker, eh? Interesting. Those two who died, their minds were maybe half that way already, I'd say. Problems, they had. And the badly wounded ones, too; the dark horses, the blokes who're never satisfied. Their own worst enemies, you might say.' He cocked a quizzical eye at me. 'And you took a bit of a bloodin', didn't you? And maybe Miss Jacquie, too. Funny 'bout that, eh? The rest of us mugs just got off with a few scratches. The skipper, he was fly enough t' whack his blade into a tree first thing. An' ole Ape there it never bothered at all. Like I say – interesting.' He grinned, though it obviously hurt. 'C'mon, cheer up! Don't go blaming yourself like that. We all knew the score, we came ready for a barney. Gold's a grand balm for a scratch or two; and they've remedies out here you'll never find back home. Just gotta get back to them, that's all.' He frowned at the truck. 'Don't think it's much use we go ask her Ladyship for those keys, do you?'

'No. Can we tow it behind the wagon?'

'Not that weight, truck an' all, it'd take a week. We'll have to winch it on. Won't leave much room for the rest of us, though. All but the real bad wounds'll have to leg it back to Yogja. Eighteen mile.'

'Or we can send someone ahead for more transport,' I snapped my fingers. 'That priest – he must have got out here somehow. Maybe he's got a cart or a carriage or something! Where'd he go?'

'What priest?' demanded te Kiore.

'But . . . didn't you see him? A native priest, in ordinary cotton gear. The one who called on me, back at my hotel, threatening me. He just popped up in front of Rangda, and barred her from the container – drove her off. I wish to hell I knew how!'

'I thought that was you!' he said. 'Or maybe Ape's little party trick – like she thought he was coming back to do it again, and slipped 'er cable. I was watching, I'd got hold of myself by then. I didn't see no priest!'

'But . . . ' I looked at Jacquie, Batang, Ape.

Ape's eyes were hooded, sunken, somehow more watchful than ever. But Ape just shrugged.

The night was a sticky curtain draped close across your face. You felt you were being stifled, yet every breath was an effort. The mosquitoes had given up their zinging assault some time back, but the cicadas creaked away in every weed patch around the wharf, and strange moths beat out the brains they barely possessed on our dim lanterns. The shore was invisible; the gangplank rested on solid shadow, out of which faint strange sounds came drifting like derelict memories. Even stranger ones drifted up from the hold, where Ape was busy renewing and adding to his protective charms on the container. Some pretty strange smells, too, and every so often a pinkish flash which lit the skeletal rigging and made the crouching sentries jump and heft their flintlocks and crossbows. We were due to sail at dawn; but dawn was hours away yet.

It couldn't come too soon for me. Then I might be able to escape Jacquie; but right now I couldn't bear the thought of my stifling cabin, or the smoke-filled saloon. We'd been warned not to stray off the ship, mostly in case we couldn't get back on in time – not that I needed any telling. If I went aloft the chances were she'd follow, and there'd be even less room for manoeuvre then. So we mooched up and down the deck, snapping at each other like sharks. She was every bit as irritable as I was, and she couldn't let go.

'You!' she hissed. 'And there was I thinking you'd changed somehow! You're just the same sleek self-centred bastard you were fifteen years ago! I thought you were so beautiful then, too! Oh, *sh*—' She stifled the word with an angry wipe of her hand, and sniffled. She'd never liked it then, either. 'You hurt me, you know that?'

I'd been trying not to say anything, but I had to come swinging back on her, I couldn't help it. 'How? Hurt you how? This time? Come on, woman! Fifteen years on, like you said. Suppose I'd asked who you were sleeping with, now? None of my bloody business, you'd have said, and you'd have had every right! We don't own each other, we're nothing to each other now – that's what you'd have said! Wouldn't you?'

'Yes!' she flared. 'So I wouldn't go sniffing after someone who looks just like you – would I?'

'How the hell would I know? I didn't go looking for this Rangda creature – she found me, and now I know why! It wasn't my fault!'

'Well, I'll just bet you didn't run away kicking and screaming!'

'You know something? I just about did, the first time.'

'The first time! *The first time?* Once wasn't enough, eh? When you're saying you didn't want it? Boy, you're really a glutton for punishment, aren't you?'

'Listen, I went to bed with her once, just once, understand? And I've been wearing my bloody throat out telling you, even that was because I was drunk.' Her smirk told me just exactly how lame that sounded. 'Drunk and mixed-up and shocked and . . . she more or less scooped me up.'

'I'll bet! And you fought her every inch of the way, didn't you?' She gave a metallic little laugh, very Chinese. 'I can just see you! Oh yes!'

I whirled on her suddenly, caught her by the shoulders. 'No! Of course I bloody didn't! I'm not sure just what exactly did happen, but sex sure as hell came into it!'

That maddening laugh again. 'And she caught you with your defences down!'

'What if she did? *What if she bloody did?* I may have messed you about, badly, yes, I'm sorry about that, but it doesn't give you any rights over me now! I've got nothing to answer to you for! Not now!'

She looked at me steadily through the dimness. 'You kissed me.'

'Afterwards, damn it! Afterwards! When I felt . . . you . . . when . . . '

'Afterwards. When you'd got what you wanted from *her*. But you got more than you expected, didn't you?'

'Oh, for . . . it wasn't *like* that! Look, so maybe I was still a bit attracted to you – did you give me one hint of encouragement, one idea you still felt anything for me? The only reason you're along here is you thought I was working some sort of con on your precious bloody project! Didn't you? *Not going to let you out of my sight*, you said! Whatever I did later, back then that was all I'd heard from you. Right?'

She shrugged, kicked at a rope's end lying across the deck. 'I suppose so. So that gives you a perfect right to behave the way you did – expect the girl you dumped right out of your life sixteen years ago to just fall flat on her back for you, the moment she walked into it again!'

'Jacquie—'

'To go on a crying drunk because you felt ever so rejected and stressed, poor thing! Poor thing!'

'Jacquie, you're jumping to conclusions—'

'Better than what you've been jumping, my boy! And worst of all, to go and . . . get your rocks off *that* way when I wouldn't give you a tumble!'

'I never asked you to!'

She yelled. 'Just as bloody well, too! For you!' Then she sighed and sucked her breath hard through her teeth, a very oriental noise of disapproval and contempt. 'To . . . to *use* another girl like that . . . To make her a substitute, a . . . a receptacle . . . Using *me*! God, the way men use a bloody *centrefold*!'

A white thrill of rage took hold of me. I could actually feel the blood draining out of my face, leaving only cold behind. My skin felt as if it had been stretched over icy metal instead of my own cheekbones. 'You ought to know,' I told her, quite brutally calm. 'You've been in enough of them.'

I folded my arms, and waited for her to try slapping me again. She didn't. Instead she just said, with a sudden rather breathless restraint, 'Just one. The others were second features. You know, I – thought you'd be proud of it.' Then, quite abruptly, she'd more or less ducked past me before I could react. There was a baffled shout from a lookout. Lightfooted and silent, she hopped up on the gangplank and with her pale hair trailing like a comet's padded down it, into the dark. I called her name. Soft steps dwindled in the shadows. I told her not to be an idiot. Silence.

Resentment held me rigid a moment. She'd been warned. Let her take the consequences. Then my obstinacy just cracked and crumbled and fell down around me. She'd been told she might not get back aboard in time, but right now that mightn't worry her too much. But nobody'd bothered to spell out that there might be other perils out there, too; after all, who needed telling? Not me, not after one long night in New Orleans. Nobody — except her. And it was my job, if anyone's, to remember that.

I looked around desperately, and raced to the plank. The lookouts were on their feet, scanning the wharfside. 'Which way?' I yelled. They shrugged. I ran down to the gangplank's end, hovered an instant, looked back in horrible indecision. A pink flash from the hold nearly blinded me; beyond the glowing saloon ports a figure rocked back and forth. The shouting, the explanations — it'd take too *long*! If I just went after her now there'd be a chance . . . and this wasn't New Orleans. I knew what I was doing, now. I had my sword. I spoke the language, a little. The lookouts shouted again as I bounced off the plank and into the dark, but I ignored them. If anything was going after Jacquie, it could take a stab at me first.

In the night substance and shadow come together, the boundaries between Core and Spiral blur. The high tide of otherness laps at the shores of settled time, washing the flotsam it carries back and forth, first one way, then another, from world to world. I ran straight as I guessed Jacquie would have, rather than down the wharves; and that would be better. That at least might carry her back into the Core, where she'd be safer. Adrift without money, papers or any kind of explanation in a suspicious state, yes; but still safer than out here. I ran, lightly, in the most obvious direction, the way that seemed to hold the sounds and lights of a modern city; that would surely draw her. Here and there I saw, reflected in stagnant puddles or rough glass panes in old plastered walls, taller buildings, well-lit windows and once a neon sign. Beneath my feet paving began to replace the ancient duckboard sidewalks, and when I saw a solitary streetlamp gleam along a side alley I turned, as Jacquie must have, drawn like any of those moths. The pull of our everyday worlds is very strong. When I saw the gleam of neon and bright shopfronts, heard the roar of traffic, I felt a leap of both gladness and dread, a tearing sensation as if I was being hauled violently both ways.

I stopped at the alley mouth, hesitating. I filled my lungs and yelled, 'Jacquie! *Jacquie!*' A gaggle of passing schoolgirls huddled together in mutual support and giggled as they looked me up and down. I could guess what they were seeing, one of those wandering Westerners who awaken both fascination and contempt among Indonesians. Hippies are practically a protected species in the rest of the world, but in Indonesia they're still flourishing. And there I was, all dark leather and bristles, with the gold brocade sweatband Mall once gave me making my hair stand up in damp spikes. Also I had a sword, but the chances were they wouldn't notice that unless I called it to their attention. 'Jacquie! *Come on*! It's bloody dangerous! Come back, dammit! I'm sorry!'

But the street was crowded, the car horns honked as people turned to look at me; they drowned out my words. A pedestrian nearby collided with another, who dropped a parcel which spilled; they started an angry chattering and gesturing at me. That distracted more drivers; cars swerved violently, there were shouts and curses. People began edging closer to see what this was about, and the pavement filled up. At least I towered above most of them, I'd be easily visible. '*Jacquie*!' I yelled again; but it got no response, except from the khaki-drab patrolman on the far side of the road. He'd come forward to break up a squabble about right of way, but everyone in the cars was pointing, at me. His almond eyes grew wider as he saw me, then he came striding across the traffic with brisk purpose, fingers flicking expertly at his holster-flap. Crazy Westerners weren't too popular with the authorities here. Defeated, I turned and ducked back into the alley and the shadow. If he came too far after me that cop might be in for some very strange adventures tonight.

It was the same story wherever I surfaced and showed my face, wherever I asked after a blond-haired Eurasian woman. One or two characters offered to show me places I could find plenty of young girls with any colour hair I liked, but I declined. Apart from anything else it sounded like a great way to bump into Rangda again. But it was deadly discouraging. If Jacquie really had passed this way, nobody remembered her. Surabaja was a bustling, modern port city with a population over the million mark, and Eurasians, even beautiful blonde ones, were no big deal. Coming from the shadows might have had something to do with it, too. No leads, then; and without them, in a place this size I could hunt for months. And I didn't want to go far from the harbour, or even if I found her neither of us might get back. I cudgelled my brain for ideas; but the roar and flash of the traffic and the cheerful crush of the evening crowds got in the way. I found a dark cool back alley, not too noisome, and retreated down it, treading very warily. To my surprise, it opened at the end into a kind of mews in a wholly European style – Dutch, probably, like the old Jembathan Merah. It was deserted, and the noise of the city had blurred into a deep bearable hum. I leaned back against some ornate railings, feeling the iron cool on the back of my tormented head, and struggled to think.

No ideas came; but after a while I realised that there was something more than traffic in that background noise, a soft, regular metallic booming with lighter clanging, chiming sounds. At first it sounded like a body-shop or some other light industry; but as my ears began to pick up the rhythmic patterns I realised what it must be, and felt my first faint thrill of hope. I came out of the mews into an open street, a row of big houses that were definitely Dutch to their high ornate gable ends. The sound seemed closer here, but still not close; as if it was drifting across the rooftops. A short walk and a left turn, and I thought I'd taken a wrong turn into somebody's garden; I was standing under a row of trees, broad, spreading European-style trees. But beyond them rose more houses, even larger, some of them a little shabby but still with immense dignity and poise. One or two of them had flagpoles above their pillared portes-cocheres, with flags drooping lifeless in the windless air, their identity hidden. They stretched out the length of a long street, and beyond the trees another row ran parallel. This had to be a semi-plush quarter of some sort, full of official residences, consulates, minor embassies even – hence the flagpoles. Even in Indonesia they wouldn't have a panel-beating shop nearby. I stopped, listened again, heard a peal of shrill laughter, and felt sure I was right. Far down the row of trees the leaves glowed dim yellow from beneath. That was where the sound was coming from, and I strode swiftly down towards it.

The pavement was rough, the flags cracked and irregular; it was easier to walk on the springy mould underneath the trees. And it kept me in shadow, too, which suited me. Embassies generally had guards, and they might not like the look of me right now. I passed silently through the trees, drawn like the moths by that warm light and the soft incessant sound, like the chatter of a river cast in bronze. A high thin voice quavered, and the voices laughed again – children and adults, such a homely sound I wasn't ready for what happened next. My breath choked in my throat, my heart gave a convulsive skip; in the heart of that yellow glow something black leaped up, cobra-fast, and seemed to swoop towards me with impossible speed, a shapeless thing of swirling tracery and skeletal limbs.

I jumped, snatched at my sword, stumbled over a root and went to one knee, gasping. But another spidery thing sprang up and capered, the high voice wailed, the chiming intensified and wooden blocks rattled; the voices squealed with delight. I gasped for breath, laughing at my own discomfiture. I'd recognised the sound of the *gamelan* all right, the Indonesian percussion orchestra. It was the booming pulse of the double gong I'd heard first, the clanging of the *demung* and *ketuk*, like bronze xylophones and bowls, I'd mistaken for metal-working. There was a reason for that; this wasn't the quiet, refined *gamelan* I'd heard before. It was raucous, dramatic, rising to swift climaxes punctuated by the drubbing of the *kendang* drum, and no wonder; that was what I hadn't expected. It was accompanying a performance of the *wayang kulit*, the immensely popular shadow-puppet theatre, and the yellow light, cast by a hissing pressure lantern on a cloth stretched loosely between two trees, was its screen.

I'd never seen the *wayang* before, and I was enthralled at the liveliness of the shadow-creatures, mere traceries of leather worked by thin sticks of buffalo-horn. But they chattered and pummelled at each other with amazing individuality as the puppeteer chanted their words in a high, stilted voice, using language so archaic I could only catch the odd word or two; so a Javanese with a smattering of English might try to understand Shakespeare. But this was more popular than Shakespeare; adults and kids alike were squatting around in the little arc of golden light, laughing and cheering at the antics of the characters on the screen.

I lingered in the outer shadows, leaning against a heavy old tree, watching. I had more than one reason for that. The more I thought about Jacquie, the less likely it seemed she'd bolt back to the bright lights, in the mood she was in. She might have looked, but then she'd have realised how out of place she was; I saw her drifting back into the darkness to be alone. The loud theatre *gamelan* must be audible all through this area, as I'd found; if she was lost and wandering anywhere around, I couldn't think of a single thing more calculated to attract her.

Besides, it was a great show.

At first I was completely lost, but then it came to me that I did seem to be making out something of what was going on. For all the cartoon-like stylisation of the puppets I could tell the handsome heroes with their dashing stride from the lumbering menace of the demons. This had to be one of the Eastern epics – not that I ever had much time for that kind of thing, but Jacquie had solemnly told me about them all, at length, years ago. Thinking of that, I suddenly found one character I did recognise, a special favourite with the children who cheered his every appearance – a hunched, long-armed shape with wagging head and tail and bounding, rolling gait. The puppeteer cackled and gibbered to accompany his capering antics. So this must be the *Ramayana*, with the distraught hero Rama and his wife the virtuous Sita, abducted by their demonic adversaries the *Rakasha*. And here was Rama's unlikely ally Hanuman, the monkey king, who sacrificed his tail to carry fire into the demons' stronghold. I found myself swaying with the sympathies of the watchers, sharing their delight at his anarchic pranks, thrilling with terror at the monstrous looming forms of the *Rakasha*. These are archetypes with which every Indonesian grows up, images as potent and instantly recognisable as James Bond or Superman in the West, and in that half-lit evening I felt a sense of gathering power about that ancient struggle between good and evil, no less terrible for its predetermined end.

Caught up as I, too, was in the action, I began to be aware of something else. The warm night air seemed to be full of moths and music and laughter one moment, with the smell of spice and sweat and nothing more. Then the next there was another sort of presence, definite, and growing stronger – like eyes on the back of one's neck. Except that with this one I had no desire at all to turn around, whatever the consequences. I was afraid to move, however much I told myself it couldn't be worse than *not* knowing what was there. I believed that, it was just that my limbs didn't. It was as if a cold breath blew around me, and every hair on my bare neck and arms seemed to bristle. I could feel my back muscles twitching and writhing slightly, as if trying to squirm away from whatever was only inches behind them. My hand was on my belt, just next to my sword; I didn't go for it, of course. I had more sense. But if I could just – if I could *only* nerve myself to spin around and draw in one movement . . .

I got no further than forcing my head about a quarter of a turn around. Someone else was standing there, to my right; someone I recognised. Recognition was a major shock; I gasped with the breathlessness of a skipped heartbeat. The rush of my breath broke the spell; or changed the electricity of it. I turned to face the figure that stood there, leaning on his glass-topped staff and contemplating the show with a keen and critical eye.

'You are enjoying the theatre, *Tuan* Fisher? I would not have thought you to be a connoisseur.'

I drew breath again. But it was a moment before I spoke, because I was weighing my words very carefully. 'I'm not, Mpu Bharadah. I've never seen it before. But yes, it's very good. It lives.'

His thin lips drew back in a dry smile. 'So do most things, in their given place and moment. This is well enough, in its way. But we have better ones on Bali. We have many better things on Bali.'

My own smile came out as a twisted grimace. 'Including one hell of a heap of problems.' I was tempted to add his name to the list, but something in his cold glance told me he'd read the thought. 'Look – back at Borobodur . . . '

'Yes, *tuan*?'

'I saw you drive off Rangda – or whatever you did. Don't for one minute believe I'm not grateful, but . . . why on earth? Why did you bother? Wasn't she going to accomplish just what you wanted? What you threatened me with?'

I expected the *pedanda* to deny the threats, if only so as not to lose face. But he shook his head in a very Western way. 'No. She was intending to lay hands upon the devices your metal case contains and . . . infect them. Control them, for her own ends, as she controlled you that night, working you like these *wayang* figures on their sticks. Control the distribution of water, and you control the sweet isle of Bali – and down many long ages that has been Rangda's will.'

'And you? What about your will? Or maybe I shouldn't ask?'

Unperturbed, Bharadah rasped a bony finger along his iron-grey moustache, trimmed to military smartness. 'Of course you may ask. Throughout those ages I and others of my kind have fought her, as you have had to. She is a creature of *kelod*, of the shore and the sea to which all evil flows. And from across the sea, always, she has drawn evil in upon these lands she desires. Once Bali was no more than a part of her empire – or her desire. All the islands of the region were to be her stepping stones, the gold of the sunrise her treasury and the scarlet of the sunset her finery. To fulfil those inordinate desires, always she has drawn outsiders down upon us, the British, the Dutch, the Japanese, who held this place – always to our ruin, and often to hers also. But it has not stopped her. Dominion is still her desire.'

I looked at him cynically. 'Of course what you want is something absolutely different, isn't it?'

He rounded on me with a glare that made me step back. 'What I want? You ignorant barbarian, how dare you presume to know what *I* want? How could you even guess at it? What *I* want, child of the wastrel West, is the days that were, and the old ways that filled them – the dream of an ancient land, unawoken by disorder, unscarred by time. If I seek control, it is on the side of mankind, and the way of life that has evolved through nature, and in harmony with it.' He regarded me with a kind of quizzical scepticism, and his voice became milder. '*Tuan*, you have asked me a question. Now I shall ask you one. You are what is called a capitalist; which do you prefer: the order of things that has evolved naturally and through consensus, or the change that is imposed from outside?' His smile was seraphic, but his eyes never left mine.

I stared. That was one hell of a loaded question to ask any aspiring politician – but that was exactly why I ought to be able to cope with it. And something told me I'd better. But at party meetings it wasn't as hot as this, was it? I wouldn't be as tired or as hungry, with a *gamelan* clanging in my ears, and the puppeteer's enthusiastic gibbering. Intellectual challenge wasn't what I'd been expecting. 'Well – that's capitalism against Marxism, isn't it? Or socialism. Nobody ever sat down and doped out a system called capitalism; it's just the way the world works, much the same in any culture. But okay, like any other human behaviour it goes wrong sometimes, or it goes too far; or other things in the world affect it. Then checks and balances have to be imposed. From inside, if possible; that's always better. But if not, changes—'

'But if it is not those who live within the system who would change it? And if those changes threaten to bring the whole system down?'

'Well . . . ' I floundered, feeling the sweat runnels pool at the small of my back and trickle down unpleasantly. He gave me no chance to marshal my objection, but plunged on with a fierce passion, jerking his head slightly to emphasise a point, but never losing my gaze.

'Change, checks, balances, they are one thing; anarchy is another. The evolved order, the ancient way; whatever its deficiencies it must be better than that, must it not? So change should be restrained, measured, weighed carefully against the other damage it might do – is that not so?'

I found myself nodding, as if in time to the racketing of the *gamelan*, and stopped angrily. What he said made sense, and yet I didn't want to go along with it; it wasn't as if I disagreed exactly, it was more as if there were swirling undertows of meaning, in danger of sweeping me away.

'But you will say – will you not?– ' he inclined his head politely, 'that at times, perhaps, some degree of change is at last found to be inevitable. Surely, then, to avoid catastrophic cultural dislocation, it is best that it filter down under the restraining hand of the older order.'

I shook my head in disagreement, but I'd nothing to say. There was a lot I wanted to parry with – about stagnation and ritual and decay and repression. But I was tired and confused, and more than a little overawed by this coolly self-possessed creature. Somehow the words just wouldn't take shape. He pressed the point home.

'Surely it is better that those whose way of life is most at risk should themselves decide? Surely, when they have the wisdom to understand the necessity of change, it is best that the means of it be . . . given into their hands?'

I swallowed. Hard to argue with that – the implications, though . . . But I found myself manoeuvred into a mental corner, nodding, dimly. His face grew a little kinder. 'Do not think I do not sympathise with you, *tuan*,' he said gravely, 'put in this impossible position, caught between forces you do not understand. How could you? The harmony we have created to live in, with nature, and each other, and most of all with our own inner selves – that you have never known. You of the West, has your material wealth, your vast store of knowledge ever found you such a balance? Yet in it lies the remedy for many of the ills that beset you – for discontent, for fear, for the troubled yearning of the inner self, the half-empty heart.' His voice sank to a whisper, and the gold-caged globe of crystal glittered between his fingers. 'The question has been asked of you also. *What profiteth it a man, that he should gain the whole world and yet lose his own soul?*'

His eyes held mine. The notes of the *gamelan* scattered through my head, like leaping fireflies, and overhead a big bat wheeled and dived in hypnotic spirals between the branches. The lights faded, the show seemed somehow to become more distant, fainter, voice and laughter and stick-figures and all; there was only the fierce old man and myself beneath the tree shadow, the glitter of his gaze and the crisp precision of his voice. 'I read it in you, how greatly your own life lacks such a way. All your life you have sought one, in your work; and yet where has that left you? Alone, weary, a success to the world, yet in your heart, in your home, a bitter failure. You have no wife, no children, no family; among our people you would be counted a thing of pity, as a man bereft of his limbs or his understanding. You feel your lack, yet you do not wholly comprehend how great it is. You could not, or you would not be aiding those who would destroy the ways that are ours. Will you not open your heart to them – to me – and be enlightened?'

'*Steve!*'

The voice was Jacquie's.

It sliced through the night, through that pinioning gaze, through my thoughts. The world leaped. There was a discontinuity, a space of shock, a rude awakening. I wasn't standing arguing civilly with the old priest; I was backed against a tree, panting, with sweat in my eyes and my sword in both hands above my head, being forced back and down by the inexorable pressure of that crystal-topped staff. Some way off, one side of her lit golden by the suddenly distant *wayang* screen, stood Jacquie, wide-eyed, horrified. But the horror that came squirming up inside me was far worse, a deepseated shuddering nausea I knew only too well by now. The late unlamented Don Petro had tried to use my commercial ambitions to do this to me; tried, and failed. Rangda had used sex, and succeeded, up to a point; or had she tapped some other, deeper vulnerability? Now this old devil was seeking his way in through my beliefs – and my weaknesses. Devil indeed, for I doubted anyone still human could even seek to possess me as this one had. But against Don Petro I'd found help that let me defend myself on two levels at once; and it seemed I still knew how. It came to me in a flash – that was why he'd changed his line of attack to the sweet and reasonable! It was only on that level I was vulnerable.

'*You – bastard!*' I screamed, loud enough to make the *gamelan* falter and the puppeteer's wailing narrative stutter. With all the revulsion that rose in my gullet I straightened up, and, aware now, dug my knee into his narrow belly and snapped up hard. The kick hurled him back against the opposite trunk with a crash that shook down leaves; his staff flew from his hands and spun off into the grove. He reeled off the trunk, and stooped to snatch up the staff. With an incoherent yell of fury I aimed a tremendous two-handed slash at him. It smashed deep into the trunk of an ancient cedar, sending me staggering.

A voice hissed, almost in my ear. '*Berhati hati, orang pemboros!* Beware, despoiler, waster! You are not yet at the bounds of my realm, and it has more barriers than one!' But as I looked around wildly there was nobody there. He had faded like smoke.

Jacquie's footsteps pattered on the leaf mould as she came running towards me, caught me and clung. She managed to gasp my name, I hers, but that was about as coherent as we got. We shivered in the grip of shock, me from my experience, she from her wanderings.

'—only wanted to get away—'
'—taking me over, right into my mind—'
'—just meant to go a little way—'
'—didn't mean—'
'—memorised the way, but it changed! *It changed*—'
'—felt I'd driven you—'
'—looking for you—'
'—looking for you—'
'—then it was hours, and I thought—'
'—bloody fool—'
'—forgive me?—'
'Me, I mean me . . . *Me*!'
'Well . . . me too . . . '

We hung there, supporting each other, while an awful lot of crust and armour crumbled away in the dark – about sixteen years' worth, maybe. It helped that it was dark; masks are useless, all cats are grey and all faces equally lost. There was nothing to ours but touch, the hot flush of Jacquie's cheek against my own, the faint brushing of her lips against my ear. I bent down and kissed the delicate slope from shoulder to neck, felt the sudden play of tension in our bodies.

Jacquie got some of her practicality back first. 'We'd better get away from here,' she mumbled. I glanced around in alarm. The performance was still going on, but *wayang* shows often lasted all night.

'Right,' I gasped. 'This way . . . I think . . . ' Still shaking, still leaning on each other, we staggered across the little park. I was casting about where the trees were thickest, looking for the avenue I'd come down, nervously aware that I couldn't be sure of it. The shadows closed around us again, and the sound of the *wayang* grew distant. The night was silent, so silent that the rustle of our footsteps was deafening in the close air. Suddenly something shot out from under our feet with a shrill croaking cry, and flapped off among the leaves – some sort of bird, but to our shattered nerves it might as well have been a cobra. We clutched each other tight, feeling the tremors that ran through us, hugging, stroking, murmuring words of comfort. But the shock passed quickly, and somehow or other we didn't stop, until some pretty unmistakable reactions brought it home to us just exactly what we were doing.

'Oh my *god!*' exclaimed Jacquie breathlessly, but she didn't stop. My hands were under her rumpled shirt, rubbing along her ribcage, rising to cup her breasts, hers delving around below my belt.

'We can't!' I said in utter horror. 'I mean . . . not here . . . we might . . . '

'Well, don't do that, then!' she mumbled. 'Oh god, don't do that!' I stopped doing that. She ground herself against me so hard I hadn't any choice.

'*You* stop!' I wheezed. She stopped, but she didn't let go.

'I've got to hang on,' she murmured. 'I can't stand up . . . '

I slid my hands down to support her, and they ended up on her buttocks, and where was the harm in that? After all, we weren't teenagers, we'd just hang on a little longer and get back to the ship in no time. And her jeans were in the way, so it'd be nothing much more if I – her belt was too tight. I shifted my grip, fumbled it open, felt her weight shift from leg to leg and her head on my chest, her half-open lips breathing a patch of heat through my shirt. Her zip gave under the strain, her jeans folded down and her panties – strong, sensible cotton – slid over my fingers; there was the warmth and the scent of her open to my hands, sliding down, sliding round, feeling the dimples of taut muscles, sliding round and down to the first light wisps. She gave a little cry, sagged as if her legs were giving out; but if she was so damn helpless, how come she was doing that to my pants – and where the hell was my sword, we'd end up falling on it if this went on . . .

It went on, but we didn't, not quite. She wasn't falling, she was pulling me down on to her, and the moist leaf mould was wondrously soft as we settled in a tangle of half-removed clothes and clutching limbs. A heady cocktail of old memories and concealing darkness destroyed our inhibitions, danger and safety alike forgotten. We buried ourselves, our senses in one another, and let what was beyond go past. To me the world seemed to be full of Jacquie; nuzzling into the warm flux of her limbs around me, nothing else existed, nothing was to be feared. Just once we surfaced, and that almost as a ploy, to suspend excitement, delay fulfilment, before the final plunge.

'Was it . . . this good . . . all those . . . years ago?' she panted into the night.

I twisted to kiss her ankles, which were either side of my neck at the time. 'No . . . ' was as much as I could manage. 'Didn't know then . . . possible . . . lose so much . . . ' I bore down on her, and her hands clawed at my hips, and the darkness jolted into exploding, coruscating light.

Then, eventually then, we fell apart, aside; and of course it didn't last. Suddenly we were aching, sticky and sweaty, encrusted with bits of leaf in all kinds of uncomfortable and embarrassing places, raw and abraded in others; my elbows were scraped, my mouth tasted foul, and at some point a sharp stone had neatly sliced the skin on my left kneecap.

'You think you've got problems,' shivered Jacquie. 'I'm not on the pill or anything.'

'Oh. Unh. Look . . . '

'Not your fault. Don't worry, it'll be all right. Why'd you think I wasn't in any hurry to get married again? Not many prospects in that direction.'

'Oh,' I said again, and hugged her.

'Thanks,' she said. 'I don't mind that much, anyhow. Not very much.'

Depression recoiled on us, and we sat in silence for a few minutes longer. A faint glimmer of moon filtered through the trees now, putting a sickly lustre on our white skins. Her flank felt cool against mine, and she shivered. 'Not so warm any more,' she complained.

'No. Feels as if the wind's changing—' I stopped. The wind! And the moon! The overcast was breaking. If dawn was coming . . .
'Jesus! We've got to get back to the ship!'

She squeaked and tried to jump up, tripped over the jeans she still wore round one ankle and fell over me. As I'd done almost the same thing, we fell in one swearing heap.

'Like bloody teenagers!' I snarled, scrabbling at my waistband, wishing I didn't have to pull clothes over skin that felt like the floor of a New York taxi. 'Off our bloody heads—'

'God! Just, just *going* at each other like that! Like a pair of alleycats – and, and – oh *damn*, what my mouth tastes of – I've got *hair* between my teeth—'

'So've I!' We stopped, both of us, hesitant suddenly. Then, rather tentatively, I felt her put her hand on my arm. I didn't say anything more, just reached out and hugged her again.

'It *was* stupid, though,' she said, glancing around. 'If he'd come back – the old man – and found us—'

'He'd have got a shock. But he didn't. And you know, out here on the Spiral emotion is a potent force like many others, if it's strong enough. So I've been told, anyhow. Love can be a strong defence in itself.'

'Love?'

I didn't say anything else for a moment, rooting around for my sword. I made as if to thrust it through its belt-loop, then thought better of it and kept it in my hand. 'We'd better get a bend on. There – see those rooftops? That looks like it.'

'Then you were going the wrong way before.'

I glanced at her, but her face was unreadable. 'Look, are you coming, or not?'

There was a brief chuckle. 'Not now. All right, love it is. Though god alone knows what sort, Steve. Let's go.'

I took her hand, swung it wide as we walked, just the way I did when we were students. Or did I? I'd been very wary of childish gestures like that, very careful not to tarnish my cool image – bloody little prig. 'What sort? Love secondhand. Revived. Reconditioned.'

She laughed. 'Retextured. Resurfaced. Retreaded – retrod? Invisible mending.' She gave a little sigh. 'Only it never is, is it? You can always see the patch.'

'That only shows somebody cared enough to mend it. Instead of throwing it away.'

She didn't answer. But she kept hold of my hand, all the way down the long avenue and back along the little street that ought to bring us out in the mews. It didn't. Another avenue like the first opened before us, evidently running at right angles to it. 'Maybe we passed it,' I said, trying to conceal my anxiety. 'One of the earlier sidestreets . . .'

'We'd better hurry,' said Jacquie, tonelessly. 'Look, the moon's down, practically. There can't be much of the night left.'

'I know! I know!'

We wheeled about, strode back towards the openings we'd passed. One did look much like another – and it'd been darker when I came through – but was it this one, or the next? Or was it one still further up?

'It's just what happened to me,' said Jacquie, with a nervy edge to her words. 'I didn't mean to go far, I was very careful to remember my way – and it changed! It *changed*!'

'I know!' I said absently, scanning the sidestreet for some hopeful indication. 'It's happened to me before. Somewhere else.'

'It has?' She breathed out. 'I thought I was going . . . How did you get . . . out, or whatever it is you got?'

'I had help. I might have managed anyway. Or I might not.'

'Steve, what'll they do, Ape and the others? Just sail away and leave—'

Her fingers clamped hard into my palm, and she gave a little shriek. I didn't need the alert. I'd seen them already, the hulking distorted shadows gliding on the stuccoed sidestreet wall, three stories high or more. Bulky distorted bodies, monstrous and troll-like, stalking forward and just hanging there, as if waiting.

That wasn't the sort of indicator I wanted. 'Back!' I said. 'Into the trees, fast! Christ knows what—' I ran down. And then I felt a laugh bubbling up. Jacquie stared. 'Well, look at them!' I burbled. 'They're not solid – see? And the way their limbs move! The *wayang* show – they're just *wayang* puppets projected on the wall! So much punched and painted leather! There must be another show going on through there somewhere!'

Jacquie gave a gurgle of delight. 'Yes, of course! Only . . .' She looked around. 'Where's the music? We should be able to hear another *gamelan* this close! And the *dalang*'s voice . . .'

She was right. We stopped, listened. It was eerily silent. And then, suddenly, one of the monstrous things half turned, stretched out an arm. It was the authentic *wayang* spidery limb, all right; but of any stick supporting it, no sign. Then I realised; it had turned! The shadow had shifted, visibly, and changed its shape and aspect. That thing was no sheet of buffalo parchment, stretched and punched; impossible as it looked, it was three-dimensional. These things were solid; and they had to be damn near as tall as the trees above us.

Jacquie'd seen it, too. We exchanged brief horrified glances, then with one accord we would have bolted. Except that, outlined faintly in the low moonlight, other giant shadows were thrown huge and quivering across the crumbling stucco of the house fronts, back along the avenue. And though nothing that threw them could be seen, they were advancing.

Then there came the voice.

'*You need not run. The kalas move fast, for all their size.*' It was the voice of the old priest, Mpu Bharadah, but strangely changed. It wasn't shouting, yet it seemed to come from far away, almost from our feet with a strange echo to it, as if he was calling from below the ground, or through it. '*Nor is there shelter for you beneath the boughs. For I am named the Banaspati Raja, the Lord of the Forest.*'

Ahead of us the branches swished and stirred suddenly, as if something large was brushing through. But wherever it was, I couldn't see anything, only branches and blackest shadow, drawing in about us like a net as the weak moon sank.

'*There is no need to fear. You need only tell me where that coffer of your devices is hidden, and how protected, and you will go free on the instant, you and the girl, unharmed.*'

'Suppose we don't?' yelled Jacquie over the rising wind. 'Killing us won't stop the Project!'

'*But help disrupt and discourage it, that it will do. And scare off any more of your contemptible kind, who grow fat in picking the bones of those they claim to aid!*'

The threat and the insult together, that really did it. I looked at Jacquie, risking her life to help a people she'd hardly ever met; I thought of how easily I could have stayed back at my office spending this much effort on safe, easy deals, of how much my time was worth to the company. The weight of the sword was comforting, but against those monsters it seemed about as much use as a knitting needle. A cedary odour still clung to it from the bleeding sap – and the spicy tang gave me an idea. Words can be turned both ways; and power can be countered with a little judicious bluff.

I shouted back, into the rushing night around us. 'A haunter of trees you seem to be – but to hell with Lord of the Forest! You know who's lord of any forest you care to mention? Man, that's who! And right here and now that means *me*! Right around the world, from the time we first reared up on two legs, we've been facing up to nature – yes, and trashing it! I've power of my own, priest. A capitalist, you called me; well, think about it. Think! About stinking chemicals stripping the leaves from these precious trees of yours! About screaming chainsaws slashing off their limbs, about giant tractors tearing up the mould as they haul them off for pulp! About brown earth drying up and blowing away to dust, till we come to plant it with roots of steel and pour concrete in its place! Well, priest? Will all your threats stop *that*?'

No voice answered. The lumbering shadows moved closer. Jacquie stared at them, and at me, saying nothing. I cast about desperately, thinking back on all the strange and sinister things I'd seen done, the actions people had gone through, the motions of summoning up some kind of power. There was Le Stryge, stripping the wind from a ship's sail with a spell – the shocking brutality of it was with me still . . .

I lashed out with the sword and hit the tree beside me, the blade sinking deep into the wrinkled old yew bark with a soft singing impact. I wrenched it free, struck again at the same point, chopping out a notch as if I meant to start felling it then and there.

'You hear that, priest?' I yelled, fighting hard not to let my voice crack with desperation. I struck again. 'This tree or any tree – this tree and all trees! All the trees on that stinking little island of yours!' I stepped back and slashed up, high up into the foliage. I meant to bring down a rain of leaves and twigs, no more; but felt the blade jar against a great limb. There was a snapping, a rush, a blur, and I barely jumped back in time as an immense branch crashed down into the mould between me and Jacquie. The wind flowing between the trees sank suddenly to a breeze, and they seemed to be chattering and whispering between the branches.

Jacquie, horrified, opened her mouth to say something. I shushed her wildly, and pointed. The shadows had come no further. Scooping up the branch, I brandished it as much as I could manage and shouted defiance. 'Demons, giants, whatever the hell you are! You're of the trees, are you? Then you can fall with 'em! And fall you bloody well will, if you don't pull back right now!'

I lifted the sword before my face, muttered over it as I'd seen Le Stryge and others do – any old nonsense, including some lines from a First World War poem that had caught my eye in a *Time* caption a week or two past, that seemed to fit somehow.

> Three lives hath one life.
> Iron, honey, gold;
> The gold, the honey gone,
> Left is the hard and cold.

Then I took aim at the tree, and swung the blade up to strike. 'You hear?' I shouted. 'This tree – all trees – '

'*Stop*! There were two voices, one beneath the earth, the other Jacquie's. Instantly the shadows seemed to sag, as if their dark substance was flowing out of them. The wind whistled and sank, a wave of blackness rolled over the treetops and was gone. The walls were blank, the mouth of the sidestreet empty. I grabbed Jacquie's wrist.

'Run for it!' For the first few steps I was almost dragging her, then she caught her stride and shook her wrist free. Together we skidded and stumbled into the street, down into the mews and along, colliding in the narrow passage, and out into another sidestreet that was deeply shadowed, but had no trees at all. We didn't stop, not until we reached a corner I remembered, and swung round it, gasping, to lean against the wall.

'We ought – to get further . . . ' I coughed.

'A minute,' Jacquie wheezed, doubled over like an Olympic sprinter. 'Or I'll throw up—'

'Don't even *say* it!'

She straightened up, rubbing her side, leaned against the wall by my side. 'What'd you *do* back there?' she demanded, half relieved, half accusing.

'How the hell should I know?'

'You didn't really mean . . . to . . . you couldn't . . . '

I exploded. 'It got us out, didn't it? Okay,' I added, subsiding, 'I'm not very proud of myself. But I was getting so goddamned fed up of everyone accusing me of being some kind of profiteering con-man, or environmental rapist, or something – I'm a shipping agent, for crissake! I didn't invent this bloody Project, I'm only trying to help!'

'I know,' said Jacquie softly.

'Well, that's nice. Okay, so I thought it might be an effective bluff to pose as one, pretend I could work magic that way. That priest creature, he was all too ready to believe it – all his worst fears coming true. Of course I didn't mean it! I like trees, dammit! I even sponsored planting one in the pavement outside the office. And I couldn't do any harm whatever I said, could I? I'm not Ape, am I? Not a bloody wizard!'

Jacquie hunched down into her shoulders. 'That branch . . . what brought that down?'

I shrugged. 'It must have been half broken or something. Or maybe I just don't know my own strength.'

'Maybe you don't,' she said quietly. 'You didn't look at it closely. The leaves were all green, it must've been still alive minutes before. But the end, right up to the bark, it was almost liquid. Rotten.'

I didn't say anything more. We hurried on, looking behind us often, though there was never anything there. The streets made way for us, almost as if they were glad to be rid of us; and the shadows were still deep and dark when a hoarse hail from up ahead made us jump. But it was only Ape, with te Kiore and a bunch of the hardest crewmen, standing at a corner ahead; and as we hurried down to them we saw the lights of the schooner in the distance.

'And that is as far as I come, by dom!' rumbled Ape. 'Further I do not stray, not with such-like enemies at our back. I've more sense! You—' He snorted at us. 'I have not the time to tell you what I am thinking, nor the words neither. But if one of you take just one little step off this ship again without my asking, I wash my hands of you! And go find some other deserving case that has got more than maybe two brain cells in the head and a whole lot less between the legs – *goed begripten*? *Goed zo*. Now, what happens?'

We told him the story as we walked back to the ship, punctuated by explosive oaths from te Kiore and the crew. When we got to the apparitions, the mate practically jumped in his tracks. '*Kalas*? Bloody hell on a frigging handcart!' He looked around so fast he almost dislocated his neck, and the crewmen bunched together around us.

'You sure they no go follow you?' muttered the Dyak bosun. 'They bunch of mean motherfuckers, they go stomp you flat you no see. They no come behind?'

214

'They no – I mean, no, they didn't, I'm sure.'

'I'd have felt it,' put in Jacquie, in a very small voice.

'Then how in blazes do you escape them?' growled Ape.

I didn't feel like telling him, till we were safely aboard. He heard me out silently, back squatting by the rail; but he rubbed a hand across his blunt jaw and rasped at his beard, while the look on his face grew darker and grimmer.

'*Dood ok ondergang!*' he muttered when I'd finished. 'Did I say these powers, they scare me? You, *jonge*, men like you I fear one thousands of times more.'

'Look, weren't you listening, or something? Twice I said it! I never meant to carry out that threat, even supposing for one minute I ever could—'

'Not unless you maybe feel it necessary?' suggested Ape quietly. 'And with intentions of maybe the best. But, have you stopped to think, you who call this a bluff to save your own so-precious life? Stopped to think what with aiding all this Project you might truly be doing?'

I stared, startled. 'Ape, I thought you'd got over your ... reservations about it. You've been helping us right down the line, after all!'

His deepset eyes glinted up at me, sidelong, a disquieting look. 'Because such power as that little box of tricks represents, better it is in the hands of the Project than of the contending forces of Bali. For I know who it is who opposes you now, and very dangerous they are, those two. The spirits of place they are, as once of all this land of islands and the ancient faiths and beliefs that bridge it; and though they are withdrawn now to one island before an alien faith, within the rest their hands are still strong, as their image is within the hearts of the people. Once, long ago, perhaps long before the Hindu gods ride laughing across the lands in their glittering chariots, before Sita is stolen or the fatal dice game played, they are men and women, these forces. The more so, since they take that shape again with ease. Rangda, it is said, she is then the wicked princess Mahendradatta; others say, the witch Kalon Arang, others yet the wife of Lord Shiva himself, Durga. Any of these she is, perhaps. Or all; for in the swirling of the Spiral even selves and souls may merge.'

'You don't have to tell me,' I shuddered, remembering what plans Don Petro had for me.

'So. But whoever they be, long ago they drift out into the

reaches of the Rim, and there they change. Or are changed, by outer forces reaching inward. Be that how it may, of the land they are, and with the land they are grown; by their contention it is shaped, and in the tension between them is its stability. Its balance they are, violent against contemplative, anarchic against reactionary. Princess against priest, still, perhaps.'

'*Kelod* and *Kaja*,' put in Jacquie softly. 'The Balinese own words for it. Governing the way a temple's oriented, a house, the direction of prayer, even the way they lie in their beds. And all in terms of water, flowing from the heart of the land towards the sea – inflow is evil, outflow good. Water – always water!'

'*Agama tirta*,' nodded Ape. 'The religion of water – so they themselves name their faith. But this balance, it may not be equal. More must flow out than in. The quieter side, the stronger it must be; but the fiercer side, it keeps its spirit alive. But then, along comes this great and noble Project – what then? That the flow may be turned this way, that way, no longer by the will of the village *subaks*, but at the behest of machine minds from oversea. These two sides, natural they try to keep such machines out. But when this is no longer possible, what then, what then? Then each seeks control. Let but one side or another get its paws upon the control of these machines, and you put more power in them than ever they have before. That power uses it against the other – it can do no else, it too is a prisoner of the pattern it long ago creates. And the other, what can it do, sooner or later, but retaliate? And so civil war is unleashed in the hearts of men, and the island's future shattered. These bandits, these guerrillas now loose on Bali where never they were before – are they not the first sign?'

Jacquie was literally wringing her hands. 'But nobody on the Project wants *that*! Nothing like it! We . . . just wanted to help, that's all! Help the old and the children who're the first to die in the droughts . . . Isn't there *any* way the system can be used for good?'

Ape rose, suddenly little shorter than me as his shoulders straightened. 'None I can conceive of. None I may enforce. Not even if we succeed. If we break the blockade, if we keep it from the hands of those twin powers, still it brings change. The new machine minds take charge, the old ways appear worthless and the young they discard them. A single culture spreads, and by so much the isle slips further out of its so-long shadow of years, that makes it what it is. It blends deeper into that mass of hard-packed human destiny you name the Core, from which emerges less and less, into which less and less enters. The isle then, it is further removed both from good and evil; and the colours of its life, very old and strong, they fade to grey. With time it grows ever more like any other place – have you not seen such things happen? Its folk, perhaps, they are even better off, with machines from another land that wash their plates and cars and clothes and maybe wipe their backsides all nice and healthier than now, and water is no longer something they worship. Better off, in material; in spirit – *pfui!* – too bad. From the ancient interplay that makes them what they are, they are cut off, that gives them an identity and a destiny to call their own, both within the Core and beyond, out upon the arms of the Spiral, transcendent. Then they share only some-body else's.' His mobile lips pursed and blew a loud raspberry, but followed it up with a deep bubbling sigh. 'But still, better that is than starvation, or the apart-tearing of civil war. If it must come thus, it must.'

'But does it have to be that, one or the other? Those are extremes! People have found ways to come to terms with change before – can't they find some way to adjust to this?'

Ape shrugged wearily. 'I tell you already – none I can im-agine. These clockwork minds of yours I know little of, what they can do, what they cannot. In the hands of men who do lies any such answer. And if I read the signs aright, those hands may be yours.'

I bridled. '*Mine?* What the hell d'you mean mine? I've never even been to this place yet! Jesus! Why drop it on me? I'm not even up to anything like this – you're so fond of telling me what I am, you ought to know that! Well then – tell me what to do! Is all this effort of mine doing one bloody bit of good at all? Should I block the Project the way all the others did? Because that much, that's in my hands all right! Should we just heave the container overside, into the deep sea, and go home?'

Jacquie's face looked ugly and rebellious. I saw she was fighting back tears, and looked away. 'Maybe we should. Maybe we should! If all this . . . all this hope and hard work, all the dedicated teams – if they're just going to tear the place apart and either way the poor Balinese get crushed . . . Screw it, then! Screw the whole lot of it, screw the engineers and the computer people and the construction gangs! Let them just turn around and go back home and sweep up their own goddamn doorsteps and never try and help anyone again!'

'*Cultivons notre jardin*!' quoted Ape unexpectedly, and even more unexpectedly he laid a ham hand on her shoulder. 'But no, this I do not agree.'

She looked up. 'You don't?'

'*Welnie*. Why would I come so far with you if I did? Bali is an island in time as well as space, but the flow does not pass it by forever. Sooner or later such a change must come. Better it comes thus, with us to steer and govern it, than blindly after much suffering.' A shout came from the bridge, and the deck thrummed and bounced to the rush of feet. We looked aloft. The mastheads showed stark and bare against a greying sky, without colour or cheer, a world without differences, inequities, unfairnesses; and who was to say which side they were on? The gangplank was hauled rattling in, and we sprang to our feet, only to duck as the mainsail boom came swinging over our heads. Ape clapped Jacquie gently on the shoulder. 'Go ahead. Follow your vision of good as you must, for in it there is much truth. But only on the Spiral do you find absolutes of good and evil, and few indeed of those; for they are uncanny company for mere men. Within the Core are only choices, that carry greater or lesser weight. You have a good choice, on balance. Defend it as you do so far, and so also will we. But it may not be enough. We must struggle to find a better – or bear upon ourselves the burden of what is to follow.' He turned away, and swung himself down the companionway with the ease of his namesake.

The wind caught, the sails cracked, a thunderous sound like a voice of doom. The bows lifted as the wind swung us out from the wharf and all the perils of the land, but my spirits didn't lift with it. Two contending powers against us – and what of the mysterious third? I looked round to ask Ape, but he was already below. The dawn was a tropical blaze, and the greyness vanished in a flare of red. The great archipelago spread out before us in that fanfare of light; but instead of golden beaches each island seemed to me encircled with red, with bloodstained shores and fire blazing across its crown. And not only to me; for Jacquie, standing beside me, gave voice to my own half-formed thoughts.

'How will it feel, do you think, Steve? To be back in a comfortable office, half a world away, reading in the morning paper about yet another little brushfire civil war? Only this time, to know that, somehow – somehow! – we might have prevented it?'

The wolves were at the gate. The run from Surabaja to Bali should have been pretty short, little over a hundred miles. But Batang Sen wasn't taking any chances. He knew our departure would be marked by many eyes, human and less so, and he set our course in a wide horseshoe sweep outwards into the Jawa sea, around the northern coast of Madura island, in the hope of circling around his Boegie kinsmen or any other ill-intentioned characters who might be lurking thereabouts, and putting them off the scent. Unfortunately not every bright idea works.

'Those little bastards!' te Kiore spat at the white *pinisi* sails rising off the port bow. 'Don't they ever give up? They must've been lying in wait just outside the bloody harbour! The whole bleedin' time!'

'Or they have wise men on board!' muttered Batang Sen significantly, glancing at Ape, sitting silent and morose by the binnacle, his long arms trailing over his knees. 'Wise men tell many things useful – sometime!'

Jacquie balanced te Kiore's long brass telescope adroitly. 'Look at them! There must be a dozen, at least!'

The mate nodded. 'You get the idea somebody's upped the ante on our heads – like that she-witch or this Charlie Chan character of yours.'

'Looks like it. Or whatever that third power might be.' I ran my hand along the age-polished rail. 'They're cutting us off, aren't they? From our course.'

Te Kiore looked to Batang Sen. 'Well, mebbe not,' he said dubiously. 'We could try and outflank 'em, steer further north . . . '

'Out into mouth Makassar Strait,' objected Batang Sen, 'south of island Sulawesi. That is my home. That is Boegie sea. We meet dozen here, we meet hundred there. Frightfully good business!'

'Oh, great. So what do we do with that lot?'

The Maori considered. 'Okay, might be we could outrun 'em, then. Head about and down through the Sunda straits, circle the island to the south. That's a hell of a lot longer, but not impossible.'

'So long as we come there within three weeks!' intoned Ape sombrely from the deck. Nobody paid him much attention.

Batang Sen showed his stained teeth. 'Brave thing is fight.'

I glared. 'We had enough trouble with three or four *prahus*! How the hell could we face a dozen?'

His grin split his face like a walnut. 'I say, is brave; not, is clever. Me, I sooner be clever, old fruit. Too right!' He turned to the bosun at the wheel. '*Sebelah kanan kapal*! We run like buggery!'

Jacquie shut the telescope with a snap. 'He has this way of putting things, hasn't he?'

So we set course away from Bali, racing out between Madura and the Jawan mainland as we'd planned, but suddenly veering back west around Tanjung Pangkah and along the coast, sometimes heading in towards it, other times tacking sharply out to sea – always the unexpected, to try to shake those menacing sails off our track. More than once we lost sight of them; but always, within the hour, within the day, they were there again, climbing steadily up the horizon once again. By night they glimmered beneath the tropical moon as we struggled to lose them among the infinite oceans of the Spiral, the waves of boundless mist which beat against the shores of a myriad realities; but at sunrise we would always see them, often closer-hauled than we could manage, scudding along like pale sharkfins in our wake.

At long last we sighted the isle of Teluk Banten and the Merak headland, and swept about them, like a hunted fox to its hole, down past the hilly green flanks of the Selat Sunda. Between Sumatera's spearhead and Jawa's shield we raced, headed out into the vast expanse of the Indian Ocean. The wind blows the same on the Spiral as in the Core, and it was against us, and it was a slow tacking this way and that, often into perilous shallows and between jagged shoals to make the best way we could. For a while it seemed the white sails had lost us for good; but out of the next dawn they rose, tipped red like deadly arrowheads by the blazing light, and the crew shrieked curses at the sight. Then Batang Sen played the last card he had, the size and ocean-going capacity of the *Ikan Yu*. We burst out of the straits, saw Tanjung Waton fall away behind us, and swung far to the southwest and the blue waters, away from the coast. We hoped that if the *pinisi* were carrying large crews they might run short of provisions, or simply willpower. But always they were there, and soon we saw they were drawing closer, slowly but surely overhauling us, never entirely out of sight now save in the grey uncertainties of twilight and dawn. And every day carried us further from our destination.

Ape seemed to feel this most keenly. He seldom turned up at meals, and sometimes even forgot to eat or drink what was brought to him. He occasionally vanished to his cabin, but spent most of the time squatting in his favoured place on the afterdeck, sombrely contemplating his feet, or something of equal interest such as the deck seams. Once in a while he would glance up at the sun, and at night he spent ages staring at the stars, with a look of inexpressible yearning on his face. You could hear him crooning strange chants to himself at times when he felt alone; when he didn't he was silent, withdrawn and morose.

I bearded him around dinnertime on the second evening, bringing him his tray myself. He thanked me, after a fashion, but he wasn't at all communicative. 'Come on!' I jollied him. 'What's eating you? Those Boegie buggers're still too far behind to get depressed about! Oh, I know you're eager to get home, but surely a day or so doesn't matter either way—'

'*Matter*!' he burst out, with such a weight of bitterness I was startled. 'How shall such as you know what may or may not matter? Or where a journey end or begin?' His huge hand shot up and seized me by my jerkin, yanked me down on my backside on the deck.

'Listen, child of a finite world, a fixed horizon! Once the Lord Amaitreya grabs me, as I grab you! Only smaller – so! A flyspeck! Then with His stern regard he fix me, so that I am afraid, I escape. To the very ends of existence I flee that look, across the clouds of the Spiral and the oceans of the night. After long travail, after much adventure, to the very pillars that uphold the universe I come, and there none dare pursue me. And there I mock Buddha, and on the tallest of the pillars I scrawl my name in charcoal, and at its foot – I piss. Then I turn to leave – and there, across that infinite expanse, the face of Buddha looks down upon me still. So, I skip about and shout insults – for do I not outdistance both His censure and His wrath? Can I not always thus evade Him and His silly restraining laws? Then He shakes His head slowly, and looking past me He lifts up His august Hand. And He smiles, a smile that is wholly gentle, and wholly terrible; and though a millenium pinned beneath a mountain I spend, no worse moment can there be than that one then. For there upon the middle finger, low above the palm, are smeared the characters of my name. And below it upon the palm lies a little pool of piss. All I do, the entire breadth of existence I traverse at such time and cost, it does but take me from one side to another of that mighty Hand.'

He snorted through his whiskers, and lumbered to his feet. 'So talk to me not of arrivals, of goings and comings. One is where one is appointed, where one must be for a purpose; and without that purpose all places are as one. For however far one flees, one's destiny . . . *that*, one can never escape.'

And leaving me staring, he shambled away down the deck, towards the companionway and his cabin. He wasn't carrying the tray, of that I'm certain; but when I remembered it, it wasn't there. I spent half the night trying to disentangle his little parable, but by morning I wasn't one whit the wiser. I gave up trying to talk him round, after that.

A day later I was in need of some talking round myself. We were well out to sea now and the white hounds worried closer and closer at our wake, standing out hard and stark in the glass-clear light. I watched the bowsprits of the leading vessels rise and fall behind us, and imagined them already training cannon on our stern. 'This running's not doing one damn bit of good!' I complained.

'That's 'cause the wind's slackening!' answered te Kiore, who had the watch. 'Been dropping ever since sun-up.'

'Great. Where's that leave us?'

Te Kiore's gesture was a suitably graphic answer. I bristled.

'Well – can't we try and outmanoeuvre them or something?'

'You got any bright ideas?' growled te Kiore. 'We'd love to hear 'em. Like about how you can outmanoeuvre twelve separate head of sail, when any one could give us some fight, and four or five good ones could eat us.' He squinted, and adjusted the telescope. 'Maybe thirteen head. There's something like another sail back there; an' it's big, maybe big as ours. Cap'n won't play against those odds, and nor will I!'

'But they're smaller, lighter. If we try to outrun them and the wind drops they'll keep going longer!'

'Yah! But all we've gotta do is make one slip and they'll be on us a damn sight surer. This isn't the time for any funny business! Just pray to whoever you think'll listen that the wind holds.'

It may have been pure coincidence that the breeze really began to flag, just about then. 'Just tell me who you worship,' muttered te Kiore, 'an' I'll go spit in the font.'

'Join the queue,' I told him. 'But it could be just a lull, couldn't it?'

'Maybe—' the big man began, but Jacquie cut him off with a curt word.

'No way! Look ahead!'

'What you found, then?' grinned the Maori. 'Icebergs?' Then he muttered something lethal, and snatched at the telescope. He focused it, stood very still, then went clattering across the deck to yell down at Batang Sen, snoozing in a deck hammock.

'*Kapten*! *Juragan Batan*! *Ara-ara*, and bloody quick! There's mist coming up!'

Amid the general cry of dismay I snatched the telescope and peered ahead. There was no mistaking those puffy, billowing swirls coiling their serpentine way in across an increasingly glassy ocean. We'd have to go about if we didn't want to get caught up in it, lose what little lead we had. White ahead and white behind, the one delivering us to the other. And behind that – another whiteness still?

'At least it's not going to do them any more good,' sighed Jacquie, her fingers plaiting nervously in her lap. 'The wind's falling too fast. Look, they're getting closer but they still can't catch up.'

'Yes, but they're almost in cannon range – and that's not all! Look back there, behind them! That sort of slanting wisp – see? Above that last masthead, the one with the large sail. I've been watching that; it must be a steadying sail. They're not going to be bothered by the wind, or lack of it. Don't you recognise it? Our enemies have upped the ante, right enough. They've put a steamboat on our tail!'

Batang Sen stiffened and peered astern. His old eyes looked red-rimmed and bleary, but he didn't make any move towards his own telescope; he looked at me and nodded. 'Is steam, yes, *Tuan* Fisher. With much power, too, I guess, to make such reekings.

Leave us no choice.' He cocked his head at the oncoming cloud. 'Enemy no longer; good friend. Mistah Bosun, steady as she go!' He snatched up the battered speaking trumpet. 'All hands! Stand by to slacken sail!'

Te Kiore exhaled quietly. 'Yeah, it's all we can do; go barging straight on into that little lot, an' try giving the Boegies the slip. But I don't much bleedin' like it!'

'Why not?' asked Jacquie. 'Are these difficult waters? Are there shoals or something?'

He hugged himself, rubbing his tattooes, as the first cool kiss of the approaching mist touched our skins. 'No, the chart's clear enough; skipper's not exactly daft, after all! But there might be the odd thing or two that ain't got charted yet 'cos no poor bastard's lived to tell of it.'

'Submerged rocks or something?'

'Yeah, maybe. But this is the Spiral, remember? Out here a cloud can hold a whole lot more than just rocks.'

Batang Sen was darting looks around, evidently calculating. He snapped his fingers to te Kiore and shouted, 'Mistah Mate!'

'Aye-aye, skipper!' called back te Kiore, and snatched up the battered speaking trumpet. 'All hands! *Kendur layar!* Aloft and stand by! *Tukang api!* Hot gang, below with you and get shovellin'! Five minutes to pressure up, or you go in the boiler instead! *If,*' he added disconsolately, 'we've got as much as five minutes. Because we're cutting it flamin' close.'

We watched in silence as the thin streamers in the air thickened into fingers, coiling and curling around the stays, billowing up around the sails as if to pull the boat in, like a sea anemone with a little fish in its tendrils. The topmen hung silent in the rigging, with none of their usual chatter. From below came the rhythmic ring and scrape of the hot gang's shovels, to a rough chant interspersed with deep gasping grunts, as if they'd no breath for more, and the clash of shovel on furnace rim.

'How much fuel have we got aboard, te Kiore?' asked Jacquie.

'I was sort of hopin' nobody was going to ask that. A bit more'n usual, 'cos we're only carrying the container; but still not much.'

Silence fell again. Batang Sen was humming a thin, eerie little song and drumming his fingers rhythmically on the rail. The air was all but still now; the sails sagged limply, and spots of dew formed on the brass trim of the binnacle. Suddenly the blackened stack belched out an uneven puff of smoke; it wavered, faltered, coughed and then streamed out again, rising straight up in the thickening air.

'This is the awkward bit,' muttered te Kiore. 'They'll see that—' No sooner had he got the words out than there was a thudding explosion – not from below, from behind us, and with it the singing screech of a shot. We tensed, staring into the murk as if somehow we could hope to spot the death whistling down out of it. Then there was an almost ludicrously small splash some way behind, and we sagged, with the shamefaced half-laughter of people who've shared a fright. Batang Sen held up his hand for silence, and was instantly obeyed. Far off in the mist, patches of duller grey seemed to float up. Drifting over to us, half muffled by the moist heavy air, came shrill angry voices and the rumble of tackle, the creak of sweeps as the *prahus* tried to get some control in the sudden calm. But nobody even bothered to fire, and slowly, maddeningly slowly, they came gliding by. If there weren't any others nearer – if one wasn't going to materialise out of the mist and ram us head on . . .

Batang Sen tapped his feet with the sublime detachment of the East. But when the speaking tube whistled and chattered and the brass telegraph rang, he jumped as high as the rest of us. A head popped out of a hatchway and chattered some more. Batang Sen howled back down the tube, and slammed the telegraph hard over. The ship vibrated, and the slow plashing of the paddles came up from overside. Te Kiore roared at the topmen; the sails were swiftly brought in and neatly gathered, ready to be flown again at the first breath, leaving only a spanker for steadying. 'Strewth, that's better!' he breathed as the paddles shifted us on to our new course, and the topmen came racing lightly down again. 'Now we're away with a chance!'

'How long till we're sure we've lost them?' demanded Jacquie.

The Maori shrugged monumentally. 'We'll need to zigzag about a bit – an hour, maybe. Chances are we'll have a nice little lead by then, and maybe clear water eastwards. If those drongoes haven't rumbled us, that is. Or that other flamin' steamboat caught up.'

It was a long hour. Ape spent it as he'd spent all the others, meditating in a hirsute heap against the afterrail. Batang Sen lit himself a foul cheroot and puffed at it as if trying to thicken the fog. Te Kiore, getting visibly more impatient, suddenly launched into a silent *haka* across the afterdeck, prancing and posturing, rolling his eyes and grimacing in the classic Maori wardance, waggling his immense tattooed tongue. It might have looked ludicrous, in other circumstances; right now, in this chill mist, with boats full of bogeymen on our tail, there was an alarming, primal quality to it which didn't seem funny at all. Jacquie and I tried retreating to the saloon and putting our feet up; we still hadn't caught up on our missed night's sleep. But after a fitful half hour, with the steam engine pulsing relentlessly up through our chairs, by unspoken agreement we got up and went on deck again. We leaned on the rail, side by side because somehow, though we weren't touching or holding hands or anything, there was an immense physical comfort in it.

Te Kiore was still twitchy, but Batang Sen remained calm as the ocean. He'd stationed himself by the wheel, listening, occasionally motioning the grim-faced bosun to spin it this way or that. Our steam power, weak as it was, gave us the edge on speed and mobility in this airless calm, but it was only too audible; we didn't dare steer a straight course, in case somebody started taking pot shots at the noise.

And just as we felt we were clear, when the hour was up and we were just beginning to relax, I actually saw us shot at. There was a sudden point of blazing red light in the mist, and an instant later a thud, as if somebody had flung open a furnace door and instantly slammed it shut. Something went screeching by in the mist, maybe fifty yards off our bow – quite wild. 'I got a fix on that!' growled te Kiore viciously. 'Skipper? We could drop one right back down their bloody barrel—'

'No!' Batang shook his head. 'No fire! We reply, give away our position. That what they want – right?'

'Aye aye, skipper,' admitted the crestfallen mate. He was about to say more when another point of red winked in the mist, and another, and a crash of thunder stirred the languid mist into startled writhings. Then a splintering crash, and voices shrieking this time, hysterically. More flashes, more bangs, from astern, but the scream of shot never came near us.

Batang Sen let loose an evil cackle and began to dance from foot to foot. 'Hihihihi! Bloody fool, bloody fool! They shoot each other, they shoot each other!'

There was a sudden deeper roar, and a really terrible crashing, and one high-pitched, sickening shriek. 'Bloody hell!' exclaimed te Kiore, aborting another wardance in midstep, 'that's no Boegie popgun! That's eighteen-pounders, a couple of 'em, or I'm *papa te pakahe*!'

'Steamboat!' exclaimed Walan hoarsely.

'Thank god it didn't catch *us*!' said Jacquie fervently.

The captain nodded grimly, blinked down at the compass and gave the bosun a curt order. He spun the wheel around, and the noise of the melee swiftly fell away behind us in the mist.

We were heading eastward now, but there seemed to be no end to the fog. Either it was an unusually wide belt, or it was travelling with us; I didn't like the sound of either alternative. Jacquie and I went off to bed early – and, despite a certain amount of mutual reconciliation in the narrow corridor outside, still separately. We were both dog-tired, anyhow, and horribly unsure of a lot of things, ourselves most of all.

All the same, neither of us slept well, and only about five hours later something woke me – a change in the thudding note of the engine, maybe. It seemed to be turning over very slowly, and the air below decks, never that fresh, was beginning to smell like a laundry. I pulled on my clothes and stumbled blearily on deck, to find the mist as heavy as ever and the deck looking like a massacre, the tired crew sprawled all over it in corpse-like attitudes. The skipper and te Kiore were in anxious congress on the afterdeck, and even Ape was showing some interest. A long hose stretched across from the main hatchway to the side, pulsing as water was pumped through it. Clouds of steam were rising from below.

'What's up?' I demanded.

'Bugger all,' was te Kiore's retort. 'Including steam. We're running low on coke, the timbers are overheating, the hot gang's half dead on their feet, and the boiler's throwing a wobbly – leaking like a rusty sheep trough, I'll bet. Just about enough pressure to keep the paddles ticking over. But you're in time for some coffee – here, get that down yer.' He scratched his backside thoughtfully. 'Oh yeah, and of course there's one other little thing – the mist. Got us out of one danger nicely, but it's becoming a danger itself, still hanging round like this. So we haven't a blind bloody clue where we are. We could use that mate of yours, the Pilot, right now.'

'Aren't you supposed to be a bit of a navigator, too?' I asked tactlessly. The huge man scowled at me, then wilted.

'Well, yeah. I've got the knowledge, fine; and maybe a bit of the instinct, too. But it's instinct you need out here, when you've no firm anchorage. Give me a sight, give me a bit of land to start from – then I could get you some places'd knock your eye out. But now . . . ' He gulped down his own coffee, and refilled his cup from the battered silver pot. 'Skipper don't know. Your mate Ape don't know. And me – I'm just enough of a navigator to be worried. This isn't where we want to be. But which heading'll take us out . . . ' He shrugged heavily. 'Hang on, though. I smell a breeze coming, less I'm much mistaken. Then we might see something.'

'Great' was about the best I could manage. The coffee tasted of steamed canvas. So did the air. That was all I smelt. I stared out at what I could see of the waters around me, which wasn't much. 'Probably run aground in bloody Shangri-la,' I muttered gracelessly.

'That'd be quite a feat of navigation,' said Jacquie drily behind me. 'Shangri-la was up a mountain, remember?'

'The way things look right now, I still wouldn't be surprised.' I gestured down at the water, what you could see of it. 'Look at that! Twenty yards beyond the ship, and it might as well be infinity out there. Probably is.'

'I know. The Spiral. Why does everyone call it that?'

'Everyone doesn't. Some philosophies call it the Wheel, with the Hub at its centre, not the Core. A turning Wheel. I've heard of others that think in terms of spheres, concentric ones. The central one's the Core, the others share its heart but grow more remote and diffuse the further out you move – or in, in some versions. Until you reach the realms of absolutes, the Rim or wherever; but by then you'd have changed a lot yourself. I've never heard of anyone ever testing its limits – nobody who came back, anyhow. But all the concepts share this ideal of movement, it seems. The Spiral's not a static place. The more you move around, the less likely you are to be sucked back into the Core.' I sighed. 'There are times I could live with that.'

Jacquie put an arm around my shoulders. There was a warm aroma around her that contradicted the dankness, a smell of sleep and secrets and soft hair, the scent of a woman newly out of bed. Little cool draughts stirred my hair; it felt as if te Kiore was right. 'You'll get cold,' I said.

'So will you.'

'I don't think so. Not where I'm going. Te Kiore! You said the stokers were all flat out!'

'Too flamin' right they are! Why – offering another pair of hands?'

'I can't do much else useful right now.'

'Yeah, me neither – hang about, though! Feel that?'

There was no doubt about it now – a breeze rising, a good one. You could see it in the mist, first swirling it about like a stirred pot, then positively scooping it up in a great fistful, pulling it off the water and sending little shivery ripples across the calm surface. A sudden breathy gust caught the limp steadying sail and filled it with a soft blossoming thud; the ship rocked, and the sleepy bosun swore as the wheel bucked under his hands with the first life it had shown in hours. I ran to help him, and together we slipped the heavy rope loops over the spokes to hold the rudder setting. He grinned a bony grin full of filed teeth, and sniffed around at the wind. '*Aduh*! Frisky one! Hard to go ride – you know – like goosed elephant!'

'Nice image!' laughed Jacquie. 'Ever thought of going into PR?'

The sudden lightening of the atmosphere caught everyone; it was as if the mist had been stifling us. Only Ape seemed immune to it, though he hadn't gone back to his brooding. He was glancing keenly about, as if he heard something; and the captain, pausing in the middle of lighting another cheroot, suddenly cocked his head as if he, too, was listening. He darted a look at me, very alert.

'You hear too? Like drum? Slow drum?'

'Now that you mention it . . . ' It rolled almost on the edge of awareness, so deep it was and soft; slow booming strokes reverberating against the sea's own note. Jacquie was listening too, nodding. Instinctively, almost, she moved closer to me again, took my arm. 'Hey,' I said, 'Wait a minute. Is that . . . surf?'

'Yeah,' said te Kiore. 'That's what I was thinking.'

'Booming like that . . . But there's none of that hiss you get on a beach.'

'No. So, chances are it's breaking over a reef.'

We stood there, silent a moment, feeling the wind gust violently at our backs; and suddenly the mist turned transparent. The white walls fell away behind us, and the ship surged forward on the first flush of a spreading swell.

Te Kiore whistled; Batang Sen bit the end off his cheroot and coughed violently. I don't know whose grip was the first to tighten, but Jacquie and I clutched at each for support. Land leaped out at us, a whole sudden landscape, as if one moment before it had surged up whole from the abysses of the sea. It sprang into our sight like a challenger or a sentinel, alarmingly big – alarmingly close, too. No ordinary landscape – vast, commanding, too large to take in at that first startled glimpse.

With the lifting of the mist the breakers sounded suddenly much closer; we could see them, a streak of white between us and the isle ahead, spouting plumes of spray like the Jascony beast, the ultimate Leviathan. Batang Sen barked out an order, and the bosun slipped the cords from the helm. I heartily agreed; that reef was too close for comfort, and the wind was still too gusty to give us steerage way. If anything it was driving us towards it. As well we still had enough power for the paddles. The mist-wreathed mountainous vista swung away in front of the bows as we pulled about; then, more slowly, it began to swing back again. The bosun unleashed a string of curses and laid the helm hard over.

'That's done it!' exclaimed Jacquie a little shakily. 'The ship's not turning back – is it?'

Batang Sen hurled his cheroot to the deck and stamped on it. He chattered out a stream of orders, te Kiore bellowed, grabbed the brass hammer dangling from the ship's bell and beat on it furiously. In an eyeblink the inert bodies on the deck were up and running in disciplined confusion for the shrouds. I watched the line of the forestays creep across the misty sky. 'It damn well is, you know – but more slowly. Maybe we can . . .' Then I saw what the captain had seen. 'No, by god! We're being pulled in a'beam! Sideways! There must be some kind of current!'

Te Kiore came running across the deck. 'That helpin' hand, mate . . .'

'Right with you!'

'Me too!' panted Jacquie, cantering down the companionway after us.

'You?' demanded te Kiore, stopping dead with surprise. 'No way, lady! I mean, thanks, but this is tough work we're talking about!'

'Well?' demanded Jacquie. 'I've done weight training! And suppose I only last ten minutes, that's still ten minutes gained, isn't it?'

Te Kiore was about to object violently, but caught the warning grimace I tipped him. 'Well, okay!' he groaned. 'No time to waste arguing! You want some practice for the afterlife, lady, you've come to the right place!'

When we looked down the ladder, we saw what he meant. There was no engine room as such, only a kind of walled platform fastened across the timbers where the afterhold had been, suspended directly above the bilges. These were fairly dry, but they still contributed their share to the stink that rose with the clouds of steam. The only light down there was the open furnace, throbbing red on figures that bent and strained like acolytes sacrificing to a hungry god, their skins striped with sweat and dust. Steam welled up from the dribbling hose that played across the overheated timbers, laying the dust in case it caught; every so often one of the figures would dash into the trickling jet, cavort for a moment, then snatch up his shovel and start shovelling again. All told, it did make a pretty good vision of hell. '*Manawa-nui*!' bellowed te Kiore as he scrambled down. 'But we need more pressure *fast*!'

The four men down there stared as I clambered after him, and positively goggled as Jacquie followed. Every one of them raised a wail of protest, but te Kiore more or less kicked them out of the way and tossed us shovels. We grabbed them and fell to, gasping and coughing as a new rush of steam came hissing over us. Te Kiore's immense shoulders bowed and bent, hurling heaped shovelfuls of coke and what looked like poor lignite into the firebox mouth. I did what I could to keep up with him; Jacquie didn't try, but shot in smaller amounts much faster and in an easy, wheeling rhythm that let her accomplish almost as much. After a while it was her I started imitating.

'Gotta admit it!' wheezed the Maori. 'Some of the *vahines* back home . . . they could heft more'n half the men in the village. My ole Ma, arms like a Barcoo shearer, she had . . . '

Waves of heat rolled over us as the boiler picked up, and sometimes a stinging wave of cinders sent us dashing for the hose. Jacquie's shirt was sticking to her as she moved, and she knotted it up under her breasts, leaving a fetching expanse of waistline that made te Kiore waggle his eyebrows and tongue in an incredibly revolting leer. I didn't say anything; I couldn't, as the bastard very well knew. Despite the steam every breath was baking my throat, and salt seawater couldn't help. And all the time the boiler shuddered and quaked with every quirk of the engine, and little jets of steam came blasting out of improbable nooks and crannies. We redoubled our efforts, but the gauges kept trembling downward. The reef grew in my imagination, rock or coral, reaching out like monstrous shark's teeth to the fragile-looking flank only feet from my head. At last te Kiore threw down his shovel with an incoherent oath.

'This bloody boiler's buggered!' he spat. 'Three times the fuel we're burning, for quarter the pressure! It must be leaking into the back of the firebox!' He rounded on the gang chief. 'Ibrahim! Quit stoking, get the hose on that door! Not on the boiler itself, mind! Abdullah, get your arse up top and tell the skipper!'

'But what can we do about it?' I demanded. The mate was rummaging in the huge tool chest at the back, and he came up triumphantly with a big ball of oily rags which he unwrapped to reveal some foul-looking putty-like substance.

'Do? Go in quick and gob it up, that's what!'

'In? *Into the firebox*? You're out of your bloody skull, man!'

He gave that horrible leer again. 'Am I, *pakahe*? Care to come along?'

Before I quite realised what was happening the other stokers were wrapping the pair of us up in great strips of damp stinking sacking – damp with bilge water, by the smell of it. But no more than damp, to stop it catching fire; too much water would conduct the heat. Then, with the hose playing over the wide firebox door, they reached their long shovels in and heaved the burning coals to either side. I was surprised to see that the fire was fairly shallow, no more than halfway down the chamber, and behind there was a blackness out of which came only steam and faint sizzlings.

'What'd I tell you?' growled te Kiore, tossing the putty in his fingers. 'Hose the floor down, boys . . . that's it!'

At first the water skittered about the hot metal in sessile droplets, refusing to settle; but soon it lay and steamed. Te Kiore bound a last rag or two round his boots and snapped his fingers, and we shuffled over to the firebox entrance. Jacquie watched, biting her lip, hunched and tense. I knew that if either of us fell (but especially me, I couldn't help hoping) she'd be in there like the proverbial greased lightning. 'Okay?' demanded te Kiore. 'In, find the leak, out – either falls, the other drags him, *but don't touch the metal*! Glad I got you along,' he added, tossing the putty stuff in his huge hand. 'Might'a been sort of nervy otherwise. Five minutes, and we're out, fixed or not – right?'

The stoker Abdullah came clattering down the ladder. 'You don't get fi' minutes! Skipper says we don't give him paddles in fi', we're on the reef in ten!'

Te Kiore looked at me, shrugged, and without further ado ducked through the firebox door. There was a fearsome hiss from inside, and Ibrahim swung the hose after him. I picked up a shovel and stepped right through the jet, but hardly noticed; my feet crunched on steaming coals, I staggered unsteadily and felt the heat clamp around me like a tangible thing.

Inside it was larger, and the still-glowing coals gave us a bit of light; we didn't need to hunch down so much. But we didn't straighten up, tall as we both were, because we knew that one brush with the metal roof would easily set our hair aflame. With the hose dribbling after us, we staggered into the slushy heap of coals at the back. They were no more than half burnt, any of them. Te Kiore nodded tautly, then ducked frantically as his curly bush brushed a rivetted joint and sizzled alarmingly. I flicked water on it, he winked, and gestured at the back of the heap. I dug the shovel in, heaved a couple of times, and saw that the coals which came away at the left side were plain black and sticky. I heaved again, cleared the heating surface, and saw, from its bottom edge, a tiny wisp of steam sizzle up into instant nothingness.

But that was enough. Te Kiore tore a lump off the ball, worked it half flat with two powerful squeezes, and as I raked more coal back he slapped it down with tremendous force over what must be a slightly sprung seam. One breathless instant we waited, the Maori clutching his hand in his damp swaddlings, but there was no more steam. Te Kiore tipped me the nod, I heaved the coals back, and we turned and bolted. Ahead of me, reaching the end of the heap, he skidded, straightened up reflexively, ducked to avoid the roof – and fell on his knees. There was a great sizzle from his wrappings, and a yell of pain. I hurled my shovel out the door, grabbed the scruff of his neck and the seat of his mummy wrappings, and heaved him up. I was so scared I hardly felt the weight; we reached the door in one stride, cursing and gibbering, and hands reached in to haul him out, and me after. But even as my heels dragged over the threshold, and the end of my wrappings ignited briefly, other hands were hurling in a bucket of hot coals, carefully preserved, and scraping back the still-hot coals from either side.

'T'ree minutes!' yelled Abdullah triumphantly. 'Up steam! Up steam!'

Ibrahim had the hose on te Kiore's legs, and Jacquie was ripping the wrappings away; they spared a moment to extinguish mine. I half expected to see his kneecaps come away with the last of the sacking; but it wasn't that bad, no worse than a good steam scalding, agonising but treatable. Other crewmen carried him up to the deck, while the gang went back to work. After a moment I joined them, but I was shaking so much my first shovelful sprayed everywhere and the shovel almost killed Ibrahim. Jacquie ordered me up the ladder; she had to come along behind and help. Up on deck I more or less fell over, but I was appalled to see how close that mountain height loomed now. To my overcooked brain the shadows on its eroded flanks began to look like a great grinning skull, so the reefs might well be its teeth.

Te Kiore, to my surprise, was conscious, sprawled against the top of the afterdeck companionway while crewmen salved and bandaged his legs. He waved cheerily. 'Good on yer, Stevie boy! There's a gap in the reef, right enough! Looks navigable! A little way, and we'll pull through it clean as a whistle!'

The telegraph clanged just then, and the paddles coughed back into hesitant life. Everyone cheered, of course. Walan swung the wheel back and forth in short arcs, whistling tonelessly through his teeth. The ship dipped and corkscrewed with a sickening motion as she fought the current and shifted her angle to the waves. Spurts of spray rose up just beyond the bows, then slid aside as another wall of green water raced under the hull, lifting it, and turned us away. We were coming up on the first line of the reef now, and the thunder of it was all around us; what it must sound like below, I didn't like to think. Suddenly the sea was transformed from the deep calm mirror we'd been gliding over into a furious beast, bucking and bellowing with unleashed energy, battering at the once-living rocks that fenced if off from the land.

A wave bounced under our bows, broke with an explosive boom, spattering the deck with spray. Then we were into the channel, with the paddles gaining speed all the time, heeling and dipping madly as we wove between the outcrops. It was quite a wide gap, easily big enough for a ship under power; but the best we could do was juggle the paddles clumsily, boosting or reversing one or both to help the rudder. A bit like trying to drive a tank down a narrow country lane – or a mountain path, with deep disaster on either side. Every so often we'd hear the coral's fingernail scraping along those sleek flanks, and Batang Sen would wince as if his own side was being gouged. But he kept his head, and we were nosing through, sometimes inch by inch.

What happened wasn't his fault, and nobody could have prevented it. The wind was gusting up more and more of a swell; and at the crucial moment, with the bows swinging out into the end of the gap, an especially fierce one struck. A low green wall of water hit the reef behind us with such force that it swept right on across it, and picked us up in its path. The ship heeled and slewed violently, one paddlewheel stuck out into the thin air, threshing frantically. Too quickly to stop, the other's blades bit deep, and pulled us sharply around. Then the wave slackened, and dropped us right on the fangs of the reef.

A tearing crash. A dreadful hollow smacking sound. Then the wave receded, and our weight pulled us free. The whole ship was spun around by its bows, and the next wave sent us gliding out into the lagoon beyond. 'Blow steam, skip!' yelled te Kiore. 'If that water hits the boiler—'

But to my horror the captain only shook his white head violently, and with a scream of rage slammed the telegraph from back to front with a resounding clang. God alone knew what the hot gang were thinking by now; but somebody had mind enough down there to hear him. The paddles spun with something like a roar, and in this newly calm water they drove us forward at full tilt. In deeper, rougher water a trick like that would have driven the bows under; but here it worked. He threw the wheel hard over, so that our wounded side lifted clear of the water, and we drove straight at the beach. Seconds – a minute – two – and then I threw Jacquie down to the deck, and fell on top of her. Barely in time; the slope was shallower than I'd guessed, and we hit sand a good way out from the tideline.

The deck jarred beneath us, and the seams sprang. The rigging thrummed like a guitar, a topmast snapped and fell like a giant javelin to the deck, trailing a tangle of rope and tackle. Batang Sen, clinging to the speaking tube, shrieked something down it – I guessed what. The dragonish shriek from below proved me right, tailing away into an explosive hiss. The lagoon at our flank bubbled up into a frothing mass, and clouds of steam billowed out of the afterhold hatch, followed by Ibrahim and the hot gang.

236

They were the heroes of the hour, but they didn't stop for congratulations; they skidded right down the listing deck and overside into the cooling lagoon waters. From below came a louder, deeper hiss, and a massive, destructive clank and crash, like a giant smashing armour; the boiler imploding as the sea lapped at its hot flanks. But at least it wasn't blasting into fragments, and the ship with it. Batang Sen's coldblooded risk had paid off; he'd beached his precious ship, and still blown steam in time.

Gingerly I picked myself off Jacquie. Winded, she raised her hands and wheezed. I eased her down to the edge of the main hatch cover, where she could hang on, and slithered my way along to the afterdeck. Batang Sen's scrawny hand reached out to help me up the tilting companionway. 'All right?' I asked the old man, and he, of course, assumed I meant the ship.

'Bad,' said Batang Sen succinctly. He swung himself up on to the port rail and motioned me to have a look over. The ship was beached in about eight feet of water, maybe less, and the tilt held the damaged hull just above the surface, so that relatively little was flooding in now. It was a nasty gash in that sleek side, about eight feet ripped out of the planking in two strips a foot wide and surrounded with splintering and cracks.

I looked at him. 'Surely we could patch that up? To last a week or so?'

'Indubitable, if I get planks. But where?'

Te Kiore was sitting feeling his neck with the air of a man unsure how securely it was attached. 'And even suppose we do,' he added, 'hauling her off this sand won't be a bloody pushover, not under sail alone. Looks like we could use some help, if there's any to be found.'

Ape, no more ruffled than usual, was shinning up into the shrouds to stare at the land before us.

'Where is this place?' I heard him mutter.

'Wherever it is,' I told him, 'we're stuck with it.'

He swung round and gave me such a look I was sorry I'd spoken. 'Best I never meddle in this business,' he said grimly, with contained wrath twitching behind every word. 'Your damn business. Best I make my own way to the island. Now there are only days remaining. How do I get there now, in any time?'

I held out my hands helplessly. 'Ape, I'm sorry. You've done so much for us already. Anything I can do, once we're off here . . . '
And then the view caught my eye, too, and I stared, fascinated.

'Where is this place?' repeated Ape, his wonder driving out his anger. '*Verbaast me* . . . I do not know it, not at all . . . '

'Well, you can't know everywhere, can you?' said Jacquie amusedly, from the companionway.

His blunt face bunched into a scowl. 'In these waters, yes, I can. But this is like no place I even hear of . . . with that mountain, surely I must know him . . . '

'You know,' I ventured. 'It's odd, but . . . it almost seems that, maybe, *I've* seen it before.'

'You've been to Jawa,' Jacquie suggested. 'So maybe that's where this is. Steve, darling, listen, it was very brave of you to throw yourself all over me like that, but honestly it was nearly as bad . . . I mean, I thought I'd cracked a couple of ribs . . . '

'Sorry,' I said abstractedly. 'No. This isn't anything I ever saw in Jawa last time. I hardly got outside the cities, anyhow.'

'In a picture, then? One of the other islands?'

'*Hoezo*? This is not Jawa,' said Ape impatiently. 'Nor Timor, Sulawesi, none of the larger ones. And none of the smaller . . . yet, of Flores it has something, of Komodo . . . Why it should, I know not at all. Neither has such a mountain-heart to it, with such cliffs – almost like a face, a dead face. *Hoe kan dat nou? Wat freemd, freemd . . .* ' He mumbled off into Dutch, then shook his head sharply. He seemed both fascinated and disturbed; and, strangely, so was I.

'As if it's somewhere I visited,' I said slowly. 'Long ago . . . as a child, even.'

'When you were at college, you'd never been further than France and Spain,' said Jacquie sharply. 'Maybe you read about it a lot, like me with Borobodur.' She glanced up at the heights, and the seabirds that wheeled around them – huge ones, albatrosses probably. Even that had something familiar about it.

'No,' I said, with an odd decisiveness. 'I feel as if I was actually here. And yet, you're right. It's just not possible.'

'Except,' Jacquie remarked sombrely, 'that as you're always reminding me, this is the Spiral . . . ' Her breath shivered into silence.

'Yeah, well.' Te Kiore's voice made us jump. He was leaning out over the lower rail, peering along the shore. 'Hate to break up the guessing games, but we're going to have to put things sort of on a practical footing. We won't get this poor old girl patched up and dragged off without a deal of help, and there's only one place we're going to find that – ashore.'

'You think so?'

'I can make a good guess.' He jerked a thumb shoreward, and grinned. And of course, once they were pointed out, they became obvious against the darker belt of forest at the mountain's foot and the long line of cliff face above it, straight roof-trees tinged with the yellowish-green of dry leaf thatching. 'Hope they're not all a load of flamin' painted savages,' added te Kiore, waggling his lace-tattooed tongue.

I was pretty flattered, not to say surprised, when Batang Sen suggested I lead the landing party; but I was also immensely relieved when Ape agreed to come along. There was no keeping Jacquie back, either, though her only justification was the smatterings of some island dialects she'd picked up in her job. I knew better than to argue, just reminded her to bring that longbow. She was horrified, though, when te Kiore hobbled up as we were struggling to get the boats lowered, assuming he'd be going as a matter of course. She didn't think he should even be standing up, but I'd seen what some of the healing they had out here could achieve; and I wasn't going to try conclusions with a seven-foot Maori, either, even one with stiff legs. So we helped him into the longboat, swearing cheerfully, gave him the tiller to keep him busy and, with pistols and *parangs* close to hand, we pushed off from the overhanging rail and dug our oars into the calm waters of the lagoon.

It looked so peaceful in the hazy afternoon light that I was surprised, looking back from my seat in the bow, to see te Kiore glancing around alertly at the water rather than the shore.

'Not expecting anything much out here, are you?'

'Well, mebbe not. But in lagoons like this in the Aru islands, down in the Arafura sea – and that's practically next door – I've seen merhorse around.'

'Merhorse?' I looked down at my supertough jerkin and trousers; I was wearing merhorse. 'Is that a problem?'

He shrugged. 'Well, they bulk like sperm whales, only with a more nervous kind of disposition. Long neck and smaller jaws, of course. Being built so much more like a seal, the shallower water don't bother them, naturally.'

'Naturally,' I echoed him hollowly.

'But 'less you throw a scare into them they'll leave you be.

Course they do scare pretty easy. Have to be on their guards for the *taniwha* . . . '

'The what?'

'Giant squid. *You* know,' he said, making tentacle gestures, and surprised me by adding, '*Architeuthis monachus*. Bright buggers, the big ones can be, the thirty-ton ones; eyes you could walk into. Come high tide they lie in the deep water just outside the reef and trail their tentacles in, try to catch the merhorses napping. You get some bonzer wrestling matches sometimes.'

I swallowed. I didn't know whether he was setting me up or not; it didn't sound like it. Somehow my clothes felt different, coming off a sixty-foot sealion or whatever it was. That gave me an idea. 'Merhorses – I'd bet nobody's ever given them a scientific classification, have they?'

'You'd lose,' he said mildly. '*Halshippus olai-magni* Heuvelmans. Well, here's the shallows.'

'Right,' I said gratefully, shaking off some appalling visions. 'You three, keep your muskets on the trees ahead, *don't* fire unless I tip you the word, right? Rest of you, stand by for beaching.' I glanced down to be sure of my depth and footing, then I swung over the bows into the rapidly shallowing water, touched bottom and more or less ran the boat on to the sand. The crewmen came swarming after me, pistols covering the forest barrier before us; any bird that flew up too suddenly risked being blown to bits. But nothing stirred, and I waved in the second boat. As soon as it landed Ape came striding across to Jacquie and myself.

'No sign of livings?'

I brushed aside the overhanging leaves. 'A path. An old-established one, by the look of it.'

'But not much used recently,' Ape nodded. 'Maybe these people do not go to the sea so often.'

'Yeah, like the Balinese,' nodded te Kiore, hobbling up the sand.

'I think we should let them know we're here,' I decided. 'Yes, I know it might be risky, but it's got to be riskier still creeping up on them with no advance warning.'

'Makes sense,' te Kiore agreed. 'Give 'em the old hail, shall I?'

Without further warning he put his hands to his mouth and let out a fearful yodelling halloo that echoed off into the thinning mist. There was a moment's devastated silence, then it was answered by a fearful outburst of croaking and shrieking from the trees round about as a flock of colourful birds burst into panicky flight. But that was all. We waited, and there was no answering sound, not even a stir.

'I'm not surprised,' said Jacquie dryly. 'After that little solo they're probably still running.'

I grinned. 'Seems they're in no hurry to meet us, whatever. Four men, stay with the boats — all right, not you, te Kiore. I haven't any irons to clamp you in anyhow. Rest of you, form up, shut up, keep your eyes open. Pistol locks closed — no, at half cock; but don't get trigger-happy. Remember, we're out to make *friends* . . . '

'Well,' te Kiore remarked a short while later, 'somebody else sure wasn't, that's a fact.' I stared unhappily at the shattered heap that blocked the path. It was easy to see what it had been, the timbered roof-tree of the native longhouse, its supporting timbers and the half-decayed bundles of palm leaves that had made up the thatch sagged drunkenly across the path.

I looked at him and Ape. 'What do you think, you two? A typhoon?'

'Pretty good guess,' said the mate. 'But that's not all it blew down. Look here!' He parted the yellowed fronds upon a ghastly grin. Several of the crewmen sprang back, making arcane signs and curses; I swallowed. Jacquie winced and looked away. There were bodies beneath that long trunk, two men by the look of them. They had been dark-skinned Melanesians, Papuan types; and though the ants and other scavengers had been at them a bit, they were in unpleasantly good condition. Bones I'd have preferred. It was all too clear how these two had gone; one lay broken under the roof-tree, the other had been literally flattened. Gingerly, in case we trod on anyone else, we picked our way through the obstruction, and into the village beyond.

It was a dismal sight. It must have been fairly large once, more than just a gaggle of dwellings; the native huts stretched out in spacious clusters among the trees. They looked quite pleasant, open and airy, most of them built on high stilt-like scaffolds, like Dyak longhouses but cruder. Now, though, a dank air of desolation hung over the whole place, and a depressing silence; and the reason was obvious.

'Oh . . . *Christ*!' Jacquie exclaimed. 'Those poor people!' I took her hand and squeezed it. The same awful jolt of sympathy shook me, too.

A great band of destruction ran right through the heart of the village, a broad corridor of devastation in which trees had been uprooted, roofs torn off and sent spinning through the air, walls smashed flat, scaffolding collapsed like a house of cards. In that great swathe half the village had been shattered; and how many of its people? How many more broken bodies, with no better grave or marker?

Beneath one unwalled scaffold, perhaps the beginnings of a new hut, we saw four or five bodies, with the fragmented remains of another in the open beside them. The scavengers had been more thorough here, but you could still see the remains of their costumes, grass skirts and high feather crowns and shell necklaces. Patterns of paint still streaked the shrivelled skin, and here and there shattered spears protruded from the wreckage.

'These were warriors,' mused te Kiore. 'Like me. Almost as if they'd gone shinning up this scaffold— to what? To bleedin' fiight?

Fight what? Defy the weather? No, that's daft.' And suddenly he looked at me.

I nodded. 'Got to you too, eh? I've been thinking the same thing. It's a damn funny typhoon that smashes a great streak through the centre of the village like this. And yet manages to leave the rest standing.'

'*And* the trees round about!' chipped in te Kiore as we advanced again, cautiously.

Jacquie looked puzzled. 'But . . . well, could a whirlwind do that? A small one? You sometimes get them . . . '

'Maybe. But I still don't see it— '

But te Kiore cut in. 'Hey! Look there!'

It was another skeleton – more or less. It lay half sunk in the muddy ground beside one of the larger huts, sagging but not shattered; and it was in much poorer condition than the others.

'Poor bastard! But what about him?'

'Jeez, I mean, *look* at the man! If that's what he was! Look at those ribs! They're flamin' well shattered! Every bone in his body looks broke!'

I swallowed. 'Thanks for pointing it out. So?'

'So what bloody did it? There's nothing around that fell on him. No roof-trees here, or anything!'

'Maybe it blew off him again,' Jacquie suggested unhappily.

I looked at her. 'And still left the hut standing?'

'Well . . . could he have fallen off it? No, that's stupid. He couldn't have hurt himself *that* badly. But then . . . what?'

'You know something?' I said, 'I have a feeling that whatever happened here hadn't anything to do with typhoons at all.'

'Well, what then?' demanded Jacquie.

'I don't know. But I also still feel I've seen this somewhere before. Laugh if you like.'

'I'm not laughing,' she answered quietly. 'I . . . I've begun to feel that, too.'

'And I,' announced te Kiore, 'have begun to feel a bloody great pain in my arse! As if my knees weren't flamin' bad enough. Why don't we have a go at finding somebody and bloody well asking them?'

I looked around. 'It's a while since this happened. I don't give much for our chances, but we'll try.'

We trudged through that gutted place, peering into every building that had any pretensions to being still usable. But we found nothing except a few gaudy junglefowl clucking and pecking around their former coops. Littered all around were other possessions broken or abandoned; some of them must have been precious to their owners, large painted earthenware pots and ornaments of hammered copper, strips of dyed bark cloth. 'You know how long this stuff takes to make?' demanded te Kiore. 'These people left in one hell of a hurry. I'm pretty damn sure nobody's here, or they'd have come back for this – this is wealth! This is like running out of the bank and leaving the safe open.'

'Abandon!' grunted Ape curtly, gazing around the place with an air of contempt. 'From fright!'

'I thought of disease,' I nodded. 'But plagues don't smash houses. Or bones. Fear it must be. But . . . what of? We're stuck here, too. I'd damn well like to know.'

Ape shrugged indifferently. I didn't like that. I remembered how he'd upbraided me for being callous; how the hell did he think he was acting now? But I let it go. 'They might have moved somewhere else on the island, then,' I suggested. 'Maybe if we could get to some higher ground we could see – look out for smoke, that kind of thing. That cliff up behind the village, why don't we try that?'

But on this island nothing was what it appeared to be. The closer we got to it through the mist, the more obvious it became

243

that it wasn't a cliff up there at all, or any other natural formation. I began to think of the Borobodur again; this was every bit as daunting. Towering some fifty or sixty feet high, stretching across the entire width of this neck of the island, it was one enormous wall.

'That,' exclaimed Jacquie bitterly, 'is absolutely bloody all we needed!'

I knew what she meant. The wall was bad enough; but just to round the whole thing off, right in the middle of it was one enormous gate. By now the sight of an ordinary subway turnstile would have made my hackles rise, but this one was really appalling. It was vast, it rose almost the entire height of the wall, with platforms some fifteen feet tall on either side. Once, when its valves were closed and barred, it must have been impassable. Now the two huge doors half hung from their ancient iron hinges, warped and smashed, it seemed, by the same force that had swept so devastatingly through the centre of the village. The huge bar that had secured them, a roughly squared tree trunk thrust along from the platforms, lay cracked in two at their feet.

'Perishin' heck!' te Kiore rumbled. 'What's done that then? A herd of elephants?'

Visions of typhoons faded from my mind. I began to see some medieval siege engine, some immense unstoppable juggernaut with the force of an army behind it. Except that a noble expanse of steps ran up to the gates, wide flights that would train the daylights out of any aspiring prizefighter; how could it get down those? And if it did, where was it now?

As we mounted the first steps, that idea too faded. Behind the gates there loomed only darkness. It was jungle out there, richer and denser than the mere forest out here, a tangled web around the mountain's roots. No machine, no army had passed that way for a long time; so what had? As if the mountain itself had stretched out a rocky limb to scrape away the human infestation at its foot . . .

But from here the wall looked as if it could shut out even that. It was made of huge stone blocks, dressed smooth and close; and it was immensely thick, thirty feet or more at the gate where the platforms stood out. It might just be stone over packed earth, like Inca walls; impressive enough – but if it was solid stone, it was a feat to rival the Pyramids. On the single gigantic capstone over the gate a mask leered out at us, bug-eyed, gape-tusked, with a suggestion of a mane – enough like that lion mask to set me wondering. Jacquie wasn't so sure.

'Almost South American, those blunt features, strong diagonals . . .' She giggled. 'Maybe Heyerdahl was right about Easter Island after all, and Incas sailing the Pacific!'

''Course he was!' chipped in te Kiore.

'Most anthropologists wouldn't agree,' Jacquie told him.

'Bugger the anthropologists,' remarked the mate amicably. 'They've never done the sensible thing, have they?'

'Which is?'

'Gone an' hitched a ride off the bleedin' Incas.'

I coughed. 'What's that on top there? That sort of gibbet thing?'

Jacquie craned her neck. 'Some sort of gong?'

'Yeah,' agreed te Kiore. 'Funny place to put the doorbell.' He peered at the collapsed piles of wooden scaffolding poles atop the platforms. 'I'd say those were the only ways up this side, or why build 'em? Maybe the other side . . .'

'Wait!' I snapped. 'It's a gate, remember? Ape – d'you think it's safe?'

He glanced at me sharply, as if startled out of some reverie; then, grudgingly, he snuffled the air through his blunt nostrils, hesitated a moment, then shrugged. 'Nothing lies in wait, not for you. Some danger, maybe, but of that kind, no. What it is . . . hard to say. Save that it is of here . . . it belongs.'

'I can believe that, all right. I'll be on my guard.' I looked up, as we stepped nervously beneath that leering capstone. I clutched at Jacquie's hand. 'I'm beginning to feel really weird.'

'Me too.' We were whispering, as if by agreement. 'And by the look of him, so's Ape!'

He certainly was. He was staring about him, his huge hands clenching and unclenching, muttering softly to himself. We poked our heads very gingerly around that gate, because we didn't entirely trust what he told us any more; but no curtain of mist closed about us. No more than a few thin leftover tendrils wreathed about an overgrown hummock at the far edge of the clearing, an outcrop of weathered grey stone with curious flecks of white. But it was at this that Ape was staring now, with a very strange look on his face. Then the details emerged for me also, like an X-ray, and the blood ran cold in my heart. More steps, a platform, higher than head height, a pillar – no, two, one had broken – all in that weathered stone, and covered in more of that zigzag carving. The bits of white were something different; they were skulls. One still grinned out from within a hollow in the stone, picked white and clean; it was a lot older than any of the other casualties here. A tangle of ropes at about five feet high on either pillar told me what they were for, with the pegs to tighten them; and I shivered.

'There's a trail of sorts there!' called te Kiore. 'A game trail, maybe, but wide for that. And well used. Maybe the natives . . . '

I drew a breath, looking around at the other crewmen padding through after us. 'Maybe, maybe not. We'll risk a short look, no more. And this time, boys, I guess you can be a bit heavier on those triggers.'

They didn't need telling. We moved out of that clearing step by step at first, like sea-creatures ready to dart back into the rocks. The guns were cocked; I had a brace of pistols in my belt, but I left them there. Somehow I felt happier about the sword that tapped against my thigh, more confident in it somehow. Jacquie nocked an arrow to her bow, a fairly pitiful precaution against the oppressive weight of that forest, a mass of greenery so dark and dense it seemed almost colourless. I kept a couple of forest-wise types up front with me, short and evil the pair of them, an Ukit called O'Halloran – there was a story to that – and an Iban with a denscr coat of tattooes than te Kiore, plus amazingly stretched earlobes. They'd never seen anywhere quite like this, either. Te Kiore I set at the rear, with a couple of huskies to scoop him up if there was trouble; he didn't protest one bit. Ape mooched along in the middle somewhere, as if his mind was miles away.

Half crouched, tense as Jacquie's bowstring, we padded along that trail. It was wide, all right; I began to think more kindly about elephant stampedes. The woodsmen pointed out broken branches and cracked saplings here and there, but none of them looked recent. The only odd thing we found was a wide shallow depression in some dried mud, as if something large had rested there. Otherwise it was deadly dull, with no sound but the rustling of small creatures in the bushes, and the croaking calls of some incredibly unmusical birds. We were climbing, consistently and unmistakably, and through the rare gaps in the overhanging forest canopy I caught glimpses of the mountain flank and the white waterfall that streaked it. There was no sign of life, or of the jungle thinning. I was thinking of giving the order to turn back,

246

but I gave in to the temptation to turn one more corner. A clearing of sorts opened up in front of us – and O'Halloran and the Iban stopped so suddenly that the rest of us cannoned up together. Jacquie almost impaled me on her nocked arrow, and I was terrified a gun might go off; but I was also tall enough to see over the heads of our scouts, and I forgave them absolutely. I didn't need their plucking at my arms and gibbering to tell me what we'd found.

I thought, at first, it was the remains of more huts, a cage of bare poles still standing among them. But it wasn't. It'd been pulled apart by scavengers, but the central bones still lay as they must have fallen, on their sides, linked by leathery wisps of sinew. A cage, all right; a ribcage. I could have walked under it without stooping – not that I wanted to. Gingerly I prodded my sword into the heaps of bones jumbled around it, flipped a few over. It was hard to believe they'd all come from one skeleton. There were enormous plaques and spikes in there, great tabletop flanges of bone, and lumps of shrivelled hide encrusted with warty nodules. You could still see the rough outline of the beast in the shattered shrubbery where it had fallen, the blackened grass where it had decayed, and it must have been damn near the length of the clearing. 'What *was* this thing?' I demanded, or rather whispered. 'God knows what kind of monstrosity – you any idea, Ape?'

He was contemplating the scene with a strange, dazed-looking intensity – not the bones expressly, just the whole scene. When I repeated my question he just shook his head and grunted something impatiently. Te Kiore only shrugged graphically and pinched his nose. Jacquie was twining strands of hair around her fingers. 'Those plates – I don't know. I *have* seen something like this. It could be some sort of . . . well, dinosaur. A stegosaur. Only it's far too big.'

'Too *big*? But I thought they were . . . never mind. A dinosaur. That's big enough to have done all the damage down in the village, just about.'

'That,' observed Jacquie, 'or whatever it was killed it . . . '

I felt the old chill go sliding like an escaped ice-cube, right down my spine. I was about to say something when I noticed Ape, staring at us harder than ever. The beast hadn't made my hair stand on end, but that look was doing it. I took a step towards him, but his gaze didn't shift. It was Jacquie alone he was intent on.

'Ape!' she demanded in an irritable whisper. 'What's the matter? Do you . . . sense something?'

Ape shook his head hesitantly, then glanced quickly around at the jungle again, as if he was teetering between fascination and hesitation. 'I . . . am drawn,' he mumbled between those massive teeth. 'As if this place, it has some claim upon me – as if somehow I belong here – or it is thought I do . . . '

'Well, it's got it all wrong!' I snapped. I'd had about as much of this as I could take. 'I'm responsible here, and drawn or not, we're going back. Think we'll find any villagers with things like *that* wandering around?'

Ape threw me a sullen glare. 'Go, then! I . . . linger.'

'You crazy?' hissed te Kiore.

'Everything says it's dangerous!' I insisted, taking his arm. 'You can't stay— '

'I do not want to stay!' He batted my hand away casually enough, but it landed as a stinging slap, and he followed it up with an angry snarl which made everyone step hastily back. He rounded on us, fury in his eyes, stiffening his back. He stood straight, his shoulders unbowing, bringing him a lot nearer my height. 'I . . . must find out what this is about! Something tugs at me. Something urgent says there is need here for me. That other duty is here to perform, *anders die erg belangrijk ist* . . . '

His accent was thickening as he got more excited, till I could hardly make out what he was saying. 'What d'you mean, something else more important? What are you on about? It's dangerous here, that's what's important!' He tossed his head contemptuously and turned away. I grabbed him by the shoulder. 'Can't you understand me, damn it? Not *belangrijk*, bloody *gevaarlijk*, idiot!'

He took a swipe at me. If he'd struck the way he did on the train I'd have been laid out flat; but though it was vicious enough, it was a clumsy, casual cuff I could dodge easily. He'd misjudged it, as if he'd expected to have a longer reach, somehow – though in this misty light he looked quite big enough.

'*Laat me met rust!*' he growled, and bared his teeth. 'Must get to the heart of this . . . ' He was scowling around at us, breathing hard, his chin down against his barrel chest, his lips drawn back over those chisel teeth. The anger in that face was frightening enough in itself, but when you thought what he was capable of . . . The crewmen evidently had; they were backing away, down the path. I remembered Le Stryge, but I stood my ground.

'We can't just leave you here alone! Damn it, Ape, what's got into you? This isn't like you!'

He snarled something incoherent and slapped at me again, then gestured us all away, turned and stalked heavy-footed up the trail. He was still mumbling on. ' . . . at the mountain, *misschien* . . . '

'Ape!' I yelled. 'At least let me come along! I owe you a hell of a lot! And you've brought us this far—'

He turned suddenly, and for an instant I thought he was going to run at me. Then his narrow eyes widened, flickered to one side. 'You—' He grunted. 'No! *You* . . . you can come!' He was staring at Jacquie. 'Might need . . . to talk . . . '

'Like hell!' I exploded. He ignored me, came stumping back towards her. She skipped away, but his arm shot out, unexpectedly far, and his immense hand clamped on her arm. For almost the first time since I'd known her, Jacquie really screamed. I sprang at him, but the growl he let loose almost froze me in mid-leap. Again it was a casual, contemptuous blow, little more than a backhand slap; but this time it connected.

In the neck it could have killed me. As it was, he thumped me in the chest, knocked me flying right into the midst of that grisly pile. I sprawled among the bones, bruised and winded, flailing my arms about to get up, to get at my sword in case he came at me again. But instead he charged off at a great loping run, both Jacquie's wrists clamped in one hand; and for all her rebellious shouts and kicks it might as well have been wild horses dragging her. Te Kiore took a couple of shaky steps, but the others just stood there dumbfounded and gaping. Ape plunged into the trail ahead, smashing twig and branch in his mad haste, and vanished.

I clawed at a boulder to pull myself up, but it turned over in the grass. It was a skull, picked clean; a monstrous skull, horse-sized or larger, though it hardly looked large enough to belong to this great beast. And above one huge eyesocket was a neat round hole; and beyond that, just at the neck condyle, a shattered mess. Unmistakably the entry and exit holes of a bullet in the brain.

I stared at that skull a moment, then, horrified, at the trail ahead. 'We've got to stop him!' I yelled. 'Once he's on top of that mountain a whole army couldn't get at him!'

Te Kiore stared at me. 'You mean you know where he's going?'

It'd been so instinctive, that reaction, that it was a real effort to run back over what I'd said and what it implied. And only then did it all hit me, the sheer terror of it.

'Get out!' I shouted at him. 'Get away! Back to the village! This place – christ, it's dangerous, all right! More dangerous than you could ever bloody imagine!' Of course they just stood and gawked. I scrambled to my feet, though my chest felt as if it was on fire. 'I'll go after the others! Didn't you even hear me, you stupid s.o.b's! Get back inside that wall, and wait! *Run like hell!*'

My turn, then, to leave them gaping. I took one deep breath, wheezed painfully and went racing after the Ape.

I hadn't done any tracking since I left the scouts, but you didn't need to be a genius to follow his trail, incredibly heavy-footed, leaving deep prints still filling with jungle ooze. He ran like a crazed mowing machine, straight into small branches and fern fronds and overhanging creepers that must have struck like whips. Either his hide was unnaturally thick or he didn't give a damn about getting hurt; I saw specks of blood on one or two, and hoped like hell it wasn't Jacquie's. Here and there she'd left clear drag marks in the soft damp soil, and I could hear her squealing and screaming in the distance. That was something, that was a spur; you've got to be alive to scream. But if I was right – and I could hardly think straight, for the sureness of it – I'd have to see to that, and soon. Because in the very near future Ape was likely to run into real trouble, and he wouldn't be equipped to cope with it. Not quite. Not yet.

As I came over a rise I caught sight of them in the little stream cutting below, him still dragging her along, half-carrying her now, while she kicked at his legs and punched and pummelled him about the head and shoulders with her bare fists, bits of branch, anything else she could lay hands on as they passed. Her self-defence classes would have been proud of her performance, it would have laid any normal rapist out; but on him it wasn't making any impression that I could see. She grabbed at bushes and branches and tried to hang on; it slowed him down, but he hauled her loose almost effortlessly and plunged on. It dawned on me as I panted after him that he almost certainly didn't know I was after them, and probably wouldn't have cared if he did. He wasn't running from me, or anything else. He was going at that pace because he was used to it, or expected to be.

Up the far side of the valley they struggled, but I was at the river, splashing across in great bounds. I ought to have been tiring; but maybe something was working on my side here, too. The insistent drumming in my ears, the singing whine of the blood in my temples and the breath in my throat only became an urgent music, spurring me on. But they were almost at the top now, where the trail passed through a sort of notch in the valley wall. Beyond that the trees loomed up again with fearful menace, even denser than here, threaded with spectral banners of mist. Ape reached the edge, fought a moment more with Jacquie, and then, snatching her practically off the ground, legs kicking, he plunged through the notch and vanished.

I came up in a rush, only to stagger and catch myself as the ground seemed to fall away below me; earth and pebbles went skittering away down the slope, into a vague wash of greyness. Those trees were even taller than they'd looked; they were rooted in a steep slope, the wall of a shallow valley between the arms of the mountain – a valley full of mist. Beyond them came the ghostly glimmer of water, patches and pools and something larger, and the humid, heavy air stank of swamp. Memory galvanised me into action. I launched myself down that treacherous mudsliding trail, and the murk closed around me like a clammy cloak. Things were getting dangerous, all right; Ape might just get through this lot, but I was fairly sure I wouldn't. Beyond the trees, as I'd expected, the ground levelled out into an overgrown swamp of swaying reed clumps and foundered tree trunks, dank and slimy; and beyond that something like a lake opened up, glass-calm and motionless save for the will-o'-the-wisps jittering here and there. Which way had Ape gone now? I heard Jacquie shouting something; but the mist made the direction hard to fix. I took a deep breath, trying not to gag.

'Jacquie!' I yelled back. 'Hold him! Hold him back! Just a minute more—'

My voice awoke a blaring cacophony of gurgles, shrieks, chitterings and hooting mockery, as if this island's minor animal life was yelling defiance in my face. And beneath it erupted deeper sounds, awful sounds, hissing bellows booming and reverberant as if they came from throats like caverns and furnace lungs. Out in the lake a humped back broke surface, glistening grey like wet slate, and a long swan-neck lifted in a shining rain of droplets, casting about. Staring at it, I suddenly saw Ape, not as far from me as I'd feared, splashing awkwardly through the first sodden pools; awkwardly, because Jacquie was still fighting him like mad. I went racing after him, leaping tangles of reed and shrub and fallen branch, splashing through the stinking mire and sending small things scuttling from my path. It was only then, I think, that it dawned on him I was chasing him. As I ran up he glanced back, then swung around to face me; and that sight alone almost brought me down in my tracks.

The transition was terrible. It was no trick of the mist; he had grown, he was huge, seven feet or maybe more, and even in the act of turning he seemed to expand, as if the rage on his face was filling him out. His shoulders heaved, and his muscles burst the seams of his coat. The ginger mop around his face had darkened, the features themselves coarsened, and the scowl upon them splintered into a fearsome snarl that bared a mouthful of huge yellowed teeth, inhumanly heavy and long.

Jacquie took one look at him, choked and started screaming the place down, and I almost joined her. The shock almost held me too long; one huge paw let go of Jacquie and lashed out at me. I only just ducked in time, it clawed past my head and seized a broken branch, tore it loose from the mire and hurled it, sending me staggering into the reeds. With a satisfied grunt Ape swung around, heaved and with the one hand that still held Jacquie he swung her right off her feet and into the air, kicking and screaming. He was about to stump off straight into the water; but Jacquie clawed out in her turn, right at his eyes. Distracted, he caught a foot and stumbled; and I was on him.

I'd drawn my sword, and swung it. Ape let loose a thunderous roar, and swatted at the blade to swipe it from my hand; but that wasn't the end I planned to use. I swung it in a different direction, his blow went wild, and I brought the heavy gold pommel up and socked him neatly under that great chinless jaw of his.

The thud was audible. With that weight in it, the blow would have decked any normal man. He howled and staggered. I winced internally, shifted my grip and tapped him smartly behind the ear. His eyes rolled, he rocked, swayed and I took careful aim, swung with both hands and hit him again. He stared at Jacquie, struggling to focus; and dangling as she was, she launched a pretty neat karate kick to the side of his head. The eyes wandered, and with a low moan he toppled forward. Jacquie swung down with him, but I caught her as she fell; and for a glorious, breathless moment we clung, arms locked tight around one

252

another, scratched and burning cheeks pressed tight. Then, panting, I shook her off.

'We're not clear yet! It could still be working on him while he's out!'

'What could?' demanded Jacquie tremulously. 'I don't suppose – before I start gibbering and tearing my hair out and everything – you couldn't just give me a little hint about—'

'This place!' There was a splash from the lake, a big one, and I looked up nervously. 'And god alone knows what all this noise could bring down on us! Those creepers there – and your belt—'

In frantic haste, with everything we could reach we trussed Ape's hands and feet. Then, constantly looking back over our shoulders at the lake and the undergrowth, we set off to carry him back up the slope. His weight almost brought down the two of us, and most of the time it was more like dragging than carrying; I've seldom been so glad as I was when we made it to the notch and could manhandle him through. We weren't out of the woods yet, literally; but we had to rest there a minute, gasping and wheezing, before heaving him away downhill. That wasn't quite so bad, and we had no more troubles, but we were pretty spent by the time we reached the bone clearing. Te Kiore and the others had obeyed my orders, but they'd managed to get somebody up one of the trees by the wall to set a watch, and when they saw us they all came streaming out. We got Ape, still crocked, back into the shelter of the wall; they'd closed one door and tipped the other across the gap, giving at least some illusion of security.

'And now, shipmates,' said te Kiore with an air of iron self-control, as we dumped our groaning burden by the little fire they'd built. 'You'd not mind telling me *just what the flyin' fuck's been goin' on here?*'

'Don't look at me,' groaned Jacquie.

'We got him out just in time,' I wheezed. 'It was really getting to him – he'd begun to change, to grow – amazingly fast – and he was carrying Jacquie already. But he was due to cross that swamp in a hurry, and it was *dangerous*! And then fight something, something big and dangerous as I remember. Like that beast in the clearing, only worse; and he wasn't big enough yet. Although, my god, the rate he was going . . . '

I faltered. I'd caught their faces. I blinked. 'You mean – neither of you – you don't actually *know*? Well . . . '

I was just wondering where to begin when we developed other

problems. The air seemed to shudder, and there was a single dull thud, like an immense footfall. But it came not from nearby, or beyond the gate, but from out to sea. We sprang up. Standing, we could all see the reef from here, and the streak of white water that marked the lagoon passage. Just entering it, its high stack streaming, its massive paddles churning, was the sleek dark shape of a large steamer; and from its starboard side the smoke of a heavy cannon was rising.

'Hell's bloody bells!' I roared. 'C'mon! We've got to get Ape down to the beach! He might recover there, and still be able to do something before they can land! That's the only hope we've got!'

'Right you are!' snapped te Kiore. 'Up and at 'em, boys!'

We reached the beach at the trot, with Jacquie flagging in our midst, myself not much better, te Kiore limping and Ape still a groaning wreck on a makeshift stretcher, but looking much more like his old self again. Things there, though, weren't quite as we'd expected. The big steamer, leaving the end of the channel, wasn't making any visible attempt to land or fight. Instead it swung about in the deeper water, just beyond our grounded schooner, dwarfing it; a three-hundred footer, maybe more, sleek and menacing. From there they could have raked ship or beach with grapeshot, but there was no sign of them taking aim at either, or lowering boats. Instead the next gunport along opened, there was a thud and a puff of smoke, but no scream of shot to follow, just the squawk of a distorted speaking trumpet speaking good English. Well, fairly good.

*'Ahoy there! You guys ashore, whaddya think you're playin' at? Get the hell outa there, y'hear? Into your boats and amscray, umpchays! It's purest poison, that place!'*

'Just want us in the boats for better targets!' muttered te Kiore rebelliously.

'No,' I told him. 'I don't think so. And staying here – believe me, every minute's one too many! Into the boats it is!'

I'd been first ashore; I was last off, heaving the bows out into the water and swinging myself up over the gunwale. 'Well?' inquired te Kiore, at the tiller. 'Back to the schooner?'

'Un-huh. Steer for the steamer.'

Instantly I was facing my first mutiny, as the oarsmen erupted. Te Kiore yelled them down, then rounded on me. 'The bloody *steamer* – jesus, you're not thinking of trying and boarding her, are you?'

'No, of course not. But . . . look, they've got us by the short and curlies, haven't they? So what else can we do? And it may not be as bad as you think. That hail didn't sound exactly unfriendly, did it?'

'If it's as bad as I think, we're mutton,' he said. 'But you're calling the shots, mate. I'm out of out of my depth, and I get the odd kinda feeling you aren't.'

'No,' I said, with a burgeoning sense of surprise, 'somehow I . . . don't think I am. And out on the Spiral here it's just about the first time ever . . . Pull away, then! Come on, pull!'

And they grumbled, those hardened old pirates; but they pulled at my command. Out over the lagoon we glided, and in no time at all we were under the shadow of that great hull. She was as beautiful in her way, that steamboat, as the schooner was in hers, and not dissimilar in her longer, higher lines. Her bows were high and sharp, the planking reinforced with a heavy strip of steel. Above them she was decked level and rigged with low masts and a steadying sail that almost symbolically gave place to the magnificent smokestack, painted a gleaming navy blue and crowned with gilt spires. The superstructure was set low, with an open bridge, astern of the great paddleboxes that rose naturally out of the hull instead of being stuck on to it, as the schooner's were.

'Beaut!' muttered te Kiore enviously, as we steered in. 'Feathered paddles, see? Uses radial rods on a cam to angle each paddle as it hits the water. Cuts the jar and makes it more efficient. That's *fast!*'

The paddle sconces were painted like the smokestack and covered with ornate gilt mouldings, and the railing of the gallery that ran round each housing was ornate as a New Orleans balcony, and gilded also. A figure was leaning over the one above us, and as we pulled up a brass-mounted rope ladder came clattering down to us.

'Or there's a boarding-ladder aft! But you've not the look of such as'd need a trimming, my brave bawchucks! Not even you, sirrah, unless you've forgot your climbing knack of old! A fair try at a tumblehome you made, for a first ever – but do you so still, without a cannon at your bum, or my blade?'

I sat there, open-mouthed, staring at the tall figure, black-clad like myself, with bare shoulders as broad as mine beneath the tumbling spray of blonde curls – and yet fiercely, lithely feminine.

'*Mall*?' I croaked.

A whoop of mocking merriment. 'Begad, a jack of rare perception, that'll spy a millstone and cry, "Out on't for a bastard cheap glass, I shaved a'morn!" Well sir, will you stand up to me hither?'

I was about to make a dive for the ladder when I looked past her to the bridge, and saw the tall figure in gold braid leaning over the outer rail. I remembered my manners, and called, 'Watch! Permission to come aboard, sir?'

The officer gave me a dashing off-the-brow salute. I grinned around at the others. 'It's okay, boys. Just follow me up – you first, Jacquie. Will you manage, te Kiore?'

'You kidding, mate?' he inquired. 'But what's all this about?'

'Damned if I know. Let's go find out.'

I ushered Jacquie carefully on to the ladder ahead of me, but she shinned up it with her usual elastic grace; her foot never slipped once, which was more than you could say for mine. Mall watched with an amused grin, and at the top she more or less scooped Jacquie in, then all but lifted me by the scruff of my neck. We stood, inches apart, grinning at one another, in my case rather breathlessly. 'So,' she said, 'how fare'st, you counting-house sailor, you?'

'And you, you . . . '

'Aye?'

'Forget it. I feel safer that way. But what . . . '

'And who's this fair one you've dragged along with you, poor thing?'

'Ah,' I said. Mall had long ago drawn the history of my love life out of me, with what might be called silk-wrapped pincers. 'Er . . . this is Jacquie.'

Of course that raised her eyebrows. '*The* Jacquie? Oh, ho, so that way blows the wind. For sure, for sure.' Jacquie looked ready to explode, but Mall unexpectedly clasped her by the shoulders. 'My lady, this is a brute of little delicacy we have here. He told me only that you were fair, and failed to work't into a sonnet at the least, as is your desert. Y'are very welcome!' She kissed her resoundingly on the cheek. 'Now come, for even a-ship this is no place for lingering! You others below, mount without fear and find refreshment!'

She led me, and a slightly stunned Jacquie, round the gallery and on to the deck, where a small keg – evidently the refreshment

— was being manhandled up by grinning turbanned crewmen. 'We'll e'en take ours with the officer of the watch,' said Mall. 'Anxious he is to meet you.'

'Mall,' I said fervently, 'you're a sight for sore eyes, but how the hell—'

'Not that way,' drawled a familiar voice from the top of the bridge steps. 'Too far off the charts even for me.'

I stared at the trim figure in dark blue with gold braid and buttons, and bounded up the steps to grab the outstretched hand. 'Jyp! Jyp, you old son-of-a-bitch! Now this really is too goddamn much! And what're you doing all got up like the original dog's dinner? And is somebody going to tell me how you got here, the pair of you, or do I have to burst all over your nice clean bridge?'

Jyp's lean, lined face twisted into a grin. 'Well, as to the uniform, now, you're talkin' to the sailing master and first officer of Her Imperial Majesty's armed merchantman *Sapphire of Hangchow*, and that's the way the skipper likes it with his officers. Kind of formal, he is; veddy veddy Bridish, you oughta get on like a house afire – well, smoulderin' a mite round the edges, anyhow.' He registered my expression, and his eyes twinkled. 'As to the rest, hell, weren't you expectin' us, Steve? You had ole Katjka put the word out for us, after all.'

I spread my hands out, overcome. 'Well, yes – but you were far away, and . . . it's been a long time . . . '

'But you must know, my Stephen,' Mall cut in, her green eyes glittering, 'that out of the very grip of the grave itself we would rise, if t'were you that summoned us?'

Jyp chuckled. 'Damn nice trick if I could swing it. But short o' that, Steve, she's right. After what we've been through, we wouldn't fail you. We still owe you our lives, don't we?'

I couldn't speak, and he saw that. 'Anyhow,' he went on, 'weren't too much of a hassle. There we was in eastern seas anyhow, and me homeward bound; so Mall signed up, and we swung it with the skipper to turn aside awhile. Not too hard to cotton on to you, after the doin's at Bangkok, but catchin' up was something else. Missed you by a hair at Surabaja, heard a pack of Boegies'd been hangin' round, sussed them out and lit off after them. But you were fast, and so were they; we didn't come within cannon-shot till you'd already vanished into that mist.'

Jacquie had been standing open-mouthed, gawping at these people, but she burst out suddenly, 'So that was *you* firing?'

'Sure was, ma'm,' grinned Jyp. 'We kind of severely discouraged 'em – cannon and ram. Guess they're still runnin'!' I thought of those looming knife-edge bows and quailed a little, but not too much. 'So then,' he concluded, 'we're here.'

I still could hardly speak. 'I . . . don't know how to thank you guys . . . we were lost, astray, and you . . . '

'Astray,' repeated Jyp, and his smile faded. 'That you surely were; and are. We'll needs settle what we can do.' He thumbed his chin. 'Best we have a word with the skipper 'bout that; he's over chewin' the fat with your captain right now. Way things are, Steve, we can spare some time to help you, but not so much. We're en route from Cathay to Lyonesse with a cargo of five-spice, *loong*-scale and – well, call 'em perishable goods.' He gave a shrug of distaste. 'To be put off at Rye. And in between you, me and the maintop, ole shipmate, the port of Rye is welcome to them. With three cheers an' a tiger. So—'

Jacquie caught him by the arm. 'I'm sorry, Mister, er, Jyp, but I don't think I – I mean, *Rye*?' She let loose a slightly hysterical giggle. 'That should be worth seeing! I mean, you docking there. It's miles inland.'

I grinned, and introduced her to Jyp, who turned on his down-home charm. 'Anyhow,' I added, this is the Spiral, remember? Rye was one of the great ports of Europe, back in Mall's day or a bit earlier.'

'That's so,' she nodded, her mane sweeping her spectacular cleavage. 'And its shadow stretches farther than might'st think. The Rye we're bound for is a port of moment *again*!' And she clapped a hand to her swordhilt, threw back her head and laughed, quietly. Mall's laughter, even muted, was as disturbing as ever.

'Again?' Jacquie insisted. 'Again? But what could possibly bring the sea to Rye now?'

I shrugged uncomfortably. 'I don't know? A rise in sea level? Or the land sinking? Mall, just how far in the future are we talking about?'

But Mall only smiled.

'Global warming!' persisted Jacquie. 'Melting the icecap. That would just about do it. Maybe Ape could—'

We both said '*Ape*!' simultaneously.

'*Ape?*' echoed Jyp and Mall.

'God,' I said unhappily, 'we've left him trussed up in the boat!'

We rushed to the bridge rail, but to our great relief te Kiore had used his head. Ape was sitting against the rail, still tied up but with every sign of coming back to life.

'Who's this?' inquired Jyp.

'A . . . a wise man. Like Le Stryge – only,' I added as I saw Jyp's face freeze, 'not so horrible. Katjka recommended him.'

Jyp looked at Mall. She shrugged. 'A meet enough judge, the little spae-witch. Who can see all things?'

'Okay, but why've you got him hogtied?' demanded Jyp.

'Something happened to him on the island . . . Look, we'd better go down and . . . '

'Sure. And I guess we might come along, Mall an' me.'

Te Kiore heard us coming down the stair. 'Hey, bonzer rum, mister!' he tossed to Jyp, and jerked a thumb. 'He's downed some grog – not too much. But I figured . . . '

'Right,' I said, and knelt down by the groaning heap of sorceror. After only a slight hesitation I cut the bonds around those massive wrists. If he turned peculiar again there were enough of us to handle him, and Mall could probably manage all by herself. He seemed more or less the same size he'd always been, though; and the eyes he turned to me were the same, except for a kind of wild, wandering look in them. He lifted his newly freed hands, peered at them, opened his mouth as if to shout something at me, then clapped his palms to his temples in anguish.

'*Waat is . . . heb je . . .* ' He finished in a hoarse whisper. 'What the bloody festering fringes of hell happens?'

'Well . . . ' I began. Ape's eyes grew wider as I told my tale; but Mall's feet tapped the deck, and Jyp gave a pretty good impression of a man being strangled by his collar, scarlet face and all. But he waited till I'd finished before he finally exploded.

'Well, in the name of . . . ' Jyp's strict upbringing back in pre-war Kansas – the Spanish–American War, this was – left him shy of all but the mildest blasphemy, but he was pretty close to it now. 'What'd you expect? What in the . . . on earth were you folks *dreamin'* of, just dandering ashore like that?' He gestured furiously up at the looming island. Looking up, I saw with a shudder that the mist had peeled back from the mountain heights, to reveal a dome top and a hollowed profile that really did look like the empty eye and nose sockets of a fleshless skull. 'On *Skull Island*? Of all the damn places!'

'Skull Island?' was more or less everybody's reaction, except mine.

'Haven't any of you ever been to the goddamn *movies*?' demanded Jyp, *in extremis*.

'Can't stand 'em,' rumbled te Kiore. 'Give me a headache reading the bloody titles.'

'I saw it once,' I admitted. 'When I was nine. And loved it – then I never went to see it again, because I thought it was childish. More or less blotted it out of my mind.' I caught Jacquie looking at me, very oddly. 'I was such a *serious* little kid, you see. So that's why it took a while to dawn on me. But you're right, Jyp, you did warn me once – what was it? That out here there's everything man'd ever imagined. But I never dreamt it could include *this*.'

Ape clutched his head again, and groaned. 'A very popular *bioskoop*, this is?'

'Very,' said Jyp, regarding him with cool suspicion. 'Seen by millions of folk the whole world over.'

'Made seventy years ago,' I added, 'and they're still watching it.'

'It's kind of authentic, too,' resumed Jyp. 'The guys who made it, they weren't just Hollywood adventurers. They'd sailed these seas.'

Jacquie, eyes as wide as they could get, snapped her fingers and made a breathy little sound of surprise. '*That* one? That's right! You said it reminded you of Komodo, and you couldn't think why! Because Komodo and Flores, and the giant lizards, gave the film-makers the idea in the first place!'

Ape groaned, more in chagrin now than pain. 'An archetype. *Een hele nieuwe arketyp* . . . I might have known, hah? In the minds of millions, yet never I hear of it. And there it stands, left vacant.' He growled with disgust. 'It just waits for me to walk right into it! Just waits!'

'You and all the others, old-timer, the longer they'd hung around – each one into whatever role best fitted 'em. And all goin' nowhere.' Jyp, leaning his hips against the rail, contemplated him with a very guarded smile. 'Well, at least you oughta be safe enough from it, off the island. But mister – if I were you I'd stay away from New York. Well away! And from high buildings anywhere.' He waggled a long finger. 'And if you've absolutely gotta climb one – you take the damn elevator, y'hear?'

Captain Sir Augustine Langley Ferris, Bart., late officer commanding Her Britannic Majesty's ship of the line *Demiphöon*, 74 guns, made a steeple of his long bony fingers – real arachnodactyls – and looked at us over it. It wasn't an encouraging look; his wintry blue eyes were set in a long equine face with more than a touch of skull about it, accentuated by his thinning dark hair and pale skin. Only a few courageous freckles spotted the thin blade of a nose and the high angular cheekbones. The cheeks beneath were hollow, lurking behind immense sidewhiskers, thick and straight, that arced outwards like twin waterfalls, only to be sliced off with mathematical precision in line with his thin straight mouth. His bony chin had that particular gleaming smoothness only a cut-throat razor can give, and his voice had the same quality; there was no trace of emotion in it as he handed me the bad news.

'I have conferred with Captain Batang, at length, and he is in agreement with me. I regret to inform you that I see no prospect whatsoever of you achieving your object.'

I took it on the chin. 'You mean the *Ikan Yu*'s a total loss? Surely she's not *that* bad!'

He shook his head. 'Oh, no. The damage to the hull is quite easily reparable. But she has lost a topmast and several major spars, and her mainmast is cracked. She does not carry sufficient spares – cannot, since she must ship cargo. And we of course carry only one spar for the steadying sail. The trees ashore do not look suitable, even if one dared go back for them.'

'Not in a hurry.' I looked at Jyp. 'I seem to remember sailing under a pretty awful jury rig before now!'

He fingered his jaw seriously. 'Yeah, but what way did we make?'

Mall, leaning against the open door of the chartroom, made an unhappy noise. 'I begin to perceive a very knot o' thorns! Neither one nor t'other?'

'Precisely, quartermaster. Once afloat, you will be able to carry only the lightest of makeshift rigs. And, of course, we can do nothing for the steam vessel—'

'The boiler, he means,' translated Jyp.

'Right,' I said unhappily. 'Well, it was done for, anyway. We'd need a whole new one.'

'Which you won't find it so easy to lay hands on out here,' Jyp reminded me. 'Hardly any industry beyond the Core, remember? Everything by hand. That's why Batang Sen let it get into that state; no choice.'

Ferris nodded. 'Precisely the problem the *Sapphire* must face from time to time. So far we have been fortunate. But I do not think you would find the necessary craftsmen anywhere in this region. So you have a choice. It will take a day or more to effect the repairs to the hull; we have a reasonable surplus of planking, caulking and so on that we will be able to spare you. Plus, of course, the assistance of my crew in every capacity. It will then be a simple matter to tow you off the sand.'

His delivery was so calm it took a moment to sink in. 'Captain Ferris,' I said, a little breathlessly, 'that's incredibly kind of you . . . you've done so much for us already.'

'Oh no, I assure you. The common courtesy of sailors. Indeed, I only wish we could do more. But you can then proceed under limited sail to some Javanese port, have new spars fitted and the hull properly reinforced, which will take two days at least, and thence to Bali. Or you can proceed to Bali directly under jury rig, which will take as long or longer. In either event, though, I see no way you could arrive there by the 3rd of May, as you wish.'

'Not wish!' said Ape fiercely, as if suddenly awoken. '*Must!*'

Ferris raised his sparse eyebrows.

I protested. 'But through the Spiral . . . '

Ferris flattened his fingers and rubbed his nose. 'Not even if I lent you the incomparable services of Mister, ah, Jyp as pilot could he steer a path through the seas of the, ah, *Spiraculum Majorem* that would get you there on time. Perhaps he would care to confirm this for us.'

Jyp ran a hand over the outstretched charts, his eyes gleaming, as if at every point the lines and symbols conveyed some new truth, and yet only served to confirm a vast inner certainty. 'Yup,' he said laconically. 'I'm sorry, Steve. That's it an' all about it. If you could sail this hour and straightway there, I might just swing it. But putting into a port, that's steering hard by the Core again, a lee shore in time. And then how long for your refit? There's no way I could make up the days you'd lose. You'd need something instant like those there Gates to do that.'

'Don't even mention them. But if we forget the refit— '

'That will lay you excessively vulnerable to wind, weather and any further assaults your enemies choose to unleash.'

'Like the cap'n says,' agreed Jyp. 'They'll scrag you for sure.'

'Then . . . we're beaten?' A weight poised over me, spinning, ready to fall.

'*No!*' exclaimed Jacquie. 'The Project won't dare impose penalty payments, not after I get through to them! What's a day or two more or less?'

'*Everything!*' growled Ape, with shocking force. 'If that container comes not to its arriving place by that midnight, and me with it, all is in peril. Other forces then come into play, other powers hold sway. Against them I am no longer a shield to you, then, when that evening comes. When that darkness falls. Those penalties can you also turn aside?'

Jacquie looked away, silent, shocked, as near uncontrollable tears as I'd ever seen her. Despair descended, a *peine forte et dure* of cold apprehension. Ferris stood up, and paced the width of the oak-panelled chartroom, idly fingering the brass-cased instruments and native curios that festooned the walls.

'Well,' I said, 'we'll press on, all the same. It's all we can do. You've given us every help you can.'

'Not necessarily,' put in Ferris abruptly. He swung himself back into his leather swivel chair, picked up a long chart pencil and began to twiddle it between his fingertips. 'We ourselves have no hold capacity to spare . . .' A sudden commotion from the deck drowned him out.

They were winching his gig back aboard, in which he'd been to see Batang Sen. Water was dripping from its hull on to the tarpaulin that covered the main hold hatchway; and beneath it something was awoken, something that rushed and rustled and slammed and thudded and scrabbled, and let out the weirdest cheeping noises. It sounds funny; it wasn't. The heavy hatchcover leaped and bounced, and the deckhands scattered in all directions.

Ferris sprang to his feet, but Mall was already leaping down the companionway to the deck, her mass of gold ornaments jingling. 'Soft, soft, my bawchucks,' she crooned over the hatchcover. 'Go to, my lusty spurcocks, go to, Sowter, go to, Tray! No more nasty cannons, is there?' A frenzied cheeping answered her, and the cover leaped again. She fetched it a hefty boot. 'Sneck up, wilt thou, thou lousy whoreson jackanapes! Hold thy peace lest I have thy lights to my pointstrings! Peace, thou poxy mooncalves! 'Tis Mall of the Clink who speaks!'

A sudden hysterical whimpering sound tailed off into silence. 'Ah!' she cooed. 'There's merry monsters all, I swear ye understand e'y word!' She let the cover fall, and tightened its lashings.

Jyp's face twisted. I'd seen him nervous before – not often, but I knew how it looked. '*That*,' he said glumly, 'is our precious "perishable cargo". And the sooner they perish, the better, if you ask me. Her and the captain are the only ones'll happily go near 'em.'

Mall, bounding back up to join us, grinned and poked him in the ribs. 'Why, man, you fodder them yourself a'times!'

'Yeah, and guess how happy it makes me.'

Ferris coughed discreetly. 'Thank you, quartermaster. Now – as I was most appositely saying – our hold space is fully accounted for. But if this container of yours is fully waterproof . . . '

'Up to 20 fathoms, this model,' I said, surprised. 'And it's buoyant, anyway, with all the packing. Could float for months – but why?'

'Very satisfactory.' He emphasised each point with a tap of the pencil. 'Then we might with ease, ah, take it on as deck cargo.' The glacial glint of his eyes became something suspiciously like a twinkle. 'Since our distinguished Sailing Master has led us so skilfully out of our way, after all, it ought to be little extra effort for him to divert us a trace further – as far as, say, Bali?'

Jyp cut loose with a rebel yell. I sat bolt upright. So did Jacquie. I guessed she'd never realised her guardian angel had mutton-chop whiskers, either.

'I was, ah, about to add,' he said, almost shyly, 'that for your esteemed selves we can find a cabin, of sorts. So if you would do us this signal honour . . . '

I blinked. 'I don't know what to say . . .'

'Why so?' drawled Mall. 'Is *yes* so fall'n from fashion?'

'No – I mean, it's not that I'm not grateful, but I don't want to leave Batang Sen and te Kiore in the lurch – not with a busted rig, and Boegies and god knows what else on their tails.'

Ferris nodded. 'I have already broached the idea to your captain, and he welcomes it – with good reason. You, your consignment, this is what the hunters seek. If you are not with the *Ikan Yu*, it will certainly be left alone; it is us they will chase.'

'And if they are truly misfortuned, why, they may catch us!' Mall's teeth glinted, and she hugged herself with delight. 'So be it!'

The captain's tight little smile spread benignly to the ends of his sidewhiskers. 'I could not have put it more, ah, pointedly myself, quartermaster. I trust that meets your objections, Mr Fisher?'

'If you promise to let me pay a fair price for passage . . .'

Ferris bobbed his head good-humouredly; he was becoming almost human. 'I long ago contrived to overcome any such inhibitions, I assure you. Then we are agreed? Yes? Then, Mr Jyp, since you persist in imitating the steamwhistle, you will please convey my compliments to Captain Batang Sen and request the pleasure of his company at dinner tonight – at which I trust all of you will join us . . .'

By the time we went back to the schooner working parties from both crews were already swarming over it like ants over their nest. Our offers of help were politely but firmly rejected; we wandered through the turmoil of sawing and hammering, feeling underfoot and in the way, with the sinister presence of the island brooding over us. The best thing we could do was pack our stuff and head back to the *Sapphire*. She had three passenger cabins, but somehow or other Jacquie's stuff and mine landed together in the large double cabin at the stern, and neither of us felt up to the fuss of rearranging matters. We were too exhausted to do more than splash on some cool water and collapse into bed, anyhow; we hardly spared each other a glance as we undressed. And yet as the night passed, we lay awake together, breathless in the tropical warmth, with our sweat trickling down and mingling under the light coverlet. The clatter and rasp of the work drifted across to us, mingled with the eerie crics of the island's night, banishing sleep. Her hand sought mine, clasped it, palm to damp palm; I looked round, saw her silhouette clear against the pale-lit

266

window louvres, her lips parted and trembling. I rolled over, touched my hand to them and ran it down her jaw, her throat, across her collarbone to the peak of her left breast. She caught it, pressed it home and pulled me after it. What it would mean, which way we were heading, I neither knew nor cared. We were ruled by the moment, and it was right, it was enough.

But in the clinging aftermath, still blind and panting, a momentary vision flashed across my eyes; of Mall, a wind of moonlight streaming through her hair, standing tall and terrible against the stars. The way she'd looked that night by the wheel, when she'd turned a mirror of ghastly clarity on the way I'd treated Jacquie, on all my self-deceptions and rationalisations, showing me the inner emptiness that spawned them. A memory, it might have been; only now, where there'd been scorn, something else blazed in those changeable eyes – mischief, maybe a touch of tenderness, but very fierce if it was. Above all, though, that disturbing spark of laughter. The vision passed; and eventually we slept.

We came on deck late that morning. By then a patch of the *Ikan Yu*'s port ribs lay bare and exposed in a great jagged strip, like a patient in mid-operation. Already they were fastening reinforcements to the damaged ribs, checking the less damaged planking and cutting replacements for the rest, while pumps spewed a jerky stream of foul water out of the bilges. Oakum caulking was teased and hammered into place with wooden mallets, pitch was boiled in pots in the engine room – nobody wanted to risk the beach – and planes and spokeshaves trimmed fine curls of wood for a neat fit. Mall, as the *Sapphire*'s quartermaster, was standing the morning watch by the wheel. She turned her gaze on us as we emerged from the stairwell; but there was only her usual look in it, challenge and mild irony mingled. She smiled a lazy, sardonic smile, and jerked a thumb at the scurrying seamen.

'A noble thing, is this labour of the hands. It physics me but to watch it.' She stretched like a cat in the dank air. 'You wear the aspect of ones well physicked yourselves. A peaceful night's watch, save that we rolled at anchor for a while, as with a heavy swell. One might avow that some danced the shaking o' the sheets below, i'faith! But who'd be about such scamblings?'

Jacquie turned a merry lobster scarlet, and maybe I did too. 'None of your damn business, Ms Frith!' I told her severely, and then a thought made me hesitate. 'Or – was it? Mall, just what were you up to last night? Not trying to meddle, by any chance? You know, putting on the old 'fluence or whatever it is?'

She rolled her eyes in injured innocence. 'Master Stephen! I?'

'Come on, Mall! I know you!'

She lowered her eyes and shrugged, scuffed one foot on the deck a little awkwardly. Mall did nothing awkwardly unless she meant to; she had the grace of centuries. 'Well-a-day . . . ' she admitted. 'Wouldst hold me blameable, that I do but take an interest? And so I did, I avow, see to it that your bags were set together i' the great cabin, true. But no more! None! All else that came to pass, 'twas your doing only, the pair of you. Coupled—'

'All right!' yelped Jacquie. 'I get the message! Mall, whatever it was you were up to, you're a low-minded, nosy, interfering cow, you're utterly bloody impossible! And now you've done spreading my sex life all across the deck, I would like some breakfast, thank you. And Mall . . . '

'Aye, sister?' inquired Mall humbly.

'Thank you very much!' said Jacquie quickly, and fled.

All that day work parties went back and forth between the two ships, but we were still left at a loose end. Skills honed over lifetimes and longer were in play among the hands who crawled in and around the opening in the schooner's flank like maggots in a wound; we would only slow them down. Ape found himself another corner of the deck to squat in and meditate, and took no further interest in proceedings. We sat and admired the amazing speed with which the gash was sutured and healed, and the masts grew upward from the deck again, sprouting spars that seemed to spin the webs of rigging anew. And in the meantime we talked. We talked of each other, of things that had been, things that might have been; but of what might still be, neither of us ventured a word. I didn't, because I was afraid to; but about Jacquie's reasons I could only guess.

By the early evening the gash was whole, and the stream of water from the bilge pumps had sunk to a trickle. The working parties came scurrying back to the *Sapphire*. I thought things would end there for the day, but Ferris, for all his languid appearance, wasn't the type to stand still. Before long the high stack overhead was coughing its first black puffs of soot, and the immense paddlewheels were beginning to churn and thrash the water. They swung her round on her cables, till she loomed over the grounded schooner like a cliff.

'Reverse paddles and shut down, if you please!' said Ferris through his speaking trumpet. The *Sapphire*'s side drifted against the schooner's fenders as lightly as a kiss, and bobbed there gently. 'Deck party! The derrick, please!'

With a rumble and a rattle the iron arm swung out over the tilted deck below, and as the pawl was thrown it spilled a rattling mass of chain down through the open hold hatchway. A few minutes of clanking and oaths below, then there was a hail, and the steam winch chugged and puffed into action. The chains twanged taut and to a great cheer from both crews, dripping wet from its flooding but still robustly intact, with Ape's hex-signs glowing brighter than a Lancaster Country barn, the container came jerking up into the dimming light. As its weight was removed the schooner's deck lifted visibly and levelled off, rocking gently; wallowing and gurgling sounds bubbled up beneath the hull. The sand was loosening its grip.

The container creaked to its zenith, and we ducked as it came swaying and spattering over to the *Sapphire*'s deck. Hands rushed to steady it, so it struck the deck with only a light bump and boom – though of course that set off the cheeping perishables again, and a burst of abuse from Mall. The container's ribbed sides looked fine, the lock was still holding. Only Ape's charms had suffered, running, smeared and peeling; but he seemed to take little interest in them now, or anything else. Crewmen swarmed around, undoing the chains and fastening them down to ringbolts set in the deck; others were already casting off the mooring cables and running a line to the schooner's stern.

The captains bellowed at each other again, *Sapphire*'s paddles began to slap, and slowly she pulled free of the beached ship, swinging her bows out into the lagoon. Beyond her stern the towcable rose dripping from the water and sang like a tautened guitar string, the engine-room telegraph rang repeatedly for more power, the paddles churned the clear water to a beery froth. There was a moment's suspense while it seemed we weren't making any headway – then a flash of sheer panic.

With an obscene wallowing, sucking sound, the schooner's bows tore free of the soft sand, and she shot sternwards into the lagoon. We all flinched, as she raced at us like a torpedo; but Ferris was ready. Over went the helm, the tow was cast, and she

269

slid easily by us, shedding momentum, till she floated free once more in the misty lagoon. Catching our breath, Jacquie and I climbed down on to the paddle housing as we moved in alongside her again.

Te Kiore was busy rigging another tow, to the bows this time; he seemed to be strutting up and down quite normally now. Batang Sen was at the helm, twisting the wheel to check the rudder action since the grounding. Everything seemed to be happening very quickly now, and I realised I didn't want to leave the schooner and its cut-throat crew behind like this; we'd been through too much. I hailed them. 'Hey, te Kiore! How's she feel?'

His face split in a pumpkin grin. 'All fast, Steve! Tight as a tick, not making enough to wet a gnat's bum!'

Batang Sen looked up and waved. '*Selamat berjalan, tuan*! Simply spiffing jaunt! Capital jollity, what? Best for many years! We do again soon, hah?'

'Yes,' I said weakly. 'Spiffing. Take care of yourselves, now!'

He laughed. 'Is hardly problem! Problem is what you got! Well, pip-pip and cheerio, hah, *tuan*? And guard your derry-air!'

'Too right!' laughed the Maori. 'Well, see you in Bali next week, as arranged, and we'll have a good spell, eh? Catch a few beers.' He blew Jacquie a kiss.

'It's a date,' I told him. 'There's just one thing more . . .'

He looked at the package I hefted. 'For us? Okay, chuck it down.'

'It's heavier than it looks!' He just flexed his muscles and laughed. 'On your head be it!' I told him, and threw.

He caught it all right, contemptuously in one hand – and fell flat on his backside. One side of the bag split with a dull clink, and a stream of little bright discs went rolling across the deck. I needn't have winced. That pack of freebooters had the conditioned reflexes of several lifetimes; not one coin made it further than three feet. They whooped and jabbered and danced around the deck, singing old tribal roundelays or possibly headhunting songs, while te Kiore sat staring at the heap, and Batang Sen came racing down the deck at a rate of knots.

'Enough here to buy the old girl twice over!' said the Maori dazedly.

'On account!' I called back, laughing. 'There's the bonus to follow, and you've bloody well earned it, you pack of sharks! Till Bali!'

That raised an even bigger cheer. Captain Ferris's voice boomed out over the megaphone. 'If your business is quite concluded, gentlemen? Very well, then. Mr Jyp? Be so good as to signal ready for tow.' The steam whistle sounded two deafening blasts, and a hail answered them. 'Will you take the helm and see us out, Mr Jyp? Quarter speed ahead, please. Very good.'

I didn't see what was so good about it. The channel looked less narrow when you'd more manoeuvring power, but the sea beyond the reef was no longer calm; the incoming waves frothed and creamed about our bows. But Jyp's hands moved with quiet confidence on the helm, and astern, bouncing in our wake, I could just make out Batang Sen in much the same attitude, with te Kiore towering in the bows, and men with long spars ready to fend off any obtrusive rocks. All the same, there were some heart-stopping moments. With a contrary wind and no power the *Ikan Yu* alone would never had made it. As it was, we emerged, after a few minutes or a century, into the swell and surf of the open ocean. Behind us, as the winds swirled, the mists drew closed like curtains over a stage and hid that deadly mountain-face and all it represented from our sight. The drumming surf thunder fell away astern, fading almost too quickly to be natural. But I found myself wondering – with a kind of weird longing, almost – what else lurked beyond that isle? What other reefs and shoals of human imaginings, within the fathomless reaches of the Spiral?

Before long even the mist was thinning, and the radiant blues of the Pacific opened out above us and below, amid the cheerful buffeting of a freshening wind. Captain Ferris lifted his long nose to the wind, and took a discreet sniff. 'Mr Jyp! Signal ready to release tow, if you please.'

The whistle blasts were met by a resounding cheer from the schooner; even as the line sagged free, lines of men went racing up into its rigging, inching along the footropes with fearful agility, and almost instantly the sails blossomed out. Even with a maimed rig she was a lovely sight, a patchwork flower where new white canvas flashed against older yellow. Ferris swivelled the speaking trumpet to his mouth. 'Coxswain's crew, raise the ensign! Gun crews, stand by to render parting honours. On the command – *fire!*'

A dark knot soared up the staff at the *Sapphire*'s stern and burst out into the red ensign; the five eighteen-pounders along the starboard side thundered in turn, heeling the whole ship. The

*Ikan Yu*'s popguns smoked in answer, while both crews cheered raucously. Then as her rudder bit she swung free, ridding herself of the entanglements and pursuits I'd led her into, and skipped like an unbridled horse over our wash, turning away eastward for the safe havens of Jawa. Jacquie and I watched her draw away, standing silent till the tall sailcrest shrank to a single pale fin against the horizon.

Her work was done; but what remained of ours?

The *Sapphire* was fast, according to Jyp one of the very fastest ships that plied these outer oceans, and I could believe that. She was close to the limits of the possible out here, where no stable industry could flourish for long, and the limit of technology lay in the hands of clever craftsmen. There were no standard spare parts for her, no machine tools to shape them; when a part wore or went wrong, it would have to be crafted anew by hand, at fantastic costs in time and money.

'That's how it was with steam mechanics when it got started, in the Core,' he said, leaning on the engine-room rail to watch the great beam arms. Their slow methodical churn and hiss seemed eerily quiet after the roar of internal combustion engines or howling warship turbines. 'Couldn't keep going that way, though, neither there nor here. How long'll ole Batang Sen be in getting his new boiler, d'you think? All that dough of yours in hand, that'll help; but he'll have to find metalworkers who can do the job. I bet he's still under sail when he makes Bali, and for a long time after. And that time'll come for the *Sapphire*, too, if nothing else sinks her first. Maybe she'll have to mount masts and sails, too; or drop back into the Core for repairs, and run the risk of never comin' out again.'

He grinned. 'And you can lay good odds I won't be with her if she does. Known guys who went that way. One I'd shipped with from New Amsterdam t'the Hesperides, heap o' times; dropped back in at his home port, got kind of daffy over a doll and just lingered. Ran into him ten years on, his teeth an' hair falling out and he hadn't a clue who I was. Going on like crazy 'bout how dull his life had been, how he'd never been anywhere worth a damn or seen anything worth seeing. Him, who'd crossed wakes with the *Argo* homeward bound and seen the very Fleece at her masthead, the blood on her stern! Him, who'd hunted elephant east of the Catskills long before the red man ever saw 'em! Never even knew he'd been away.' He gave a deep sigh, and shook his head.

Jacquie held my arm and said nothing; and the look on her face was even harder to read than usual.

Mall snorted disdainfully. 'It's these sweltering arms of steel that drag your thoughts Hubward! Back beneath the open heavens, and breathe free again!'

She herded us up the ladder ahead of her, keeping Jacquie and myself carefully together, as if even a momentary intervention might break the fragile bond between us. Maybe she was right. We weren't quite sure what it was ourselves, this sudden intensity of feeling – old love renewed, or a wholly new relationship between two very different people. But then, neither of us cared that much. Maybe Jacquie had picked up a little of that vague heedless euphoria the Spiral triggers off in some people – the feeling that because anything can happen, why not enjoy it? Maybe I had too, because I was content to just bask in the sheer delight of her, and enjoy the company of two old friends I'd never been sure I'd see again. The friends didn't encourage us to think overmuch, either. Mall, no doubt remembering how she'd upbraided me about Jacquie, kept a sardonic but kindly eye on us; Jyp plainly found the whole business mildly hilarious. But for me those few days' passage were as close to an idyll as I'd ever come.

There was almost nothing to cloud them – no more hunters, no more opposition of any kind. There were worries for the future, but only one I couldn't easily let slip by – our arrival in Bali. Jyp and Mall couldn't stay to back me up; Ferris had allowed them to stretch their articles of service far enough already, and they weren't the types to let him down. Te Kiore and the rest would take days to catch up. That left Ape, and right now he wasn't inspiring much confidence, a subdued, blanket-wrapped heap, meditating, or moping, at the rear of the bridge. He barely ate or drank now, and his little eyes looked tired and red-rimmed. It was as well the voyage was going so quickly.

By day we rode an empty ocean, by night the clouds of the Spiral billowed beneath our hull and the steadying sail filled with moonlight. Jyp's guiding eye pierced the veils of possibility to set our course, and Mall's firm hands held our bows true to their leading stars. But glad as I was of that, waking with Jacquie beside me, brushing up my swordplay with Mall or hearing her viol conjure up tunes that were old in Shakespeare's day, joking with Jyp after a marvellous *rijsttafel* dinner, sharing volcanic

273

curries and deck-shaking dances with the foc'sle hands or single malt and hymn-singing with MacAndrew the chief engineer – or *arteefeecer*, as he called himself – I had an aching wish that it could go on forever. Even the captain was surprisingly good company, in an academic sort of way; his hobby was marine biology, and he was full of strange tales of life in the depths. Some of them had you looking long and anxiously over the side. Also, he'd once known my boss Barry's grandfather, the founder of our original firm, and was impressed to hear how it had developed; we talked shop over billiards into the small hours, and I soon decided the old-time smugglers and other badhats had nothing to learn from their modern counterparts. A good few tricks I'd never heard of came up, and security was in for the tightening of all time when I got home.

That was another grey cloud across the horizon. Home was something I didn't want to face. Home was demands, decisions, distractions that ate up the tiny ration of seconds in every minute, the meagre hours and scanty dole of days. And home, too, was loneliness, a solitude I could hardly contemplate from here; or had I found my answer to that at long last? I lay there in the darkness of our last night, too anxious to sleep, too leaden to waken, till an insistent hammering forced its way into my mind, and then the steward's scrannel voice. 'Cap'n's compliments, sir, and we've land in sight. Shall I bring your hot water now?'

It was still dark. We groaned ourselves awake, untwining numbed limbs, our common scent rank in our nostrils. Silently, almost ignoring one another's nakedness, we sponged our aching bodies clean, pulled our clothes on and went on deck. Jyp greeted us with a wave towards the bows and beyond. At first I saw nothing, till my eyes caught the starlight's glitter on a thread of smoke; it was rising from the highest point in a jagged outline, a tooth in some fossil monster's jawbone. 'Gunung Agung,' said Jacquie softly. 'The Holy Mountain.'

'More than that!' said Ape roughly, making us all jump. He'd barely stirred from his place by the rail all the voyage, or spoken; now he stood like a wall of shadow, his gaze fixed. 'The summit of *kaja*, the right-hand path of good, as the sea is of *kelod*, the left-hand way of evil. Evil comes from the sea to Bali. What is it that you bring?'

'The best they know.' It was Mall who spoke, quietly, from her place at the wheel. 'What more can any of us? Not even at

274

the farthest Rim, they say, can those who dwell there perceive all the threads of fate and destiny in any action.'

'Then is it not better not to act?' he rumbled, though in his dulled eyes something seemed to stir and shine. 'Better not to banish the desire for action, let those threads entangle further?'

Mall snorted. 'Then still would Sita lie 'neath hundred-armed Ravana! Take Krishna's word for thine own, my Stephen, and act as you see you must!'

'As I must?' It had a bitter taste to it, that morning air. It seemed for a moment as if great forces rode the soft breeze, as if a mighty axis poised in the darkness above us, that the faintest breath might swing. 'If the Project founders, along come famine and death. If we succeed, we bring—'

Ape growled in his throat. 'Worse than death.' His long arms twitched, his shoulders hunched. 'Men die. Women die. Children die. All things they die; even those outermost forces you invoke, they have their endings as their beginnings were. Yet they look with a longer view. Lives are leaves in a furnace – *poof*! They flutter and are gone. Yet the fire goes on, others they come to sustain it in their turn. What gives its meaning to their living and their dying, what feeds that fire but the ways their ancestors bequeathe them?'

'Yet think on this,' sighed Mall, her voice soft and sad. 'You, Sir Ape, you thing of wisdom, you feeder of fires – will you tell the child who cries for a grain of rice to ease her famine-bloated belly that the ways of her fathers are made safe instead? Will you say that to the mother who weeps over a grave scratched i'the parched earth? *Well?*' she snapped, in sudden anger, and for a moment, though the velvet darkness clung around us, I seemed to see her clearly, legs planted wide, head thrown back as if to defy the looming mass of Ape before her.

'I will not,' he answered shortly. He bowed his head, which somehow diminished him. 'No better answer have I, nor the forces that would stop these two and their Project. So I help, then and now, as I can. But I ask them, find me that answer!'

'That's unfair!' protested Jacquie. 'Find what you and all these, these *forces* can't?'

'More easily, perhaps, than they, my lady,' said Mall. 'For they see only the tangle of threads, and are no longer of it. 'Tis you may twine them together to make a stronger – or find the one they were unravelled from, and make it whole.'

Ahead of us a sudden point of red swelled for an instant; and over the freshening wind I became aware of a soft rumbling sound, a tremor felt more than heard through the very timbers of the hull and the sea beyond. 'Gunung Agung is restless,' said Ape quietly; and I realised then how much lighter the sky had become. Yet still there was no other colour in the world.

Nor had it come when the *Sapphire* chugged into the shallow bay of Padangbai, exchanging casual whistles with one of the early ferries to the outer islands. If anybody on the ferry noticed something odd about the incoming vessel they probably just put it down to the dimness and forgot about it. Half an hour back we'd passed a Chinese junk that belonged in the Ming dynasty; every port has its strange passages at dawn and sunset, when perceptions blur, and the doors between Core and Spiral stand ajar. We came in smoothly alongside the high quay where the cruise liners usually tie up; and even as our fenders were scraping the concrete piles the derrick was being made ready.

The sky was still grey when the container swung up against it, a blocky foreboding silhouette, swinging outwards and down to land, at long last, with a scrape and a creak upon the dusty concrete jetty that was the outmost fringe of the ancient realm of Bali. I looked at my watch for about the hundredth time; there it was – Thursday the 3rd of May, 2:47 a.m., EST. There were no cheers, and no more ceremony than that. The blockade was broken, and our work was done.

'I regret I can leave you so little time for farewells,' said Ferris, hauling his huge half-hunter from his waistcoat fob. 'But if we are to catch the dawn—'

'You've done more than enough already,' I told him. 'And you two!'

Jyp clapped a lean hand on my shoulder. 'It's never enough! But jehoshaphat, Steve, it was good to see you again – *and* those best duds of mine! You're wearin' them as if you were born in 'em now! In them – and to them. Maybe I'll be looking for you again soon, out here.'

'You think that's wise? You've warned me off before!'

'It is,' said Mall shortly. 'You grow, Master Stephen. Fuller than you were, you become; and for good or ill, you may not now be held back. I, I pluck no prophecies else from the stars – but I also will be looking for you, ere long. Yet watch every corner! For if naught else, there is still one lurks around each one to trip you

276

up anew. Stephen, beware Stephen!' As suddenly as that she reached out her arms and caught me, drew me to her and all but wrapped herself around me, so that once again I felt the litheness of her and the fierce energy of the life that blazed within. Her lips touched mine, but it was not a kiss, more a breathing between our parted lips. Then as quickly she released me, with liquid fire running along my nerves.

'And you, my lady,' she said, so intensely that the wry smile faltered on Jacquie's lips. 'Look to him, and to yourself. For who knows, but your fate also may lie along the Great Paths of sky and sea, and in the lands of legend and shadow. Better so, that such rare flowering loveliness be not left hostage to that meddling tyrant Time, such breadth of mind and heart for him to mar with scant experience. I'll listen for your feet also.' She embraced Jacquie also; the touch of lips was sisterly enough, the brush of hands against breasts as she released her mere awkwardness. With no more ado she stalked back up the gangplank, and out of our sight. Jacquie blinked dazedly. Jyp smiled cynically and kissed her hand with a flourish.

'Your servant always, Miss Jacquie,' he said. 'And you look after yourself, y'hear?'

'I . . . think I'm learning,' said Jacquie. She touched the bow she'd brought out with her in a sailcloth duffel bag. 'I hope I see you both again.'

'Couldn't hope it more than I do, ma'am. Well, Steve . . . '

Nobody said goodbye to Ape. He squatted, blanket-draped against the dawn air, against the wall of the container, like some uneasy parody of a Buddha. The spray spattered him as the paddles turned, but he didn't even look up. The light swung in balance now, an even greyness over sky and sea, with only the faintest line between them; and for that line the *Sapphire* set its bows. We watched in silence, and in minutes, it seemed, it was itself a thing of shadow, devoid of detail – save that, at the stern, shining as if with inner light, a figure stood out clear. Blonde hair blew in the wind; an arm waved in farewell, waved till even that light dwindled to a point, and a brighter one crept into the sky. From below the world's edge it shone, and the streaks of cloud above it took shape, grey isles upon a blinding sea of light, as golden as the path that spread towards us down the ocean below, turning the steamer's stern to a silhouette of blackness. Their pale margins became golden shores streaked white with breakers;

277

their billowing crests the tossing tips of forests in the warm winds. The sky was full of islands, like the shadows of some distant archipelago; and into it, along that brighter road, the shadow we'd sailed on, solid beneath our feet, raised its bows and dwindled, sailing away into the depths of the sky.

We huddled together as we saw it, awed and diminished, like small animals at the bounds of their own familiar wood, seeing for the first time the incomprehensible vastness of fields stretch out beyond it. 'Like a dream,' said Jacquie softly.

'Not to me.'

'Not that. This. As if only once in my life I'd been properly awake.'

A sudden shrilling made us jump, like a furious giant insect. 'It's coming from your bag!' Jacquie gasped.

I was already rummaging furiously through it, making hay of all the steward's elegant packing, right to the bottom. With a grunt of triumph I seized the vibrating shell, hoiked it out in a shower of socks and underpants across the quay and cracked it open in my palm.

'*Steve? Hullo, Steve? Jesus H Christ, man, is that you?*'

'Yes, Dave,' I said resignedly, clapping the earpiece to my ear. 'All present and correct.'

'*Present where, you son of a bitch? Where's the container? Where's that bint from the Project you went waltzing off with? Don't you know today's the contract deadline?*'

'I'm on Bali, Dave. With the container.'

'And the bint,' put in Jacquie over my shoulder, and kissed me on the ear.

There was a moment's dead silence. '*You said you'd let me know the absolute bloody moment you arrived, you jammy bugger.*'

'This is the moment, twit. You know what time it is here? About four-thirty in the morning, the sun's only just coming up.' I glanced around at the sleeping rows of bright aluminium-sided sheds. 'We haven't even moved off the bloody Padangbai quay yet, everything's closed up, customs, immigration, the lot. Listen, since you're on the line, this official who's supposed to be picking us up—'

There was a sound suspiciously like teeth grating. '*Un-huh. The Interior Ministry liaison man. I have had him on the line, yes.*'

'Then I hope you told him what I said – that I was seeing the container in by a very roundabout route and I'd call him today when I got in.'

'*He wasn't too happy. Didn't have my touching faith in you. Wanted your phone number himself.*'

'I don't think he'd have got through, somehow.'

'*That's what I told him. Listen, where'd you get to, anyhow? Nowhere with a satellite link, that's for sure. Every time I tried to get hold of you I kept getting these crazy wrong numbers you wouldn't believe!*'

'Jokers, probably,' I suggested, wondering just who he *had* managed to get through to. 'Hackers – you know.'

'*Guess so. Anyhow, we arranged that the Ministry man would get down there as late as possible today – thought I'd give you as much leeway as I could.*'

I sighed. 'Well thought of. But that means we've got to hang about for hours, then.'

'*Shouldn't be so bad. They've put in some nice new tourist facilities, he says; you can get a shower and meals and so on. And he's made sure the port boys are expecting you; they'll look after things till he gets there. The lad done good, huh? Huh?*'

'Yes. Yes, thanks, Dave. I'll call you back later. I'm kind of tired now.'

'*I'll bet. Anyhow, it's another triumph for Stephen Fisher the shipping wizard – how does he do it, nothing up his sleeve and not a mirror in sight. My love to the b— the lady. Sayonara!*'

The port boys were expecting not only us, but our ship; they weren't too pleased to find it had come and gone without them noticing. Our link with the Project gave us instant VIP status, and we already had our business visas, of course, which circumvented the usual day-long battle with the *Kantor Imigrasi* bureaucrats; Ape produced a moth-eaten Jawan passport in the name of Pendek Dewa, birthdate unknown. But none of the officials liked the idea of ships being able to come and go undetected and unaccounted for, and landing foreigners into the bargain. The *Syahbandar*, or harbourmaster, and the *Kantor Imigrasi* chief, both Jawanese, were close to apoplexy; in the current terrorist emergency that could get them into deep slurry with the military, a very unhealthy place to be.

But when Jacquie diplomatically explained we'd travelled on a Boegie ship – 'Well, part of the way, anyhow' – they calmed down considerably. It let them off the hook. They'd been watching for a modern ship, and what could one expect from Boegies? They went everywhere, and were a law unto themselves at the best of times, but they were highly unlikely to carry terrorists. 'Flea, food poisoning, *ada*!' joked the *Kantor Pemeriksaan* man, scratching his well-padded backside idly as he covered every page of our inch-thick wad of customs clearances in rubber stamps as bright as Ape's charms. The others commiserated; but the Interior Ministry and the *Kantor Gubernoran* had booked rooms for my party at the good Western-style hotel on the waterfront. We could rest there today, and the Ministry man would come and pick us up later.

When? I should have known better than to ask. Round here, the more important an official was – or wanted to look – the more he took his time; they called it *jam karet*, 'rubber time'. The most anyone would say was *'berapa jam*!', a few hours, which could mean afternoon or evening. The harbourmaster would have armed guards posted on the container meanwhile. The hotel began to look very tempting; but Ape declined. He preferred just to stay there with the container, guard or no guard, even though it ought to be safe in broad daylight. He didn't want any food; when I pressed him he let me buy him a cup of *baijgur*, a sort of dilute rice pudding and coconut milk, from a quayside stall, but went shuffling back to his place at once.

'He looks ill,' said Jacquie anxiously, looking back.

'I'd have said . . . old. But you should have seen him on that train! What's changed him like this?'

Jacquie shivered. 'There's something else governing him, some other law. The things he was saying, about tonight, not being able to help us later . . . ' She turned to Pujawan, the young man the harbourmaster had sent to help us with our bags. '*Ma'af*! Is there something special about today? Or tomorrow?'

He grinned. 'You don't know? Tomorrow begins big festival, whole island celebrates. Galungan, it's called.' He shifted his grip on my bag to stick out his thumb, the polite way to point in Bali. 'Them, they celebrate already. Not good luck.'

They were a group of young men, anything from late teens to early twenties, rolling off the quay from one of the early-morning island ferries, to the accompaniment of an incredible row. Four or five of them had gigantic tinny blasters on their shoulders, each one playing something different with the volume turned up all the way, so that most of what you heard was shrieking discord and distortion. Their cheap surfer shorts and shirts, crinkling and faded, were spattered with ineptly copied English slogans like *Hip*! and *Crazy*! and *Spunky*!, though one or two boasted slogans like *Bali Breaks*! Their threadbare caps had baseball logos or the names of Bali chain hotels. Several carried battered full-gun surfboards, one with BALI HYATT, SANUR still readable through a crude paint-job. Most of them looked all right, just noisy kids with big goofy grins and a few beers too many in the cooler. One or two, though, had a look that's the same the world over, one I'd seen on Berkeley panhandlers and Polish skinheads and *Pamyat* race-thugs in Moscow, on Glasgow football hooligans and the Times Square pimp who'd slashed a girl's face with a switchblade; they wielded their boards like 'dozer blades to clear people from their path. Altogether they looked like cheap, crappy parodies of the worst things Western, walking casualties of culture shock. As they passed they yelled at us, and I caught an acrid whiff from the joints they were smoking. Pujawan stared straight ahead.

'What was that about?' I asked, but he didn't appear to hear.

'Winding him up,' said Jacquie softly. 'About carrying a European's bags.'

Pujawan heard that all right. '*Lupakan saja*!' he said softly. 'Don't bother about them! They're no good. No use.'

'Even so,' I said uncomfortably, in my halting Malay. 'I could—'

He wasn't to be put off; and nobody wins a war of politeness with a Balinese. 'I do not mind! I carry bags once, it is an honour. Them, they live off foreigners all the time. Let them get jobs, joke about me then!'

But I held the doors for him at the hotel; and when we'd checked in, we made him stop for coffee with us, and felt a bit better.

'Those little creeps!' said Jacquie bitterly, when he'd gone.

'You know, that priest character, that *pedanda* – he warned me about the surfers.'

'They can't all be like that.'

'No, some of them didn't even look too bad, but I sort of begin to see his point. This place was an idyll once. If it's all going to go like that . . . Or this hotel even. I stayed in another of this chain in the Seychelles, and it was exactly the same. If it wasn't for all those bug-eyed masks on the walls you'd never know we were in Bali.'

'That's right. But for better or worse, Steve, we are. The *pedanda*, and the woman, whoever she was, or whatever – you've beaten them both.'

'We. You, I, te Kiore, Batang Sen, Jyp and Mall – lots of people. And lots of luck.'

'But you held it all together,' she said crisply. She hauled herself up, a little stiffly. 'Not many people could have done what you've done. Now you deserve a rest. You look half-dead.'

'It's hotter than Jawa here. I'm not acclimatised.'

'Wait'll midday gets you; you'll be nothing but a grease spot. Come get a shower while you still can.'

Fortunately the Ministry man had a high sense of status; he didn't show up until almost six o'clock. By then we'd had a good rest in an air-conditioned room, and the sea breeze was making outdoors almost bearable again. Until, that is, his convoy and its army escort pulled up in a billow of dust. He came bounding with fearsome energy out on to the shaded verandah where we were sitting, a thickset little man in a spotless safari suit straight out of Abercrombie & Fitch. 'Mister Fisher? Doctor Jusuf Pasaribu! And Miss Kang-Svensen – how do you do?'

Another Javanese, with that Muslim name; there was a slight emphasis on the 'Doctor' – of economics, we found out – and his English was fluent. Too fluent; he chattered. God, how he chattered; and he positively radiated a go-getting sort of energy that made me want to shove him into a sack – and I was used to the type. I was one myself, if it came to that; some of the time, anyway. He gulped down the drink we offered him – a highball, presumably to show off his lack of Islamic prejudice – and, barking orders at the hotel staff and his own men alike, bundled us and our gear out of the door in about five minutes flat. The soldiers spilled out of their truck to salute, he handed us into his personal car, barked at the driver, and we were off to the dock.

Within minutes he'd made all the final clearances and had the container winched on to the flatbed truck he'd brought, painted the same dusty military dun as the soldiers' canvas-topped truck; but his car was something else, a glossy great two-tone Japanese four-wheel drive with louvre blinds all round and air-conditioning. He blenched slightly when we introduced Ape, looking dusty and haggard after his vigil, and very obviously ushered him into the spare seat in the luggage space; he seemed to assume Ape was some sort of derelict interpreter we'd brought along, and would no longer need with him there. He never even bothered to ask if we spoke the language ourselves, just leaned over to us from the front seat and chattered on and on; he let up only to bark at the driver, or for some answer from us. Not that he listened; comments rolled over his head and were overwhelmed in the flood of his enthusiasm. He didn't seem to notice our reactions; like many Easterners he probably found Western faces, even blendings like Jacquie's, hard to read – inscrutable, in fact. That was probably just as well.

The island rolled by outside, while he talked about it as if we were just some more know-nothing visiting firemen. The buildings of the town, sun-bleached and pleasantly shabby with their peeling paintwork and bright shop signs, gave way to greenery – flat paddy fields, glistening algae-green under the sinking sun, through which the convoy passed on a raised causeway fringed with low shrubbery. Flowers shone in the fields like scattered jewels, waving in the wake of the escort truck: marigold, hibiscus, bougainvillea and frangipani red and white and pink, dark blue butterfly-pea and flowers with only native names, *kapaka* and *manori*, lavender-shaded, and the orange *dadak*. Hillsides carved out into neat terraces, whose wavy edges and vivid, almost artificial greenness made the whole landscape look like some giant contour model of painted flock. And splashing down narrow stone-lined channels in between, the coffee-brown turbid water that fed them and the little whitewalled villages scattered along our route.

I remembered what the old priest had told me, and later Jacquie. To a Balinese a village is a living thing, a body much like his own, to be addressed as *I Desa*, with the same respectful title he would expect for himself – and so is every house in it, from the family shrine at its head to the arms which are its rooms, the legs and feet of kitchen and larder, and the rubbish pit at its rear. Life within life, surrounding life, each house, village, temple a living being made up of those within it, the very island itself a divine living creature, a macrocosm with the water system as its pale yet vital lifeblood. I felt it too, I thrilled to it, this first glimpse of what the Project was all about, the ideal that had brought me all this way, the vision I'd been afraid to fail; and I wasn't disappointed. I squeezed Jacquie's hand, and she squeezed back, her eyes shining.

And then he started talking about it. He talked about it as if we were complete outsiders, even Jacquie. And the more he talked the more he laid bare of himself, of how he thought, and no doubt those behind him. Early on I managed to get in a question about this Galungan festival, and he fizzed and sputtered in reply.

'Oh, Mister Fisher! Half the days on this island are festivals of some kind. They have a special kind of rotating calendar, even, to keep track as they come round – each more superstitious than the next. A thirty-week cycle, would you believe? Galungan, it's the worst; like Christmas, kind of. One day, but the celebration lasts a whole ten days and ends in another, Kuningan, and can you get one goddamn thing done during that time? Fat chance. All the offices and shops and schools shut up tight, all the roads gummed up and god help you if there's an accident or a fire or something. Everyone pushing off to their home villages, you see; very village-minded, the Balinese, even the town dwellers. It's the Descent of the Ancestors, you see; when they think the ancient powers of the island hold sway again. That's why the deadline was set – and why I'm so very glad you made it. One minute after midnight tonight and you'd have walked into a madhouse.'

I looked sharply round at Ape, but he seemed to be asleep there in the back, his eyelids drooping, his mouth half-open in a silent snore.

'Not that the run-up to it's any better,' added Pasaribu scornfully. 'They think the week or two before is a bad-luck time, when the *kalas* and the *butas* – the local ghosties and ghoulies and long-leggity beasties, that is – can come up from the underworld and bugger everybody about. So everything important gets screwed up, then, too. Can you believe it?'

'After the voyage we've had,' I put in, 'I just about could.' But he wasn't listening.

'You know, that's what I really look forward to,' he rhapsodised. 'Breaking the back of all this feckless Balinese nonsense at long last. It's a fossil, really; primitive Hinduism, the only backwoods corner in the whole goddamn country where it's hung on. Demons and googoos and whatever everywhere, and don't so much as cross a road without choosing a propitious day from the calendar – it's as bad as Tibet or Nepal or somewhere like that. And the endless damn etiquette! Having to use a different *language* when you're speaking to someone of a higher or lower class. In this day and age that's a feudal obscenity!'

'Don't you speak differently to your boss?' inquired Jacquie sofly. 'Or the President? Or a *haji*?'

'Oh, sure, but that's different!' he laughed, as if it should be self-evident. 'That's why I expect great things from the Project. It'll do so much for the island, in one fell swoop as it were.'

'Feed it,' I suggested, peering out through the blinds. We were climbing now, up the valley flank. Almost all of it was cultivated, with only the odd clump of overhanging trees between the field margins, as often as not around the greystone peak of some temple or minor shrine, mimicking the blue-grey mass of the mountains beyond. 'Save all this from droughts. Let people support themselves without ravaging the landscape any further.'

He gave me a patronising smirk. 'Well obviously, sure, and that's very good. But the Project can achieve so much more – it's a sharp sword in the hands of progress, as Ho Chi Minh used to say. On the most basic level it'll strip the power from these priest-ridden villages and put it in the hands of the democratically elected government, where it belongs.'

'Elected by the whole of Indonesia, not Bali,' murmured Jacquie.

'Absolutely! So what will follow from that? They'll have to get used to dealing with a proper centralised government for their resources. They'll see us controlling their water supplies efficiently with computers and electronics, and they'll think less and less in terms of priests and temples and primitive deities. That'll make room for a spot of clear-headed religion – nothing fundamentalist, of course,' he added apologetically. 'Absolute toleration and everything. But bit by bit it'll whittle away at the superstitious foundations, the way the West has at the cultural ones.'

He gave me a knowing wink, such an un-Indonesian gesture he must have deliberately practised it. 'And I have got to admit, it'll do a great deal of good for the administration here. Put new life into it. Bali's been kind of a Siberia posting, for some departments, but that's all changing now. The Project will really set the ball rolling – or should I say the Bali? A businessman like you, you must see the kind of opportunities public-sector development opens up for the private sector, following in its footsteps.'

'I begin to think I do,' I murmured. 'You mean, in terms of construction, land use, property development for mass tourism, industry even, that sort of thing?'

'Right!' he smiled, delighted to find me so quick on the uptake. 'Who's to say otherwise?'

'Who indeed?' I grinned back. *When Greek meets Greek, they smile* . . .

I hadn't seen any of this before, but it seemed so obvious now; and to judge by the flash in her eyes, Jacquie had got it too. Water was the key to land use. If farmland suddenly became less cost-efficient, perhaps because the water to keep it fertile had become too expensive, then it would have to be converted to some other use, wouldn't it? The peasants would have to sell it for what they could get. Or else there was compulsory purchase, eminent domain . . . In a country where *korupsi* was practically the basis of a government official's income, where a child couldn't go up a grade in school unless the teacher was sweetened, the potential profits were enormous. 'But all the rest of this, the breaking of superstition and so on . . . I suppose this is government policy?'

He smiled again. We were equals, confederates practically; we moved on the same elevated, sophisticated levels. 'Of course our political masters cannot afford to be so explicit, not in these . . . ' he shrugged,' . . . sensitive times. You as a cosmopolitan Westerner must have seen how Third World governments are constantly at the mercy of minority parties with disproportionate influence – and of course there are sentimentalists even within government. It's we, the administrators charged with the everyday business of rule, who have to come up against these barriers, these obstacles to progress; and therefore it's we who have to break through them.' He chuckled. 'After all, we know there's no such place as Shangri-la, don't we?'

'I wouldn't be too sure,' said Jacquie venomously; but fortunately we lurched over a pothole just then, and he turned to berate the driver. Then he turned back and went on about the duty of the intellectual classes to take the lead.

'. . . and drag, if need be, these charming, yes, but indolent islanders into the realities of the new century!'

It got too much for me, too. 'You mean like the secondhand surfer culture?'

He gave a wry laugh. 'Them? Just another way of being feckless. Though we don't exactly discourage them; good for tourism, the free-and-easy style. Keeps up the tropical paradise image. The government spoiled that a bit when it cracked down on peasant women, made them dress decently, cut out the traditional topless styles altogether; and nude bathing. That used to draw the Yankees and Aussie tourists. At least the surfers are decent. Fancy a cold soda?' He dug out cans from somewhere beneath the front seat, and tossed them back to us. 'Sorry I've nothing stronger. Anyhow, within limits, what's good for tourism is good for us – foreign exchange, cheap service industries bringing more people into contact with more sophisticated ways. We can crack down on the surfers, too, when the time is ripe. It all hangs together.' He took a luxurious swig of his Pepsi, choked as the driver went around a corner too fast, and started yelling at him again.

'I hope they do,' breathed Jacquie, seizing my arm in a death grip. 'Hang together, the bastards! In a row! Steve, you can't be going along with this – this—'

'It's your Project,' I whispered back. Pasaribu was off on some tack about road improvement.

'No! No, it isn't, not mine! None of our people think of it like this! They just want to, to help! Nobody's ever come out and talked like this! It must just be this . . . this little shit's imagination!'

I shook my head, speaking out of the side of my mouth like Bogart in a prison movie. 'You lot are idealists, remember? So they've been talking to you like idealists – telling you what they know you want to hear. But now he thinks he's talking to someone who matters, someone who can help him – a contact. Probably got you tagged as just a glorified secretary.'

She was almost in tears of rage. 'But . . . you wouldn't . . . would you? Not help . . . '

I grimaced behind my can. 'Like hell. But there's plenty of others who'd jump to.'

There were more trees as we climbed, feathery palms, sometimes in small plantations for coconuts and copra, bright acacia and great ranks of mimosa, its sweet scent scrubbed out by the air-conditioning. Here in the south of the island some of the trees were shrines themselves; there were offerings set out at their foot and even clothes draped and fastened around their branches and trunks. That gave our man the opportunity for some mordant comments. I hardly noticed; my mind was going into overdrive. It tends to when I get angry enough, and right now I was quietly steaming, reinforced by Jacquie smouldering at my side. 'I could still block the Project,' I reminded her softly. 'This is the key load—'

'But he's signed for it!'

'He's just signed for its import and transport. Technically it's still in my firm's custody, till it's delivered to the Project site. In theory, if I see fit I could have it shipped right back.'

'But the soldiers!' hissed Jacquie, looking at the back of the escort truck.

'In theory, I said. But soldiers or no soldiers, I could still raise Cain. Court actions, that kind of thing; stall every shipment till they're sick of it or some effective opposition can be raised. Damn it, maybe that's the answer I'm supposed to have.'

'No, it can't be. That just ruins the Project and leaves the island to starve anyway—'

'Well, maybe it's part of it. I've got to work out a strategy of some kind. Quiet and let me think!'

We were getting into real hill country now, and the villages were fewer and fewer as the evening drew in. The road meandered like a dusty scar through an increasingly dense overhanging jungle, nothing visible beyond the tangled green weave. But over it the mountain slopes hung vast and slaty blue, and closer by the minute; and above them, seen through occasional gaps, a crown of volcanic smoke shimmered gold in the low sunlight. The escort truck leading the way braked suddenly as we passed one, and I craned my neck for a longer look; but then I saw the barricade of palm trunks across the road. A sudden burst of stuttering explosions shook the air, the truck's canvas cover twitched and bucked; we jumped as the car's hood dented and the driver's window shattered.

'*Perusuh*! *PKI*!' screamed Pasaribu. Terrorists; we'd forgotten all about them. The soldiers were poking their AK47s over the truck side, returning the automatic fire that swept the little column. The noise was incredible. Flinging open his door, on the safe side, the Ministry man leaned out, low down, and bellowed at them and the truck behind. Its driver flung it into gear, and with the corporal beside him sniping out of the window, he pulled out and moved past us. Bullets zinged off the bulk of the container, but we were shielded. The officer with the soldiers screamed an order, and half a dozen of them leaped up on to the truck as it overtook them. Revving up, the huge vehicle smashed into the barrier with a smash of grille and headlights, and sent the logs rolling away like so many pencils. Our driver put his foot down and we swerved out after it, weaving to avoid the new hails of automatic fire. A brief crimson flower exploded on the road behind with a deafening crash; an anti-tank rocket, bazooka or Karl Gustav or something, aimed at the truck. A row of holes were punched in the car's bodywork, my seat erupted inches from where I was hanging on – and then both vehicles were through and away, leaving our escort to keep the terrorists busy. In clouds of dust we went careering heavily away up the road, swerving violently around the potholes, hanging on for grim death. Pasaribu, pulling himself up from the floor, looked back to us with a white and haggard face.

'Terrorists!' he said unnecessarily, swallowing hard. 'I hadn't bargained for— but the troops will deal with them. And anyway this is a crowded island, the next village won't be far and those bastards don't fight near them, in case the villagers turn against them. Hang on and we'll get through double-quick!'

We didn't need to hang on long; just around the next bend we nearly rammed the container truck as it braked hard – before a human barrier this time. Right across the road, sitting peacefully cross-legged on the mats, chattering and smiling among themselves, there was a triple line of very ordinary-looking Balinese men and women, clad mostly in the traditional *sarongs* and chequered headscarves. And beyond them, in a clearing among the trees, rose the buildings of a very ordinary village, as tranquil as any other we'd passed through. I could see all the features Jacquie had pointed out, the neat, delicate *kampungs*, family compounds clustering round the higher roofs of the public buildings, the *banjar* or council pavilion and the three temples, celestial *pura puseh*, mundane *pura desa* and demonic *pura dalem* – for even the darker forces must have their due, so that balance be maintained.

And here nothing seemed to disturb it – nothing, except the rows of humanity sitting in the dust. To the left of the road was thick undergrowth and trees, and beyond them terraced rice paddies deep in mud; to the right the same, with the main irrigation channel and at its head the *subak* water shrine. There was no other way through. And behind the villagers, from the shady seats at the foot of the *alun-alun*, the banyan tree in the centre of the square, rose the tall figure of the priest Mpu Bharadah. Leaning on his staff, he glided through the ranks of villagers. With that familiar toss of his head he stepped in front of them and stood, immovable.

Pasaribu leaned out and shouted at him, and the remaining soldiers jumped down off the container lorry, chattering angrily. In the soft evening light, surrounded by modern weapons, the priest looked momentarily less formidable. Pasaribu gazed around angrily, scratching his head. I heard him ask the soldiers where the hell this dirty little rathole was; he couldn't remember any such place along this stretch of the road – if it still was the right road! When they didn't answer he shouted at the priest, even more insultingly; but the old man only smiled grimly, and answered him in his cold English.

'This village?' he repeated. 'This is any village, or all villages. The shadow of all villages, the image of what you most imperil.'

Pasaribu choked at this impertinence; but I shivered. To reach so openly into the Core while it was still light, this priest, or whatever lay behind him, must have great confidence, or great power – or both.

So it proved. For, reaching out his staff, he brushed Pasaribu aside, speechless, and gestured straight at me. I leaned over to the back, where Ape was awake, peering about with red-rimmed eyes, and grappled furiously with my baggage. I hauled out my sword, leather-wrapped, and trailing it in one hand I touched Jacquie's cheek and baled out of the car.

'Well, *Tuan* Fisher?' demanded the old man, as I strode forward. There was iron menace in his voice, but also an odd note, almost of resignation or even sorrow. 'In your arrogance you thought yourself safe, surrounded now by the instruments of your forces of stone and metal and abstract riches. You ride in my realm now, and you are in my hand. The stony force you call upon will not serve you here. You face the power behind my power, the strength that raises my green forests to the clouds.'

His staff lifted as if to dash out my brains. The soldiers didn't need Pasaribu's yell; half a dozen Kalashnikovs would have cut the old man in two, but even as their fingers tightened on the triggers, that crystal sphere caught the gleam of the setting sun. The wooden stocks seemed to writhe and contort in their hands, as if seeking the shape of the tree they were hewn from; one gun jerked skyward and went off, loosing two harmless rounds, before the distorting wood bent and jammed the mechanism. They fell from the soldiers' hands and writhed in the dust, thrusting out feeble attempts at twigs, leaves even, no longer weapons of any kind. And as they fell the villagers surged up, twenty men or more falling on the soldiers in a thrash of limbs. As the dust settled I saw them pinned in wiry peasant arms, with pitted *kris* blades held to their throats. Pasaribu leaned out of the car with a little automatic in his pudgy fist; the priest simply angled the focus of his sphere, the sun flashed and Pasaribu screamed and fell out of the door, clutching his eyes. The pistol dropped into the dust.

'These are my people, fools that they are,' said the priest quietly. 'Even that one is bound to me by his blood, though he follows another faith and betrays all faiths. I will not harm them. But with you and your friends from across the seas – with you I will not hesitate.' The sun touched his staff again – and suddenly the container lorry shimmered like a summer noon. The driver and his guard leapt out screaming, crashing through the bushes into the paddy. The windows shattered, the paintwork blistered, the tyres smoked and stank. Only the smudged flanks of the container seemed untouched, though the paint should have burned and blistered with the rest.

'Stop!' I yelled. 'Or it'll explode!'

The staff angled slightly, just as I expected – towards the car, with Ape and Jacquie still inside. Mpu Bharadah shook his head. 'I would take no delight in this,' he said sombrely; and I didn't altogether disbelieve him. 'But if you will wipe the remnants of those charms from that accursed metal coffer . . . '

'No,' I said. Something clicked, something of what Ape had been saying. 'I might, now – but not for you. Not you alone. That'd just make things worse – destroy the ancient balance just as badly, wouldn't it?'

I wouldn't have thought the old beast could gape in surprise, but he did, and his staff faltered a little. Then, collecting his wits, he shook his head. 'The balance no longer matters. Do not hide behind it! I alone can safeguard my country, as I have done these fifteen centuries and longer. Nature in the hands of man, that is my power alone.'

'And the other force, that's just nature, isn't it? Man as one more animal in it, ruled by senses, not brains.' My chuckle sounded bitter. 'No wonder she got through to me.'

The old man inclined his head. 'I see you begin to understand. Learn, then, that mine is the only way. You have seen the future of my country.'

'How so?'

'You have seen the idlers of the surf. The wielders of terror who assailed you but minutes past. You have seen – *him*.' He jerked a yellow claw of a thumbnail at Pasaribu. 'It is not only that the surfers are vulgar, or the terrorists cowardly and cruel beneath their slogans of idealism, or that he is corrupt. It is that they all have nothing that is truly theirs. They are poor imitations of Americans or Australians or North Koreans, he of his masters. They are too ignorant to know it now, but one day they will – when they find themselves fit only for the scrapheap of history. That I cannot permit. You know more than I suspected, perhaps; but whatever your intentions, you are helping to make this possible. I tell you this because I regret what I must now do.' He drew a long, shuddering breath, and over his high cheekbones his eyes took on a green glitter, his white moustache bristled and stood out straight, his gnarled hands crooked as if their nails would tear at me where I stood. 'But destroy it or control it – I *will* have that machinery!'

I'd made him hesitate; I knew I didn't dare. There were no second chances here. All this time I'd been shifting my grip, slowly, subtly, to angle my sword a particular way. So that when I flicked free the wrapping, and swung—

It went just as I'd aimed it, around and up in a singing curve. Right into the old man's staff it struck, slicing off the top, smashing that glass sphere and, because I couldn't stop it, cutting a wicked gash in the old man's shoulder. The glassy fragments tinkled across the hard-packed yellow earth – and blood sprayed after them. But as it touched the ground, it hissed, smoked, and burst into flame. The priest's eyes narrowed in anguish, his mouth opened, and behind his yellowed fangs he roared, a great rolling roar that seemed impossible from that slender frame. And indeed, as it swelled out of him he swelled with it, rising, expanding just as Rangda had. As if some vast power contained in human shape was breaking gladly free.

With fire on my blade I swung it, ready to strike again. The villagers shrilled their horror, and the nearest men flew at me, lips foaming, *kris* slashing. Something hissed in the air, there was a thump like cut wood, and the leader stopped dead, dropped the knife and grabbed at the arrow in his shoulder.

'*Pergilah!*' yelled Jacquie, and sent another arrow from behind the car door, into another man's leg. '*Pergi!*' They hesitated, and she stepped out and ran towards me. But I wasn't staying; I staggered back to the car, waving her away. Behind the flames the thing that had been the priest swelled and bellowed, a nightmarish vision even more monstrous than Rangda's true shape. This wasn't human at all – four-legged, slab-sided, a shaggy thing with a fell that shimmered golden among the flames. Like a tiger, a Sumateran tiger even, but the size of a Shire horse. And the countenance, fierce-fanged and bestial though it was, was no tiger's; I'd seen it before. The mask that had hung before Dave and myself in that Bangkok alley; the beast-shape that had pursued me, driven me through that first of the Gates to where I might be crushed or made away with at ease. Wide-eyed, saber-fanged, it fixed its baleful gaze on me and tossed its high-crowned mane in an uncannily familiar gesture.

'*The Barong!*' screamed Jacquie, over that incessant roar.

'What? The *what?*'

'*Barong Keket!*' babbled Pasaribu, grovelling at our feet. '*Banaspati Raja*, Lord of the Forest, Protector of Men! Forgive me, forgive me!'

'The Barong!' repeated Jacquie dazedly. 'I should have known, should've expected it – but he seemed so human – the Balance, Ape said!' She stared at me. 'He's been telling us what this is about all along, if only we'd thought! Rangda – the legendary figure. In the dances she's always defeated, never wins – because another powerful spirit takes the side of men!'

'That's right! That's right!' Pasaribu, weeping from half-dazzled eyes, grovelled and goggled, white-faced, at the brute that roared and reared in our path. He gibbered at us in a weird mixture of English and Indonesian. 'Lord of forest, lord of field! Lord of the greater harvest and the smaller! Master of the tree giants and the *kuro-i* of the undergrowth and of all the lesser *barong* spirits! Champion of life, defender of fertility.' His voice shivered into hysteria, a high sing-song storyteller's tone, as if he was mimicking a tale told him as a child. 'The witch took shape, as the beautiful widow Kalon Arang, and sought to seduce and corrupt the *raja*. So he became human also, as the wise counsellor Mpu Bharadah, and broke her power and drove her out into the blackness and the sea. Mpu Bharadah, *Barong Keket, Banaspati Raja, jangan' memarahkan kepada sahaya!* What'll he do to me, after all I've done?'

A question we might have answered, any minute. The

transformation was complete. The creature rolled its awesome head at us, champed jaws that could gulp down a well-grown calf, and with its great tail lashing, saliva threading from between those sabre fangs, it hunched down as a cat does, poised to spring.

But in shattering the Barong's staff, in checking its power, I had unwittingly unleashed something else. The first I knew of it was the villagers, who'd fallen to their knees at sight of the Barong, leaping to their feet and pointing back with shrill cries of dismay. The mirror calm of the paddies clouded suddenly, the precious plants bent and flailed, the trees lashed. The Barong's great head turned, its jaws parted and it roared at the air. A great chill gust rolled in, and on it rode the smell of the sea, that these people loathed and feared; to us it carried the crack and spatter of gunfire and screams, not far off, and a hint of acrid smoke.

It buffeted the limbs of the banyan, bent them till they creaked, tore its trailing tendrils loose and sent them snaking through the air. It curled around the village temples, toppling vessels, spilling offerings, tearing away garlands and garments set to decorate them for the coming festival. But as it touched the summit of the little *pura dalem*, the underworld temple, there came a sudden crack, far louder than any gunfire, and a slow muted grinding I had heard before, at the Borobodur. From gate to summit the little greystone enclosure fissured and split, and its two halves slid majestically apart. From inside, this time, that arc-like blaze of blue-white light sprang out; and through it, casting gigantic shadows within it like some monstrous *wayang kulit* puppets, stepped an inhuman figure.

Rangda, the alluring and the monstrous mingled, embodiment of nature destructive, nature unrestrained. At her heels her dead dacoits gathered, stooped and scuttling, and behind them stalked the creaking suits of armour of a bygone era, of the time when Bali bathed in blood. If blood filled them now it was too little; for behind those masks I could see no glint of eyes. With a shrill banshee shriek no human throat could have matched, she rallied them; they swarmed around her and flowed like a column of ants down the steps, out into the village square, long *kris* and sabres gripped in nerveless hands.

The villagers screamed and scuttled back towards us, and we backed hurriedly behind the car, dragging the weeping Pasaribu with us. Only the Barong stood his ground; he tossed his head, and a roar burst out of his jaws like an exploding shell, shaking the ground. A great paw clawed deep troughs in the brown earth, scattering stones, tearing up roots. Then it lashed out, caught one of the advancing warriors, and its explosive impact literally shattered him where he stood, in a spray of armour segments and dry flesh. The Barong roared again, like thunder, and this time the villagers rallied, brandishing *kris* and sickle, threshing flail and sledgehammer. Even we stopped, with that battlecry vibrating in our veins; and the soldiers snatched up their weapons and ran to join the villagers at the Barong's side. Only Pasaribu was left, weeping in the dust; and ourselves. Outsiders who'd jarred the balance violently, and now stood caught in its destructive swing.

A bitter shock came bubbling up in me, harsh realisation caught at the back of my throat. What had lain at the bottom of all this, for me – the real desire to help, or simply to achieve? At long last I understood why Ape had been so ambiguous, so uncertain whether he was truly doing good. By barging my way through to Bali in the face of that fierce opposition I'd achieved one thing only; I'd forced my way in with that container and its complement of Western thinking electronically preserved, where angels or their like might well fear to tread. The two great forces that had acted together, after a fashion, to stop me, I'd given a greater reason to fight – and something to fight over. I had unleashed open war, that might tear the island apart. And I had landed myself, along with Jacquie, and Ape, and the promise of a more peaceful future, right in its midst.

Next moment that became all too true. The fight eddied back around us, a wash of screaming soldiers trading blows with blank-faced dacoits, jabbing and clubbing with gun-butts and bayonets because they were packed too close to shoot. Blinded by the dust they kicked up, I was knocked staggering, and Jacquie whirled from my side. Eyes stinging, I flailed around with the sword, left and right, parrying a blow from a short Kalashnikov bayonet one moment and a rusty *kris* the next, kicking and punching and gouging with my free hand, desperate to get free of the scrum. At last I managed, or it rolled past me, but as I ducked away a foot caught my ankles, I bit the dust and rolled over as the dacoit stooped to me, and his blade seamed the air above my chest. There was a flat popping crack, hardly audible above the uproar; his head jerked, he spun around and fell sprawling. Like someone killed in a movie, no blood, but the small crater in his face was real enough. I scrambled up. So did Jacquie, kneeling on the ground with Pasaribu's pistol. Its owner's legs were disappearing over the edge of the road towards the irrigation ditch.

'He's got a point!' I yelled in her ear. 'Back to the car! We'll get Ape!' But as we struggled back towards it, knocking dacoits and villagers and screaming fanatics aside, I saw him standing by the car and looking up and around. No longer apathetic or depressed, but baleful, terrible; the wind pressed his coarse hair flat to his skull, showing the heavy outline of sloping brow and massive jaw as he stared into the skies. Not even on the island had he looked so inhuman. Above us the storm yelled, shaking the trees; yet louder still as they rode it were the taut battlecries of the *garuda*, the warbirds of the gods, their black feathers iridescent in the hellish light as they circled lower and lower above the fray.

296

Dustdevils danced and whirled around among the swirling fighters. The earth shook; the creature that had been Rangda stamped by us, so close I could smell her, that same cloying scent turned musky and animal. We cowered back, but she ignored us, glaring eyes fixed upon her adversary. Legs akimbo, long curved claws flexing, beastman and beastwoman circled each other in a tense dance of hate, hissing, bellowing, foaming at the jaw, running saliva from their fangs. The ground shivered at their tread, and volcanic rumblings shook them where they stood.

A wild yelp came from the irrigation channel. Pasaribu hopped out like a cricket and ran; its turbid surface was bubbling suddenly, it seethed, lifted and surged in a steaming wave across the path. The spray stung; it was close to boiling, and we had to skip hastily back. I looked to the trees for shelter, but the undergrowth was stirring, the gorgeous flowers were thrust aside or stamped underfoot by milling shadow shapes whose high chittering cries brought back the immediacy of that crawling nightmare on the train. The *kuro-i* were gathering to support their forest lord, to seize the container as they had failed to months before. And behind them other shapes moved, the vast tree-shifting shapelessnesses of the Surabaja night, while the howling seawind bent the trees back about them, lashing like whips, blocking their passage. The high-sided car rocked on its suspension as fighting men clashed and tumbled against it, and the wind shook it like a toy.

'Any stronger and it'll go right over!' I yelled to Jacquie. 'The truck—'

She nodded vigorously rather than waste breath, and together we seized Ape, who didn't resist, and propelled his bulk across to the scorched container truck. The cab was still full of smoke, so we bolted around the back, panting, momentarily free of the uproar. But even as we sank down behind a rear wheel the wind shrieked again, there was the crash of a heavy body hitting the earth, and the earth seemed to hump beneath us as if some vast thing burrowed. All along the canal bank the hard-packed soil cracked, collapsed and went pattering down in little landslides that cut back into the road – one of them right under the truck's front wheel. As suddenly as that the whole huge thing lurched and tilted, looming above us, I clutched at Jacquie, hoping to leap free with her; but we slipped and skidded on the loosened soil. The truck and container came ponderously down on us, and beyond its leaning flank I caught a brief glimpse of the sun's rim against the cloud, a circlet of molten gold sinking in a furious welter of fire – the last thing, I knew, that I might ever see.

Then the wheel ground to a halt, the container slid no further. Jacquie, looking over my shoulder, was a picture of slack-jawed, goggle-eyed amazement. Letting her go, I scrambled around, feet sliding out from under me, and saw what she'd seen. Right there behind us, feet planted ankle-deep in the loose soil, stood Ape. He had one long hand almost casually on the edge of the truck's flatbed; but the fingers were clamped tight. He was holding it – the whole damn thing. And as I watched he placed his other hand someway along and, with an almost insultingly negligent heave, he shoved the whole immense weight bodily back on to the road. Then he rounded on us, as we tried to get up. But as we saw the look in his narrowed eyes, our feet slid from under us again. Deep in their depths an awesome glitter shone, like a single shaft of sun striking some underground river in the vast depths.

'*Het vallt de zon*! The sun sets at last!' he said, and for all the wrath of the air about us his deep voice resounded like an organ. 'The Descent of the Ancestors has begun!'

He reached down, and just as he had back at the railway, he caught us up in those fingers and set us effortlessly on our feet. 'Yet what I feared has come to pass. So very little time there is remaining. *Mynheer* Stephen Fisher, if you are to find an answer to all this, then it must be soon – very soon!'

'*Me*?' I screamed at him over the tumult, coughing on the swirling dust. 'Me again! Why me? Why always me?' Anguish and anger burned away in me at the sheer bloody unfairness of it all. 'You bloody dare go on telling me I'm responsible for an island full of spooks and lunatics and lousy bloody leeching bureaucrats? In any way? Sod the whole pack of them, and you with it! Let them solve their own damn problems, you hear me? Just get off my back – leave me alone, you hear – *alone*!'

I coughed on the dust I'd breathed in – or was it fear that dried out my mouth like that? 'What the hell use am I among all these monsters, anyhow? I don't know anything about them – or you, for that matter! Whatever in hell *you* are, wizard or warlock or whatever! Suppose I did have some shadow of an idea, you think I'd dare suggest it? What'd it be worth? How'd I get anything done about it? I could just make things a hundred times worse! I don't know enough, you hear? I don't bloody *know*!'

'That is so.' Ape's voice was surprisingly gentle. 'And that is why I brought you here, that you might see and learn. *Why you,* you ask? As so many, caught in the toils of the world, have asked; but you are lucky. For you there is an answer to be given, and this is it. This chance I took with you, because you are wise in the ways of your world, as am I in mine – and this is a conflict between them. Surely only one who knows both may find its resolution.' His eyes flashed again, and his fists clenched. 'And learn you have! You have encountered the ruling spirits of this place, the masters of its shadow, the weights of its balance, its spirits of place. That is more than most have ever done. You have felt their presence, and gone up against them. You have traded words and blows with them, and known defeat against them, and triumph. You have felt them within your soul. Is that small knowledge? No mind even tries to occupy another without leaving much of itself behind, an image, an imprint. You may know more of them than you realise, if only you will search within yourself. Search hard!'

I looked hard at him. 'Two powers – but Katjka said there were three! And you agreed, didn't you? Shouldn't I know something of the other one, as well?'

'Do you not?' said Ape softly. 'I had hoped you might, even a little, by now. I looked to give you more, days of time to see and consider, here upon the island. I looked not to stray so among the shadows of men's minds that I almost lost what I truly am, and was left to linger in weakness as the time drew closer, arriving only in the last hours. I looked to have the answer by now; for there is little time left. But if truly you still do not know enough, then there is a way you may learn that also, even yet. A way that is open here and now, while I have yet the power, and the time. I have used up much of what remained to me.'

I gaped at him. '*What?*'

'Do you not yet understand?' he said fiercely. From somewhere across the fields, borne on the wind, came a crackle of gunfire. It sounded nearer. 'If still you have not enough within you . . . It has been forced upon you, yes. But once before, as you have told me, you took it upon you, by instinct and desperation. Now you must embrace it by will and openly. For otherwise I have not the strength. But you – have you the courage?'

'*You*—' I choked. I was beginning to understand. From

299

beyond our shelter came the Barong's coughing roar and a crash of masonry, and above the squeals of the *kuro-i* a high-pitched shrilling laughter, wholly unhuman.

Jacquie wrapped an arm around my shoulder. 'Steve . . . what's he want you to do? Why are you looking like that?'

I said nothing at first, only leaned on the side of the truck and fought to steady my breath, to collect my thoughts. 'I . . . can't explain, Jacquie. It's . . . everything I've ever been afraid of.' Everyone has them, deep-rooted terrors and horrors and phobias. Mine had been worse, if anything, since the Rangda episode; and they all came bubbling and festering up to strangle me there and then.

'It is hard, yes!' said Ape. 'But you ask, *why you*? And this also may be your answer. The Pilot, your friend, he told you, did he not, that rarely for no purpose do the Gates of the Spiral open, for good or bad. For this, perhaps, they were opened to you; this, perhaps, is the price of your wider world. This – or more, much more, of which this may be but a part. For price there always is!'

Ape's hand closed on my other shoulder. Though the touch was light there seemed to be no end to the strength I felt in those massive fingers, so much it barely seemed to be contained within the mere flesh, but blazed and tingled like some invisible aura, cooling, calming. 'This much I can give you,' he rumbled, 'these few minutes, this touch of strength; but only this. Think, man! Remember! Fight down your fears! Was there nothing else – nothing better?'

And of course there had been. A memory, of how it'd felt once to be no longer empty, no longer alone within myself as every human being is alone; but one with something vaster, higher, greater than myself. Filled; fulfilled. Not only possessed, as I had been by Rangda, as the Barong had sought to, but also possessing. Not even Rangda, not even the Barong, could wholly destroy that.

'You, afraid?' whispered Jacquie. 'You thought you were, once – afraid of everything, of what people might think of you, of what might happen to all your glorious plans. That was why you did what you did to us, I know, that was why you let me down. But that was only a dream, a delusion, Steve! I've seen you as you really are, now – as I always thought you might be, underneath. This, whatever it is – if you really need to do it, you can!' And from her embrace, too, a strength seemed to flow, a greater energy even than Ape's, a bright blaze that burned as steel does in an oxygen blast, that seemed to temper me with the strength of her belief. And why not? This was the outer reach, this was the Spiral, where such things could be, as truly as the monstrous forces that raged above our heads now.

'Steve!' she said urgently. 'Steve, whatever masters you, it can't be fear!'

With a vast effort, as if the darkening air around me was thickening to smoky glass, I forced my arms up from my side, put one around her waist and clutched tight. But the other I reached out, though the resistance was terrible, grinding my teeth with the effort, slowly, desperately forcing my hand across a space that seemed infinite. I felt my hair lift, my skin tingle, as if mighty energies played about us; sparks seemed to crackle from Jacquie's floating hair. '*I'm ready!*' I shouted; and with one tearing lunge that twisted my arm agonisingly in its socket, I caught Ape by the shoulder.

My hand went through him like smoke.

The next instant, with Jacquie tight against me, I was rising, spiralling upwards like a leaf from a bonfire, above the thrashing slopes of green below. And in my ears, though I couldn't see him, was the voice of Ape. 'See, see! How wildly swings the balance, this way and that, beyond control! Rangda and the Barong, in the shadows they strive – but already their strife spills over into the Core! This is madness unleashed – this is *puputan*! See!'

Flashes of scarlet and gold lit the dusk below. The firefight between the terrorists and our escort had spread into the paddies, and by the look of it there were heavy weapons in play. Both sides must have called up support, and evidently the guerillas were in greater force than anyone had expected. Across the mountainside, swinging wildly in the wind, an Ilyushin attack 'copter was battling towards the scene, its weapons pods clustered like ripe fruit along its flanks, its nose cannon already sweeping the trees below; others were rising over the distant hills. Suddenly a red glare flashed right across a paddy as some kind of missile exploded. From the brooding blue-black summit of Gunung Agung there came a rumble, as if in answer, and out of the caldera sinister gases boiled up to join its trailing stream of clouds and panting puffs of hot ash. And across the miles, on the distant summit of Gunung Batur, the shining surface of the mighty caldera lake shivered suddenly like a clouded mirror, and spat a column of boiling mud and steam into the sky.

'Between them they will lay waste the isle! See, Stephen Fisher – join your eyes and mine! See, and be wise!'

As if a monochrome image flushed suddenly with blazing colour . . .

As if a flat image sprang suddenly into three dimensions . . .

As if a picture on a wall reached out and wrapped itself around me . . .

As if a stream of gibberish suddenly resolved into Shakespearean verse and soaring plainsong . . .

As if a dry stalk suddenly swelled with sap beneath my fingers, and burst into leaf and flower, and filled my nostrils with its scent . . .

As if, as if a million things grew, filled out, expanded with apocalyptic force in one moment of awesome understanding; as if the world became suddenly even more immense than I had imagined, as if vast avenues of knowledge opened up behind the least passing thought – and even greater avenues of ignorance. For you need to know a vast amount even to begin to comprehend how much you still have yet to know; and like the empty arches of a derelict cathedral that ignorance reared over me, terrifying, dwarfing my tiny human scrap of intellect, my fragmentary existence. In panic I veered away from it, clung desperately to my own self and stared down at the island that still fell away below.

I saw.

A whole thing, a macrocosm. A single unified system, a living thing, a single body laid out below me against the blueness of the ocean like a sample stained upon a microscope slide. A body like my own. The island of Bali was alive. The wonder and the glory of it, that vision, struck me with thunderbolt force, sent me spinning and whirling as I hung there, while before my blurring sight marched all the lands and countries of the world, all the massive continents crawling with less than glacial slowness about the planetary face – all, all living, all alive. Not mere dead rock with live things on it; for whence came their nourishment but from that rock, that soil? And both were full of things that had lived there before, would be full of life that returned to it in the end. The lifeless was part of the living, the living of the lifeless; each moved to the other in its turn, and there was no divide between them. And the very planet itself, moving among the stars that wheeled above me now, itself a thing of life, itself an integrity of its living landmasses. And what then? The stars themselves? And beyond?

But my flight steadied, and Bali swam into my view once more. I thought of *I Desa*, Mr Village, and the house laid out like a man. So it was, this living organism below me – not just a concept, an overlay upon the real, the physical Bali, but part of it, indissoluble, inseparable, a joint creation shaped by nature and by man. Constantly living, constantly dying, the living things of the island, from humblest algae to most august Brahmin, they were its constituent cells. But a body is more than a mere complex assemblage of cells; it has vital organs, to keep the system functioning. So if Bali was alive, where lay its heart, this great Jascony beast, this stone and soil kraken below me – and where was its brain?

As I wondered, so I knew. Water was its blood, the water system, part natural, part man-made, the veins it ran in; and the heart that kept it going was the *subak* system. Governed, in its turn, by the brain. That was the network of *subak* temples and all the others which constantly monitored and governed every aspect of the island's intricate inner life, maintaining a delicate but elegant balance.

Or did. Until the irruption of outside culture, the coming of tourism, government regulation and the explosive growth of population. Like a body invaded by viruses, its immune system failing, its physical resources dwindling, the isle was sick, racked by turmoil, fever and distress. I thought desperately of a man whose circulation is poor, whose heart is failing – surely it must have help? Yet what I was bringing it was an artificial, outside heart, a semblance, a simulacrum beyond the body's control, that could not respond as it responded, quicken or relax in harmony with all the billion tiny reactions of a living thing. A transplant, against which the body's own defences would strike – so they had to be nullified, at a cost. The red sparks of tracer below, the springing tongues of fire around the little village, told me what that might be; and if that was the shadow of all villages, what was the island's future? I saw war and fire haemorrhage across the land.

'*Ape!*' I shouted aloud. '*Ape!*'

'I hear already. I hear your thoughts even as they are voiced; I

303

need delve no deeper, yet. You have seen. Have you an answer? Then tell me! *Tell*!'

I still felt Jacquie at my side, the pounding of her heart, even; but I couldn't see her, couldn't see myself. There was only the island beneath us, a rough green jewel, slowly turning against emptiness, and wheeling above us in their vast slow dance, the tropical stars. Where I was, how I could be speaking in air too thin to breathe, I didn't know. I gasped and stammered, incoherent.

'A truth – maybe! A beginning – but I need to think! I can't, not while they're butchering each other! Ape, we've got to stop them!'

'That I may do, with the last minutes of power left me for this cycle. But soon they will fight again, worse than before; and I will be powerless. Unless your thinking turn up some answer they'll accept.'

'It can!' I gasped. 'I know it! All I need's that last piece of the puzzle! And I won't get it with this holocaust going on!'

There was a searing shriek from below, a crash of gunfire.

'Then I will trust you, and take the risk. The island's fate is within your grasp. Reach out with me, Stephen, and take it!'

Suddenly I saw my arm, my hand, stretched out into the void as if it still pressed through that unseen barrier. Or was it mine? It seemed huger, heavier; and yet when I flexed it I felt, with a new fountain of awareness, a burgeoning strength within my fingers that could crack whole worlds like dry nutshells. And in my open palm lay something tiny yet heavy, immensely heavy, a rod, black and glossy, gold-capped. I clutched it, flicked it, spun it like a pencil and saw it blur, expand, lance out at either tip to the mighty staff Ape had wielded. Words came to me, old words long buried beneath others, and there grown powerful; I spoke them, and fire flashed from the gold – but pink no longer. Scarlet it blazed, ruby light, no longer the force of a single mind embodied, but of two.

Down I plunged those hands, down, down into the heart of that green jewel, to where points of fire awoke; and it was as if my sight went with it, piercing the gathering clouds about the crest of the holy mountain. Across its nightbound bulk thin fireworms crawled, seams of steam puffed out, threads of red and greyish white that traced the rugged cliff like livid veins – rivulets of glowing lava and steaming mud-ash, scouting the path for the lethal floods at their heels, ready to rain down upon the land. And beneath it the night raged brighter yet. Across the fields beyond helicopters ranged like hellish insects, while the broken body of one lay smoking among the remains of a once-rich rice paddy, now scorched to sterility. Hails of tracer bullets curved up the sky from the jungle beyond, and the brighter streak of a missile. A 'copter plunged violently to avoid the airburst.

The little village we'd left lay already ablaze, its roof-trees bare and blackening, its temple towers cracking in the heat. The narrow streets were thick with contorted corpses, many with hands at each other's throats. The banyan tree was a pillar of fire that cast a malevolent light across a trodden morass of blood-soaked mud, where two ignorant armies milled and thrashed around the massive shapes that cuffed and clawed and snarled and shrilled, trampling friend and foe alike to gain the slightest advantage of position, blind to all else but the mirror image of their mutual hate. And at the margins of the light, looming like the threat of every destructive destiny embodied, the squat angular shadow of the container they fought over, to destroy or to possess and control for their own ends. The container I had brought . . .

'NO!'

Whether the voice was mine or Ape's I could hardly tell, whether there was Jacquie there also, whether it was English or Indonesian, *tidak*! But the wind from the spinning staff burst like a thunderclap over the battle beneath, blasting men off their feet, blotting out the blazing tree like a guttering candle, blasting the fire from the roof-trees. Into the midst of the battle I reached like plunging lightning, and unleashed the fires that were my own.

Like a dog torn from its prey the Barong's mighty bulk went spinning, bowling helplessly over and over, kicking and biting and snarling, into the forest's edge.

Rangda, caught by that trailing mass of hair, shrieked and threshed; but off the ground she was lifted by it, swung and hurled, down to the margins of the river falls. She landed with a mighty splash, and the water plucked at her, eager to sweep her away seaward; but those mighty talons anchored her to a rock, and she scrambled ashore, glaring.

In the near dark men grovelled and sobbed, while the stump of the banyan smouldered and smoked. Over the electric air the sound of the gun battle came crackling. Beneath the shadows of the first overhanging branches the Barong crouched and snarled; but I brandished the staff, and he quailed. He; for suddenly, without any perceptible change, I saw him as the old priest once more.

'A strange alliance!' he said, stalking forward. 'Still stranger treason; but your power will not last forever, Ancient.' I swung the staff, sowed an arc of flame at his feet, and he stopped.

'Stephen Fisher!' he said urgently. 'What you feared most has come to you! Yet soon, you may throw it off. What you lack most, I can give you! Have I not found it for my people here, throughout many long centuries – till your people disturbed it? But trust me as they have done, and together, with the powers of your world and mine united in our hands, you and I could banish all that we did not desire! And you would have peace at last, the peace of mind you so desire, amid the ancient harmony that reigns here once again!'

'Harmony!' laughed a soft, sensual voice. 'Ancient boredom! Centuries of rust! You are a man, Stephen – and a strong man seeks better things than mere timeless vegetating! Life is stronger than death, change is stronger than stillness – peace is in the grave! Reach out, trust me and take all that a man most desires!'

It was Rangda again, human again – and yet, cleverly, not so, not quite. Her shape was still slightly larger than life, her skin, still running bright droplets from the river, faintly pearly, opalescent, her eyes bright and warm. She was herself; and then, quite suddenly, she was Clare. Still standing there, still wearing loincloth and heavy pearls; but Clare, from head to foot; and then, shockingly, Jacquie – a stranger, magical Jacquie, alluring and perfect, an image of love. Then, even more devastating, Mall – Mall, half naked, with the fire of divinity blazing about her in a dazzling coronal. Her arms reached out to me, she stepped closer – and I laughed Ape's nasty belly-laugh, and trailed flames at her feet also.

'Beware!' shouted the Barong. 'You cannot delay, you cannot keep these devices within your own hands forever. Into another's you must give them. Into the government's? You have heard their voice – can they be trusted?'

He seemed to be well aware of what had been going on in the car – and of my reaction to it. It came to me suddenly – could he have been working on Pasaribu, very subtly, to make him reveal as much of himself as he did?

'Not the government, then,' he said, and he too laughed, a cold brief laugh, a carnivore sound. 'Into whose, then? The hairy one? I would not trust him. Was he not striving to slay you, as hard as any of us? That third power you feared so – do you not know that it was he?'

That almost made me falter, like a physical blow. All my fears boiled up once more. '*Ape?*' I yelled, though I knew he could hear perfectly well. 'Is that . . . '

The voice within me was sombre. 'It was true, Stephen. It was with just the same purpose as the others I came westward, I who could travel far where they could not; for all around the world am I known, and in many lands my roots lie. Many of your troubles I made; those Bundler creatures, apt to my hand, I drew upon you. But when the little witch brought you to me, and I found you neither cruel nor corrupt, but only a little empty, a little lacking in understanding of what you dealt with . . . then I decided I would aid you, protect you from the long reach of the native powers. For it took no great foresight to believe that such a man, with knowledge I and the others totally lacked, might come on some way out of the impasse. A man of two worlds, a man risen high in one and fast finding his feet in the other – a rare blend. Was I right, Stephen? Tell me now, show me – was I right?'

The Barong seemed to hear him as well as I could. 'And suppose he is not? He has turned his coat once – will he not again, if he is displeased? Can you trust him?' He tossed his head in regal contempt.

Rangda's voice cut him off. 'And you, old greycoat, senile and sterile, who will trust you? What can you offer them that sets the heart a single beat faster, or promises one day different from the last? Trust *me*, Stephen!' She was pacing back and forth, just beyond the arc of my staff, like a caged cat. The Barong was pacing and shouting, too; but her clear voice overrode his, sensual, seductive, beautiful as Bali island itself.

'Only *I* can set the blood flowing; only I can make this living grave come back to life again! Only I and those who fight in my name, only they can keep the government vultures at bay! This cobwebbed old fool has let them march all over him for dignity's sake sooner than stir a limb, only to find energy enough for *puputan* at the end. What does he know of life or love or the joy of the fleeting moment! Remember how it was with me, Steve; it

307

can be so for eternity, if you do but trust me. Trust me! Trust me! *Trust me*! *Me—*'

The Barong was shouting the same words. Their voices came together in a terrible unison, a barrage of sound. I fought to think, to see; the heavy staff faltered a touch – and equally as one, they sprang. But Ape's reflexes were behind my own. I flung the staff across my shoulders as he had back at the railyards, and felt the leaping surge of power to either tip, even as clawed hands snatched out to tear it from my grasp. Scarlet fire erupted in great spurting shields, enveloping them, buffeting them as they clung to it; I tipped the staff back and forth, with them still hanging on, swinging from side to side like an embodiment of the balance they'd endangered.

'Trust *you*?' I yelled at them, and flung them free in a shower of crackling radiance. 'You stupid bastards! You blind bloody pair of idiots! Who'd trust *you*? You're just a pair of overgrown infants whoring after your own ends, your own stupid selfish obsessions! You're not really thinking of the people here, are you? If I trusted anybody, hell, it'd be *them* . . . '

The silence was instant, so complete I could almost hear my own heart pounding within my chest. Artificial hearts, transplants; those were last-ditch remedies doctors applied, when all else had failed. What was better for a human body, one of those – or its own, mended, healed, strengthened, restored?

For a moment I thought my own would stop. Then, that it would tear itself loose from my chest, battering at my ribs as if they were a carnivore's cage bars. I was still panting with the power I had exerted, with the weirdness of the forces that flowed and coursed through me, the thoughts of another being that lurked at the borders of my own, infusing them with the dark tang of strange knowledge, unheard-of experiences.

I'd looked, I'd seen, and – I couldn't voice it. I was stammering like an over-excited child.

'*Then open your thoughts to me, and I will give them form. I see, already I see – that the Project is the island's heart . . .* '

'Yes! Too big a thing – too much a part of it for outsiders to run. A surgeon can intervene to fix a heart – but he doesn't go on pumping it, does he? Soon as he can, he lets the body take over again, he hands back control; that's all that makes it worthwhile! And that's what's got to happen here. This isn't something for a national government – or for outside do-gooders, however well they mean. They can help, yes; but they mustn't take control. Or the body will forget. The nerves will wither. It'll never learn again!'

My mind whirled upon the wind, into the gathering dark. Was Jacquie still with me? I couldn't feel her any more, couldn't feel anything; and yet I knew, somehow, she was there still, wherever there was.

'*This is so. But to whom may that control be given?*'

'The ones who've always had it! Don't you see? The government wanted to train a whole new generation of irrigation engineers – well, why shouldn't it? Only through the *subaks*! This generation of *klian subaks* are using computers already; why shouldn't the next ones be fully fledged engineers? Wielding their modern power – but under the eyes of the *subak* councils and the ancient laws!'

'*The next generation? But till then? The need is now!*'

'For now, the Project engineers can do the work – as they always planned to! But answering to the *subak* councils and the *klians*, not the government! Can't you see, damn it? The older men will jump at the idea, so they can keep their power and prestige. So will the young men! They get to learn on the job, while the engineers pick out the best of them for the training schemes – so they won't get stuck with the sons of government officials! And none of this bull about breaking down traditions! It'll strengthen the old ways, not weaken them! Because the *subak* laws are fair; they won't allow any manipulation of water rights, or any other kind of corruption! They evolved with the island and weren't imposed from outside by a load of so-called social engineers; and if they need amending, it'll be by the people who live under them! The island's heart – and the island's brain! Able to work in concert again! Made whole!'

Blackness and silence, an awful silence. The voice that spoke was Jacquie's, calm, controlled, considering – and yet underneath it a growing tremor. 'I think . . . I believe the Project will accept this. The men on the ground will, I know that. If we can sell it to the trustees, the college itself will have to go along; and without the college and the trust, there's no Project. But the government . . . '

I gathered my strength, tried to open my mind as freely as I could, speaking into the vast void around us, starless and moonless night. 'If the Barong and Rangda keep up their blockade, go on stopping shipments – then the government'll have to agree! They'll have no alternative! Either they do things our way, or nothing gets through!' Still silence; but I pulled the last of my courage together, and spoke again.

'But those two powers, in the state they are – will they pay any attention to what they hear? Will they be convinced? Because we've got to have their help – and the islanders, too – and that mysterious third power, Ape? So what does it think, now it's got by my defences? Will it change its mind again? Will it destroy me, the way the others want to? Or will it help me persuade them, if it can? Stop the fighting, calm them down, undo the damage? Will it? And can it? Can you, Ape?'

'*Not alone*!' said the voice within me. Ape's voice; but I realised suddenly it had changed. From the moment of our merging it had changed. All trace of Dutch had fallen from it now, as if it had been adopted only to hide how strange those guttural accents really were, and how inhuman. It was a single voice, but behind it were the echoes of a million. '*Not alone. For midnight approaches, and with it I must become what it will make me, take on another form for a season, to be renewed and refreshed among my people. For this is the hour of the Ancestors – and I am an Ancestor. The Ancestor! I am He who stole the Undying Peaches of Heaven, who won therewith great powers of sorcery and still greater punishment. Who paid his penance and earned his freedom when he helped a holy man to spread a new faith from India to the East. I was Hanuman, who brought his army of kin to the aid of Rama, to rescue his wife from the demon Rakashas, who went before to burn their rooftops, and who in doing so lost his tail. A loss that was its own great reward – for then I was Monkey no longer, but became Ape. Ancestor of Ancestors I am, the First that came to this corner of the Earth, and peopled it with his children. Who earned himself a true name even in the West's most sacred tongue . . .*'

'Yes!' whispered Jacquie, in awe. 'I should have known! When I first saw him. *Pithecanthropus erectus* – Apeman who walked upright. Java Man. Ancestor of all the East. *My* ancestor. He has the right. He has the power.'

A sound began, grew, swelled, the harsh thudding of the *wayang* drum, to which I'd seen the monkey-shadow dance. '*I have. And I will use it. For, Stephen Fisher, you have fulfilled the purpose for which I sought you. Your answer is the true one! And my nature, my power will end the conflict, will heal the hurts, will make them listen! But only through you, Stephen Fisher, can I wield it. Only you still hold me together as one. Now you must set me free – free! FREE!'*

All the sullen weariness and age I had seen grow upon his features in these last weeks were in that voice then, all the longing for release. The drum drubbed and thudded like an unsteady heart. Like a mind trapped in a maimed body, like a butterfly in its chrysalis, he longed to leap free; I felt it with him. But how? How, in any way that would let him still help us?

I meant to rub my chin; but my free hand halted in horror as I touched it, felt the harsh bristly hairs, the heavy contours, the massive jaw. There was no chin. It was Ape's face I touched, in this dark world; and in the ultimate fear of loss, of my very identity, I snatched at those hairs, tore them out and hurled them away.

The drumbeat rose to a climactic rattle, and redoubled. Suddenly the darkness was full of drums. I held up the staff, and in the scarlet glow from its tip I saw other shadows there, sturdy, dancing a strange half-squatting dance, a comic, grotesque dance, a dance of happiness, of liberation. And each one clutched a staff; and each one, as the drumming raced again, tore at its face and sent a tuft of hairs scattering on the wind. And again, the drumbeat was redoubled, and redoubled – and redoubled – till the whole darkness was dark no longer, till it was one frenetic, chattering, crashing infinite dance that caught hold of Jacquie and myself, and whirled us around and around till we saw only flashes . . .

Of the dance enveloping the battle, of squat shapes leaping among the combatants, hopping grotesquely around the stabbing swords and slashing bayonets . . .

Of the dance sweeping over the last embers of the fires and kicking the ashes into a billowing, almost solid cloud . . .

Of the dance leaping across the paddies, among the terrorists and the troops who raced and sniped and skirmished there, tripping them, kicking the weapons from their hands and stamping them down into the fertile mud, to clog and rust and decay . . .

Of the dance falling on the woman and the man, the hag and the half-beast who tore and clawed at each other, barging them, yanking a robe, tweaking a loincloth, pulling a tail, swinging on strands of hair, twanging a tusk with impudent bravado, scattering ropes of pearls and goosing their wearer with earthy, irreverent gestures . . .

And then, abruptly, there was only darkness again, still, empty, silent. Except for Jacquie's trembling breath; but it was excitement that made it tremble. She spoke, as if she was answering some voice she heard naturally, even when it wasn't directed at me. 'Then . . . then it's all right?' she demanded. 'They'll accept Steve's idea?'

*Look*, said Ape's voice. It was fuller now, yet more diffuse, as if it came from a great distance, as if it was merging somehow with that immense echo, becoming a part of all those myriad other voices. *Listen* . . .

Darkness covered the island. The tearing wind had died down, the rumbles of the volcanic heights were silent, their hellish glows no longer visible. Where the opposing armies had trampled and struggled over the smashed remains of their comrades, there was silence. Where the firefight had torn the air over the peaceful paddy terraces, there were still points of red light floating around; but somehow they no longer looked angry, they no longer had the terrible arcing purpose of tracer rounds. At first I thought I could still hear the distant cries and the clamour of metal, the bursts of rattling explosions; but slowly, as if coming into focus, the voices resolved into a rhythm, a chanting line of many voices. And the crash of combat resolved into the gentle, ordered clangour of the *gamelan*.

Jacquie and I were standing, embracing, in the darkness beneath some overhanging trees. The hot and humid air of the tropical night clung like a damp silk veil about us, weighed down by the heavy scent of their flowers – some kind of mimosa, maybe. The droplets that hung on the leaves were glittering red and yellow jewels in the light of lanterns through the trees. We clung, savouring the moment; and when at last we had to breathe, we looked up together to the skies, clear now, alight with the glittering southern stars and a blazing crescent moon. Under their steely light we kissed again, for how long I don't know; but soon, drawn, we walked hand in hand down the narrow path towards the light.

It shone upon the branches of an ancient banyan tree, that had not the slightest trace of fire upon it; and on the walls of the little temples round about, the only marks were those of lichen, and where offerings of paste and scent had been smeared throughout the centuries.

'Oh, there you are!' said Pasaribu, turning towards us. Somehow in the warm lanternlight even he looked more benign. 'That was a fierce little shower, wasn't it? Rare for this time of year – but never unwelcome in our business, huh? And it certainly didn't put them off. I came down here because I hoped I'd be able to introduce you to this.'

He was watching – and enjoying, unless I was much mistaken – two masked figures in a slow, circling dance to the tapping of the *gamelan*. One was a grotesquely animalistic she-witch, in a costume of white striped with red and black, almost hidden behind immense trailing yellow hair. Her eyes bulged balefully, fangs and tusks sprouted from her jaws, and a waist-length wagging red tongue; and her fingers bore immense white nails which the dancer twisted into malevolent and menacing gestures. A horrific figure; yet also a figure of fun, the hostile compressed into the comprehensible. And against her, played by two dancers in a magnificent carapace of gold plates with tawny hair sprouting beneath, was a four-legged beast with the lithe magnificence of a tiger. On his head a tall peaked crown bobbed, encrusted with golden flowers; behind his wide cat-ears rose a great collar of flaming gold, like a stylised mane. His open red mouth also spouted fangs, fewer but larger than Rangda's, and behind him lashed a sweeping golden tail. Pasaribu went on to explain rather laboriously that these were ritual characters who appear at almost every festival dance – the two rival powers who are the guardians of the villages. The Barong, it appeared, was friendlier; but Rangda had her place too. '*Yin* and *Yang* kind of thing, you know . . . '

His voice tailed off. Despite his pretence of showing it to us, he was evidently fascinated by the dance, representing the last shreds of a culture that had been swept off Jawa centuries past by outside invaders and missionaries, and yet was in his and his ancestors' blood. I wrapped an arm around Jacquie – a bit of a breach of manners here, but I was too happy to care – and whispered to her. 'You know, we may have seen this island's heart and brain, back there; but a body needs more, doesn't it? Rangda, the Barong, all these lesser spirits and things – they purge its conflicts, they keep its peace. They're its soul.'

313

'Kind of a shame we shouldn't linger,' said Pasaribu dreamily, after a while. 'Sometimes some of the villagers will join in – in trance, you know. They think they're possessed, that kind of thing.'

'Yes,' I said, a little grimly. 'Rangda goes in for that kind of thing, doesn't she?'

'Oh!' exclaimed the little official, startled. 'You – er, you take an, an interest in, uh, folklore, do you?' he inquired, almost shyly, quite unlike his usual glib manner. It seemed to please him. 'They pretend to attack her, you see, drive her off. She fights them, makes them turn their own weapons against themselves; but it's all ritual. They never hurt her, she never hurts them. Everybody just retires peacefully for another day – an eternal struggle. Nobody ever wins – but nobody ever loses, either. All absolute superstition, sure; but I have got to admit, when you see them like this, these old, uh, expressions of the people's consciousness have a certain charm – mmnh? A certain charm,' he repeated, a little shamefacedly.

He sighed, and looked at his watch. 'I guess we'd better be moving along soon. Er – where has your friend got to?'

Jacquie looked around sharply. 'Yes! Where *is* Ape?'

'I shouldn't worry,' I said. 'He said he, er, was expected somewhere along the way. He'll look after himself; he's quite at home here – or anywhere else in these islands.'

'Oh?' chuckled Pasaribu. 'Goes native, does he?'

'To the point of overdoing it, sometimes,' said Jacquie drily. 'But he's a good friend.'

Back at the road the convoy were waiting for us, alert but calm, their side arms resting across their knees. They grinned as Pasaribu clucked unhappily over the bullet holes in his car. 'You know how long it'll take me to get this damn thing resprayed out here?'

Evidently Ape had forgotten to undo some damage – with malice aforethought, I suspected.

'No more trouble?' I asked the corporal in the container truck. He laughed.

'Some terroris'! Frighten 'way by shower of rain! Didn' even wait for 'coptah!'

From out of the trees came a sudden explosive chatter of voices, almost derisive, a complicated chorus chanting what seemed to be nonsense sounds beneath the wailing high notes of a soloist; he sounded a lot like the *wayang* narrator. 'Ah!' exclaimed Pasaribu wistfully. 'That's the *kecak*, the monkey dance. With the chorus imitating the *gamelan*, you hear? And dancing.'

'It tells the story of the *Ramayana*, doesn't it?' mused Jacquie softly.

'That's right!' said Pasaribu, pleased. 'But the real hero's Hanuman, of course; if you know who—'

'Yes,' I said. 'Quite well.'

He smiled, looked back. 'It's quite a sight. I wish . . . but no, we'd better be going. At least it's kind of a nice farewell.'

I agreed. His driver, one arm bandaged but otherwise cheerful, slid the car out into the road and away. We wound down the window and listened as the chant dwindled behind us. Ape was there; but we both knew that he was elsewhere too. He was all around us now, in the hearts and minds and souls of his descendants, spirit of the last remnant of an ancient people, who had reached halfway round the world and back again to bring them the protection they needed.

Now that Pasaribu wasn't playing the worldly cosmopolitan quite so thoroughly, he happily told me all about this Descent of the Ancestors. 'They believe they stay here on the island all through Galungan, for a week or so – till Kuningan, the closing festival, when they're given specially honoured offerings of yellow rice. But in the meantime everybody wears their best clothes, makes offerings, decorates the whole village with these *penjor* poles like Christmas trees – in fact the whole atmosphere's a lot like Christmas. Only it's for the Ancestors they push the boat out – and how!'

'Good for Ape!' whispered Jacquie softly, snuggling up to me in the back. 'He deserves it.'

'Yes,' I smiled down at her. Pasaribu was chattering on obliviously again, but it sounded almost likable now. 'But what about us? Haven't we earned something, too?'

Jacquie sighed. 'Well, I don't know. Thanks to you I'm going to have my work cut out for a while to come. This bright idea of yours – you realise how many people I'm going to have to sell it to? The Project, the trust, the college, the government, the *subaks* – dear god! And see that they stay sold? It's going to be the PR job of all time. And then we've got to start getting the scheme organised more or less at once, and can you imagine what *that's* going to take?' She rubbed a hand up and down my chest. 'And all the way here you've been saying how much work'll be piling up for you at home.'

I pressed the hand to me. 'Dave can take care of that a little longer.' But even to me that sounded unhappy. I didn't want him to; he might handle things too well, and leave me feeling superfluous.

'So you won't just throw that away and stay out here, not even with me – oh, don't worry!' she smiled as I protested. 'I wouldn't ask you to. You might do it, and it'd be cruelty. But I love *my* work, too. I won't go; and you won't stay.'

Unhappiness crawled over me like a cowl. 'I suppose I'd hoped . . . '

'That we could start again, forget the past? It won't forget us, Steve. We live in different worlds now.' She grimaced. 'And I don't think I can face yours.'

'You lived in the West long enough. You look European, damn it!'

'I don't feel it – not very. But it wasn't Europe I was talking about. Your world – or worlds. Remember what Jyp said? Something about people who get a glimpse, and step back into their own world again. The Spiral—' I felt her shiver. 'Wonderful, terrible beyond belief! The things that must be out there, that I'd love to see – but there must be other things, too. For one extreme there must be the other. Ultimate beauty, ultimate horror; endless good, endless evil. I can't take that – that possibility. You're incredibly brave, that you can.'

I felt my mouth twist, petulantly. 'Incredibly unimaginative, more like. That's been said before. Or just plain thick.'

'No! You have got imagination, more than most, if only you'll unleash it. I always knew you had. I'm the limited one; I know where I'm best suited to be.'

'I was warned to stay away from the Spiral,' I said sombrely. 'To forget it, for my own safety. I almost succeeded. Maybe I should have.'

'Mall said you could look after yourself now. That there was less risk you'd get hurt.'

'I don't think she had this way in mind. I know how much I hurt you, Jacquie. But Christ, you're well repaid now. Maybe I ought to just forget all this, too.'

She stroked my cheek. 'I hope you don't. You might still go on blaming yourself. Whatever you did, you more than made up for

316

– remember that, at least. So we can get on with living our lives, without being yoked to the past, the way we would be if we stayed together. Wouldn't we?'

I shrugged. It was a dull pain now; and I really had no cause for complaint. I'd gone into this, haring after a name that might be Jacquie's, and a bit of easy do-gooding. Easy! I'd expected . . . what? I didn't know. But no reward, certainly. The trouble was, I had thought I'd found one.

'You've found something,' she insisted softly. 'A better way to say goodbye. Don't you see? You're not a slave to the past any more – to us, to our breakup. Steve, that was my fault too, in a hundred stupid ways. I could have made a better play for you, I could have hung on to you, if my own stupid pride hadn't been hurt. You opened the gates for us again – that's good. But that they close again, that's good too. That's healing!'

And miraculously, as if the magic of the Spiral still clung about us on this enchanted midsummer night, it was. A load I'd hardly even realised was there was lifting from my shoulders now, as if I'd been carrying a second container on them all this way – all these years. I bent down and kissed Jacquie, long and deep; and that, too, was happiness, an astonishing happiness, free from bitterness and guilt at long, long last.

'Wow!' she giggled, when at last we surfaced for air. She sounded just like the girl of all those years before. 'Steve . . . '

'Hmm?'

'Those Gates . . . they don't have to close just yet, do they? At least you should take a holiday. Somewhere nice and relaxing.'

'Like – oh, a tropical island paradise? Like Bali?'

'Wonderful idea. I think I will, too. Know where we can get any yellow rice?'

I would have jerked a thumb at Pasaribu, but she'd trapped my hand neatly between her thighs, and she wasn't letting it go. 'He'll know. He seems to know quite a lot. As if he's picked up just a touch of somebody else . . . '

'Mmh. Steve . . . back then, when I said I believed in you . . . '

'Mmh?'

'I did. I always have, even against every better judgement in the world. If you ever seemed empty in some ways, maybe it was because you have room for so much. Maybe you had to go further than most people to find it.'

'How do you mean?' I was too happy to care. And yet there

was a quiet intensity in her words that was to linger long after Bali was only one more memory, however bright, falling away beneath an airliner's wheels.

'I mean . . . maybe it's not up to you to stay away from this weird world of yours, dangerous or not. Maybe you were really meant for it, all along, as Jyp or Mall seem to be; maybe you do have a purpose, as Ape was hinting. Steve, darling – do you think it's going to stay away from you?'

This book, like its predecessor *Chase the Morning*, is set some years in the future. It assumes, for example, that Indonesia is under a different and perhaps more repressive government. However, *korupsi* and the other problems facing the country are firmly rooted in the present day.

Equally, it assumes that Bangkok's current epidemic of concrete and glass will continue and expand down along the Chao Phraya towards the sea; and that despite the looming threat of AIDS and promised government crackdowns, an almost entirely European and Australian clientele will go on flocking to Phatphong and places like it.

Finally, it goes without saying that the aid organisations in the book do not exist, and bear no relation to any that do.

The song on page 158 is a traditional chant from the Trobriand Islands, collected by John Kasaipwalova.